MW00683232

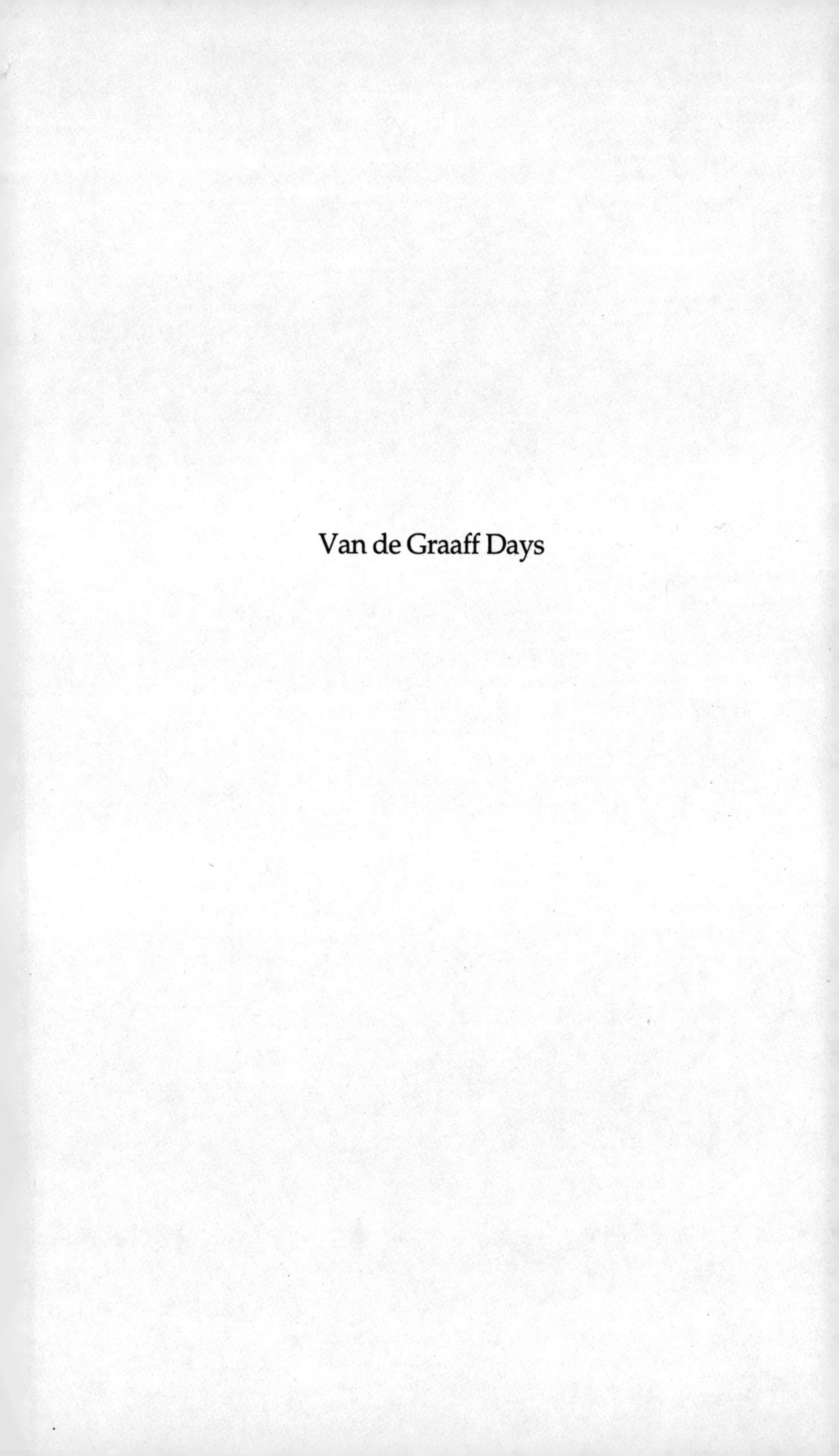

# Van de Graaff Days

# Van de Graaff Days

*Ven Begamudré*

**oolichan books**
Lantzville, British Columbia
1993

Canadian Cataloguing in Publication Data

Begamudré, Ven, 1956-
Van de Graaff days

ISBN 0-88982-126-7

I. Title
PS8553.E342V3 1993 C813'.54 C93-091373-6
PR9199.3.B43V3 1993

Publication of this book has been financially assisted by the Canada Council and Multiculturalism and Citizenship Canada.

Published by
**OOLICHAN BOOKS**
P.O. Box 10
Lantzville, British Columbia
Canada V0R 2H0

Printed in Canada by
Hignell Printing Limited
Winnipeg, Manitoba

*for Lloyd and Irene Sopher*
*and once again for Shelley*

## Acknowledgements

An early draft of the chapter "Holiday Father" appeared in *Saskatchewan Gold* (Coteau Books, 1982). An early draft of parts 1 and 2 appeared as the novella *Sacrifices* (The Porcupine's Quill, 1986). Brief scenes have been broadcast on "Ambience" (CBC Radio, 1986), KFJM (North Dakota Public Radio, 1991), and "Cloud 9" (CBC Radio, 1993).

This novel was written with financial support from the Saskatchewan Arts Board, Multiculturalism and Citizenship Canada, the Canada Council, and the Banff Centre's May Writing Studio and Leighton Artist Colony.

Equally generous moral support and advice came from people too numerous to name: colleagues at the Banff Centre, the Saskatchewan Writers'/Artists' Colonies, and the former Saskatchewan School of the Arts; members of the Bombay Bicycle Club prose group and Common Ground; writers-in-residence at the Regina and Saskatoon public libraries; and editors at Oolichan Books. Finally, I am indebted to my parents for their love of history and mythology, engineering and music.

. . . we tell one interminable tale.

—Raja Rao, *Kanthapura*, 1938

—J.S. Bach, *Goldberg Variations*, 1742

# Contents

# Part One

# Chapter 1

# Museum Pieces

The one thing Krishna liked more than solitude was space. He sat with his feet on his desk and tapped his teeth with a pencil while correcting a student lab report. When he leaned farther back, he felt the handle of a filing cabinet press into the base of his neck. He tossed the report onto his desk, then the pencil, and crossed his hands behind his head. Except for the whirring of a ceiling fan, his office was quiet. Solitude was useless without quiet.

This was his favourite time of day, afternoon. Others had abandoned their offices for the faculty canteen, where they complained over bottled drinks about students and teaching loads. A close room was no place to remain when the temperature passed ninety degrees, but this was the only time of day he could call his own. Even in his large house, with his wife away, there was still the servant. As for space, Krishna had little of it here though he shared his office with no one. Boxes of equipment covered the floor; circuit diagrams cluttered the corners; textbooks overflowed his bookshelves. For now, he was a senior lecturer but one day he would have a storeroom, a private entrance to his office, and a glass door marked, "Head of Electrical." All he had to do was work hard and bide his time.

Time.

Glancing at his watch, he pulled his feet off the desk. He was late. He rose, took his suit jacket from the back of his chair, and switched off the fan. Then he walked out onto a balcony which ran the length of the second floor. With his cream linen jacket hooked over his shoulder, he stood at the railing and surveyed the *maidan*. Withered grass, trodden almost lifeless, fringed the expanse of packed dirt. He had hoped to have the space to himself but a groundskeeper was dismantling wickets on the pitch. Well, Krishna thought, a man can't have everything.

He descended by the nearest stairs and waited in the shade of the balcony. His goal was the faculty club, not the canteen. He could reach the club by keeping to the shade of adjoining buildings—sandstone buildings which absorbed more heat than they reflected—but he did not want to encounter anyone, especially one of his colleagues. They would ask about his wife and he would have to admit he had heard nothing yet. They would grin with anticipation. If they were older than him, and most of them were older, they would make some jocular remark about fatherhood changing a young man's life. Not just yet, he thought; and why should it? Having two sons had not changed his father's life; he had kept on with his surveying, his building, his superintending.

When Krishna thought of his father, he caught himself wishing the boy—and he was sure it would be a boy—could be born old enough to learn things. Cricket, for instance. What use could a father be to a baby? The thought disturbed him but he had always felt exasperated in the company of infants. He left the shelter of the balcony. He barely noticed the sun beating down on the back of his neck, and he could not see the clouds of dust rising in his wake. No matter how slowly he walked, though, the groundskeeper moved even more slowly. He was scooping up bails and balancing them on stumps held in the crook of his left arm. Krishna recognized the old man when he straightened. It was Mali. He scratched at his backside; he shook a fist at the sun; he spat.

Mali waited until Krishna reached the pitch before calling, "Hallo, Yuvaraj-sir!"

All the workers referred to Krishna as the *yuvaraja*, the crown prince, but only Mali was bold enough to address him this way. Clutching the dismantled wickets to his chest, Mali squatted to pick up a cricket ball, then rose and touched his brow. Even if Krishna was a Brahmin—a South Indian at that, his dark skin out of place here on the Northern plains—Mali worshipped him. The groundskeeper had watched two generations of lecturers come and go, yet none of them had such poise. None of them could meet the British professors on their own ground the way the *yuvaraja* could.

Krishna laughed self-consciously. Crown prince indeed. "Here," he said. "Let me carry something."

"I am not so old!" Mali cried. This was true. He was only sixty and his forearms and calves were still taut. But what he meant, and Krishna knew it, was, "You remember your place." When Mali turned away, a bail slid off his load.

Krishna caught the bail and laid it next to the others, nestled among the topmost stumps.

Mali grunted his thanks. "You keep on," he ordered. "It is hot." He faced the club and pulled at the crotch of his short pants. The fly was fastened with safety pins.

"Then you take rest after this," Krishna said. He continued toward the club. The sandstone facade was whitewashed; the door and shutters were red. He had covered only ten paces when he heard Mali shout:

"You remind them! Seven years, seven months and one day—we have been free. You remind the fine gentlemen we shall be keeping our grounds when all of them are long gone!"

Without turning, Krishna waved and called, "Righto!" But if all the fine gentlemen left, who could he meet for a drink? Certainly not his Indian colleagues, who complained non-stop.

He liked his students and his teaching load was light. Pausing at the edge of the *maidan*, he pulled on his jacket, tugged the lapels flat, and adjusted his tie. His father would never enter such a place. He would sooner wear a yoke than a tie; he wore dark grey tunics buttoned to the neck. Nor had he much use for the homespun wisdom of groundskeepers, though he did have a favourite proverb: "Live far from relatives and near water." Krishna liked his relatives—especially his in-laws—as long as they kept their distance. He turned to look at Mali, washed out now by the glare. Yes, Krishna thought. We're free now.

*

Stuart McAulay was halfway through his first brandy and soda of the afternoon. The club protected him not only from the heat but also from the insolence of Indians who wished he would pack up and leave. Like any good Scot, he did not think of himself as a man who had helped the British rule their empire. He considered himself a man who had helped the Indians and he saw no reason to stop. He had no desire to return to a cottage in Kent, where he would spend the rest of his days growing roses and dreaming of bougainvillaea. That was for sad, old Englishmen. Besides, he had no intention of leaving until he could pass his department on to capable hands, and there was only one man here he considered worthy.

Through the window he watched Krishna pause at the edge of the *maidan* as though reluctant to leave it. He looked at home out there. He was such a good sportsman, the students often invited him to join in their casual games. If the students had any complaint, it was that he never took their games casually. He played to win. He was also the only man in the department eager to earn his keep; yet McAulay could not shake the feeling that Krishna was wasted here.

"Wasted," McAulay said after Krishna entered the club. "Like good whiskey on a sepoy."

Other department heads looked up from their drinks, and Krishna acknowledged the few nods in his direction. None of the men smiled. Most of them ignored him. He knew what McAulay was talking about—Krishna would never advance without further studies, preferably abroad—but he tried to keep the conversation to more immediate problems. "One of my students asked about radio interference this morning," he said. He sat on a sofa with his back to the window. He sat off-centre so as not to block McAulay's view.

Their favourite waiter, Chota-Wallah, brought Krishna's usual tonic with lime cordial. Then he lit McAulay's Dunhill and stationed himself nearby.

"I told him the theoretical problems have yet to be solved." Krishna frowned at his dusty Oxfords. "If we could do that . . . if we had a proper Van de Graaff—"

"And if you were Maharaja of Mysore!" McAulay scoffed.

This was Krishna's home state: Mysore, in the South. It was a quiet if enlightened backwater—quiet because it was far enough from the strife-torn North that life remained peaceful; enlightened because the Maharajas of Mysore had early on introduced schooling, roads and electricity. Krishna's father had built and managed some of Mysore's finest power stations.

"Damn it, man," McAulay said, "I could get you into any university in Britain! You could read for your doctorate. Perhaps even replace me when I retire. Don't pretend it hasn't crossed your mind." He snorted when Krishna shrugged.

They both knew the *perhaps* was deliberate. Northerners might not take kindly to a Southerner heading up a department. Especially not someone who got on so well with his former masters.

"My travelling days will soon be finished." Krishna sipped his drink to end the discussion but he wished he had remained silent. The mention of travel seemed to fuel McAulay's resolve.

"Becoming a father won't hobble you for life," he said. "Look at me: two children and I still saw my share of the world. My first wife managed fine without me, though it was hard at times. . ." No, he had better not get into that. The lengthy separations had led to disinterest and an expedient divorce. Only then came the happily settled years with Mildred. "Did I ever tell you my father was a prisoner of war when I was born? I remember he returned from South Africa—I'd just turned three, if you can imagine!—with a Boer hat he'd stolen."

When McAulay laughed, smoke eddied from his mouth. The smoke rose toward a ceiling fan, then slanted away from the blades. "You won't learn what you want in Britain, though. Americans won the war. They can teach you everything you need to know for this passion of yours. Radio interference indeed, as if there weren't more pressing problems! Now take the power losses from DC transmission to, say, an island with no local source of—"

"I would not be able to take my wife and child," Krishna interrupted. "Not as a student."

McAulay waved off the objection. He frowned at ash flaking onto the mat, then ground the flecks into the weave. "Hundreds of Indians have left their families to go abroad. It's a small price to pay considering the salaries they draw after they return. Nearly as much as we hangers-on."

"I do not like Americans," Krishna said.

The admission took McAulay aback. Krishna rarely volunteered information about himself. McAulay had not even known Krishna's wife was pregnant until she had left, over a month ago, to rejoin her people in the South. She had told Mildred that Benares, on these unshaded plains, was too hot. "Well?" McAulay asked.

Krishna studied the potted fern next to him. Even here, in the welcoming coolness of the club, the edges of its fronds were fraying brown. The soil was dry like dust. "I had enough of Americans in Japan. I remember it was the Fourth of July. The Korean War was in full swing. For everything one had to go cap in hand to General MacArthur's office. Or whomever replaced him after . . ." Krishna stopped. The events of a life should be kept to one's self, he thought. Not bottled up, but guarded, because disclosure could be misread as a sign of weakness. Besides, incidents in themselves rarely held much significance.

"Do go on," McAulay said. "You mentioned it was the Fourth of July."

Krishna spoke slowly. "I saw a jeepload of GIs throw firecrackers into a crowd of school children." He paused. He could feel his face growing hot and he forced himself to sound calm. "The soldiers laughed when the children shrieked. All the Americans I saw in Japan acted as though they were fighting the North Koreans single-handedly . . ." He hesitated, thoughtful, and tried to fathom the meaning of what he had seen. He could feel himself growing intense, even angry. "Yet it was only Japanese children who were terrorized."

Was that all? McAulay wondered. The incident was silly, if not typical, and Krishna's response exaggerated. He did not seem particularly fond of children. He looked abashed when Mildred once teased him about manhandling the little one—his hands were so large. Still, McAulay nodded. The Americans he met in France, forty years ago now, also acted as though they alone could humble the Kaiser. And during the last war, they once again remained aloof until the embarrassment of Pearl Harbor goaded them into action. Granted, they turned the tide, but they displayed poor sportsmanship. As they so often did. But back to the problem at hand. One diversion—what else could this story of firecrackers have been?—deserved another.

"Tell me," McAulay asked, "have things really changed since Independence? I don't mean the stamps and coins." He straightened in his chair and looked pleased with himself. "Got a set of those outlawed *Azad Hind* stamps last night, by the way."

"At last," Krishna said. McAulay had been searching out these stamps for years. One last souvenir, perhaps, of his years out of station.

"Hmm. The rebels did such a poor job of printing them, the ink from the bottom layer's dried on the one above." McAulay paused. "No, I mean are you happier or simply free?"

He knew the answer. He had seen too much not to know. Independence never brought happiness. Ask any young fool who thought life would be easier when he left family and friends to make his fortune elsewhere. But Krishna said:

"Both."

What else would he say? McAulay had heard from the college principal, who came here from Delhi, that Krishna was the first student leader to wear *khadi*. This was during the Quit India campaign ten years earlier, before homespun cotton became fashionable, as it was now. In those days it had been eloquent: a slap in Britannia's face.

"Problems exist," Krishna was saying, "but as Gandhi insisted, they were, and are, our own problems. This is the price, and also the reward, of Independence."

McAulay was hearing nothing new. He tilted up his glass and found it nearly empty. Glancing at the bar, he frowned. No doubt Chota-Wallah had already told Krishna about the surprise lying in store. Still, McAulay could not resist asking, "Heard anything?"

Krishna glanced at his drink and then out the window, across the *maidan*. The air wavered in the heat and he imagined a cricket match under way behind the movement. McAulay did not usually switch subjects like this. But then, Krishna supposed, McAulay's wife was after him for news of the birth. Women seemed more fascinated than men by birth, by babies. He shook his head.

McAulay returned his gaze to the bar. The moment he crushed his Dunhill out, Chota-Wallah removed the ashtray and brought a clean one. McAulay decided against another cigarette. He toyed with his trench lighter. If Krishna smoked, the lighter would be his, a mark of sincere regard from a superior. McAulay gave Krishna much—friendship, advice—but he wanted to pass on something tangible before passing on the department itself. Yet Krishna did not smoke. Nor did he drink. He seemed to have no vice, unless obsession counted as one: first with Independence, now with the Van de Graaff. Then there was his obsession with games. Even when seated, his frame betrayed no trace of fat. Why he married that girl, that mere slip of a girl, McAulay could not imagine. She looked pretty enough the one time she had come to tea before leaving for the South, but she had chattered away while Krishna had been more reticent than usual. She had also looked frail compared to him. He was six feet tall and broad in the shoulders, unusual in a Mysorian. They tended to be even shorter than the girl, who was of passable height. And darker. McAulay remembered her complexion as a milky brown. He put the lighter away and finished his drink.

Something blurred outside. Now what the deuce? A *chaprasi* was running across the *maidan*. One rarely saw *chaprasis* run in this heat. One rarely saw them run. When the man shot into the club, department heads scowled at him for leaving the door open. Quite right. He turned to close it before gasping:

"Sir!" He panted over Krishna's shoulder like a fagged-out pony. "Telegram-sir-arrived-this-instant!"

Chota-Wallah gestured for the envelope and offered it to Krishna, who studied his name, scrawled in purple ink. "At last," he said.

To keep from snatching the envelope away, McAulay clutched his empty glass with both hands. How could anyone be so casual at a time like this? As you were, he reminded himself. How could anyone appear so casual? "Give it over," he said, and Krishna obeyed.

No time for decorum, this. A quick tear and out came the telegram. McAulay handed it back without unfolding the coarse, grey paper. He crumpled the envelope into a ball and tossed it up to Chota-Wallah, who dismissed the *chaprasi* with a backhanded wave. Krishna gestured to the man and handed him a coin. The *chaprasi* smiled triumphantly at Chota-Wallah before leaving.

McAulay watched Krishna's brown eyes scan the telegram. Was it merely a trick of the light or could McAulay detect a gleam? If a gleam, then of what, pride or disappointment? A similar note from home reached him in Malaya: "Twin girls." His disappointment did not last long. Six flares later he burned his hand on the Very pistol. A binge followed to end all binges, then the bloom of a hangover with the awful realization of fatherhood, of responsibility. There might be no fireworks this time but there was still the surprise hidden for this moment, this occasion.

Krishna read the telegram twice but it made no sense to him. Each word made sense but taken together they made none. This was not how he imagined he would feel, not numb like this. He cleared his throat. He read aloud and the full meaning of the message came to him through the sound of his own, hushed voice: "Your wife Rukmini delivered a boy, four pounds, ten ounces, at nine-thirty last night—"

McAulay blurted a laugh. He handed his glass to Chota-Wallah and said, "Another! Nothing but the best."

"Mother and son doing well," Krishna continued. He stopped when Chota-Wallah exclaimed:

"Of course, sir!" Chota-Wallah was grinning at McAulay, who was scowling good-naturedly. "The best of news!"

Krishna finished with, "Congratulations from all here." He folded the telegram and tucked it into a pocket. He allowed himself a proud smile and adjusted his tie.

A boy, McAulay thought. Lucky devil. Both his girls were married but childless. Trying not to think about the grandsons he wanted, he examined Krishna's tie. McAulay owned one much like it: Japanese calligraphy handpainted on silk. McAulay's tie was a bold red. Imperial red. Krishna's was the colour of sand.

"It was sent by my wife's brother," Krishna explained.

"What?" McAulay asked, confused. "Oh, that! Not very expensive, eh? Four pounds, ten? Dear, nonetheless." He rose and waved for Krishna to surrender the telegram again, this time so McAulay could show it to department heads wandering over to investigate. When Krishna also rose, McAulay grasped his arm. Krishna frowned and McAulay released him. Quite right. "Remember," a messmate warned McAulay during their first posting overseas, "speak loudly so they understand you, but never touch them. So they also understand you." McAulay exaggerated his fatherly growl when he asked, "Where do you think you're off to?"

"I must cable my acknowledgement," Krishna said.

"It can wait." McAulay joined his hands in a hollow clap. He gestured at two waiters, led by Chota-Wallah, making their way among the department heads. Chota-Wallah held a bottle of VSOP, another waiter a box of Havanas, and the third a tray of snifters. Hands, most of them sunburnt but a few still pinkish white, reached for snifters and cigars. The snifters clinked in polite competition for the cognac Chota-Wallah poured. "Fancy that," McAulay said. "You won't smoke, will you?"

Krishna shook his head. No, not even now.

"You'll join us in a drink just this once?" McAulay suggested. "That's an order, Mr. Krishna-Rao." Let the man look preoccupied; McAulay abandoned himself to his mirth. "Gentlemen," he declared, "I give you the finest lecturer at Benares Hindu University and, now, the proud father of a boy. Four pounds, ten!"

"Here, here!" said the chorus.

"Sterling?" someone quipped. It was Carruthers, newly arrived from Manchester to head up mechanical engineering.

The chorus chuckled.

Krishna obliged with a smile. Instead of swirling his cognac as the others did, he held his snifter steady. Matches flared while the department heads lit cigars. He backed away from the smoke and wished he could leave. He would rather be outside, in the heat, than suffocate in here.

"So," McAulay asked, "what're you planning to name the boy? Not Stuart, I hope!" When he mused about the possibility only last week, Mildred said, "You do dream."

Krishna glanced at the other men. He could see they were only mildly interested. "After a great Indian statesman," he said. He added, "If I have my way."

McAulay wagged his head over the feeble attempt at humour. The gesture was one he affected despite swearing he would never go native. It meant, "Maybe yes, maybe no." He had to prompt Krishna by raising an unlit cigar.

The reply was a hesitant one: "Gopal Rajagopalachari."

Loosening his tie, McAulay nodded a grudging approval. The Gopal was Krishna's family name. It came first because Mysorians insisted on placing their given names last. The backward practice no longer confused McAulay. C. Rajagopalachari, also a Southerner, had been the first Indian governor-general, a worthy successor to Mountbatten.

"Gopal-what?" Carruthers piped. "Gopal Gopal?"

Krishna ignored him but McAulay summoned up his most withering gaze. It was lost on Carruthers, who raised his glass in a casual toast. McAulay looked back in time to see Krishna pour his drink into the potted fern. Such a waste. McAulay would say so, too, first chance he got. For now, other department heads, trading reminiscences about fatherhood, were closing in, cutting him off from Krishna. Flushed with excitement, McAulay collapsed into his chair. The wicker creaked.

Carruthers took Krishna's place on the sofa but sat dead centre, blocking McAulay's view. "I must say I'll never forget seeing my firstborn," Carruthers mused. "The unexpected result of a leave in Brighton of all places!"

That a woman could arouse passion in Carruthers intrigued McAulay. He had assumed, wrongly it seemed now, that the new head of mechanical was something of a poof. Declining Chota-Wallah's offer of a match, McAulay caught sight of Krishna heading for the door. "You realize you're on leave as of today?" McAulay demanded.

"Thank you," Krishna replied. "For everything." His grin was broad, almost boyish. "There is too much to do here. I shall leave for the South after *karmachario*. At the end of term, I should say."

"That's another two months!" McAulay exclaimed. True, he had not seen his own girls for two months—it had taken that long to ship home—but how long could it take Krishna? First the express to Madras on the coast, then the express inland to Bangalore. Twenty-four hours at most barring layovers.

Krishna raised a hand in farewell. He felt no obligation to explain, and he certainly could not explain in the presence of others. Although constantly thrown together like this, with solitude elusive in such a crowded land, they all lived in their separate worlds. His wife would claim they were characters in one another's dreams but he preferred the certainties of engineering to the vagaries of mysticism. Besides, even McAulay might not understand his ambivalence. Krishna still did not know what use he could be to the boy. Better to let the boy's mother—she was no longer merely a wife—have him to herself for a while. Krishna opened the door and gasped. After the coolness of the club, the heat struck him like compressed air forced into the bottom of a blast furnace. He was careful to pull the door closed behind him.

"Odd chap that," Carruthers said. He gestured over his shoulder with his cigar.

McAulay had to lean sideways to watch Krishna, who strolled away across the *maidan*. The old groundskeeper had long ago found shelter from the sun but Krishna seemed immune to the heat. He walked with his hands in his trouser pockets and looked unusually relaxed.

"Don't know why you waste your time on him," Carruthers said. "Too deep for his own good. Be an iceberg if he weren't black."

McAulay slapped the arm of his chair. The gesture startled Carruthers. McAulay let him squirm before saying, "The name Krishna may mean dark or black, but most natives here aren't black." He lit his cigar. "They're brown." His lighter clinked when he snapped it shut. He watched Carruthers mulling over his gaffe.

Exhaling toward the fan, watching the smoke rise, McAulay thought he finally understood why he cared so much about Krishna. They were trapped in the way too many men—thinking men—were trapped: Krishna by his Anglo-Indian sensibilities, McAulay by his Indian sympathies. Newcomers like Carruthers could never understand such things. McAulay wagged his head again. Maybe yes, maybe no. Dark, black, brown—what did it matter? Of course, it was rarely politic to antagonize colleagues on behalf of a native. On the other hand, a man had to find his fun where he could. Faced with someone like Carruthers, an insipid Englishman to boot, how could a good Scot resist?

"Leave in Brighton," McAulay said, pondering the outcome. "Low season, was it?"

*

After sending his telegram, Krishna dawdled in the university post office while wondering what to do next. He did not want to spend the rest of the afternoon correcting lab reports and he was not about to return to the club. Nor did he want to go home, where his servant would make a fuss over news of the birth. He wondered whether to visit a temple, but he would not know what to do there. His wife and her family could deal with the naming ceremony at the proper time. At any rate, he disliked the noise and bustle of temples. Aside from his office, there was only one place he could find the solitude he cherished. He passed no one on his way there.

The sign on the door, a door painted an uninviting ash grey, read, "Engineering College Museum. Visitors Most Welcome." As far as Krishna knew, he was the only visitor. The museum was tucked in the back of a building, in a room which might better serve as a lab. There was not one proper lab for the faculty's use but this was a minor obstacle compared with his colleagues' indifference. "Why experiment?" they asked him. "Is there not already too much to teach? Besides, what can people like us discover?" The museum was stifling but Krishna closed the door. He ignored the buzz of flies and skitter of cockroaches. The attendant, as usual, was in the workers' canteen.

While Krishna's eyes adapted to the poor lighting, he took out a kerchief and dabbed at the sweat pooling above his collar. He folded the kerchief and passed it from palm to palm until each felt dry, then put it away. He began his tour, stopping first at a bulky electric motor. In better days the motor might have powered a lathe in a factory, even an irrigation pump, but now the motor was forever still. One side of its housing had been cut away to reveal its workings, caked with grease and dust. He caught himself massaging his left wrist. He pressed with his thumb until the scar flamed.

The scar was a memento from his student days. Ten years ago. In another time, at another university, young men like him had thrown themselves into the freedom struggle. In Delhi. In the very shadow of the Raj. Speeches, pamphlets, boycotts—and that final march, the police charging on horseback, the broken wrist, the weeks it had taken to heal, the months he had spent in hiding. He had never suspected he would one day feel nostalgic. Even now he was too young for such things, but he often thought, "It was the season of light, the spring of hope." He would tell his son about this one day—the boy who would plead, "Appa, tell me again how you helped rid India of the British." Krishna would say, "I was not the only one. There were thousands of us. Millions." The boy would nod then, as though the British should have known they could not have won. Krishna caught himself grinning at the motor. Imagine: he a father; he of all people, who had sworn that as long as India needed him he would never settle down.

Continuing his tour, he made his way to the back, where a sphere mounted on a column dwarfed the other displays.

The Van de Graaff stood by itself in a corner. On his very first visit Krishna found it covered with dust and suggested the attendant clean it. "Why, sir?" the attendant asked. "It is no longer operable." He did clean it, though. He brushed away cobwebs for Krishna's benefit alone and polished the signboard: "An electrostatic generator developed in 1928-29 by the U.S. physicist Robert Jemison Van de Graaff." The words told everything yet nothing. One day Krishna would show his son how the generator worked. The boy would be nine or ten, old enough to understand. Krishna heard himself say, "Van de Graaff conceived of this machine while finishing his PhD at Oxford. Then he built a working model. By the early 1930s, at MIT, he was using it to accelerate atomic particles for research."

Krishna heard his son ask, "Appa, how does it work?" The boy would point, correctly, at a small motor on the platform. Wooden blocks held the platform off the concrete floor. In a lab these blocks would be a hard rubber.

"The most elegant things in the world work simply. You see this column which supports the sphere?" The visible part of the column was five feet high; it rose into the sphere, which was seven feet in diameter.

The boy would nod.

"Inside the column, attached to the motor, are belts made of rubberized fabric. Also inside, near the base, are sharp points which press against the belts."

"I see no points," the boy might say. He might even pout. No, he would not be that kind of boy. He would be the kind who delighted in mysteries, in discoveries. Precocious yet well-behaved.

"They're in the column, remember? We call these points a comb. As the motor runs, a power supply of ten thousand volts transfers electric charges to the belts through corona discharge—" Krishna stopped.

The boy might puzzle over this. Even if he knew what a power supply was, he would not understand corona discharges. He would know about friction, though.

Krishna heard himself ask, "What happens when you comb your hair without water?"

"It stands up," the boy would say, lifting strands of hair. "It stands up like this!"

Smoothing the hair down, Krishna would relish the way the bumps on the boy's head nestled under his own palm. The hair would be thick and curly and black.

"Yes, your hair stands up because you're charging it with static electricity. The belts carry the charges from the lower comb to another comb. At the top. From here they move onto the surface of the sphere. It stores them the way a tank stores rainwater. A similar thing happens in your clothes when they rub together on a dry day."

The boy would nod again. He would be a quick learner.

"The sphere continues collecting charges until the ten thousand volts at the bottom becomes a million volts at the top. The larger the tank, the more water it can hold, correct? And so, the larger the sphere, the more charges it can hold. Engineers at a place called Los Alamos, in America, have built a Van de Graaff which can generate twelve million volts. Can you imagine?"

The boy would grow wide-eyed at this. Rightly so, Krishna thought. Such things were possible in places like Los Alamos, where a physicist named Robert Oppenheimer had developed the first atomic bomb. And yet, only last year, Oppenheimer had lost his security clearance and was hounded out of government work. The FBI called him a Communist because he now opposed developing a hydrogen bomb. Krishna grimaced at the pitted metal of the sphere. Rust did to metal what politics did to science. The boy would learn this as well.

Krishna's eyes returned to the motor. Its housing had not been cut away. Instead, someone had painted the motor green. It was the same green as the lower third of the Indian flag, a green meant to pass for the fertility of this land. The connecting shaft was frozen under the paint. Worse, the power supply was missing, likely scavenged by another department, and the sphere was not only pitted but also dull. On a proper Van de Graaff, the sphere would be so shiny it would reflect the boy's upturned face. This one was clouded like an old mirror. It could barely reflect the light streaming through the barred windows. Not that there was any need for bars—there was little here worth stealing.

On the wall between the nearest window and the Van de Graaff hung a grounding rod. Its hard rubber shaft was narrow and also ended in a sphere, a tiny one. This tiny sphere was to the large one what the moon was to the earth, or the earth to the sun. Krishna pulled the grounding rod out of a clip on the wall. He heard himself say, "If we want, we can discharge the Van de Graaff and cause arcing. Remember how if your clothes are dry and you touch something that's metal—"

"It goes snap and I jump!" The boy would clap his hands and laugh. "It makes a spark!"

"Because you're discharging the static your clothes have built up. On a Van de Graaff we can pull the charges off the large sphere so you won't get a shock when you touch it. The charges arc to this rod. Then we're once again at equilibrium, at rest, but only for a moment since the charges build up as long as the belts run."

The boy would look proud of himself because he would understand how simple it all was. How elegant. He might even be proud of his father for working with such a splendid machine.

Krishna looked up from his son and tapped the large sphere with the tiny one. The noise was dull, not resonant, because the tiny sphere was not metal. It was a cricket ball, fixed in place with twine. The relative proportions were wrong. A sphere this size was too small to discharge the Van de Graaff without being buffetted by the charges, perhaps even split.

Of all things, he thought: a cricket ball. It was one of his own. He had asked the attendant to paint it silver but the attendant had been unable to find silver paint so he had painted the ball orange. It was the same orange as the upper third of the Indian flag, a yellowy orange meant to pass for the saffron of spirituality. This was the India he helped free for his son and his son's sons—fertile and spiritual. Where once, he believed, anything was possible. Not now; not any more. Rust had set in. The flaws had been painted over. Cobwebs reappeared. Perhaps one day someone would also paint the large sphere and column and repaint the cricket ball. If there were still no silver paint to be found, he hoped they would at least use white.

Krishna snapped the grounding rod into its clip and turned to leave. He took a different route this time, through the civil engineering displays. He stopped at a model of a dam with its reservoir; a small-scale turbine, generator and transformer; and a model of a transmission tower. Grandiose labels, brittle and cracked, tried to explain hydroelectricity: generating power from water.

Once, when he was six, he visited his father at a power station he had built in the hills. His father showed him how water, falling through intake tubes, pushed the blades of the turbines, which spun the generators to produce electric power. Transformers boosted the power further and transmission lines took it through the hills to substations at nearby towns and faraway cities. The equipment was breathtaking, gigantic; yet Krishna understood nothing. To keep his father happy, he nodded each time his father said, "Are you following me?" Afterward, standing on the dam which held back the calm waters of the reservoir, Krishna asked if he could go swimming. His father snorted. "Do you want to be sucked into an intake tube? We will have to shut down the turbines to pick pieces of you out." Later, in college, Krishna wondered how his father could have imagined that a boy of six would understand such things. Now, turning from the models, Krishna promised himself he would never make the same mistake. The secret of being a father was to know the precise moment at which a boy was old enough to learn.

Krishna headed for the door. Just as he reached the cut-away motor, he sneezed. He had not realized his footsteps were raising so much dust. When he stopped to blow his nose, his eye caught a calendar picture on the back of the door. The image pleased him.

It was a picture of Ganesha, the god of wisdom. The god sat cross-legged on a cushion. He had the body of a pot-bellied man, the head of an elephant with one tusk broken, and four arms. His four hands clutched a shell, a discus, a goad and a water lily. His skin was yellow. Children liked him because he ate as much as he wanted, especially fruit and sweets. Adults liked him because he was the remover of obstacles, a god to be worshipped before every undertaking: building a house, leaving on a journey. Below the picture was a calendar for 1955. The months were grouped in four columns of three, with a list of feast days separating the two halves of the year. Unlike the western calendars Krishna preferred, with their days of the week across the top and the dates running from left to right, this local calendar was printed with the days along the left and the dates running from top to bottom. Most of the dates were in black. Red-lettered days were for feasts. Skimming a fingertip across the thin paper, he finally located his own red-letter day: yesterday, March 15th. How odd. The boy had been born seven years and seven months after Independence. So had a thousand other children, no doubt. Krishna wagged his head. If he mentioned this to Mali, even in jest, he might say something foolishly wise like, "It is a sign, Yuvaraj-sir." But a sign of what? Mali would shrug and say, "We must give this much consideration."

This time, when Krishna opened the door, he did not gasp in the heat but he did loosen his tie. A cockroach scuttled out of the light. He crossed the threshold and pulled the door shut. Shading his eyes from the sun, he looked across the *maidan* and squinted at the cricket pitch. He clenched his fists and laughed at the brilliant, blue sky. A son! The things they could do once the boy was older: the things a man could do with no one except his son.

# Chapter 2

## *The Good Brahmin*

With every passing week, Saroja had to stand farther back and bend farther forward to clear the table. She reached for a plate stained with lime pickle and curds. A muscle in her back clenched. It felt as though tiny hands were squeezing the base of her spine into pulp. Biting on a knuckle to keep from crying out, she eased herself into a chair. She massaged the knuckle and rocked to ease the spasm. From the front room came the squeaks and squawks of a violin tuned by someone oblivious to her discomfort.

Saroja traced the grain of the tabletop. The lines within the whorls turned in on themselves but the lines around them joined the outer lines of neighbouring whorls—just like the lines in her fingerprints, just like lines joining and circling members of an extended family. In another month, she too would be a mother like her sister-in-law, Rukmini, who lay upstairs with her baby. It was nine weeks since Rukmini had given birth. With Krishna's arrival imminent, the time had come for Saroja to reveal her latest plan. She rose with care but the pain did not return. Silently cursing her waddling gait, she entered the front room.

Her husband, Rukmini's brother Prakash, sat on the floor and toyed with his violin. He was naked from the waist up. His Brahmin thread, crossing his chest from one shoulder to the roll of flesh at his waist, clung to the sweat. The pipe clenched in his teeth remained unlit.

"I have been thinking," Saroja announced in Telugu. "If this child of ours is a girl, we should name her Chandramati."

Prakash's lips curved around the stem of his pipe. At the same time he stopped tuning the violin long enough to show he was listening. "Simply because my sister named her son after King Harischandra," Prakash teased, "you want to bring tales from the *Markandeya Purana* to life? Why not a true epic like the *Mahabharata*?"

"If this child of ours is a girl," Saroja declared, "we should promise her to little Harish."

Prakash's belly quivered while he laughed. He had not had the paunch at their wedding, when he had immersed himself in water before changing to sit next to her at the sacred fire. Even then she thought he needed to put on weight. Now he blamed her for what he called her plot to kill him with savouries and sweets.

"You are dreaming too much, I say," he declared.

"It is all I can do these days," she reminded him. She stifled the "Oof!" that came to her lips when she dropped the last few inches to the floor. She sat with her spine pressed against the wall to ward off more spasms. "No-o, I have been thinking," she repeated. "We are now joined with Krishna's family. This is why Rukmini named her son Harischandra. Krishna's father is still called—"

"—a modern Harischandra," Prakash finished for her, "because he always keeps his word. Just as Harischandra, King of Ayodhya, renowned throughout the land for his piety and his justice—"

She clucked her tongue, and Prakash stopped. She scowled to remind him he should not make fun of the old stories. The tale of King Harischandra was one of her favourites. During long years of hardship brought on by gods who wished to test him, the king lost his throne, his wife, and their son. And yet he remained so true to his word, so steadfast, that the gods declared he and his family had conquered heaven itself. Only when Prakash chuckled his apology did she continue:

"So why not name our daughter after King Harischandra's wife? It would be a good omen. Rukmini would look favourably on the match."

"Krishna does not believe in such things," Prakash warned. "He wanted the boy named for Rajagopalachari, remember?"

"What do we need with statesmen in this family?" she demanded.

"But kings and queens," Prakash said, "that is another matter." He finally put down his violin and bow. He also took the pipe from his mouth.

"The boy is not some king," she said. "He will become an engineering teacher like his father."

"And our daughter Chandramati," Prakash said, "if the child proves to be a girl—why so pessimistic, I say?—will become a storyteller like you."

Saroja leaned forward to stare into his eyes, eyes so much kinder than his tongue. "Look at Krishna and Rukmini," she insisted. "Are they not like Lord Krishna and Princess Rukmini themselves?"

"More legends?" Prakash groaned.

"Did they not marry in defiance of tradition because they were in love?"

"The princess and the lord," he asked, "or my sister and her husband? Many people from different states marry now. It is a modern tradition. Besides, only my sister was in love. Krishna was obeying his father's wishes to get settled."

"Oh, you know so much," Saroja declared. She knew she could convince him, though. "If Krishna had not been in love also, why did he win the tennis tournament?"

Prakash slapped his forehead. "Leave me alone, I say! Go back to your room and dream."

Her room indeed, she thought; the room he entered only if he were hungry. She rose by pressing her palms flat against the wall. "I shall leave you to your violin. Perhaps one day you will learn to play it."

Jingling her bangles, swishing her sari, she returned to the dining room. No matter what Prakash said, she knew Rukmini and Krishna's marriage had been foretold by poets; that her sister-in-law and her brother-in-law by marriage were merely acting out a play composed centuries before. Why else were Hindus reborn if not to keep playing out the same roles, as though each life were a rehearsal for the next? Perhaps it was not enlightenment that would bring an end to rebirth but a final, perfect performance.

Saroja sat down at the table and once more traced the swirling grain, the lines within families and those joining families.

It had all been so simple, she thought; so clearly pre-ordained. Rukmini had come to Bangalore from Madras to meet a man named Reddi, whom Prakash had chosen for her. Their parents had died some years ago, so he was acting in their stead. From their first meeting, Saroja did not care for Reddi and she said as much. Everyone called him Reddi-or-Nought, because though he never played cricket he always knew the latest test match scores. One day Krishna dropped by for a visit. He rarely spoke about games; he played them. He defeated Reddi in the Institute tennis tournament, then won the singles championship and unwittingly stole Rukmini's heart. How spectacular! Saroja was glad for Rukmini. Had Rukmini's parents been alive she would never have questioned their choice of a husband. Families knew what was best for their children. However, as Saroja told Prakash then, he had been mistaken in his choice of Reddi. Poor Reddi-or-Nought. He had settled for a girl from another Madrasi family, rich but dark.

And even if everyone laughed when Saroja pointed out the legendary parallels, she enjoyed herself at Krishna and Rukmini's wedding. There were differences between real life and legend, of course. For one thing, Krishna had not abducted

Rukmini from her wedding the way Lord Krishna had abducted Princess Rukmini from hers. For another, no one could compare Reddi with the prince to whom Princess Rukmini had been promised. But the parallels were close enough for Saroja. And now, if little Harish could be promised to a girl named Chandramati, named for King Harischandra's queen, their own play could begin—the gods willing, for one last time.

"Finally!" Prakash exclaimed in English. Saroja's heart leapt. She had not heard the front door open but now she heard it close.

"Krishna has arrived!" Prakash shouted.

Saroja pressed her hand to her fluttering heart. She was becoming overly sensitive to noise, that was all. But here she dreamt. Here she was, caught without a clean plate on the table. She combed the pleats of her sari with her fingers until the cloth lay smooth over her belly. Ignoring an impulse to look for a mirror, she rose and walked as gracefully as she could into the front room. "*Yelaunnavu*?" she asked. She switched to English. "How have you been? How was the journey? Tiring? These trains become less comfortable with all these villagers crowding—"

"Too long," Krishna sighed. He dropped his suitcase and flopped gladly into Prakash's reading chair, the only chair in the front room. Krishna crossed one knee over the other. He did not consider himself a slave to comfort—he liked his surroundings simple—but he did prefer western-style furniture to Indian floors.

They made such a pair, Saroja thought: Prakash with his paunch and Krishna, so tall and slim, looking like Lord Krishna himself. It was a pity Rukmini did not have the poise of her legendary namesake, but that would have been too perfect. When a present life imitated a past life too closely, it was not a good sign. The play always told the same story, yes, and with the same characters, of course; yet if there were no differences the gods would lose interest.

But what was she thinking of when the poor man likely had not eaten? "You are hungry?" she asked. Even if she had to send Prakash to the First Class Hotel, no one would leave her house without eating.

"I ate near the station only now," Krishna said.

"You have not seen your wife in over three months," Saroja cried, "and you dawdle in some second class eating place? Who knows what kind of flour they use! Rancid, or mixed with chalk!"

"How is she?" he asked.

"She has got over it," Prakash said, "but for some time we were both worried."

Krishna noticed Saroja's warning glance and sat up. Now what? Perhaps he should have come sooner, after all. He felt compelled to apologize for his delay. "There was nothing in her letters."

"Well, she—" Prakash began.

"*Yenraja*?" Saroja scolded. "Why do you try to explain matters you know nothing about?" She turned to Krishna. "Your wife had no milk. She became hysterical and asked us to send a cable. We did not. What was there to worry? We hired a wet nurse from my village itself. Her name is Helen. She will travel to Benares with the two of you if you wish. With the three of you. Only, she will have to return to our village for the planting."

Krishna did not know how he should act: whether to show shock, which he did not feel, or concern, which he did feel. Only a callous man would not be concerned. "May I see her?" he asked.

"They are upstairs taking their nap," Saroja answered.

Krishna sat back and clasped his hands on his knee. "I will not disturb them then." What could a man say to his wife about her problems? He needed time to prepare.

"What?" Saroja cried. "You have not seen your wife in months, and you keep her waiting even longer? Do you not want to see your son? What kind of father does not become so excited that he makes a fool of himself! Even in the company of others."

Krishna grinned while straightening the creases of his trousers. They were flecked with soot from the train. Of the few women he knew, Saroja seemed to know him best. He enjoyed her teasing but he did not like being mistaken for a book, open for anyone to read. He looked to Prakash for support and Prakash shrugged as if to say, "You see what I put up with?" Krishna rose and headed for the stairway. At the bottom he stopped and asked Saroja, "Will you come up also?" He was not good at reunions.

Saroja followed him. "It is hot in Benares?"

"A hundred in the shade." Krishna ducked to clear the sloped ceiling at the foot of the stairs. "No wonder all those people remain in the Ganges all day. No wonder the water is so filthy."

She clucked her tongue at his sacrilege. She knew Krishna had worn the Brahmin thread for the first time in years at his wedding. Even then, after the immersion and the ceremony at the sacred fire, he had given the thread to Prakash, who kept it safe in case Krishna might ever need it. Prakash wore his own thread at all times and went to temples with her, yet he drank at the Institute club like a westerner while Krishna did no such thing. Who then was the better Brahmin?

When Krishna stopped at the head of the stairs, Saroja passed him and rounded a corner. Helen lay asleep in the corridor. She was a Christian and called herself Helen after the heroine of a Greek legend. As long as Helen's breasts held plenty of milk, Saroja could tolerate her dislike of Brahmins—a dislike verging on distrust. Moving quietly, Saroja opened narrow, louvred doors and waved Krishna in ahead of her.

Her sister-in-law turned on her cot. "*Yem*-Saroja?" Rukmini sounded like a drowsy child. She seemed to have grown younger and more frail since her son's birth. She spent hours in the third bedroom, where Saroja stored her doll collection—hours with the girl from Holland who wore a pointed, lace cap and pointed, wooden shoes; the boy from Scotland with his checked skirt, which Prakash called a kilt; the girl from America with her red face, her black braids, and her beaded leather dress. Rukmini showed them all to the boy even while he slept. The upstairs room was as far as she had taken him by herself. She would not carry him down the stairs for fear she might stumble. Helen carried him then and sometimes Rukmini seemed reluctant to take him back, as if he were not the same baby downstairs as he was upstairs alone with her.

"*Yem*-Saroja?" Rukmini repeated.

"No one special," Saroja replied in English. "Your husband only. The father of your son." She did not know what to expect. Surely any reunion between a man and wife would be strained after so long? Still, Rukmini's first words to Krishna astounded Saroja. She glanced at him as if to say, "You see why we did not bother you."

"Oh Krishna," Rukmini cried, "it hurt so much! I thought I would split open and die!"

Saroja bit her lip. Even if childbirth nearly killed her, she could never admit such a thing. Certainly not to a man.

Krishna hurried to Rukmini's side. His weight threatened to tip the cot when he sat on the edge, so he rose. The legs on the far side met the bare floor with a thump. He squatted beside the cot to wipe a tear from Rukmini's cheek. He did this with a corner of her sari, and he did it gently.

Saroja moved to the hammock near the open window. From here she could see Krishna's face better. If anything, she saw only sadness in his firmly set mouth. Did he feel this way for putting his wife through such an ordeal? Or for her weakness? He did not tolerate weakness in himself, so why would he tolerate it in others, even his wife? Saroja turned her back on the cot and looked at the baby. He lay asleep in his hammock. She twirled it on the single rope hanging from a hook in the ceiling. He had his grandfather's perpetually worried eyes. Yet why had Krishna's father not visited the boy? She thought Prakash had been joking when he claimed the old man had washed his hands of all relations. But she felt it was a strange family, whose members rarely saw one another. She had met few of them—and only Krishna's father, who no longer lived with his wife, and some distant cousins. Krishna's mother lived in Mauritius. Saroja had never even met Krishna's elder brother, who lived in London. The boy had been disowned for marrying a low-class English girl. What had he expected, a knighthood?

There, it happened again. Each time Saroja looked at the baby while he slept, he opened his eyes and feebly waved his fists. Prakash could chide her but she knew this boy possessed the sixth sense of those born in March. It was as though the shock of birth had been unable to drive the memory of his past lives from his mind. He even appeared to know his tears would be wasted, and so he rarely cried.

"Come," she told Krishna. "Your son is calling." While Krishna approached the hammock, she squeezed herself behind it, then leaned against the sill to rest her back.

His expectant smile changed to a frown.

"You are not pleased?" she whispered. "The limbs of all babies are crooked. Over time they will straighten. My younger sister, you remember she is at Maharani's College—"

"Of course," he muttered. He shook his head at the way Saroja went on at times. "Only the boy is so . . ." Krishna ran a finger along the narrow ribs and flat brown belly. Tiny, he thought. Surely neither he nor his brother had ever been this tiny? "How will he play games," Krishna asked, "if he is so small?"

"Listen to this," Saroja called toward the cot. "Your son is not three months old, and your husband wants him to become an all-rounder! Team sports," she asked Krishna, "or individual sports? You will teach him cricket, hah? Batting and bowling? You will teach him to keep your wickets?"

He tried to chuckle at the fond scolding but he glanced at Rukmini and his smile faded. He felt as helpless as the child looked. Krishna resented feeling this way.

Saroja turned to look out the window. A passing bullock cart loaded with sugar cane dropped leaves into the unpaved street. They swirled above the dust. The driver seemed to have forgotten that the season for sugar cane was long past. He seemed not to care. Someone would buy his crop if only to feed to cows. She turned to look at the tall man frowning over his son and at the girl-woman who had finally risen. Rukmini's unbraided locks fell to the small of her back but Saroja did not offer to braid them. Only this morning she told Rukmini she must look strong for

Krishna. Rukmini lowered her eyes and made a face as though she could never be pretty again.

There was nothing more Saroja could do for now. "I will be downstairs if you require anything." She squeezed herself out from behind the hammock. After opening the doors, she closed them behind her, but she could not leave the corridor. She could never resist eavesdropping. How else had she learned, outside her parents' door, that children were conceived not from love but from desire? And not always desire for children.

"Krishna," she heard Rukmini say, "I do not want another child. I cannot go through that again."

"What is there?" he asked. "Millions of women have gone through it."

The voices came clearly through the louvres.

"The day before my brother brought me home from the hospital," Rukmini said, "a woman died while delivering her tenth child."

"Oh, I say!" Krishna exclaimed.

Saroja nodded. There was a big difference between bearing three or four children and bearing ten. She glanced at Helen, who snored. The dead woman must have been a villager, yet how could she have afforded a hospital unless the child had been a landowner's? Everyone knew the way of villages. Things were not always as innocent as people liked to pretend.

"*Yenraja*?" Rukmini said. "Not every woman wants more than one child. We have a son now, that is enough. I spoke with the doctor and she said there are a few days, better to leave a week to be safe, when we should resist temptation. Sleep in separate rooms if need be."

Saroja clapped her hands over her ears. She would be struck deaf listening to such things. After moving carefully past Helen, Saroja went down the stairs one step at a time. In another month she would be able to run again. She had never seen Rukmini run, not even for a lark. What if she and Krishna were mismatched, after all? What if she had loved him more before the wedding than afterward? Such things were known to happen with love matches. From the foot of the stairs, Saroja watched Prakash tune his violin. She could not call him handsome, but he was kind. He had understood her need to escape the village yet never acted as though he had rescued her; as though she owed him any more than he owed her. This is why she loved him already, only three years after their wedding: for the things he left unsaid.

"How did it go?" he asked.

"Fine, fine," she replied. "How else?" Annoyed with her lie, she turned away. "I shall be in my room if you want anything." She reached the dining table, sat down heavily and ignored the uncleared dishes. She had been looking forward to Krishna's arrival so much, perhaps too much. How could she raise the subject now of promising her daughter to Harish? As it was, Krishna and Rukmini faced too many obstacles to think clearly about their son's marriage.

Saroja looked about the room and sighed. Soon this would no longer be her room. But no place in any house would be sacred to children except one. If Prakash secured a permanent appointment—she had made him apply for one in Hyderabad—she would have him build a house for her with a godroom. It would have a door of brass bars. This way everyone would know to leave her in peace while she did her *puja*: while she lit the flame, arranged the flowers, and made her offerings. It was such a little thing to ask, one every mother deserved: her very own godroom.

✵

Madras Central Station was as busy as usual. And July was a hot month. Still people travelled in spite of the discomfort. Jesudas Fernandez puffed his cheeks, blew a soundless train whistle, and snapped his pocket watch shut. The Delhi Express would be pulling out in twenty-seven minutes.

From across his desk a woman named Meera-Bai glared at him. Within seconds of marching into his office, she had soured his entire day. He wanted to tell her to get out. He wanted to ask her, "Who do you think you are addressing?"

"Well?" Meera-Bai clutched her furled umbrella like a field marshal's baton. "Are you simply going to stand there, or shall I cable the Prime Minister?"

Fernandez glanced at Meera-Bai's secretary. The man was a gaunt Muslim. He wore a knee-length coat called a *sherwani* and tapered trousers called *churidars*. He remained silent and dropped a ten-rupee note on Fernandez's desk. Fernandez pocketed the note and pulled on his tunic. Then he led Meera-Bai down from his office, which overlooked Buckingham Canal. Her secretary lagged behind for he walked with a slight limp, which slowed him on the stairs. Poor Madrasis and villagers began arriving hours before departure. They spent the time squatting in dark corners where flies buzzed over banana peels. Next, the second class ticket holders arrived to fill the waiting rooms. At the last moment, the first class passengers sauntered through the gates. Fernandez clucked his tongue. Those Americans again, with their saffron robes and canvas shoes! Americans, preaching the joys of Hinduism to Hindus. The world continually amazed him.

There were twenty-five minutes left.

When he caught sight of the man standing on the platform outside D compartment, Fernandez slowed. Station master or not, he dreaded the upcoming confrontation. It was one thing to tell porters and conductors to go to hell; it was quite another to quarrel with a man so tall he resembled a Sikh except for his cleanshaven face and bare head. It helped to stay on the good side of such men. Glancing at his clipboard, Fernandez read the name *G. Krishna-Rao*. Good name for a Hindu, Fernandez thought. Beside the man stood a young woman in a turquoise sari. Behind her stood a much older woman, who held a baby. The grandmother, no doubt. A servant was rearranging luggage in their compartment. To remain on the safe side, Fernandez made *namaskar*. He joined his palms in front of his breast and bowed while introducing himself.

Meera-Bai began tapping the tip of her umbrella on the platform. The umbrella clicked like a clock.

Elsewhere in the station, someone beat a steel bar and the Madurai Express pulled out. It was a mere six minutes late. After glancing at his clipboard again, Fernandez said, "I am sorry, sir, but I am going to have to ask you to—" He told himself to stop whispering, for God's sake. Was he not in charge here? "—to leave your compartment. This lady and her secretary would like your berths." There, it was out. Fernandez had said the same thing many times over the years; yet his mouth had never felt so dry. He held his breath when Krishna stiffened. Fernandez exhaled when Krishna slipped his hands into the pockets of his white flannels. Even in this heat, he wore a college blazer. Fernandez could not place the crest.

Both of the women with Krishna cried, "What!"

Fernandez ignored them for the time being. He could deal with them later, not to worry.

"I am Mrs. Meera-Bai," the woman beside Fernandez announced. She raised her umbrella like a signalman's flag, a red flag. "I am a Member of the *Lok Sabha,*" she said, speaking Hindi now. "My secretary and I must reach Delhi the day after tomorrow for a special sitting. Called by Pandit Nehru himself."

Fernandez heard a shuffle and felt her secretary back away. The secretary asked no one in particular, "Is there no berth in another compartment?"

Fernandez knew the answer. All the same he consulted his clipboard. "One only," he announced, "in A compartment."

"I shall take it then," the secretary said.

"Nonsense," Meera-Bai snapped at him. She said to the gathering at large, "I travel with my secretary at all times."

A vendor pushing a cart stopped nearby. It was loaded with bananas, oranges and biscuits. The group on the platform ignored him but people in the carriage tried to open their windows to get his attention. Most would not budge. Fernandez also tried to ignore the vendor but the smell of oranges began overpowering other smells: the axle grease, the urine on the tracks.

"I fail to see the problem," Krishna said. Sometimes problems in this newly constituted country could be magnified out of proportion. He wondered how anything got done. There was enough tension stored in the people to power several hundred Van de Graaff generators. The thought amused and sickened him. He looked at the servant who now stood on the carriage step waiting for the baby. "We have reserved only two berths."

A wet nurse, Fernandez decided. Her breasts resembled sacks of copra. Between them dangled a crucifix. He briefly touched his own, safe beneath his undershirt.

"She will sleep in the corridor near the attendant's place," Krishna said. "That leaves two berths for the lady and her secretary. At any rate, we shall be getting down at Benares and they can have the compartment to themselves."

"This is what I was telling her!" Fernandez cried. "You see, Madame, there was no need to worry. No need at all." He longed to be back in his office with his tunic unbuttoned; with some curds to cool his stomach; with his paper and pencil and plans. His stomach was churning from the effects of too much fried food during the day.

The umbrella clicked even louder now. Sparks might just as well have flown from it—the platform was growing unbearably hot. "You said a child would be in the compartment?" Meera-Bai asked him, abandoning her Hindi. Why could she not leave him out of this? Ten rupees, that was why. "I cannot have a child crying all night."

The older woman hugged the baby closer. Her marigold sari was made from Kanchi silk. Something about her worried Fernandez but he could not decide what it was. Her apparent indifference, perhaps? Her confidence everything would work out? The polite disdain, he thought, of someone from the upper classes.

"I need my sleep," Meera-Bai declared.

"The boy will not cry all night," Krishna said.

"He never cries," Rukmini added.

Fernandez glanced at his clipboard. Her name was listed as *Mrs. G. Rukmini.*

Meera-Bai insisted, "All babies cry."

When she glared at Fernandez, he nodded in agreement. How many nights had his own son kept him awake in earlier days? Now the boy was grown up and Fernandez still lay awake nights because the boy refused to marry that nice girl from Old Goa. Fernandez had grown up with her father. He was no mere station master; he was a gazetted civil servant.

Meera-Bai took a step backward and raised her chin in a brave attempt to look taller than she was. "Do you people not realize who I am?" she demanded. "I represent you in Delhi."

"We do not vote in Madras," Krishna said. "We are only passing through."

Fernandez suppressed an urge to chuckle. Meera-Bai was succeeding only in looking ridiculous. Worse yet, she seemed to know it.

"I spent five years in prison," she told him, "so people like this could have their precious Independence. You see how I am treated?"

Fernandez nodded again.

All this time, Krishna had been polite, almost offhand, but the word *precious* irked him. He took his hands from his pockets and said, "Do not talk of prisons!" Even as he felt his temper flare, he knew he could do nothing to stop it. Who did this woman think she was? Member of the *Lok Sabha* indeed. Member of the House of Commons, more like.

Fernandez kept his eyes on those large hands. He was the only one within their reach. The secretary stood too far back. Perhaps Fernandez could use his clipboard as a shield—he saw this done in a Bombay talkie once—but the hands remained open, thank God.

People in the carriages were peering through the dirty windows. Some people were asking questions; others were shrugging. The vendor was all but forgotten.

"When you Congress Party people were making martyrs of yourselves," Krishna continued, "my friends and I remained on the outside so we could—"

"Then you are a Communist!" Meera-Bai said loudly. Fernandez nodded for a third time, gravely now. Only Communists and terrorists had refused to go to jail as Mahatma Gandhi had asked. Besides, Krishna's fists had clenched. "What did I say?" she cried. "A *goonda*, that is all he is. Just another hoodlum."

"Do not excite yourself, Madame," Fernandez pleaded. He glanced at the platform clock. Seventeen minutes to go.

The older woman, the one who remained silent after demanding, "What!" handed the baby to his mother, then adjusted her own sari. The fine silk was wrinkled at the shoulder. "I have heard enough. This girl is my husband's niece and Mr. Krishna-Rao is therefore my nephew by marriage. No one removes them from their compartment. Not Pandit Nehru himself."

Fernandez peered at her, then searched for her name on the passenger list. Who could she be? More important, who was her husband? A drop of sweat blurred the ink.

Krishna felt his brow knit. He needed no one's help with this, least of all from Rukmini's aunt. Not that he resented her wealth, and she was wealthy—the Madras House in which he had spent the past week left no doubt of this. It was just that the quarrel was between Meera-Bai and himself, and he needed no assistance.

When the vendor moved on, the smell of oranges moved with him. From the windows of the first class carriage, passengers who had ignored him now waved for his attention. Too late. The wet nurse, tired of standing, closed the door and retreated to the attendant's folding seat.

Meera-Bai jerked her head backward in mock fear like a starlet. "And who is your husband, may I inquire?"

Krishna plunged his hands into his pockets and turned away. The debate was no longer his to win. He could not compete with the reserves on which Rukmini's aunt could call. Especially her husband, even in his absence.

"Was," the aunt said. "He is no more."

Fernandez was about to offer condolences when Meera-Bai inclined her head in exaggerated respect. "And who was your husband, may I inquire?"

"Sir S.V. Ramamurthy," the aunt said.

Oh, God, why? Fernandez felt bile rise to his throat. His teeth were beginning to ache, something they did if he went too long without a *beedi*. If only he had brought one, but he could not smoke in the presence of first class passengers. Not even Americans. It was time to switch sides, ten rupees or not. Fernandez tucked his clipboard under his arm and wrung his hands.

"A thousand pardons, Lady Ramamurthy," he said. "I had no inkling, none whatsoever, not one iota!" He glanced at Krishna, whose back was still turned.

Meera-Bai handed her umbrella to her secretary and made *namaskar*. She bowed more reverently than Fernandez had. "Why did you not intimate this before?" she asked. "I met your husband after he was knighted by the Viceroy. I do not suppose he mentioned my name? My secretary and I would be honoured to travel with the niece of such an illustrious man. This is your baby?" she asked Rukmini. "Such a sweet thing," Meera-Bai crooned. She wiggled a finger at the sleeping child until Rukmini joined Krishna, who then turned to face the gathering.

Fernandez glanced at the clock. Fifteen minutes left and yet another problem solved. He had not become station master through influence alone.

"No you will not!" Krishna snapped. He flicked his hand at Meera-Bai and said, "I do not want this, this viper sleeping near my son."

What now? Fernandez wanted to cry. Why could these people not take their petty quarrels elsewhere?

"Who do you think you are," Krishna asked her. The words welled up in him the way they had years ago at rallies, at marches. "Demanding that people make way for you! If not for my classmates, no one could have fought either the British or the Communists." He raised his hands level with his head. It was throbbing from all the noise in the station. Fitters were inspecting the engine now, clanging their crowbars against its wheels. "You, your kind played Joan of Arc and pulled your hair and cried, 'See how we are suffering in prison!' while thinking people . . . while patriots like Ashok Mehta and Purnima Banerjee kept up the freedom struggle." There had been many others Krishna could name, men and women he never thought to call heroic.

But wait, Fernandez wanted to ask; had not Gandhi and Nehru kept up the struggle? Had not the Congress Party alone freed India?

"So, you are a good Socialist," Meera-Bai declared. Her raised eyebrows signalled Fernandez, "What did I tell you?"

There was silence on the platform now. The people in the carriages, who could not hear any of this, waited for something dramatic to happen. Something violent, perhaps.

This was the last thing Fernandez wanted. He looked about for a railway policeman but none was in sight. He forced himself to remain calm. Fortunately, Krishna dropped his hands. Fernandez knew nothing of Mehta or Banerjee but every Indian knew about the Socialist Party and how Gandhi had opposed its methods.

"I was a patriot," Krishna exclaimed. How dare this woman presume to judge him, to sneer at him like this? "Now you Hindi-speaking people are acting just like the British did." He wrenched open the carriage door and climbed the steps. He turned in the doorway and snapped, "You are nothing but a brown memsahib!"

Fernandez paled at the insult. He glanced at Meera-Bai, who seemed beyond reaching with fists let alone insults.

She grabbed her umbrella from the secretary and shook it at Krishna. "You cannot keep me out of that compartment!" she shouted. She turned first to Fernandez, who looked away, still embarrassed for her, then to Rukmini. "Your husband is being unreasonable," Meera-Bai pleaded. "The VIP quota stipulates—"

"I shall be more reasonable." It was Lady Ramamurthy again. "Sir," she said, addressing Fernandez.

He straightened the baggy hem of his tunic. He imagined telling his son, "Lady Ramamurthy herself called me sir."

"I shall buy the remaining berths," she said, "and let Mr. Krishna-Rao decide who shall have them."

Fernandez threw up his hands. His clipboard fell to the platform. He heard himself cry, "Jesus-Mary-Joseph! Please, ladies, there is only—" He glanced at the clock. "—twelve minutes remaining!" He longed for a sip of curds, even some soda. Anything to calm his churning stomach. Hindi-speaking, English-speaking, Congressman, Socialist—they were all the same to him. He had a station to run.

The secretary picked up the clipboard.

"This will not be necessary, Sharada," Rukmini told her aunt. The baby opened his eyes and clutched at his mother's breast. She moved his hand away. "I am sure Krishna will not mind if Mrs. Meera-Bai's secretary travels with us. She could still travel in the other compartment."

"In A compartment." Fernandez nodded at his saviour. "It is at the far end of the carriage from the child," he told Meera-Bai.

She looked away and her brow furled. She wondered whether to send her secretary after the vendor. He was wheeling his cart toward the second class carriages. First class passengers were descending now to clamour for his attention. They waved for him to return.

"Splendid," Fernandez cried. "All our problems are solved!" He made *namaskar* twice to Lady Ramamurthy and accepted his clipboard from the secretary. "This way, please, Madame." Meera-Bai was tightlipped now, silent in defeat. He pushed aside a hovering porter and ordered, "Make way for the Member of Parliament!" He waited until they reached the carriage step before taking the ten-rupee note from his pocket. Then he slipped it back to her. Oh well, the saffron-robed Americans had a saying for it: "Come easy, go easy." After his son collected the girl's dowry, if the boy ever settled down, they would found a booming business. "Fernandez and Son (Madras) Ltd.," their sign would read. "Manufacturers of Quality Tuning Knobs."

Dreaming of all the foreign currency the business would earn nearly lightened his mood, but he still had to hurry the fitters inspecting the engine. There were only ten minutes left.

❋

While the train rolled through the countryside, Muhammad Azad lay on an upper berth with his face to the wall. A fan in a wire cage spun inches from his head. All evening he had been trying to apologize to Krishna for Meera-Bai's thoughtlessness but Azad still felt like an accomplice. Once, trying a different tack, he remarked, "Your wife's uncle was known to have a keen legal mind." To this, Krishna replied:

"So I have heard."

Azad left to pace in the corridor and look for distractions in the passing landscape. There was little to see. After returning, he took refuge behind his tattered copy of *The Life of Mahatma Gandhi* by the American Louis Fischer. The title elicited no comment from Krishna.

Now, chafing in his close-fitting *sherwani*, Azad turned and rested his head on his right arm. He squinted at the luminous dial of his wrist watch, swaying on a hook under the fan. It had been two hours since the sun had set like a blazing poppy, two hours since Azad and the others had climbed into their berths, two hours since the attendant had locked the glass and wire mesh windows into place. Rukmini wanted them shut to protect her child from the draft, so Azad said nothing. He switched on his fan and it still whispered accusations into his ear. Sleep evaded him—like the right words to dispell the tension which followed him like unwanted luggage into D compartment. The cause of all the fuss.

By daylight the compartment had seemed welcoming: the promise of a quiet journey sheltered from passengers in second and third class, even passengers in other first class compartments. With darkness the space seemed to have shrunk. His bent arm was jammed against the compartment's outer wall, which felt cool. The soles of his bare feet pressed against the wall with the corridor, which still felt warm. He estimated the compartment was eight feet from front to back yet he could almost reach out to the opposite upper berth. This was only an illusion, one heightened by the dark well between the berths. Is this how his grave would feel one day? He had heard of Christian monks who slept in their coffins to remind themselves all things would pass. Now all things were passing rather too slowly for his taste.

It was not Krishna's fault, Azad decided; it was Meera-Bai's for dragging him hither and thither. Hospital teas, poor house openings, these constant trips to Delhi—Azad was growing invisible in his employer's wake. Not completely, though. With his Muslim costume, he suited her image as a champion of minorities. What would she think if she knew of his ambitions? One of these days in Delhi he would attract the attention of an enlightened patron; perhaps even contest a seat in the *Rajya Sabha*. Even if he had to salaam a thousand times, it would be less demeaning to bow to a fellow Muslim than to scrape for some petty local goddess. Could Meera-Bai ever bring herself to address him as Senator Azad? Would their paths even cross? He hoped not. He would not know what to say.

He opened his eyes and peered at the opposite lower berth. He hoped no one could see his face in the darkness. Krishna lay with his knees bent. He had unlaced his shoes but still not removed them. They were fine Oxfords, not Kashmiri slippers like those Azad had left on the floor. As the latecomer, Azad was relegated to a berth facing backward.

He felt himself roll toward the wall. The train was slowing. He nearly rose but heard Krishna's shoes meet the floor. Azad watched him sit up and momentarily cover his eyes in the glare of a platform light.

Rukmini looked down to ask, "Where are we?"

"At some station in the middle of nowhere," Krishna suggested. "Taking on water, I suppose."

"You cannot sleep?" Rukmini asked.

"*Alla,*" he said in Kannada and repeated himself in English: "No."

Azad frowned at this. Why did Krishna insist on speaking English when it was obvious he knew other languages? The man was Indian, was he not? Azad grimaced. Yes, they were all Indians, but they still slept in their separate berths. Some were higher than others; half of them faced backward.

When Krishna helped Rukmini down, Azad stared at her narrow hips, then squeezed his eyes shut. She wore only her petticoat and blouse. He had never seen his own wife undressed. Even after eight years of marriage, Alia waited until he turned off the light before struggling out of her tentlike *burka*. He had to imagine what she looked like while skimming his hands over her shoulders and breasts, her waist and thighs. At such times he pretended he was a sculptor, a blind sculptor. He opened his eyes a fraction and watched through his lashes while Rukmini pulled on Krishna's blazer.

The couple sat on Krishna's berth, far enough apart that no one could accuse them of displaying public affection. Krishna pulled at the front of his shirt and blew a stream of air onto his chest. The shirt was damp with sweat. He would have to sleep in his undershirt but he would not remove his trousers. As a concession to comfort, he unbuckled his belt and eased it from the loops. He curled the belt into itself and tucked it in a corner of his berth. Then he removed his shoes but not his socks. The shoes went next to Rukmini's sandals, well away from the slippers.

"What is the matter?" Rukmini asked. All this time, she had been caressing the embroidery of his college crest.

Azad listened closely. With his right ear pressed into his forearm, with the fan whirring past his left ear, he could just follow her words.

"Nothing," Krishna replied. His deep voice carried well. It was a voice for putting fools in their place. "I know your aunt is used to getting her own way," he said at last, "but I would prefer she not step in like that."

Good thing she had, Azad thought. Nothing made Meera-Bai more intolerable than getting her own way, unless it was not getting it. At such times she took her anger out on him, and he could take his out on no one. Even her Madrasi clerks barely tolerated him. They called him Cow-killer to his face. He was used to this, but he still felt tempted to apologize for every Muslim left in India.

"Aunt Sharada was trying to be helpful," Rukmini told Krishna. When he grunted, she asked, "Is this all?"

Krishna rose to grasp the topmost bar of the window. He could see nothing outside except the light. All summer in Bangalore he had never mentioned his career to Rukmini, and Prakash had been of little help during their private chats. "Professor McAulay has been urging me to go abroad," Krishna admitted at last. He found himself speaking not to her but to the world outside. "So we can live better when I return. He came right out and said so in the spring, but he has been intimating as much ever since I joined his department."

"How much better?" Rukmini asked. "We already have one servant. Now we have this wet nurse. Will we find another when she returns to her village?"

"I am sure there are wet nurses in Benares," he said, "though I have heard North Indians produce a different kind of milk." He looked over his shoulder to find her frowning at him. He laughed to set her at ease. It surprised him how often even she could not guess when he was joking.

"You still feel out of place," she asked, "after all the time you have spent in the North? They are decent people, Krishna, just like us. You were not so intolerant before."

He pressed his forehead onto the bar. Shaking his head against the pitted iron, he stared at his feet. "It is not what you think," he said. "We are South Indian Brahmins—that is all anyone sees in Benares—and we can never forget it."

When she asked, "What is there to forget?" Azad nearly groaned. He watched Krishna turn to sit on the sill with his heels dug into the wooden floor. When Krishna reached up with both hands to clasp a bar behind his head, his left elbow hid his face from Azad's view. Pity; a man could almost gain confidence by gazing at such a strong face, as Hindus did by gazing upon their gods.

"Did I ever tell you about my first interview after I left Delhi?" Krishna asked. "This was eight years ago now. Imagine!" He watched the compartment door. The curtain was not fully drawn and he glimpsed a figure passing, likely heading for the toilet. Or perhaps someone else could not sleep. Perhaps the whole train was awake. "I forgot about it until this evening," he said. This was a lie. He rarely forgot affronts. They lay in the back of his mind like cankers in his mouth; all it took was someone like Meera-Bai for the canker to swell.

"You have told me so little about yourself," Rukmini said. "I did not even know you were hunted by the police until my brother told me just before the wedding." She laughed softly. "I think he was trying to test whether I truly loved you. Poor Prakash, it only made me love you more. Were you frightened?"

Krishna wagged his head. He did not like talk of love. He had married her; that was enough. Now she was asking him:

"Was it exciting?"

"What," he demanded, "slinking from house to house while the CID inspectors came to question my friends?"

Azad wished Meera-Bai could hear this. Then again, she would likely gloat. He nearly started when Krishna glanced up at him. Azad closed his eyes and pretended to sleep.

Krishna lowered his right arm to look at Rukmini. He kept his voice low at first so as not to wake either the baby or the extra passenger, but even as Krishna spoke he heard his voice rise with passion.

"When I went looking for my first posting after Independence—this was once I knew the police no longer cared about arresting me—the personnel officer asked me point-blank, 'Are you a Brahmin?' Foolish question. What else could I be? 'Well,' he said, 'we have nothing for you.' I was annoyed but I simply asked him to look at my application and handed it over. He got as far as reading where I studied and said, 'Why did you attend Delhi when we have perfectly good universities in the South? We have nothing for you.' This time I stared at him and reminded him of the quotas. Of how some of us were denied entrance everywhere in the South merely because all the Brahmin seats were filled. He looked embarrassed then, likely because he was a Harijan and secured his own post under the quotas. Children of God!" Krishna muttered. "Renaming an Untouchable does not make him any more touchable, but I suppose Gandhi—"

Krishna stopped to refocus his thoughts. There was always so much to tell and never enough time, or the right time, or the right person to tell. Too often this last. Not since his college days had he known true friends, who listened while he paced in their hostel rooms. Where had all his friends gone? Had they simply grown up? Were they too busy now to laugh late into the night?

He continued, in words he had been rehearsing ever since the train had left Madras. "The fellow finally gave my application a proper reading. Suddenly he leapt from his chair and cried, 'Why did you not tell me? Please, please sit down!' Then he shouted for the office boy to bring coffee double-quick. I thought he had seen my marks from Delhi but, no, it was not that at all. He asked, 'Why did you not tell me who your father was directly you entered? Where do you want to work?' I told him Jog Falls, and he said, 'No one goes there, it is out-of-the-way.' Precisely why I chose it. Within two years, at twenty-four, I would become assistant station manager and be accepted by the Institute, then go on to Japan for my factory experience."

It amazed him how easily his career had progressed, no move a waste, each building on the last. Then, remembering MeeraBai, he pursed his lips. "I have been thinking about the interview all evening," he admitted.

"Your father's name has nothing to do with how well you have done," Rukmini said. "Imagine: a senior lecturer at twenty-nine! Assistant to a great man like Professor McAulay."

Azad groaned. Here he was, at thirty-six, a mere secretary, and not to some important commission but to an individual concerned only with re-election. Was it all her fault, though? In his youth he blamed his invisibility on the limp left by his childhood polio. Now Alia insisted the limp remained magnified in his mind. She even claimed he enjoyed playing the laggard. He bit the inside of his cheek until it stung. How could she say such a thing—his own wife?

"Do you not see?" Krishna asked. He glanced once again at Azad, who forced himself to breathe evenly. "Wherever I go in the North people will say, 'You are a South Indian. Go back to your *sambar* and rice.' Wherever I go in the South people will say, 'Oh, you are Mr. So-and-so's son.'" He glanced at the upper berth, on which the child lay. "I do not mean to say—" He sighed. "I admire Appa. I did everything he told me." Even marry, Krishna thought, but his father had once again been right. Marriage settled a man. It simplified so much. "'Everyone is going to England,' Appa said. 'You go to Germany or Japan. They are rebuilding, so you will secure a good post and learn more.' Professor McAulay believes I should go to America. But it is so advanced I will likely have to begin at the bottom once more. In Japan they treated me like a prince—they were so glad for the help. They were so utterly defeated. Besides, I do not like Americans."

"Why?" she asked.

He looked down and flexed his toes. "It does not matter," he said.

Azad heard the rustle of a petticoat and opened his eyes. Rukmini had reached out to touch Krishna's knee. "What do you want to do then?" The lapels of the blazer separated to reveal, in the light through the window, dark nipples under her white blouse.

Krishna remembered the first time he had helped her undress while she stood with her back to him. How smooth her skin had felt between her shoulders. He had turned her to face him. How small her wrists had seemed when he circled them to pull her arms about his neck. He had thought she might never release him. He reached out to cup her cheek with one hand. She kissed it before drawing away, and he withdrew his hand.

Azad watched Rukmini clutch the lapels closed with her fingers hooked around the top button. He shut his eyes again and wished she would get dressed. He had come too close to giving himself away.

"Perhaps I should go to America after all," Krishna wondered aloud, "and get my doctorate. But I am not sure now whether I want to return. Whether the boy should grow up here." This was the India we freed, he thought; for our sons and our son's sons. "What happened to the country we fought for?" he asked. "Everyone now claims, 'You Brahmins helped the British rule us. Now it is our turn to tell you what you can or cannot do.' Brahmin quotas, Harijan quotas. Can we reverse five thousand years of history in less than a decade? The British had their faults, oh yes they had their faults. And yet they rewarded talent and hard work. I see this now. The Americans also have their faults, but they will not care what caste I am from. To them a foreign student is a foreign student." He shrugged. "It is true I shall begin at the bottom, but there may be no limit to how high I can rise. Not like here."

"My brother has done well for himself," Rukmini said.

Krishna nodded. She was right, but she did not see why. She understood little about careers, ambition—the things which mattered to a man. "Prakash knows the value in being settled," Krishna told her. "If he gets this new post in Hyderabad, he will remain there for life. Delhi, Jog Falls, Tokyo, Benares . . . They were mistakes. A person should go to one place and remain there no matter how difficult it seems. This is the only way to find security. Moving about is the problem, following the first sweet smell north, or east. Are we human beings or cattle?"

Cattle, Azad thought; different breeds of cattle. But it did not have to be this way. Were they not humans with names and faces and God-given talents? Did they not, within the larger scheme of things, have free will?

"It is karma," Rukmini said. "We reap what we sowed. Even the Christians know this. Perhaps you left something unfinished in your previous life."

Krishna laughed. He preferred to think of his moving about as a law of nature. Even particles at rest were in constant motion—a random motion which appeared regular only in the long-term or to the distant observer.

"I shall come also," she said. "I shall begin my graduate work as I planned before. Before we had Babu."

A man could never accuse Brahmin women of lacking ambition, Azad thought. Once, when he urged Alia to work in a friend's school to pass her time, she accused him of wanting to flaunt her in public. He said nothing more about it. There was more than one way to lag.

"The chances of getting into the same university are slim," Krishna said. "We should each go where we will learn the most." Then he looked at the berth above his and checked his rising spirits. Marriage simplified a man's life, yes, but not fatherhood. "What about the boy?" he asked. "I have heard Americans do not look kindly on students bringing families. Should we leave him motherless as well as fatherless?"

"I thought we were doing this for him," she said. "We can leave him with Aunt Sharada. He will get nothing but the best in her house."

How lucky these people were, Azad thought. How willing to take risks. Perhaps he should simply leave Meera-Bai and take his chances in Delhi. But Alia would languish in Madras until he could send for her. The long letters she wrote him when the House was sitting would grow even more plaintive. What to do? What to do? Azad started when Krishna said:

"No!"

Azad moaned and turned to face the wall. His face lifted into the dusty breeze of the fan and he wiped at his nose. The light from outside picked out a spider's web in the corner by his feet. Did spiders sleep at night? Would he never get to sleep?

"No," Krishna repeated softly. "I do not want the boy being spoiled. Being driven everywhere and living in the Madras House. Your aunt is too generous. We can leave him with my mother."

"In Mauritius?" Rukmini asked. "It is so far. Why do even the close relations in your family act like distant relations? What are they afraid of? Saroja still asks me why your mother did not attend our wedding. Why we have not seen your father since. She likes him—he is kind like you. And she speaks about lines on a table and fingerprints."

Krishna puzzled over this. Saroja confused him as well, the way she tried to find connections between everything. There were no rational explanations for dealings among humans; only for the forces among atoms and molecules. At that level, yes, everything was connected. Anything could be explained given time.

Azad heard Krishna sit next to her. Did they touch now? Did they hold hands?

Krishna propped his feet on the far berth. "Your brother was right in calling you Bookworm," Krishna said, chuckling. "It will be good, I say! We can spend our holidays together."

"Can we go to Ni-ga-ra Falls?" she asked. "I have heard so much about it."

"We can visit Niagara Falls and the Grand Canyon," he exclaimed. "Alaska itself, why not?"

Plans, plans, plans. Azad could contain himself no longer. He did not want to be continually left out like this. He did not want to see the spider. After allowing a reasonable length of silence to pass, he turned and rubbed his eyes. Careful to use Hindi, he asked, "*Kya baja hai*?"

"Late," Krishna replied. He wondered how much the fellow had heard. That was another thing about America: it was said there was more privacy in those vast, uncrowded spaces than anywhere on earth.

Rukmini rose. She turned her back on Azad, who averted his eyes, and climbed onto her berth. She checked on the baby sleeping between the compartment wall and a pillow.

Even as Krishna looked out the window and said, "How long do these people need to take on water?" the whistle shrieked. The carriage lurched, the curtain swayed, and Azad clung to the edge of his berth. The compartment plunged into darkness. Suddenly, the child began to cry. Neither Rukmini's caresses nor her reassurances could stop him. "I am sorry," Krishna told Azad. "Would you like to read a while longer?"

"*Dhanyawad*," Azad replied. "Thank you," he repeated. He climbed down from his berth and switched on the light. He ducked his head in apology when Krishna squinted in the glare. Azad sat on the lower berth, found his book, and looked across to see Krishna eyeing the frayed cloth of the spine. "I was in Bengal," Azad said, "when Gandhiji arrived to stop the riots. In Noakhali itself. I remember watching him step out of the car and walk toward the stones people threw. When they froze I remember thinking, 'Surely this man is immortal.'" Azad dropped his eyes to the book. Never had he felt so betrayed as on the day Gandhi had proven to be mortal, the day he had allowed himself to be killed. "I was still in Noakhali," Azad said, "on thirtieth January."

Krishna was nodding at the book. It was the only time he could remember being so angry he stalked off a pitch; the only time he could remember weeping since childhood. "I was in Bangalore," he said, "in the midst of a crucial match—"

"I was still in Madras," Rukmini said from above. "I cried all night because I thought every Muslim in India would be murdered. Then we heard a Hindu madman shot Gandhi and I cried for our own people."

"It would appear the boy also intends to cry all night," Krishna said. He smiled at Azad, who chanced:

"Good thing Mrs. Meera-Bai is not here."

When their eyes met, Krishna began to laugh.

Azad also began to laugh, so hard he rocked backward and struck his chin on the edge of the book. It had been years since he had laughed like this, years since he had felt this close to any man. He wanted to remind Krishna that wherever Gandhi had gone he had carried a Koran with him; that in spite of their differences Indians were brothers. Azad could not get the words out. Even as one man's laughter fell, the other man's laughter rose until they began laughing at one another's tears. Azad dropped the book. Hunched over, he clapped his hands, then threw back his head.

From her upper berth, above the men, Rukmini half smiled and half frowned. She wondered what this stranger could possibly have in common with her husband. Still, it was good to hear Krishna enjoying himself. While the two men laughed and the train rocked, picking up speed, she turned her attention to the crying child.

*

One year later, in Benares, Krishna left his own farewell party. He suspected he would not be missed.

His Indian colleagues had streamed into the faculty club to wish him well, but their envy of his going abroad discomfited him. The department heads had come only for the drinks, courtesy of McAulay. Now the heads were gathered along the bar. McAulay was scoffing at Carruthers, who predicted dire consequences if Egypt nationalized the Suez Canal. Other heads were discussing Britain's new Clean Air Act. The Indians occupied the rest of the club. They lounged in the wicker chairs or crammed, shoulder to shoulder, on the sofas. One group of laughing, gesturing men was debating the meaning of elegance in mathematics. Another was applauding the recent discovery of the neutrino. Krishna marvelled at how much less space Indians needed than Europeans. Most Indians, he thought; he needed more. After bidding Chota-Wallah farewell, Krishna slipped out and went back to his office for his bicycle.

He had planned to go home but found himself drawn to the museum. He propped his bicycle next to the door, pulled the clips off his trouser cuffs, and hung the clips on the crossbar. He entered and closed the door behind him but now he was not sure why he had come. Certainly not to look at the displays, such as they were. Not even to look at the Van de Graaff, hulking in the far corner. Turning to leave, faced with the closed door, he blurted a laugh.

The calendar for 1955 had been replaced with a calendar for 1956 but the picture was of the same old Ganesha, god of wisdom, remover of obstacles: a god to be worshipped before building a house, as Prakash hoped to do one day, or leaving on a journey. There were some differences, though. The yellow skin of this year's Ganesha looked saffron, more orange than last year's, and this year he was accompanied by his vehicle. Every god had his vehicle—Brahma his swan or goose, Shiva his bull—but Ganesha's vehicle was, of all things, a rat. Not a fearsome rat; one mischievously eyeing the round sweets. They were piled at one side of Ganesha's cushion into a glistening pyramid. The pyramid was flat on top as though Ganesha had been unable to resist the sweets. His elephant mouth was curved into a smile.

As a boy Krishna had listened, enthralled, to legends about the origin of the elephant head. According to one of them, Ganesha's father often surprised his wife while she bathed. One day she mixed the scurf of her body with ointments. She formed a boy and brought him to life with water from the Ganges. Setting him outside her door, she hoped Ganesha would guard her. His father found his way blocked. Not realizing Ganesha was his own son, the father cut off Ganesha's head. Ganesha's mother grieved so bitterly, her husband sent messengers to find another head. The first creature they saw was an elephant. It willingly sacrificed its head, which the father then attached to his son's neck. Krishna shook his own head at the nonsense children believed; the fantastic nonsense too many adults still believed. He liked the picture, though. He liked its simplicity: the triangular shape of Ganesha, cross-legged, echoed in the truncated pyramid of sweets.

Krishna took the calendar down. It left a rectangle of silvery grey on the door, a patch shinier and less dusty than the surrounding ash grey.

He laid the thin paper on a table with the calendar over the edge and slowly tore it from the picture. Even as he did this, it occurred to him he should take the whole thing. Then again, the numbers running from top to bottom would look primitive where he was bound. He pinned the calendar back onto the door and slowly rolled the picture to take with him. Once outside, he retrieved his bicycle and began walking it to the edge of the university grounds. Perhaps one day he would tell his son the story of Ganesha. The boy was still too young for stories. One day, Krishna promised himself, he would tell his son about Ganesha. His American son.

# Part Two

# Chapter 3

## *A Green, Sweet World*

Four-year-old Hari was listening to the radio play a Telugu song. He liked the music better than the words because the words made no sense to him. He could not even guess where one ended or the next began.

> *Manulo, manuloko, padawadakay,*
> *Pa, padawufa, padawadakay,*
> *Manulo-oh-oh-ohohoh.*

Once the song ended, the announcer said, "Port Louis and Poudre d'Or can expect clearing late this afternoon." Hari recognized only Port Louis, which was where he lived. The announcer's voice came from far away and sounded tinny. "The remainder of the island will experience cloudy conditions until sunset. Next, a French song for all of you who enjoy motoring."

Hari enjoyed motoring, especially with his friend Devraj, the doctor who lived at the end of the lane. When Hari was bigger he planned to have his own motor car. Then he could drive while Devraj sat in the back like a prince and they could sing together.

Part way through the new song, Hari sat up so he could hear it better. He could not understand this one either, but he liked the chorus. The second verse ended,

*Dansleparc cebeau après-midi,*
*Nousnous balladonsenauto trèsjoli.*

Then came the words he liked:

*Hey, bébé, hey-yay, bébé.*

Clapping, he sang along:

*Hey, Harish, hey-yay, Harish.*
*Hey* (clap) *Harish, yay* (clap) *Harish.*

He stopped. His grandmother, the woman he called Ajji, was standing in the doorway.

"That was you," she asked, "singing with the radio? Good boy, sing some more."

He shook his head.

"All right then," she said kindly, "go to sleep. We are leaving for the airport after supper only." Poor boy, she thought; he had been excitable ever since she had told him his mother was coming. Ajji could not bring herself to explain the real reason for his mother's visit: she was coming to reclaim him.

"Cannot sleep," he said.

"Get dressed then," Ajji said. "Your best clothes only." She knew she sounded ironic when she added, "Your mother likes nothing but the best."

Ajji was glad for him—children should not be separated too long from their parents, she thought—but it surprised her these days how often she felt sorry for herself. She had reassured his mother the time would pass quickly, but Ajji wished it had not sped by like this. He had come to her as a toddler, grown into a little boy, and even learned to speak. Thanks to her. She was supposed to teach him English because his parents planned to raise him in America, but she also taught him a few words of Kannada. It was her mother tongue, after all. And he had also learned some Creole from his ayah. He had the ear of someone whose first language was music.

Hari grew tired of waiting for Ajji to lift him from the cot. He slid off and straightened his underwear while she watched him with a sad smile. He had no idea why she should be sad. Today was a happy day for him. She had told him so again, this morning, while showing him an aerogram written in green ink.

Ajji took his best shirt and short pants from the Godrej and began dressing him. She squatted to do this and he looked at the careful part in her hair. It smelled of coconut oil and was streaked with grey.

His ayah, Marie, had jet black hair but Marie's was short and felt like a sponge. Ajji wore her long hair braided and twisted into a bun, held with bobby pins. Not the pretty woman, though; the one whose picture stood on the radio and whose photograph was the only one in the house. No matter where he stood in the room, her eyes followed him. He could not see whether her hair, pulled back from her face, was also braided and twisted into a bun.

Ajji often said the woman was his *amma*, his mother. This confused him until, one day, he asked, "Ajji, are you not my mother?" She said no, she was his grandmother, and he finally understood. A boy owned two mothers, an old-mother like Ajji and a young-mother like his *amma*. She was coming all the way across the sea. Not by a boat; by an aeroplane, just like the aerogram, and he would finally get to see an airport. To quell his growing excitement, he pressed one bare foot on the other and placed his hand on Ajji's head for balance.

She often sounded harsh when she spoke about his *amma*. He did not know why, unless his *amma* had done something terribly wrong the way he had, only this morning. He had been playing outside, barefoot as usual, and wanted to ask Ajji whether his *amma* would bring him a gift. He had been in such a hurry, he had forgotten to wipe his feet on the mat. Ajji had scolded him for it, then hugged him so hard she frightened him.

Ajji finished buttoning his shirt and short pants. "Your *chappals* are being polished. Put them on when we leave for the airport." Even as she rose, he ran into the main room. She followed him, sat at her desk, and picked up a red pencil. "You play while I finish correcting these papers," she said. A stack of them lay on the floor next to her chair. "Do not get dirty, though."

Shaking his head, Hari wandered out of the house. Fronds of coconut palms rustled in the wind while the grey sky turned blue. A crow caw-cawed from the wall surrounding the compound. Hari did not like the noise. It was too loud, and each caw sounded too much like the last. When he heard the sound of a motor, he ran to the gate. Devraj's new car was bumping over potholes in the lane. The car stopped.

Devraj stretched his arm through the open window and waved. "Do you want to come to the lagoon?" His voice had a rasping sound like the crow's. "I have to see my patient there."

"Lah-goon," Hari said, singing the word.

Devraj climbed out and opened the gate. He stepped aside so Hari could run to the car. Even as Devraj closed the gate, Hari climbed into the driver's seat. He pressed the horn with all his might. It honked, and the crow cawed again. Clutching the steering wheel to keep from sliding off the seat, Hari flicked a switch next to the steering column. This time, when he pressed the horn, it beeped.

"All right, little driver," Devraj said. "Let us go."

Hari slid away from the steering wheel so Devraj could get in. The car smelled of smoke just like Devraj's suit jacket, which even looked a smoky grey. Then they were off, bumping down the lane between houses in the layout. Seated far back with his heels dangling over the edge, Hari watched the tops of palm trees flashing by. Streaks of blue widened beyond the thinning grey. The car turned onto a smooth surface and rattled along a trunk road out of Port Louis.

On their very first trip to the lagoon, in Devraj's battered old car, they stopped on a cliff covered with margosa trees. Devraj called them *neem*. He pointed across the peacock blue sea and said that on clear days a boy could see the island of Réunion. Even Madagascar. Hari, squinting into the sun, could see only fishing boats. Devraj twisted a twig off a tree. He split the twig with his thumbnail, chewed the end until it frayed, and brushed his teeth. Hari did the same thing with the other half of the twig. His lips tingled sourly, as they did when Marie made him suck on a lemon for luck.

"*Neem* is good for you." Devraj laughed at Hari's puckered lips. "It cures fever. Never mind. On the ride home I will buy you a pink ice."

The car turned off the trunk road and wound along a path toward a shanty town which bordered a lagoon. Beyond the lagoon stretched open water, but Hari could see neither Réunion nor Madagascar. He looked at the shanty town instead. Unlike the concrete houses of their own layout, the houses here were made of wood. Loose sheets of corrugated iron banged in the wind. Specks of tar flew from the seams like soot. A lorry sat, without tires, on blocks of wood.

Devraj stopped the car, climbed out, and patted at the wrinkles on his jacket. He straightened its cuffs and buttoned his shirt at the collar. Then he combed his fingernails down his small rectangle of a moustache. "You stay on the beach." He pointed at a strip of dark sand hugging the lagoon. He took his medical bag from the back seat, turned and added, "I shall be in that hut."

Hari jumped onto the ground. He looked at the lorry first but it promised no fun. Pieces of its motor lay scattered everywhere. Then he spied a canoe. He left the road to run along the beach. Looking back, he saw Devraj enter a hut perched on stilts.

Long and brown, the canoe was shaped from the trunk of a single tree. It sat on blocks like the lorry but these bristled with bark. Beyond the canoe, a dark boy was placing a shard of coconut shell on a sandcastle. Safety pins held his shirt closed, and he was naked from the waist down. Searching for a shell to offer, Hari approached the sandcastle.

"*Mon shato-sabelle*," the boy said. He spoke Creole like Marie. "*Papa*," the boy added.

Hari understood: the boy's father had built the castle for him; even a moat. Hari felt envious. Devraj never built castles when they went for picnics on the beach. Neither did Ajji, who always complained that the sand got into the food, clothing, and mats.

A stick from a pink ice lay near the boy's feet. Hari scooped up the stick and wiped sand from it. After plucking the coconut shell from the tower, he planted the stick with the pink end up. "*Drapo*," Hari said, but the boy screamed:

"*Mon shato! Papa*!"

Hari backed away while the boy scrabbled for a fistful of sand. Even after the boy threw the sand, Hari refused to leave. He watched, puzzled, while the boy planted his feet in front of the castle. The boy was grinning now. He was peeing into the moat. The pee flowed out to form a puddle at his feet.

Hari wrinkled his nose in disgust. He ran back to the hut near the car and ducked between the stilts. Searching for a spot free of refuse, he crawled onto a palm frond, then wiped his soles up and down his calves. No radio played in the hut but he could hear the jingle-jingle of anklets, the pad-pad of bare feet, and the clomp-clomp of shoes.

A pair of dark feet stepped onto the sand. The woman wore copper anklets. Hari sat perfectly still while she walked toward another hut. Then, bending to one side, he saw a baby on the woman's hip. The only other person in sight was the dark boy. Hari did not like children who peed—who did what Ajji called number one—anywhere except in a toilet. He sat up, drew his knees to his chest, and shrugged. He had his own castle now, a splendid one made of bamboo. It even had a rug of palm fronds, and there was plenty of room for friends.

A tawny mongrel pup poked its head around a stilt.

When Hari held out his arms, the pup wagged its tail and came to him. He giggled when it licked his hands with its pink tongue.

He smothered the pup to his chest until it yelped. Instead of scampering away when he released it, the pup burrowed under the frond. It looked up when a clomp shook the wooden steps. The next moment, a pair of scuffed shoes appeared on the sand. Hari held his breath. He clapped his hands over his mouth to stifle a giggle, but the pup yapped and the shoes turned.

"Is that you, Harish?" Devraj asked. He put down his bag and bent until Hari could see the moustache. It looked tiny next to the large nose. "Do not play with dogs!" Devraj scolded. "*Thup,*" he said, pretending to spit. "They eat lizards and rats! Do you want to catch some disease?"

No, Hari did not. He crawled out as fast as he could.

Devraj pulled him to his feet. Devraj slapped sand and leaves from the back of Hari's short pants, took his hand firmly, and headed for the car. This time he did not wait for Hari to play beep-honk before setting off. Devraj drove so quickly, shifting gears so often, that the tires spun. Once he reached the trunk road, he sighed. Visiting patients, especially old ones he could no longer help, always left him feeling this way. And yet there were compensations, like healing their children. "Would you like to be a doctor when you grow up," he asked Hari, "and drive a new motor car?"

A double-decker bus rumbled along the trunk road. The driver honked his horn. The bus was heading straight for the car. Hari held his breath. At the last moment, the car swerved onto the dirt shoulder. The bus swerved onto the opposite shoulder, and they passed. Hari breathed only when the outside tires of the car skipped onto the blacktop.

"My motor car big as a bus!" he said.

Devraj laughed, mainly with relief. "A double-decker motor car? Why not!" From the breast pocket of his jacket he took a cigarette. He struck a match on the sun visor and lit the cigarette with the match cupped in his hand. "Here," he said, offering the flame.

Even as Hari took a deep breath, the match went out. He sat back. For the rest of the trip he rolled the wooden match in his palms and watched the sky through the windscreen. He hoped Devraj would stop for a pink ice but he drove back to the layout without stopping. Longing for the pink ice, Hari forgot all about the airport.

When the car stopped at her gate, Ajji ran from her house. The loose end of her sari snapped in the wind. "Harischandra, where have you been?" She had completely lost track of the time. She had told him to play outside; not wander away like this.

Her worried expression puzzled Devraj. "We went to the lagoon only," he said. "I had to see my patient there." His voice dropped. "I fear there is little more I can do."

Ajji had no interest in excuses. She rounded the front of the car, opened the passenger door and lifted Hari out. He clasped his arms about her neck while she carried him back to the gate. "You are fine? You did not get dirty?" Hari shook his head. Ajji turned back to Devraj. "You will please remember to tell me in future."

"There will be few more such outings for the boy," Devraj said. "Did you like the beach, Harish?"

"Long brown bird," Hari began.

"The canoe, he means," Devraj explained to Ajji.

"Cannot fly," Hari said.

"Why not?" Devraj asked.

Hari pointed at a parrot swooping over a tamarind bush. "No feathers."

"Incorrect," Devraj laughed. "I told you once. No wings." He put the car in gear. "Ta-ta."

"Ta-ta," Hari called. He squirmed in Ajji's arms to watch the car grow small.

"You are hungry for a snack?" she asked. They entered the house and she set him down in the main room. The stack of papers on the floor was higher now and her desk was almost clear. "Ovaltine and a biscuit."

"Two biscuits?" he asked, searching her eyes for a promise.

"We shall see," she said.

He ran into the kitchen. His brown sandals gleamed next to the back door. So did Ajji's black sandals. Marie was squatting against the far wall to heat milk on the hot plate. It stood next to an earthenware jug.

Water came from a tap behind the house but Ajji let him drink only from this jug. She said it breathed goodness into the water; that he should never drink straight from a tap. She said it was unclean.

"*Alo, mon petit*," Marie crooned. She switched off the hot plate, lifted the pan, and set it on the concrete floor.

Hari backed away because the coil still glowed. Ajji said it was a snake. She said it would bite if Hari touched it and once she even held his finger over it to feel the stinging heat. "Never play near a hot plate," she said, shaking her own finger. "Even if the coil is black and the snake is asleep."

Marie pried the lid off a tin of Ovaltine. A malty smell rose to mingle with the smell of warm milk. She spooned brown crystals into the pan.

With one hand on Marie's shoulder, Hari leaned forward to watch the crystals sink. They left reddish brown traces on the white skim of the milk. She stirred with a spoon until the milk turned a pale brown, not as dark as the Ovaltine yet not as light as the milk. He breathed in the warm, malted smell. He grinned up at Ajji because he thought that, like him, she could smell the change in colour.

✷

The Air France aeroplane looked like a long, hard, silver bird caught in the glare of floodlights. It had no feathers, but it did have wings. So did the strange animal on the aeroplane's tail. Its curled bottom looked like a fish but its torso and head looked like a horse. It was a winged seahorse. Devraj was saying, "The plane will wake if people climb into it only, just as a canoe will wake once people step into it. Then the plane's propellers will lift it into the sky."

Hari stood between Devraj and Ajji on the roof of the airport terminus. It was well past his bedtime but he felt wide awake. He squirmed with curiosity over coming to an airfield with its taxi cabs and buses, its wind socks, the rise and fall of propellers revving on the tarmac. Best of all he would finally meet his *amma,* his mother.

He looked up at Ajji and touched her hand. She smiled down at him but she did not look happy. She had changed her rumpled sari for a freshly ironed one, and she wore her good sandals. Even Devraj had changed his grey jacket for a shiny, black one. Hari looked down at his own sandals and nodded with satisfaction. His *amma* liked nothing but the best.

Ajji asked, "Will you miss us, Harish?"

She had asked him this in the car, on the way here. As he had then, he frowned at her. What did it mean to miss someone, and why should he? They would all be together: Ajji, Devraj, and his *amma*. They could go on picnics and his mother would build him a sandcastle.

Hari looked at the aeroplane. People were picking their way down a wheeled staircase set against a door near the nose. From the foot of the staircase they crossed the apron toward the terminus. He had eyes only for the women but from up here they all looked alike. Most of them, like Ajji, wore saris and short blouses; a few, like the air hostess at the top of the staircase, wore longer blouses tucked into tight skirts. The saris flapped in the breeze yet the women wearing them walked gracefully.

"Let us go downstairs," Devraj said. He pulled Hari back from the damp railing.

Hari patted the wet spots on his shirt and wiped a bare forearm across his brow. Everything felt wet on this hot night. His sandals made sucking noises on the terminus roof.

Once downstairs, he stayed with Ajji while Devraj bought cigarettes from a vendor. Ajji sat on a bench and frowned at grey hairs she plucked from her head. When she dropped them, they drifted in the breeze of a ceiling fan before settling on the unswept floor. "There!" she said and sighed. It was over now. It would be a relief not to have a boy underfoot, tracking dirt into the house, but there was much she did not want to give up: his songs, for instance. Not that she had any choice. She was only the grandmother. She rose to lead him toward a man in khaki.

The man was stamping the passports of two beautiful women. Both of them wore saris and both carried identical flight bags. On the side of each rode the winged seahorse of Air France. Hari's hand was beginning to hurt—Ajji was clutching it so tightly. At last she released him. When the women took back their passports, Ajji nudged him forward with a harsh, "Go."

Hari walked through a stream of passengers. A few of them smiled at him but most were looking for people they knew. He continued, then waited while a second man in khaki asked the two women questions. This man chalked Xs on their luggage and waved the women past a low gate. A porter pulled the luggage off the table and stood awaiting orders. The woman on the left was beaming at Hari. The woman on the right, hanging back to adjust her turquoise sari, looked tired. She wore specs. No one he knew wore specs, and neither woman looked like the one in his photo.

"Amma?" he asked the first woman.

Her sari was wrinkled and grey. Her teeth flashed like Ajji's ivory fan on hot, hot days. "You are very handsome, Master," the woman said, "but I am your *amma*'s new friend. We met on the way from Nairobi. Do you know where that is?"

Hari stopped listening. He looked at the second woman, the one who wore specs, the one who hung back. She draped a green sweater across her flight bag, then dropped the bag at her feet. She bent toward him and held out her arms. Now Hari hung back. He looked for a gleam in her eyes, a gleam that promised more than biscuits, but he ran to her and let her lift him. She hugged him so hard, he could barely breathe. Her cheek felt soft and wet.

Again he asked, "Amma?"

"Oh, yes, Babu," she replied. "Yes!" Her face smelled of powder, her hands of lemon soap, and her hair of roses. "Here you are," she said, opening one of her hands. "The hostess gave me a sweet especially for you. Sing a song for us first. Your *ajji* wrote you are a fine singer."

He began to sing, "Happy birthday to you-u."

Rukmini laughed and tried to wipe away her tears. She took off her specs and rubbed her cheek with the back of her hand.

The friend took the specs and moved away.

"Your birthday has passed," Rukmini said, "but we shall celebrate your next one at home. Here you are." She unwrapped the sweet and pressed it between his lips.

Long and white, the sweet made his lips tingle. Not the way the *neem* had; not sourly. This was a different kind of tingle, a sugary one with a hint of pepper. The peppermint clicked against his teeth. When Rukmini hugged him again, he pressed his face against her shoulder until the border of her sari tickled his nose. She rubbed her cheek against his. She rubbed her powder and tears onto his face.

"Babu," she crooned. "Did you miss me?"

Why did everyone ask him this strange question? He turned to look for Ajji. She stood with her back to him and spoke with Devraj, who was nodding sadly. Hari did not understand. This was no time to be sad. He looked into his *amma*'s eyes for the answer. She was still crying, but he knew she was happy—as happy as he was, here in an airport at last, with his very own mother. When she hugged him again, the sweet snapped in his mouth.

Gasping, Hari gulped for air. His entire world, this island in a peacock blue sea, tasted minty and cool. Not pink, not like pink ice, but green. The world was green and sweet.

# Chapter 4

## *Holiday Father*

Buffalo Bill was on his way.

Hari looked at the sky, rumbling with thunder. He saw a hunter on a white horse stampeding a herd of water buffalo through a grassland.

Hari was making a kite from a Hindi newspaper. He liked English papers more. Their print looked plain compared to the curlicued Hindi script but he could at least spell out the English words. He put the half-finished kite and his plate of rice glue in a corner of the veranda. He frowned. The glue had stuck together two fringes of his black sheriff's vest. Rukmini had brought the vest back from America and it was now too small for him. The pin of the silver star, once over his left breast, scraped at his shoulder through his shirt. He struggled out of the vest and dropped it on the kite, which rustled. He sat with his chin cupped in his hands and his elbows planted on his knees. He could smell rain in the air. The smell rose from the house as though the rain would seep from the walls themselves, not fall from the clouds.

Thunder boomed in the sky again, lower this time. Buffalo Bill was chasing a herd of elephants through a jungle. Large, round drops splattered in the compound and threw up fountains of dust which fanned outward. Before long the rain came hissing down on the coconut palms and flat rooftops and turned the compound dust into mud.

Hari pulled his feet close to his thighs and wiped his wet toenails. Rukmini had made him wear his good clothes today so he stayed in the dry veranda. Mother ducks let their children play in the rain, Rukmini said, but not with their good clothes on. Once, in Mauritius, he had seen ducks in a pond. The pictures and sounds and smells from those days floated in a shiny, silver bubble. Hari remembered the car a doctor friend had driven. Its horn could honk like a goose or beep like a—what? Not a duck; they quacked.

On their way back to Bangalore, their home now, Rukmini took him on a safari through Nairobi National Park. From the olive green Land Rover they watched zebras and antelopes thunder away beyond clouds of dust. Later they saw giraffes munch the tops of trees. The guide promised to rouse a hippopotamus from a river by throwing stones. It did not work. Pink flamingos fled screaming from the bank into the sky. Rukmini kept photos of the safari in Hari's orange album. On its cover stood a golden-haired boy holding flowers behind his back. Her own album, a green one, had a golden-haired girl in a frock hiding behind an umbrella.

Hari stretched his right arm to catch some rain. A warm drop fell on his palm and ran down to his wrist. He drew a wet bangle around his wrist and thought about food.

What would Ajji have for her snack today? Deep-fried *bondas*, perhaps, or spicy *wadas*. If he visited her she would send to the Kwality Restaurant for sweets, but today was his ayah Elzabeth's day off so Elzabeth could not take him to Ajji's new house. It was on Halsur Road, near Halsur Lake, on the east side of Bangalore. Rukmini refused to take him there because she did not trust Ajji. Rukmini said Ajji would not feed a crow if it came starving to her window sill. Hari found this hard to believe. Had she not brought a tin of biscuits at the start of the rainy season?

But Rukmini and Ajji quarrelled about an aerogram from America and Ajji swore she would never visit this house again. There was so much Hari did not understand. Ajji was his grandmother but she was not Rukmini's mother. He knew this. Rukmini's mother had died before he was born. But if Ajji was his grandmother, whose mother was she? His father's, Rukmini said, but this meant nothing to him—just as it meant nothing when she added, "Your *ajji* won't be able to follow you much longer." She had retired to Bangalore after his fifth birthday, two months ago. Now she did little except scold her new servant. Rukmini never scolded Elzabeth even if she arrived late some mornings, when Rukmini hurried to get ready and had little time to fix breakfast.

Rukmini studied engineering at the Institute, the Indian Institute of Science. It was in a far corner of Bangalore between Sankey's Reservoir and Mattikere Tank. Hari had been there only once. Today she had stayed home although it was Saturday, her day for laboratory work. On Sunday she stayed home all day. Elzabeth made carrot *halva* and Rukmini took Hari to the Ganapati Tea Room in Cantonment district for cold pineapple juice. She was the only mother he knew who went to the Institute. His Saroja Auntie stayed home with his cousin-sisters. His Prakash Uncle taught at the Institute. He taught astronomy, which Hari could not spell. He could spell electricity, though, because Rukmini spelled it aloud once while scoring under the letters. Her long fingernails looked like parrots' beaks.

The rain stopped. The air still felt warm but it smelled fresh, as it did in the morning before filling with dust. Rain dripped from the trees and ran down the walls of the house.

Hari stood and slapped at the back of his short pants. Squishing mud between his toes, he walked in a slow zig-zag to the big house on the far side of the compound. He knew no one would answer but he slammed his palms against the door. The latch rattled and the padlock thudded against nicks worn into the wood. The big house family was at a wedding. Even the parakeets which often twittered in the trees had fled, chased by Buffalo Bill.

Hari and the big house boy were the best of friends. The boy's name was Srinivasan. Every morning Elzabeth took them by bus all the way to Cluny Convent in Malleswaram district. Every afternoon she came to fetch them. At Cluny Convent, Hari and Srinivasan sat in Mrs. Kamala-Bai's class, the first standard, and learned the English alphabet. They also sang nursery rhymes like "Lavender Blue." Hari enjoyed listening to Mrs. Kamala-Bai when she played the piano, but at such times he often sat in a corner with his slate. From the pictures nailed on the walls, he copied down numbers with his orange chalk. Then he tried to multiply them. Three blind mice times two little pigs made how many? Sometimes five, sometimes six. "Why do you not wait until you are in the second standard?" Mrs. Kamala-Bai once asked. Hari shrugged. By the time he reached the second standard he wanted to know how to spell long words like astronomy.

"Is your mother home?" someone called.

Hari turned to find a man standing on the other side of the gate. He wore a creamy suit spotted with rain. On his shoulder was slung an Air France flight bag like the one Rukmini owned, a dark blue bag with a winged white seahorse. Even the clip on the man's checked tie was a winged seahorse. It was silver, not white, and it gleamed as if new. His broad smile frightened Hari, who ran back to the veranda to stare silently at the man.

"Is your mother home, I say?" the man asked.

"Amma!" Hari called over his shoulder. "Amma?"

Her voice came from the main room, where she sat reading. "Yes, Babu?" Her voice was musical because her mother tongue was Telugu, the same as Prakash Uncle and Saroja Auntie's. They both claimed Telugu songs were the finest in South India. They said Kannada songs were fit only for dull films. "Yes, Babu?" Rukmini repeated.

"There is a man-uncle at the gate," he called.

Rukmini appeared at once in the doorway of the main room. She adjusted her specs and touched the vermilion dot on her brow. Then she retucked the end of her turquoise sari in front of her bare midriff. She rarely wore this sari. She said its embroidered border of silver feathers might fade if she wore it too often. Hari was glad she had worn it today. It was splendid. Now she smiled the way she did when she saw him after school. "All right, Babu. Let him come in. You play for a few minutes more. Then come in also."

Hari ran to the gate and lifted the latch. The man-uncle entered the compound. When he held his left hand above Hari's head, Hari backed away. The man-uncle chuckled. Hari had never seen such a large hand or such thick arms and broad shoulders. The man-uncle was a giant. He had to duck to enter the house.

Hari turned to close the gate. He looked down the lane running between Srinivasan's house and the high wall to the right. Pieces of glass were embedded in the top of the wall so thieves could not climb into the compound.

A yellow and black autorickshaw roared by on its three wheels. It buzzed out of sight like a wasp. Then a Dunlop cart rolled into sight. Bells jingled on the white bullock's horns. How strange, Hari thought; the wooden cart had rubber wheels even larger than the autorickshaw's, yet the cart moved slowly. Instead of roaring, it creaked. Instead of a motor it had a bullock, which pulled a load of flat, brown cow-dung patties bristling with grass. He could not smell them, but he could almost smell the refuse in the gutters. He could almost see the flies. Across the road a beggar asked for alms outside the Chettiar Store. He had only one good arm, his left one. A hand on a baby arm hung from his right shoulder. He held this hand out with the fingers curled for coins and gazed at passers-by with cowlike eyes. He stood there every day at this time. Once, he waved to Hari with the baby arm and Hari turned away, frightened. Now the beggar pretended he did not see Hari at the gate and Hari pretended to ignore the beggar.

When Hari looked at the sweetshop next to the store, his stomach growled. It was time for his afternoon snack. He ran back to the veranda, wiped his muddy feet on the coir mat, and entered the main room.

An electric bulb cast a cone of light onto Rukmini and the man-uncle. They sat in wicker chairs on opposite sides of a low wicker table. He had hung his jacket over the calendar someone had sent from England. Rukmini said it was Hari's London Uncle but Hari was not to speak of him in front of Ajji. The calendar showed the Queen inspecting red-coated troops. She too wore a red coat, but her hat was not as splendid as the tall black hats of the troops. When the Queen and Prince Philip came to Bangalore a few months before, Rukmini took Hari to watch, from a crowd jamming the Institute grounds. Most people waved saffron, white, and green Indian flags. A few old people waved smaller flags with red, white, and blue crosses on them. The Union Jack, Rukmini said. Everyone yelled, "*Rani, hai*!" Hari was so busy admiring the turbaned Mysore Cavalry, he missed seeing the Queen and Prince Philip.

The man-uncle turned toward Hari with a smile and Rukmini gestured for Hari to come closer. He ran to her and played with her bangles while staring shyly at the man-uncle. She bent until Hari could smell the rose water in her hair. "Babu," she said, "this is your father."

Hari did not believe her. Prakash Uncle lived in the same house as his two daughters. Srinivasan's father lived in the big house. This man did not live here. Perhaps, Hari thought, he was a different type of father.

"Hi," Krishna said. He did not know what else to say.

Hari heard it as "*Hai.*" He clutched Rukmini's arm when she tried to nudge him around the table. People only shouted "*Hai*!" to the Queen, not to little boys. Hari did not like people teasing him the way children at school did because he wanted to learn multiplication.

Krishna's eyebrows joined in a frown. He knew children were shy with strangers, but he also knew what children liked: stories and sweets, games and toys. Supressing a grin, Krishna leaned forward to push a brown-paper packet which bumped along the wicker tabletop. "Here," he said. "I brought you this."

Only when Krishna sat back did Hari reach for the gift. "Thank you, sir," he said. He sat on the stone floor to open the packet. It held a post card of a long, black ship with two red and black funnels. The clear paper covering the post card crinkled under his touch. He turned the card over to find squiggly lines stamped into the back.

"It's a jigsaw puzzle," Krishna explained. "That's the ocean liner I took. It's called the *Queen Elizabeth.*"

Hari frowned at the jacket hanging over the calendar. Both Queen Elizabeth and Elzabeth, his ayah, were women, not ships. And what should he do with a jigsaw puzzle?

"Your father has come all the way from America to see you," Rukmini said. "He has not seen you since you were a baby."

Hari found this hard to believe as well. He could not remember having been a baby. He looked at this man-uncle—at his father—and asked, "How is America spelled?"

"A-m-e-r-i-c-a," Krishna said. "Why?"

Hari spelled it aloud. He nodded with satisfaction and tore off the clear paper. When he squeezed it, the paper hissed like rain falling on coconut palms. The puzzle broke. It fell in a dozen pieces into his lap and his mouth turned dry. How could he have broken a new toy so soon? Perhaps he could mend it with rice glue.

"That's right," Krishna said. "Now lay the pieces on the floor and fit them together. If you need any help, your mother—" Before he could finish, Hari pieced the puzzle together.

Krishna's eyebrows rose. "The boy is clever for his age," he told Rukmini. "Then again, he is your son." He meant it as a compliment but she took it the wrong way and said:

"Harischandra is also your son." She rose and left to work in the kitchen.

Hari took the puzzle apart. He put it together upside down and even backward with only the squiggly lines showing. He did not speak to Krishna, who rose to switch on Rukmini's Murphy Radio.

On it stood a statue of Ganesha, the elephant god. It had belonged to Prakash before Rukmini and, before them, to their mother. Krishna wished he had brought the calendar picture back with him. It might have impressed Hari more than a mere jigsaw puzzle. Krishna turned when Rukmini entered with a tray and they both sat down, still on opposite sides of the table.

Hari drank his warm Ovaltine and leaned against Rukmini's legs. His stomach felt full and so did the house.

While Rukmini and Krishna chatted about his journey, Hari fell asleep. He slept curled like the fish tail of a winged seahorse. He slept curled like the baby he could not remember having been.

*

On Saturday afternoons Hari waited for Krishna to come to the house. Elzabeth called him Holiday Father because he came only on her day off. When she asked about him, she sounded jealous of Hari for having a relation in America. Hari wanted to learn all about America. He wanted to tell Srinivasan about it but Krishna rarely spoke about anything. He often appeared lost in thought.

Rukmini laughed at the name Holiday Father. She told Hari to call his father Appa. It sounded strange, since this *appa* did not live with Hari. Krishna lived with Ajji near Halsur Road. Krishna was her son, then, Hari decided, but he was not sure if he really were Krishna's son. Krishna had not hugged Hari when they met—not the way Rukmini had—but there was much Hari did not know. Krishna had stood watching Hari in the compound; he had seemed too shy to try anything more than touching Hari's head. Hari was also not sure if he were Krishna's son because Krishna called him Boy. It did not sound as musical as Babu even if they did mean the same thing. And so Hari, who called his mother Amma and his grandmother Ajji, avoided calling his father Appa.

On the first Saturday after his arrival, Krishna took Hari to Ajji's house by autorickshaw. Hari sat in the back with Krishna while the driver, alone in front, beeped the horn on one handlebar. Ajji ordered a meal from the Kwality Restaurant. Her new servant, Maura, served Hari and Ajji's food on stainless steel plates. Maura served Krishna's food on a white china plate because, he explained, he ate meat in America and so should not defile Ajji's everyday plates. For this reason, he also drank from a glass tumbler instead of a stainless steel one.

Hari had eaten only half a *masala dosa* when Maura asked, "*Sakkare beda*?" She stooped over him with a paper cone.

Hari looked at the sugar next to his curried pancake. "*Sakkare beka*," he said, shaking his head.

Krishna stopped eating and looked at Ajji. "We agreed the boy should be taught English," he said.

Ajji poured *sambar* from a tumbler onto a mound of rice. She mixed the reddish soup into the rice with her right hand. "When Harish began talking in Mauritius," she said, "I taught him English first. His mother also talks to him in English only." Ajji threw a moist ball of rice into her mouth.

"Then where did he learn Kannada?" Krishna asked.

The lines deepened around Ajji's mouth when she pursed her lips. "*Yenappa*?" she asked. "His schoolmates speak Kannada. The boy is not deaf."

"He won't need Kannada to live in the U.S.," Krishna said. He looked at Hari and imagined him coming home from school. Hari would go straight to his room and finish his homework before going out to play. Baseball, basketball, American-style football—Hari would become an all-rounder. Team sports, not individual ones. Tennis was all very well, but it taught a boy nothing about working with others.

"At this rate the boy will be fortunate to start secondary school there," Ajji said. "Are you planning to be a student for ever?"

Krishna glared at his plate. Nothing he did pleased her. It had, once, before his brother had settled in England. If only Ravi had not married an English woman, especially a shopkeeper's daughter. Such things did not bother Krishna. He had met Ravi's wife once and liked her—she took good care of him—yet how long would Krishna have to keep paying for Ravi's escape?

Krishna deflected his anger from Ajji to his superiors. "They use me," he said. "They know they can get cheap labour from foreign students so they make us mark all their papers." And then question the marks we give, he thought. "Where's the time for research?" he asked. "Don't worry, I'll get my doctorate soon and I'll have my pick of jobs. The very day I get my landed immigrant status, I'll send for the boy and his mother." Krishna smiled at Hari. "You'll eat like an American and grow even bigger and stronger than me. This rice and curry won't put flesh on your bones! You need chicken and beef and fish."

Hari could not imagine anyone bigger than Krishna. His head had pressed against the canvas top of the autorickshaw. Nor could Hari imagine anyone stronger than Krishna with his thick lips, broad nose, and hair as dense as flies on a sweet. When he raised a glass of curds to his lips, muscles flexed on his bare forearm. A scar on his left wrist twisted like a pale snake. Hari wanted to ask Krishna how he got the scar, but most of the time Krishna kept it covered.

Krishna lowered his glass. "It's all right. The Kannada will be useful for now. But I say," he exclaimed, "what other languages do you know?"

"Telugu," Hari replied. He sounded justly proud. "I knew Creole also, but I have forgotten it."

"The Creole he learned from his black ayah," Ajji said. "The Telugu he learns at his Uncle Prakash-Rao's house." She found a grey hair dangling across her forehead and plucked the hair out.

"You mean from his mother?" Krishna asked.

"You knew that when you married her," Ajji said. "Your father had so many good Kannada-speaking girls chosen for you but, no, you make a love match and now you live apart. What happened to you both in America? Why are you both so unhappy?"

It was not her business, Krishna decided. Some things were best left between a man and his wife. People drifted apart when they lived in different cities; when they thought only of their studies; when the one thing binding them was beyond their reach. He glanced at Hari, then back at her.

"I'm happy," Krishna said. "I share the upstairs of a nice townhouse near the university. I drive a fifty-five Chevrolet with an automatic transmission. My friends and I go to Broadway to see the shows. We even go golfing, and next year I'm driving all the way to Canada for a holiday. Who says I'm not happy?" When he bit into a *bonda*, the tip of a black chilli fell into his rice. Frowning at it, he tried not to think of what he could not tell her: the curfew in the house because his landlady wanted to protect foreign students from American women; the mechanics he could never trust with the car; the hours spent in lines for cheap seats; and the golf which was not real golf because none of his friends belonged to a country club. Those endless rounds of mini-golf.

Hari pushed his plate away and squirmed. Something was wrong. His *masala dosa* had grown cold, and the sugar tasted like salt. He felt snakes slither through his ears and down his throat. The snakes were knotting in his stomach. He wanted to go home.

"What is the matter?" Ajji asked.

"I am full," he replied.

"After half a *dosa* only?" she asked. "Do you not want any sweets?" Maura, who stood watching from the kitchen, brought a wet banana leaf tied with brown string. She set the leaf on the table and picked the knot apart. "Harischandra," she crooned, "look," and peeled the leaf aside.

The snakes in his stomach vanished. Piled on the leaf, inches from his nose, were hard Mysore *pak* and soft *gulab jamun*. He could smell saffron under them. He eased the yellow and brown sweets aside with a spoon to find three spiralled *jelabis*. He took the largest. He bit through a narrow tube of orange dough, sucked the syrup from the *jelabi*, and began to eat. Round and round he went until only the syrup-filled centre remained. He placed it on his tongue and pressed the sticky centre against the roof of his mouth. Syrup trickled down his throat.

Not to be outdone by Ajji, Krishna said, "We'll get you a mango later, too, from a stall near your house. You have to share it, though. If you eat an entire mango by yourself, you'll get a stomach ache." He ignored Ajji's look, which said, "Do you expect the boy to believe such rubbish?"

"Can I give the beggar with the baby arm part of the mango?" Hari asked.

"Why not?" Krishna exclaimed. "Why not, I say!" He tousled Hari's hair with his clean, left hand.

Hari felt happier than he had since that night in Mauritius Airport; almost as happy as on the safari in Nairobi National Park. He liked Krishna.

On the following Saturday, Krishna took Hari to Cubbon Park, this time in a taxi cab. They sat in the back on the leather seat, Krishna on one side and Hari on the other. Hari stared out his window at the hand-painted film hoardings, at the stern policemen directing traffic through busy crossroads, at the buses and bicycles and bullock carts. In the park he played on the lawn while Krishna sat on a bench. He read newspapers: *The Statesman, The Guardian*. Sometimes he glanced up at young women pushing perambulators past the bench. Hari thought Krishna wanted to look at the babies. Hari did. When he asked whether he could go to the zoo on the far side of the park, Krishna nodded.

Hari set off. He felt like a big boy. He had never been here alone. With his fingers curled through the wire mesh, he watched the white rabbits. They turned round and round with nowhere to go. Their eyes and ears were pink. He wished he had some carrot *halva* for them. Mrs. Kamala-Bai said rabbits liked carrots. He sang to the tune of "Lavender Blue":

> Horses like oats, dilly-dilly,
> Kittens like milk,
> Rabbits like carrots, dilly
> I-I like . . . silk!

He ran, clapping, back to the bench.

"Finished, Boy?" Krishna asked. From under his newspapers, he took an *Illustrated Weekly* and opened it.

Hari nodded. He wanted to sing the song for Krishna, but he thought Krishna disliked music. Hari had still not heard Krishna hum, let alone sing.

Hari climbed onto the bench and leaned against Krishna's arm to look at the magazine. An entire page contained an advertisement for jam. "Strawberries from Panch-gani," Hari read aloud, scoring under words with a fingernail. "Mangoes from Ratna-giri. Allaha-bad guavas. Trichur pineapples. Papayas from Dahanu and Jalgaon bananas. All picked for the sun-blessed goodness of Dipy's Mixed Fruit Jam. When it's Dipy's, it's got to be the finest."

Krishna was impressed. Still he said, "You can't believe all advertisements," and turned the page. "Sometimes they tell lies." Now here was something. He tapped a black and white photo of an actor. The man wore shiny chains on his shoulders and chest and a temple-shaped crown on his head. "Do you know who this is?" Krishna asked.

"A liar?" Hari said.

Krishna found this so funny he began laughing and Hari also had to laugh. "This is King Harischandra," Krishna said at last. "They're making another Bombay talkie about him. Do you go to movies, to films?"

"English ones only," Hari said. "I have seen *Dumbo* and *Bambi* and *Sleeping Beauty*. It had a terrible dragon. The prince threw his sword into its heart, and it died. The prince rode on a fine white horse. It had no wings, so it could not fly." The horse reminded him of something but he could not remember what. "Amma said all these films are made by a man called Walldisney. Do you have Walldisney films in America?"

"That's where he lives," Krishna said, "in a huge castle called Disneyland."

Hari thought Krishna would begin talking about Disneyland. Instead, he tapped the photo again.

"This is the great man your mother named you for," Krishna said. "Actually, she named you for your grandfather, my own father, who is still called a modern King Harischandra. Because he was such an honest civil servant. Have you heard the story about the king?"

Hari tilted his head to examine the photo. It did not look like his grandfather. He lived all the way out in Jayanagar district on the very edge of Bangalore, nowhere near Halsur Road. It made no sense, but then his own parents did not live in the same house either.

"What is it?" Krishna asked.

"Amma does not have time to tell stories," Hari said. "She is studying always. I like songs better, like the ones Mrs. Kamala-Bai sings. Will you sing me an American song?" Hari clutched Krishna's arm. "Sing about Buffalo Bill!"

"Sorry, Boy, I can't sing. Except in the shower." Krishna smiled self-consciously.

Hari was disappointed but he also wanted to know about the shower. Before he could ask, Krishna said, "I'll tell you about Harischandra, though. He was the King of Ayodhya a long time ago. He was a great and noble ruler who conquered many lands. But more important than this, he always kept his word. To this very day, to call someone a modern Harischandra means he is an honest man."

Krishna's voice droned on to mingle with the rattling of the black pods on a *gulmohur* tree, what Hari called a sword tree. On the way home, he sat yawning on Krishna's lap. "Will you sing me a song next time?" Hari asked. "Sing about . . ." He felt gentle fingers pushing the hair back from his brow. The last thing he remembered was floating out of the taxi cab and into bed.

That night he woke to hear whispering outside his partly open door. After turning onto his side, he saw a strange sight through the fine mesh of his mosquito curtain. His parents were standing in the main room on the edge of the cone of light. Krishna held his jacket hooked over one shoulder. His tie was off, half tucked into his shirt pocket. Rukmini wore only her petticoat and held her blouse in front of her breasts. Krishna placed his hands on her bare shoulders and pressed his cheek against hers. While Hari turned away from the door, he decided to ask

Rukmini why Krishna had remained so late. In the morning Hari said nothing because he thought he had been dreaming. His parents looked happy together at last, floating in a bubble.

On the third Saturday, Hari and Srinivasan played hoops until Rukmini came home from her laboratory. After lunch, which Hari ate in the big house, Srinivasan insisted on leafing through his father's atlas. Hari waited for Krishna in the veranda of the little house while Rukmini read in the main room. He played with his jigsaw puzzle; he cleaned the rice glue from his sheriff's vest; he made a tail for his new kite. Each time he heard an autorickshaw slow on the road, he ran to the gate. Krishna still did not appear. Even the beggar was missing. At last Hari asked Rukmini to take him to Ajji's house.

"If your father wants to see you," Rukmini said, "he will come." She began preparing their afternoon snack.

Ajji arrived just as Hari and Rukmini sat down to curried eggplant and rice. Ajji's white petticoat showed below the hem of her sari. She smoothed its pleats when she saw the food on the wicker table. Hari sat cross-legged on the floor and she took his chair.

"Where is Babu's father?" Rukmini asked. "*Brinjal*? Rice? Mango pickle?"

Ajji nodded several times before saying, "He has left. He finally located his best friend from his Delhi days. The one who smuggled him out of the North and was himself arrested." She shook her head, recalling how the CID had expected her to betray her own son. How long ago it seemed: young men playing games in which to be beaten meant more than to lose. Krishna had never been caught, thank God. He had never been beaten. "After this," Ajji said, "your husband will fly to London to see his brother. He will take the *Queen Mary* back to New York."

Rukmini pursed her lips but she was not thinking only of herself. "He could not say goodbye to his own son?"

"What is there to worry?" Ajji said. "They will meet again soon." She bit into a mango pickle, then licked the oily sauce from her lips. The chair creaked when she sat back. "What happened to my boys?" she asked. "One lives far away and never sees his son. The elder marries some low-class Britisher and never returns to visit. It is true their father was strict, but was I such a bad mother? Always I marked my papers at home." When Rukmini looked sorry for her, Ajji remembered herself. "What would have been so wrong for all of you to remain in India?" she demanded. "Even you left the boy to pursue another degree. For two and a half years he had no parents. Why did it take you so long to finish? Why all this madness?"

Rukmini wanted to say, "My supervisor made trouble for me as well," but she did not want to give Ajji yet another reason to criticize her. "You know why," Rukmini said. "My husband wants Babu to have a better life."

Ajji wagged her head while leaning forward. For a moment Hari thought she and Rukmini might touch across the table. Ajji reached for the mango pickle. Rukmini reached for the salt.

Hari frowned at his plate, which he had balanced on his ankles. How could he have a better life than this one? Elzabeth made carrot *halva* on Sundays. Ajji ordered sweets from the Kwality Restaurant. Mrs. Kamala-Bai played the piano and sang. All he needed was someone to sing him American songs. Suddenly his eyes felt moist. Tears welled up from his jaw and he clenched it to keep from crying. Unable to eat, he put his plate on the floor and quickly wiped his eyes. He knew Krishna would leave one day but why had he left so soon? How could Hari sing American songs for Srinivasan or Mrs. Kamala-Bai now? Even when Rukmini sang, it was in Telugu, and often the words made little sense. It was simply music.

*

Hari looked up from his favourite birthday gift, a wooden cart and horse. He stared at the pale blue sky. Buffalo Bill had left so the sky no longer rumbled. Hari sat on the veranda step and waited for rain but Elzabeth said this was not the season of rains. He knew better. Buffalo Bill had dropped the rain somewhere else today.

After placing the horse and cart in a corner of the large veranda, Hari wandered into his garden. It was not a real garden like the one in front of Ajji's house. Only one row of ferns and margosa trees—what Elzabeth called *neem*—surrounded the compound. It was paved with stones but Hari could easily imagine it as a garden or even a jungle, one in which he could stalk tigers with the new pop gun his cousin-sisters had sent him. They lived in Hyderabad now, in another state, so Hari and Rukmini rented Prakash's old house. It was in Malleswaram district.

Rukmini's godmother, Lady Raman, lived nearby. Some weeks earlier, Rukmini had taken Hari to pay his respects. Lady Raman had half a dozen servants, a driver and even a mechanic. A yellow Chevrolet stood ready at all times under the portico. Inside, in the middle of the sitting room, there stood an inlaid piano, but Hari was afraid to touch it. While Rukmini and Lady Raman chatted, he played on the grounds, which were as large as the playground at Cluny Convent. His school was now only two furlongs away. It was even closer than Lady Raman's house, which was hidden from the road by a high wall. The wall was topped with barbed wire instead of broken glass.

A wall also surrounded Hari's new house but a wide gate allowed a good view of the quiet road. Hari's new best friend, Jagadish, lived down the road. His father was a banker and drove a Hindustan Ambassador but he never took them for rides. Moving through his jungle, Hari rubbed the rough, hairy trunk of a palm tree. Perhaps Elzabeth would knock down one of the green coconuts. Perhaps she would serve its cloudy milk for a snack. But today was Sunday. Rukmini would take him to the Ganapati Tea Room for cold pineapple juice.

Elzabeth rounded a corner of the house. She shook an insect spray pump and stopped to spray poison on the single rosebush. The poison smelled oily and she coughed from the spray. It drifted toward Hari, who held his nose. A string of rosewood beads, tucked into the waist of her sari, clicked when she turned.

"*Aré, baba*, nothing to do? Where are all your new toys?"

"In the veranda," Hari answered. "Will you guard them from the tigers while we are gone?"

"Of course. Any tiger comes in here is finished. I shall spray him like this." Elzabeth pointed the pump at the gate.

"Was it not a grand party we had yesterday?" he asked. Rukmini had bought him a cake with blue rosebuds. Silver pellets had spelled, "Happy Sixth Birthday," on the white icing. She had invited a dozen children: Jagadish the banker's son, and sons and daughters of lecturers at the Institute. She had also bought a tin of biscuits for Hari to give out at school. She had told him it was a custom—to give on one's birthday as well as to receive.

Elzabeth nodded. "Lovely party." She looked out through the gate. "Extremely lovely." The gate shrank. To Hari's eyes she dissolved like Ovaltine.

A battered car in a silver bubble appeared on the other side of the gate. A man waved through the open window. "Do you want to come to the lagoon?" he asked. His voice rasped like a crow's. Then he asked, "Is your mother home?"

"Amma," Hari heard himself call, "there is a man-uncle at the gate."

"All right, Babu," he heard her say, "let him in."

When he reached out, the bubble burst. Rainbows shot through the garden. He tried to glue the bubble together but the pieces would not fit. There were too many to make a single picture. One showed a car, another an ocean liner, yet another a flying seahorse.

Rukmini came out wearing her good green sweater. She was carrying a beaded purse. "Are you ready?"

"Ready!" he said; then: "Where did I live when you were studying in America?"

"In Mauritius," she said. "Do you not remember?"

He tried to remember but he could not. The bubble was like a silver one around the zebras and antelopes and a Land Rover. Both bubbles were beautiful but everything in them looked blurred. The bubbles floated like dreams.

# Chapter 5

## *The Madras House*

In July of the same year, Rukmini and Hari took the Brindavan Express to Madras, where Sharada met them at the station. She kissed Rukmini on both cheeks. Sharada's youngest daughter Usha, the only child still at home, made such a fuss over Hari that he hid behind Rukmini. Unlike the women, who both wore saris, Usha wore a frock, and her braids were not pinned behind her head. Sharada gave Usha two four-anna coins to give the porters. They made *namaskar*. Dawdling outside the station, Hari waved to the porters. One of them made *namaskar* again while the other grinned. Hari wished he had two annas to give them. Rukmini said, "Come along, Babu," and he climbed into Sharada's car. It was a sandy yellow Buick. Standing on the hump in the back, he watched autorickshaws and horse-drawn *tongas* wheel aside when the driver honked his horn. The car turned onto Poonamallee High Road. When the car reached Sharada's house, a sentry touched his yellow and gold turban before opening the gates. The car stopped in a portico, its white columns festooned with pink and orange bougainvillaea. Water lilies and lotus grew in a pond. Ivy shaded the veranda. All the rooms had creamy, patterned rugs, ferns in clay pots, bamboo blinds, and ceiling fans.

The next morning, Sharada and Usha took Rukmini and Hari to Marina Beach. While the women sat in canvas chairs shaded by umbrellas, Hari searched for shells and Usha built a sandcastle near the water's edge. When a wave came too near the castle, Usha ran screaming and giggling with her black braids whipping the air. Even if she was twice his age, Hari thought her silly. Did she not see the waves would wash her castle away? Collecting shells made more sense. He spent most of the morning sifting through the velvety sand for shells as large as those in the Madras House. Some were speckled, others spiked; some were the colour of ivory, others orange and pink. But the sand yielded shells no larger than a four-anna coin. While the sun climbed and grew hot, he spent more time staring out to sea. It was the Bay of Bengal, Usha said. It began at the Mouths of the Ganges in the north, stretched past this coast—the Coromandel Coast—and ended at Cape Comorin in the south. He liked the sounds of these musical names: *Cor-o-mandel, Com-or-in*.

A long ship sailed north. It moved so slowly, it appeared to stand still. He remembered playing next to a canoe on a dark beach, one shaded by coconut palms, while a man helped him search for buried treasure. Someone had taken a photo of this, and Rukmini kept it in her green album. Only the week before, she had pasted a new photo, Hari's first coloured one, into his orange album. In the photo Krishna leaned against the front of a huge, black car. Hari could barely make out Krishna's face, but he could see the grin. The car grinned as well. It had silver teeth—its grille—and two large headlamps. Rukmini said everyone in New York City drove cars. Soon she and Hari would go there, but first they would have to visit Madras for their medical certificates. She told him sick people could not go to America. Everyone there was healthy like his father. Now he told Usha, "Everyone in America is big and strong, did you know? Where does your father live?"

"He is no more," Usha said. "He died before I was born."

At this, Hari looked away at her sandcastle. Then he coughed. Unlike the dry air of Bangalore, the air in Madras felt salty and wet and smelled of smoke from all the cars. But the sky seemed larger. Even as it spread upward from the beach, the sky changed from grey-blue to real sky blue. Then it turned yellow-white near the sun. Looking up burned his eyes. He lowered them and blinked at dazzling, purple spots bobbing on the waves.

After lunch Hari took a nap, something he rarely did now.

He woke with his fists clenched. He felt hungry but his legs ached, so he lay still and listened to the ceiling fan. Through the closed door, he could hear voices and music from the front of the house. He sat up and rubbed his eyes. They were burning. His hands felt clammy, and sweat drenched his hair. Worst of all, his knees felt so stiff it hurt to bend them. When he switched on the light, it stabbed his eyes like the sun glaring on the beach. He buried his face in the cool, soft pillow but he still felt hungry. He also wanted to find Usha. He slid half-heartedly over the edge of the cot. Tomorrow he would take his medical exam. He climbed onto a stool next to the washbasin and, careful not to hit his head on the tap, leaned over the basin to wash his face. Then he climbed onto his cot, switched off the fan and light, and hurried from the room. His legs ached but his face felt cool.

Rukmini and Sharada were chatting while Telugu songs played on the gramophone.

"Why she gave up medical school to marry him," Sharada said, "I will never know." They were speaking about a distant relation. "And after four years," Sharada added, "they still have no issue. So, tell me: *bagunnava*?"

"*Paapam*," Rukmini said. "I told you this morning. Fine. A little back pain, that is all."

"Reading cannot be good for the back," Sharada said. "You must learn to enjoy life a little more. You can always finish your doctorate in America."

Hari did not want to bother Rukmini about his aching legs. He turned and walked slowly down the corridor into a dining room. In the middle of the room stood a long, teakwood table covered with a lace cloth. Golden birds embroidered on sandy yellow velvet covered the high chair backs and the seats. The chairs were also made of teak and the carving on their legs matched the carving on the table's pedestal. Careful not to touch anything, Hari entered a second dining room. It was bare except for a framed Mysore painting of Ganesha. Bits of coloured glass were pasted like old jewellery about his neck, and his crown was made of gold leaf. Sharada used this room only on feast days, when people sat on the floor with their backs to the walls and ate from plantain leaves. On the far side of this dining room, a long ramp led down to a kitchen. In a corner stood a stone for grinding grain. Next to it, a servant named May bent over a kerosene stove. Hari stopped at the foot of the ramp. The stone floor felt cold beneath his feet. He turned away quietly so he would not disturb May. Now he faced a closed door. It was made of unpainted wood. It had an iron latch instead of a silver handle like other doors in the house. He opened the door and stood on the threshold.

To his left, a window barred against monkeys let in a shaft of sunlight. Dust danced like fairies. The room smelled of incense and camphor. In the far right-hand corner, a platform held tarnished silver utensils and statuettes of two gods with flowers at their feet. Hari knew this was a godroom of sorts, but whose? Sharada's godroom was upstairs. Even as he blinked, the drooping ends of incense sticks dropped ash on the flowers. He noticed movement out of the corner of his eye and faced the window. There was someone beyond the shaft of light.

It was Sharada's mother-in-law, Muttamma, but Hari did not know this. She spent her days lying or sitting on her bedroll. When the door opened, she was toying with her long white hair, which fell over her shoulders. She looked at the door but could see nothing beyond a beam of soft, slanting light. She measured the passage of time by the angle of this beam. It shone through her window each afternoon and, like the light of the past few hours, moved too quickly for comfort.

How strange, Hari thought; the old woman was looking straight at him yet he felt invisible. When the door creaked beside him, she sat up cross-legged and dropped her hands to her knees. Now she looked like Lord Buddha seated on a lotus but Hari puzzled over this. Lords were men.

Muttamma asked in Telugu, "Who is there? Are you making mischief, Usha?" When she sniffed, she detected hair oil and sweat, the smells of a boy. Girls also smelled of sweat—it came from all their running about—but their hair was more fragrant even when they did not wear flowers.

"I am Harischandra," Hari said. He added, plaintively, "I do not make mischief." He watched the woman reach out. Her eyes were like ivory beads. He stepped all the way into the room and closed the door behind him, careful to leave it ajar.

"I recall no one by that name," she said. "Such a grand name. Who is your father? What is he?"

"He does not live with us," Hari said.

"Your mother's name?" Muttamma asked. "What is she?"

"Rukmini," he replied. "She studies engineering."

"*Aré, baba*!" Muttamma exclaimed. She clapped once and left her palms closed with the tips of her first fingers touching her crinkled lips. "Gopal Harischandra, no? I recall when you were born. Seven years after Usha. You are now . . . five years old?"

"Six," he said proudly. "We had a birthday party and ate cake and played jute."

"Come closer, Harish," Muttamma commanded. "Let me see you." She watched his form pass through the light. There was another light in the room now, a faint orange glow which outlined the grey of his body. It was an orange so pale, so yellowy, it verged on saffron. Only one kind of child could have an aura like this: he had been a saint in his previous life. This life would not be easy for him, she knew, but he would always be lucky. He would always be charmed.

Hari stood so close to her, his toes touched the bedroll, so close he could smell the cloves on her breath. Her thin, gentle fingers ran over his arms, then squeezed his hands. When she lifted his left foot to trace the lines on his sole, he clutched her shoulder and giggled.

The foot told her much. "You have the *Chakra*," she said. "Do you know what this is?"

"A wheel," he replied.

"A special kind of wheel," she said. "It is the *Dharma Chakra* which appears below the lions on Ashoka's Pillar. It is Lord Buddha's wheel of cosmic order."

"The blue wheel on our flag!" he exclaimed.

"You have the *Chakra*," she repeated. Then: "It means you must travel far."

"I have been to Mauritius!" he declared.

"Ah, and what are you doing here?" she asked.

"I must pass an exam," he replied, "and go to America to see my father. I have my passport already. It is not like my baby passport, which was also Amma's passport. This is my own, with my own photograph."

Muttamma moved her hands up to his chin and traced the line between his lips. They curved downward. "You are the image of your mother," she said, "but you must learn to smile more. Last time I heard of Rukmini, she was studying in America. Why did no one tell me she had returned? I have not seen her these six years." Muttamma stroked his nose. "This is not from your mother," she said.

Hari's legs were throbbing. He locked his knees to keep them from shaking.

Muttamma could sense something was wrong. A smell of weariness followed him. "What is it?" she asked. When she ran her fingers down the backs of his legs, he cried out and fell against her. He was much lighter than she expected. He was small for his age. The saffron light quivered against her shoulder now but it felt too warm. She stood him upright and pressed a palm to his forehead. It was hot. "May!" she called. "Ma-ay!"

The shouting startled Hari. He was biting his lips to keep from crying. The backs of his legs burned. He tried to turn away, but the old woman clutched him with her free hand.

"Donkey," she called, "why are you so slow?"

May's sari swished when she ran into the room.

"Where is my daughter-in-law?" Muttamma demanded. "Bring her here! And this boy's mother? Bring her here also!" Muttamma pulled him into her lap. He lay against her like a bundle of rags.

Hari heard feet running, then the voices of three women and the jingle-jangle of jewellery. Someone bumped into a chair in the front dining room. Smiling, the old woman revealed toothless gums. "See how they run?" she whispered. "Like three blind mice." When she laughed her clove-scented breath into his face, he tried to smile.

The women entered in a flurry, all of them speaking at once:

"How did he come to be here?"

"Babu, what is this!"

"Just now I was boiling water and—"

Muttamma silenced them with, "Where are you, Rukmini?"

Someone stepped forward and Muttamma watched the grey form bend into itself. Rukmini was making *namaskar*. The green outline pleased Muttamma, as it had years before. Rukmini had the aura of someone who was both spiritual and practical, the best of both worlds. She had also been a saint in her previous life, a courtly singer-saint. Rukmini said, "How have you been, Muttamma?"

"My son the governor is forgotten," she replied, "so his niece no longer visits her grand-auntie?" Muttamma clucked her tongue. "How long have you been here?"

"We arrived yesterday and went to the beach this morning," Rukmini said. "Babu likes the beach."

Muttamma snorted. What child did not like the beach? "This is what comes of getting an American degree," she said. "This boy only comes to pay his respects. Will he speak to me after he returns from seeing his father?"

"Harish will not be returning," Sharada announced. "They are going to America to live."

Muttamma's eyes widened. "Why so far?" she asked. "Still, how fitting. The governor's niece leaves us again. What is this exam the boy must pass?"

"Nothing to worry yourself about," Sharada said. "There is no place to obtain the proper medical certificate in Bangalore, so—"

"Go back to Bangalore then," Muttamma told Rukmini. "The boy will fail with this rash. He has a fever also."

Rukmini and Sharada said together:

"Babu! Come here."

"May, bring hot lemon for Harish!"

"Where will we find lemons now?" May asked.

"Donkey," Muttamma snapped. "Send Driver to Bazaar Road."

Rukmini pulled Hari to his feet and turned his back to the window. The light picked out splotches of red on his skin. When she also saw the beginnings of boils, she sucked in her breath. "My god!" she exclaimed. "You are so brave, you would not tell me? What shall we do?"

Hari did not know what she was talking about. His legs ached, that was all. He wanted to lie down.

Muttamma laughed dryly. "Take him to the doctor," she suggested. "Let him cure the boy instead of examining him."

"But he will fail," Rukmini said. "We will have to wait another year for the exam." She made a spitting sound at the window. "*Thup*! Such an idiotic rule!"

When Muttamma waved her hand, Hari watched the fairies of dust dance out of the sunlight.

"Is this not the same child who fell ill in Benares?" she asked.

Hari looked at Rukmini. She had never told him about this. Now she was avoiding his eyes.

"We joined my husband there," she replied. "He was a senior lecturer at—"

"He must be a brilliant man," Muttamma said. "Too brilliant to raise a son?" She remembered him now. She had met him only twice and could see all in his aura: a deep, dull blue. He was a man of much ambition and little luck. He must have been a pilgrim in his previous life: a pilgrim who had lost his way.

"Babu could not stand the heat," Rukmini said. "The doctors gave up all hope so I took him back to Bangalore on his first birthday. He slept three days. When he woke he was fine, totally."

Muttamma nodded. "It is true what they say," she said. "Those born in Bangalore can never live anywhere else. Even in Madras we know this. Give me the boy."

Rukmini finally released him and he folded into Muttamma's lap. He did not know what this talk was about, and he did not care.

Muttamma turned him to face the far corner. "Do you know what gods these are?" she asked. "Lord Venkateswara and his consort. Do you see the lord's eyes are hidden?" Hari could just make out white lines covering Lord Venkateswara's eyes.

"This is so he cannot see all the evil in the world," Muttamma said, "for if he did, he would destroy it with a blinding flash."

She drew a corner of her white cotton sari over her head. When she thought of her own husband, dead these many years, she felt young. Only when she thought of her son did she feel old; only at such times did she feel like a widow. She spoke slowly now, as much for Sharada and Rukmini's benefit as for Hari's:

"Every morning my son rose at five o'clock to make *puja* to his gods before going to the high court. Then, when the governor died during the war, the Viceroy made my son acting governor. Suddenly he had no time for *puja*. He began to live like the Britishers, and the British ways killed him. Why is everyone so proud he was knighted by the Viceroy? Were the Britishers gods? Did they make him immortal?" She paused. "He never saw Usha born, just as your father did not see you born. I thank the lord I could not see by then. But I could feel my son grow thin and pale even after he returned to the high court. Stay in India!" she said, tightening her grip on Hari. "You are from a great family on your mother's side. With your father in America, you will be nothing."

Rukmini pulled Hari into her arms. He wondered why she was taking him from such a kind woman. Muttamma would make him better, he knew it. Rukmini stopped to give May instructions on how to make hot lemon. "The best lemons only," Rukmini said. "And a sprinkling of jaggery."

Still in the room, Sharada was scolding Muttamma, who refused to be silenced. "We are Hindus," she said. "God did not create us to learn foreign ways." Surely even Sharada knew this? But no, she did not concern herself with such things even though, or perhaps because, she had lost her husband to those ways. Muttamma covered her ears until Sharada left.

Outside in the kitchen, even as Rukmini took Hari up the ramp, even as Sharada gave May further instructions, he could hear Muttamma's voice. She was chanting:

> Oh Lord,
> Remove the mask from your eyes,
> So I may behold your magnificence
> Even as the world ends.

✸

The following day Hari sat in the front room with his feet on an ottoman. Usha had wrapped him in a cashmere shawl. The bamboo blinds were down. The doctor had given ointment but Hari's bandaged knees hurt so much he could not bend them. He traced the sandy yellow patterns on the rug with his eyes. Every Sunday Elzabeth made designs on the floor with a white powder called *rangoli*. She did this to bring the house luck. He never played near the designs in case he might smudge them, especially the lotus flowers with their many petals.

"What shall we do now?" Rukmini asked. She slapped at the bothersome leaves of a fern next to her teakwood chair.

Sharada lifted her hand and let it fall back into her lap. Her fingers were curled as though waiting for alms.

"I told the doctor it was only a rash," Rukmini said. "He claimed he must do his duty. I told him Babu's father would be angry. Still the idiot refused to sign the certificate!" Her voice sank and she toyed with her bangles. "*Ayoh*, we were so close."

Hari looked at a conch shell next to the silent gramophone. The large, black horn stared at him. Even the mouth of the shell stared at him. It was not his fault his eyes still burned, or that Sharada's driver had had to carry him to and from the Buick.

Usha entered with a stainless steel tumbler of hot lemon. She blew on the liquid and gave the tumbler to Hari, who held it by the hot, metal rim. Usha left the room once more, then returned with a net bag as large as a coconut. It was filled with shells. "Here, Babu," she said, placing the bag in his lap, "you take these back to Bangalore."

He fingered a cowrie shell. It was the size of his fist and spotted like a leopard. He did not want these shells. He wanted someone to tell him everything would be all right.

"What do you say?" Rukmini asked kindly.

"Thank you, Usha," he whispered.

"*Aré!*" Sharada gasped. She was staring at the door and everyone turned to look.

Muttamma tottered on the threshold. She was leaning on May. "Move forward," Muttamma said. "Donkey, can I not enter my own son's sitting room? I was mistress here once." She told Sharada, "I will wear white and remain out of your way, but I will not shave my head, and I will not wait for you educated people to tell me what has happened."

May looked as though she might collapse under the weight. She brought Muttamma as far as Hari, who moved his feet so Muttamma could sink onto the ottoman. Usha took the shells and backed toward a window.

"So, Harish," Muttamma said, "no one is laughing in this room. You must give me the news then."

He threw himself into her arms. The tumbler struck her shoulder and the hot lemon spilled onto the rug. "We shall never go to America!" he sobbed.

"Don't cry, Babu," Rukmini said. "We shall try again next year. These things happen. They are nobody's fault."

He did not care. He did not want to return to take the exam. He wanted to return only to see Muttamma.

While he sobbed, she crooned, "*Paapam*, poor boy. It is karma only. It is fate. I told you people: those born in Bangalore can never live anywhere else. Still, a boy belongs with his father. Do not cry, Harischandra. America will wait. Your father will wait also."

Hari nodded and wiped an arm across his eyes. Muttamma stroked his hair and he took a deep breath. He never wanted to lose the memory of her scent, of camphor and cloves. But now the room was filling with the scent of hot lemon. Lemon and jaggery with a pinch of saffron—they soaked into the rug.

# Chapter 6

## *Sacrifices*

Hari's grandfather, Ajja, got down from the bus on Margosa Road. After opening his umbrella for shade, he straightened the towel draped over his shoulder. He was ready now. He rarely left his house on the outskirts, but he considered these weekly forays into Malleswaram district a duty. His only grandchild was not well and at such times a boy needed a man about. A woman could provide comfort but only a man could provide inspiration. Ajja fingered the coins in his shirt pocket. Parting with one anna would not bankrupt him, he decided, so he bought some ginger mints at a stall. They were his only vice.

An autorickshaw in search of a fare slowed nearby and the driver beeped his horn. Ajja ignored him. He had spent much of his life on foot, even when he rated a car and driver, and he could not allow himself the luxury of being transported a few furlongs. The autorickshaw driver shrugged insolently and followed two women burdened with infants, but even the women ignored him. Ajja lengthened his stride to pass them. He did not like following people. There would be plenty of time for that when he began to dodder.

Ajja was in the third stage of a high-caste man's life. The first two stages had been less enjoyable than this one. His days in *brahmacharya*, as a student, were challenging ones. He learned much, though as a modern man he spent more time on his civil engineering than on the *Vedas*. Even now he preferred the elegance of mathematics to the irrelevance of Sanskrit. His days as a householder had not been as satisfying—his wife had cared more about her own career than the children. However, Ajja had something to show for himself besides his good reputation: a son in America, a high-class daughter-in-law, a clever grandson and, when Ajja allowed himself to think about his one failure, a son in England. Now Ajja was a hermit, a suburban dweller rather than a forest dweller. He lived in his bungalow in Jayanagar district and meditated. Not on the *Vedas*, not yet, but on the latest developments in science. Lasers, microwaves—they would change the face of the earth as surely as he had changed Mysore State with his dams and power stations. At a crossroad he stopped for a bullock cart. The stone marker here said 4th Cross, and he smiled. In the fourth stage of his life he would become an ascetic: wander like a beggar in search of knowledge to free him from rebirth. But given that he was a modern man, perhaps he would travel abroad instead. Perhaps he would take a ship through the Suez Canal and the Mediterranean Sea all the way to England where, as his last act, he would forgive his wayward son. Then again, perhaps not.

❋

While Ajja walked from the bus stop, Rukmini helped Elzabeth make carrot *halva* and Hari played in the main room. He could not climb the stairs, so he spent his days on the first floor and even slept in the veranda.

Rukmini had taken her statue of Ganesha off the Murphy Radio and placed the elephant god under the table. "You pretend it is a Ganesha temple," she said. "You play with him all you want. He is a remover of obstacles."

She did not explain what she meant, but Hari knew Ganesha was one of many animal gods Hindus could worship. Just now Hari was pretending to be Hanuman, the monkey god, who liked playing tricks on demons by changing his size. Hari had shrunk himself to the size of a rat and was visiting the temple in his horsedrawn cart. "You must be patient," he told Ganesha. "The *halva* will take some time." Hari placed a slice of carrot on a plate and slid it under the table.

When the gate creaked open, he slid across the floor toward the veranda. Using the rope Elzabeth had tied in the middle of the doorway, he pulled himself to his feet. From here he watched Ajja look about the garden and scratch his head. Hari giggled. He and Ajja played this game every Sunday: Ajja pretended he did not know Hari spied on him.

"Where can he be?" Ajja said, closing his umbrella. "Has he vanished?"

Hari released the rope and tottered forward. Fire stabbed through his legs and his knees buckled. He fell with a cry. At the last moment, just before his knees struck the floor, he grasped the white bars of the veranda window. He heard Ajja hurry across the garden and into the veranda.

Ajja hooked his umbrella over the open door. He scooped Hari up so he could lean, trembling, against the veranda wall. "*Yenappa*," Ajja demanded, "why do you walk?"

"Why not walk?" Hari asked. "I have legs still." He pouted at the bandages covering his legs from his ankles to his thighs. He looked at Ajja for the answer. His breath smelled of ginger mints. He had yellow teeth as stubby as the white hair on his head.

With one end of his towel, Ajja dabbed the sweat from Hari's brow. Then Ajja sat in the nearest chair. "Does it not hurt you to stand?" he asked.

"No," Hari replied.

"You know it does, Babu." Rukmini stood in the doorway to the main room and held a knife with her fingers stained a yellow-orange. "Welcome," she told Ajja. She tucked the rope out of the way.

Ajja took off his wire-rimmed specs, wiped his face, and threw the towel across his shoulder. "Things are no better?" he asked. He pulled up one end of his white cotton *dhoti* and polished his specs.

Rukmini watched him closely. Without his specs he resembled Krishna. It was said that if a woman wanted to know what her husband would look like when he grew old, she should look at his father. Rukmini liked what she saw. Then she looked at Hari and answered Ajja's question. "He has stopped getting worse at least," she said. "This new doctor in Palace Orchards is smarter than the others. He gave ointment to soften the skin. Still the boils ooze. I will tell Elzabeth to begin your coffee."

After Rukmini left, Hari crawled across the floor to Ajja's feet and unlaced his heavy, black shoes. Hari tugged them off and placed them toe to toe, heel to heel under the chair.

"Thank you," Ajja said. "At home I have no one to remove my shoes."

"You can live with us," Hari suggested.

Ajja put his specs on to gaze out at the garden. He needed no more family problems, no more illness in the house. He shook his head.

Rukmini returned to sit in the far chair. "Elzabeth will bring food soon," she said.

Hari's right ankle began to itch but he could not reach the skin under the bandage. Instead, he rubbed one ankle against the other. There were many things he could not do now, like playing jute with his friend, Jagadish. Then there was the play at school. Before they went to Madras, before the rash began, Rukmini had stitched him a soldier's uniform: a splendid red coat with brass buttons, a pair of black trousers with a red stripe on each leg, and a black cap. He was to have worn the uniform in the school play, but he had sat with other children on the ground while watching a first standard boy wear the uniform. The boy had played a Britisher named Lord Mountbatten in a story celebrating Independence Day.

"Why so many tribulations?" Ajja asked Rukmini. He began toying with Hari's long, curly hair.

"God knows," she sighed. "The school van drives him and we live so close. It costs five rupees a month. Elzabeth goes to carry him from class to class. I have hired another servant to come each afternoon to cook supper."

Hari looked up in time to see Ajja flick his free hand. "We have money," he said.

When Rukmini muttered, "It is not the money," Ajja nodded and pursed his lips.

Hari wondered why everyone made such a fuss over his legs. He would get better one day, he knew it. For now he could still enjoy things like riding in the van.

The olive green Cluny Convent van looked like a jeep in front. The driver always picked Hari up first and dropped him off last so he could have the longest ride of anyone. Each morning Rukmini snipped a pink rose off the bush in the garden for the driver and he tucked the rose above his mirror. From it dangled a string of sandalwood beads, like the rosewood string Elzabeth wore, and a garland of jasmine. Hari thought it splendid: to drive all over Malleswaram, miles and miles, in a van smelling of jasmine and sandalwood and rose. Being unable to walk was not so bad. Besides, when all the children gathered in the school compound after lunch to recite the Lord's Prayer, Hari sat in the shade near the statue of Saint Joseph and pretended to conduct them.

Elzabeth appeared with a tray holding three tumblers. When she bent in front of him, her string of beads swayed out from her waist. He took the only tumbler of Ovaltine and grinned. Her large teeth were stained black from chewing coal to keep them healthy. Why did she not use toothpaste? He did. He used Colgate, the world's finest toothpaste.

Ajja nodded at Hari's legs and asked, "May I see?"

"Bring the olive oil and ointment," Rukmini told Elzabeth. "Also find clean bandages."

Elzabeth placed the tray on the wicker table and left. She returned with a bottle of olive oil and a round tin of ointment, which she handed to Rukmini. Elzabeth left the veranda once more.

Rukmini knelt next to Hari and undid the knot above his right knee. As she poured oil along the bandage, he squirmed. The cool oil tickled. After the gauze turned yellow, she began unwinding it. When she reached his knee, she let him pull off the rest of the gauze while she trickled oil down his calf. Once, when he pulled too quickly, a scab tore away and he flinched. "Careful," she said. She took the end of the bandage from him and unwrapped it until she reached his ankle. After patting more oil into the gauze, she let him unwrap the ankle himself.

Gaping, red wounds covered his swollen leg. Not an inch of normal skin showed between his thigh and his foot. But the wounds did not hurt nearly as much as the boils around his ankle and behind his knee. They smelled like sour, yellowing milk.

Ajja peered at the boils and shook his head. "Why?" he asked again.

Rukmini twisted the lid off the round tin. Now an odour stronger than the pus filled the air. The ointment smelled like tar bubbling on hot summer roads.

When Ajja took the tin from her, Hari cried, "You must not!"

Ajja's knees cracked when he knelt on the floor. "You get down to remove my shoes," he said. "I shall get down to apply your medicine. Here, turn the leg. How can I reach?" He pressed a fingertip into the black ointment and dabbed it into the red wounds. He screwed the lid onto the tin. Wrinkling his nose at the tarry smell, he gently smeared the ointment around Hari's ankle and knee.

Elzabeth returned with two rolls of gauze.

"We need one only," Rukmini said.

Elzabeth grimaced at Hari's leg. She turned away with a hand covering her nose.

Rukmini wound a new bandage around the leg. The gauze sank into the wounds. It stuck to the red circle where Hari had pulled off the scab.

Soon the ointment softened the skin behind his knee until he could straighten his right leg. His left one lay stiff and bent. Clutching his Ovaltine, he pulled himself into his favourite place near the steps. From here he could see into both the garden and the main room.

Ajja also pulled himself backward, into his chair. He wiped his hand on the towel, picked up his tumbler, and blew across the rim. He sucked in more air than coffee when he drank and it amused Hari. Today, though, Ajja did not wiggle his ears as though he and Hari shared a secret. Ajja gazed at the garden while he drank. At last he told Rukmini, "I think you should tell my son about this." He said this every week.

She rose from the floor and took her chair. "I still do not want to worry him."

Ajja wiped his lips with the towel. True, he had been against this match—marriages between people from different states rarely lasted, especially when the wife was of a higher class than the husband—but he had to admit Krishna had made a good choice. It remained to be seen whether something as tenuous as love could keep this marriage together. Ajja frowned. He could not tell Rukmini such things.

He admired the way she handled everything. Not only was she studying; she was also looking after a sick boy. Still, he felt it was time to speak his mind. After turning his chair to face her, he rubbed the purple splotch on the back of his neck. It was beginning to itch, a sure sign he was venturing beyond his guarded life. "I have been giving this matter a great deal of thought. I feel doctors cannot help the boy. We must fall back on other ways."

Hari looked from the purple splotch to the dot on Rukmini's forehead. It winked when she frowned, but Hari did not laugh. Everyone was being so glum today. Ajja had even forgotten to offer Hari a ginger mint.

"What ways?" she asked.

Ajja put his tumbler on the table and placed his hands on his knees. "Many years ago, I cut myself badly while shaving. The wound would not stop bleeding. I went to every doctor I could find. I tried all the different cures. Allopathy, your western medicine. Ayurveda, healing with herbs. Even German homeopathy, which I learned out of books. Yet none of these methods worked so my friends told me, 'You are such an educated man, a twentieth-century fellow! What of your ancestor, Raghavendra Swami?'"

"The faith healer?" Rukmini asked. She turned to Hari. "He was your ancestor, too."

How lucky, Hari thought: a real swami for an ancestor. Hari pulled himself closer to the table so he could listen.

Ajja looked down and touched Hari's head. "Raghavendra Swami was more than a faith healer," Ajja insisted. "When he was young he was a poor, simple villager. One day he had a vision, so he left his wife and child. He lived like a *sannyasi,* alone in the forest. He fasted and prayed until finally he understood the ways of all men. Only then could he begin his great work. He passed on his knowledge to his disciples, but the ordinary people revered him for his powers of healing. Leprosy, cholera, blindness—there was nothing he could not cure. Except ignorance, so you learn your times table!" Ajja shook his finger at Hari. Growing serious once more, Ajja continued: "When the time came for Raghavendra to die he went into a trance. His disciples built a stone hut around him. The Britishers call it a cairn and even some Britishers claim he never died."

Hari looked at Rukmini but she kept her eyes on Ajja and nodded. Hari decided it must be true.

"I was in despair," Ajja told her. "Day after day I bled like that Russian prince, so I went to Raghavendra's shrine and did all the proper things. I bathed in the river and circled the cairn in my wet clothes. I fed all the poor people sleeping nearby. I even swore to keep proper Brahmin traditions for the rest of my life. This is why I also believe Raghavendra never died. I was cured in one week."

"Truly?" Rukmini exclaimed. "And did you keep all the Brahmin traditions?"

"Oh yes," he replied. "For one whole year. Then I went back to my modern ways." He laughed so heartily, she too had to laugh, though not as hard.

Hari frowned. It was a fine story, but what did it mean? And what was so funny? Still, he liked the way Ajja laughed, with his eyes screwed shut and his specs glinting in the light.

Rukmini picked up her coffee. She thought she understood what Ajja was getting at, but it was a big step to take—falling back on local superstitions about swamis. Only a god could help her now. Not Ganesha but her family god. "You are advising me to take Babu to be cured by his ancestor?" she asked. When Ajja nodded she said, "My people do not go to mere swamis."

Ajja's neck grew hot. "Is your family so much better than mine?" he demanded.

"I am not being ungrateful," she said. "You have shown me what I must do. Babu must go to Lord Venkateswara. He must make the sacrifice."

Hari looked from Rukmini to Ajja, who was gazing at her in disbelief. What was all this talk about sacrifice? "I can give the lord my sheriff's vest," Hari said.

She smiled and stretched out her hand. He pulled himself from Ajja's feet to hers. "Lord Venkateswara demands more than a costume," she said. She buried her fingers in Hari's hair.

Hari crossed his bandaged legs, the right over the left. What more could he give? "My pop gun also?" he asked.

Of all the ridiculous things, Ajja thought. Surely she was jesting? And there was the boy to think of. It was one thing to bathe in a river and circle a shrine. When it was done it was done and a man could go back to his normal life. But a sacrifice to Lord Venkateswara marked a man for weeks, perhaps months—it was so primitive—and the god could be so fickle. "The other children will laugh at him," Ajja said angrily. "Times have changed too much."

"Let them laugh," Rukmini said. "Can he play with them like this?" Her voice dropped. "I am getting worried for him. I have not heard him sing in weeks."

Hari frowned once again. What should it matter that he did not feel like singing because his legs hurt? He still heard music in his head. It simply would not come out.

"My son would be displeased," Ajja said.

"Your son is not here," Rukmini declared. "What good can he do from America?"

Ajja turned his palms upward on his knees. She had an answer to everything. He should have left the healing to doctors and time; he should never have mentioned Raghavendra Swami. Why did he even bother to visit? Because of the boy.

"Elzabeth!" Rukmini called.

Elzabeth appeared with a plate. "It is ready," she announced. "Just now ready!"

"Has *dhobi* brought back our washing?" Rukmini asked.

"Tomorrow he will come," Elzabeth replied. She put the plate on the table.

Hari dug his fingers into the orange paste. How good it smelled: of carrots and pistachios. Sunday was his favourite day even if he could no longer drink cold pineapple juice in the Ganapati Tea Room. He barely chewed the *halva* before he swallowed.

Ajja picked up a morsel, which he tucked into his cheek. He did not like soft foods. His teeth were fine.

"We will leave the day after," Rukmini told Elzabeth. "We are going to Tirumala."

"To the temple?" Elzabeth demanded.

"I shall need you to help me with Babu," Rukmini said. "It is a long way to the holy hill." She toyed with his hair and twirled a lock around her finger. "What?" she asked when Elzabeth scowled.

"You send him to a good Christian school," Elzabeth said, "and now you take him to a Hindu temple to—"

"The doctors have done nothing!" Rukmini snapped.

Elzabeth drew herself up and stared at Rukmini over Ajja's head. He slumped in his seat as if wanting to be out of the way. "My littlest brother is hoping to be a doctor," Elzabeth said. "He will cure Harish."

"We cannot wait so long," Rukmini scoffed.

Elzabeth tried to say, "This Venkateswara is evil—"

"*Hogu,*" Rukmini ordered. "Go!"

Elzabeth moved so she could look at Ajja.

He slumped even lower. He stared at the *halva* as though it had upset his stomach. This was exactly why he lived out in Jayanagar, so he could avoid becoming embroiled in other people's troubles. Now look what he had done. And to be caught between a mistress and an ayah? It served him right. Still, order must be maintained, and an ayah had her place. "It would seem your mistress has made up her mind," he said.

"It is true what I tell you," Elzabeth cried. She glared at Rukmini. "I know what mothers did with their girl-childs before the British passed their laws. What mother in her proper mind would throw her girl-child into the offering pot so this 'lord' would give her a son? My auntie told me. She heard it from the taxi driver in our village. He drove rich people all the way from Chittoor to Tirupathi, up the hill itself to Tirumala. When the priests cleaned out the gold from the pot, they would find bones mixed in. The girl-childs died from having no air, smothered under all the jewellery."

Hari stared at Rukmini. He knew she could never do such a thing—she had such gentle hands.

Rukmini's chin trembled with anger. It had been decades since a mother had thrown a girl into the offering pot. It was ancient history, long gone, like the British themselves and their laws. Her chair creaked when she straightened. "I am Babu's mother, not you," she told Elzabeth. "Our family has worshipped Lord Venkateswara for generations."

Elzabeth ground her black teeth. "There is only one lord," she said coldly, "and his name is God. He sacrificed his only-begotten son to die for our sins." She crossed herself the way she did when reciting the Lord's Prayer at school after lunch. "Yea, though I walk through the valley of the shadow of death—"

"Enough of this," Rukmini interrupted. "You recite things you do not even understand. Like a parrot."

Elzabeth turned abruptly. Her cotton sari, an old one from Rukmini, swished loudly. Her beads clicked all the way to the kitchen.

Rukmini stared at Ajja as though she might scold him, too.

He spread his hands. "You are the boy's mother, yes," he said. He pushed the plate of *halva* closer to Hari. Enough was enough.

She nodded once, twice, three times.

Hari breathed in the sweet, carroty smell. The *halva* sank into the valleys he gouged. What more could he offer than his sheriff's vest and pop gun? There was always the horse and cart. Perhaps the lord even wanted Hari's orange album with its coloured photo of his father. No, Lord Venkateswara could have anything except the album. And the splendid new uniform, of course.

✱

Two days later, in the evening, Hari, Rukmini and Elzabeth reached Tirupathi by train. While they waited for the Tirumala Link Bus, Rukmini bought Hari a plastic wrist watch. It was either this or a balloon, and a balloon would be impractical on the bus. When the bus arrived, people swarmed about the door even as others got off. Using Hari's small suitcase like a battering ram, Elzabeth cleared a path through the crowd so Rukmini could carry him on. People rubbed their shoulders and scowled until they saw his bandaged legs. Then the people made way, only to close in behind Rukmini and shove her into the bus like a bundle. She chose a seat halfway back and held Hari until he fell asleep. Thank God, she thought; she did not want him awake during the ride up the hill.

At first the journey was smooth. Then the bus began its climb. The road up the holy hill coiled like a snake and bristled with retaining walls. It was a masterpiece of engineering, but equally a road meant to test faith. The bus yawed about curves while passengers clung to the seats in front of them. It rolled when the wheels on one side encountered dirt. It pitched when they struck potholes. The ride was all too familiar. The first time Rukmini took the Link Bus she was nine. The journey left her in tears. She sat on Prakash's lap and screamed if he loosened his grip on her. It was her father's idea they come—he said every good Hindu should visit Tirumala at least once—and she swore she would never forgive him. She did, though. Now she clung to Hari. She held him so his head could not strike the side of the bus, or the metal back of the seat in front of them. She would never let him go. He moaned but remained asleep. Elzabeth clung to a handhold and kept her eyes shut.

There was a loud bang. The bus swerved. The driver braked so suddenly, a net bag of coconuts flew down the aisle to strike an old woman. Neither her curses nor the cries of other passengers could drown the hiss of steam from the motor.

Elzabeth opened her eyes and crossed herself. "Good thing it was not a puncture," she said, and crossed herself again. She wondered what else might go wrong.

People got down to stretch and scratch. After the driver reattached a hose, he ordered two men to help him refill the radiator from jerry cans. The men had to climb onto the roof for the cans. The rest of the passengers remained on the right side of the road. On the left, the ground dropped like a cliff. Four young men dared one another to stand on the retaining wall. Elzabeth also got down but Rukmini did not move.

Hari woke and sat up to look at the view. He found himself staring down onto a stony plain. The sun hung over it like an orange rubber ball. He pushed the rolled-up canvas flap higher before poking his head out the window. Rukmini held him by the waist.

"How much farther?" he asked.

"I think we are nearly there," Rukmini answered. "Are you hungry?"

He shook his head. Looking across through the far windows, he caught sight of Elzabeth but pretended not to recognize her. She was squatting on the roadside with a corner of her sari draped over one eye. She was making number one, and everyone politely ignored her.

He grinned at the face of his new wrist watch. He moved the hands. "Ask me what time it is."

"What time is it, sir?" Rukmini inquired.

The driver slammed down the bonnet. Empty jerry cans clattered onto the roof. The conductor blew his whistle.

Hari sat down and declared, "Time to move on!"

The bus rocked while people climbed aboard to reclaim their seats. The driver yelled to a straggler, who buttoned his fly even as he hurried back. The old woman refused to move from her place on the floor. She cursed anyone who kicked her. The motor roared, gears grated, and the bus jerked forward.

While the bus resumed its climb, the orange sun shimmered out of sight.

Hari nestled against Rukmini and closed his eyes. When he woke once more, it was pitch black except for a single streetlamp near the bus. Rukmini said they should wait until everyone got off, but passengers bound for the foot of the hill were already boarding. Once again Elzabeth beat a path with the suitcase.

All around them rose the dark shapes of low buildings. When Hari looked past the rear of the rocking bus, he could picture the scene. In one of the photos in Rukmini's green album, her parents walked barefoot on the hill. Her father looked at the camera but her mother walked with her head bent and her sari lifted out of the dust. Rukmini and Prakash sat on a stone wall. It curved down behind them until the path narrowed like a lizard's tail. The stony plain stretched away in the background.

"Let us find the Ramamurthy guest house," Rukmini told Elzabeth. "You hold Babu while I search."

The moment Rukmini set him down, he cried out. His knees had stiffened from sitting in the train all day and in the bus all evening. He could neither straighten nor bend them. Elzabeth dropped his suitcase and stooped toward him. He raised his arms and felt himself rise, higher and higher until he thought he could touch the stars. The next time he opened his eyes, he found himself surrounded by a mosquito curtain. Sunlight streamed into the large room. From outside he could hear the rise and fall of chatter as people passed the guest house. He looked at his wrist watch. The hands had fallen off in the night.

"What time is it?" he asked.

Rukmini was seated on her bedroll with the mosquito curtain folded back. "Nearly nine o'clock," she replied. She set aside her textbook. "They have finished feeding the lord."

Hari sat up. She never let him sleep so late. At home he woke at seven, in plenty of time for school. Today, though, he would not be giving the driver a pink rose. He would be giving something up, something he owned, but what?

The front door opened. Without entering the guest house, Elzabeth asked, "Shall I bring the—?"

"Yes," Rukmini replied quickly. She did not want Hari frightened. "Also bring some food for Babu. Not too much. We shall order *thali* plates afterward." She told him, "You can go in the back."

Waving the mosquito curtain aside, he rolled onto unpainted concrete. Still in his underwear, he crawled out the back door. It was already hot and flies buzzed about the latrine. Here he made number one and washed his hands. Then he drank some water. He held his right hand under the tap and drank the water from his palm so his lips would not touch the spout. That would be unclean. He crawled back into the guest house to find a man seated, cross-legged, in the middle of the room.

The man hummed to himself with his eyes closed. He did not look like a priest. When Hari tried to hum the tune, the man opened his eyes. "This is the one?" he asked. He spoke Telugu but it did not sound musical. It was gutter Telugu.

Rukmini nodded. "Come, Babu. Drink this hot milk and eat the bun. This man is going to shave your head. Your hair is the greatest gift you can give Lord Venkateswara."

A barber? Hari shrank against the door. The lower hinge scraped his shoulder. How could she do this to him?

"Oh, Babu," she cried, "you cannot keep crawling like a baby! Your hair will grow back." Her mother had said this as well. Three of them had given their hair to the lord—Rukmini and Prakash less willingly than their mother—and it had grown back thick and dark. Their father had refused. He had reminded them he had never promised to give his hair; he had merely said every good Hindu should visit Tirumala at least once.

Hari did not know any of this. He only knew he hated barbers. He simply hated them. Just before the trip to Madras, Elzabeth had taken him to a new barbershop near Maharani's College. The shop was a painted stall with a large, shiny mirror and calendar pictures of gods. Among them hung a black and white photo of a man with wavy black hair and a pencil-thin moustache. The barber had called the handsome man, "Clar'-gable, my filmstar friend." Elzabeth had put Hari on a board laid across the arms of a high, padded chair. "Shall I cut it short?" the barber had asked. He had snipped the air in front of Hari's face and grinned like a demon. Hari had squeezed his eyes shut. The barber had hissed, "Shall I cut off your royal nose, Little Lord Fondleroy?" When the barber's own nose touched Hari's cheek, Hari had lashed out so hard he fell onto the floor. He had fallen among black and grey curls. Elzabeth had shrieked. Hari had been unhurt but she kept babbling and crossing herself. After she had led him from the shop, the barber had called him a name that sounded like "Pinoach-yo." A mango vendor near the shop had laughed.

Now Hari searched the room for the board and the photo of Clar'gable. He looked for the long scissors with their sharp points. "No," he shouted. "No!" He began to cry.

"What is the matter with you?" Rukmini demanded. "Where is my brave little boy?" She picked him up, and he pressed his face into her blouse. "What is all this?" she whispered. "You never cry. Even when the rash began, you hardly cried." She set him down with his back to the barber, who draped a towel over Hari's shoulders. Then she opened a bag. She took out the bottle of olive oil, the tin of ointment, and two new rolls of gauze. "I will change your bandages while the nice man works," she said. She told the barber, "Be careful not to let hair fall on his legs."

Strange fingers drummed on Hari's head. He shivered when a hot breath stabbed the back of his neck. The barber smelled of betel nut and *pan*. "Such thick curly hair," the barber said. "Pitch black and curly!" Clear paper hissed. The barber held a wooden bowl full of hard white soap under Hari's nose. "Yardley's Shaving Soap," the barber said proudly. "I use nothing but the best for the young master."

"I brought the soap with us," Rukmini told Hari. She spoke in English so the barber would not understand. These fellows: they tried to get away with the least little thing. She shook her head at her own annoyance. It would not do to see the lord in such a state. She undid the knots on the bandages, then poured oil onto them.

When Hari's legs began to tickle, he stopped crying.

The barber swirled a wet brush on the soap. Soon lather bubbled up and the sharp smell of soap mingled with the smooth odour of olive oil. Hari shivered again when the barber soaped his hair. Even as Rukmini unwrapped the gauze, Hari heard the barber suck in his breath. Then came the k-chuck, k-chuck of a razor sharpened on a strip of leather. The barber tilted Hari's head so he faced the bare ceiling, took a handful of hair, and sliced through it. Hari felt trapped—just as he had in the fancy barbershop. At least this barber did not grin like a demon. When curls fell on Hari's shoulders, the barber brushed them onto his own lap.

Now something stronger than the barber's breath and the sickly pus filled the air. Rukmini had opened the tin of ointment. When the barber released Hari to sharpen the razor a second time, Hari looked down and watched her paint his red wounds black. Again the barber pulled Hari backward. This time Hari sniffed and tried to smile. Nodding and humming, the barber worked with one hand while clutching Hari's head with the other. The tune seemed to have no melody, none which repeated itself; none which Hari could also hum.

"Almost finished." Rukmini put the tin of ointment aside.

"All-must-finish-it," the barber chanted. He released Hari and sharpened the razor for a third time.

Rukmini wound the bandage to the k-chuck, k-chuck. Black lines appeared on the gauze where it stuck to the ointment. Hari moved his leg. His knee bent easily now. Perhaps she would let him walk to the temple. The bandage rasped when she tore it down the middle. She made a knot to keep the gauze from tearing any farther and tied the two frayed ends around his ankle. She worked on his other leg more quickly.

"Hold the bowl for me, young master," the barber said. He handed it to Hari. Again the wet brush swirled on the soap until lather covered its soft bristles. The handle of the brush was chipped like the barber's nails. When he soaped Hari's head again, Hari giggled. It felt bristly like the brush. Then he stiffened. A cold steel edge rested on his scalp.

"Such a brave boy," the barber crooned. He pressed his thumb into the hollow at the base of Hari's skull. "The lord will be happy, so very happy." When the razor skimmed across Hari's scalp, the blade rasped like tearing gauze. The barber's eyes darted while he scraped the blade over nearly smooth skin. He finished, dipped his hand in a bowl of water, and dribbled it on Hari's head. Hari squirmed while the water trickled down his neck and back. The barber dried him with a clean towel and uncorked a bottle. It smelled of coconut oil.

"I shall do that." Rukmini took the bottle from him carefully so their hands would not touch. Then she poured the clear oil into her left palm and put the bottle down. After rubbing her hands together, she caressed Hari's head. It felt cold.

Hari breathed deeply and sighed. The room smelled of soap, ointment, betel nut, *pan*, and olive and coconut oil.

Rukmini wiped her hands on another towel and gave the barber a purple one-rupee note.

He rose and made *namaskar*. He piled the black curls onto his towel and tied the four corners to form a bundle. "The lord will bless you very much for giving your hair," he told Hari. "The lord will like your offering." He hurried out.

Elzabeth, who was waiting outside, stopped the door from closing behind him. She watched while Hari pulled on his short pants and shirt. "Poor Harischandra," she clucked. "He looks like a monkey."

"I do not!" he cried. He felt strange bumps on his skull.

"What is there to worry?" Rukmini squinted at her round compact mirror. "Even a monkey mother loves her child," she told him. "Good boy. You cried once only." She stretched out her arm as though to give him the mirror, then frowned and snapped the compact shut. She fit the wooden lid onto the bowl of Yardley's Shaving Soap and held it out to Elzabeth. "Here, you can give this to your littlest brother. A budding doctor deserves nothing but the best."

Elzabeth smiled for the first time since leaving Bangalore.

"We will go now," Rukmini announced. "Do you not want this bun?"

Hari shook his head. He wanted to see the lord.

"Drink this at least." She handed him the tumbler and he drained it of the lukewarm milk.

✷

With Rukmini holding Hari's left hand and Elzabeth holding his right, they joined the people streaming past the guest house. Rukmini and Elzabeth moved slowly, because Hari could walk only by jerking one foot in front of the other like a boy he had once seen. The boy's legs had not been bandaged, though. They had been withered and bare. He had walked on sticks lashed to his forearms with hemp.

The stream of people on the road quickly turned into a crowd. Few of them were dressed as well as Rukmini or even Elzabeth. Most called greetings and insults to one another and acted as though they lived on the hill. Who could have dreamt of such noise? A baby shrieked each time its mother tossed it high into the air. Pale men, spinning in saffron robes, played cymbals, flutes, and drums.

"*Ver-u-sen-a-ga*!" a man squawked. He sounded like a parrot. Even after he lowered the glass box of peanuts from his shoulder, his head remained tilted to one side. "*Ver-u-sen-a-ga*!"

"*Chai, chai*!" other men called. Golden-brown tea poured into glasses so quickly, the tea vendors' hands blurred like wings.

"*Bee-di*!" a woman called. "Smoke a *bee-di*!"

The road leading through the square looked more like a market than the path to a temple. Shops and stalls, all named for the lord, surrounded the square: Venkateswara Tea Room, Venkateswara Tailors, Venkateswara Gifts. Everywhere Hari looked, he saw the lord painted on calendars and picture post cards; chased in silver on copper plates; carved from rosewood, sandalwood, and stone. There were statues of Lord Balaji preparing for a wedding, Nirmala paintings, inlaid boxes, enamelled brass hookahs; sandals, saris, umbrellas; shirtings, suitings, Bata shoes; *beedis*, bangles, toys, and mounds of *tilak* powder—not only in vermilion like the dot on Rukmini's brow but in more colours than the widest rainbow could ever hold. Then came the food stalls, packed so closely the smell made him too dizzy to move: cinnamon as thick and gnarled as walking sticks; mountains of *pan supari*, ginger, and cloves; peanuts, dates, figs; cardamom seeds both white and green, chillies both green and red; plantains, tangerines, stubby Nanjangud bananas; lemons to squeeze on papaya, salt to sprinkle on pineapple; saffron, garlic, coriander leaves; fried *brinjal* and okra; stacks of *chappatis* oozing *ghee*; *bondas, wadas, poppadums*; pomegranate chutney, coconut chutney, mango pickle, lime pickle; *bisleri* soda in marble-stoppered bottles; capped bottles of Fanta, Limca, and squash; cane sugar, sugar cane, honey from Coorg; *barfi* stamped with glistening foil, *jelabis* dotted with flies; *rasagulla*, *gulab jamun*, English toffee, *badhu shah*. He wanted it all.

At last Hari, Rukmini, and Elzabeth passed through high stone walls and the commotion stopped. Here the only noise came from crows cawing on the walls and the k-chuck, k-chuck of razors. A dozen barbers sat scattered about the compound. One of them caught Hari's eye, glanced at his bald head, and looked away to spit at a monkey. It sneered back. Behind a second ring of walls, above the silver doors, the temple rose into a golden dome.

"Lord Venkateswara was Lord Vishnu in heaven," Rukmini told Hari. "Just as Lord Krishna was Lord Vishnu in heaven. But then Vishnu borrowed a huge sum of money to pay for a friend's wedding. He came to earth as Lord Venkateswara so people could help him repay the loan. What?" she asked Elzabeth.

Elzabeth was refusing to release Hari's hand at the silver doors. "I am coming too," she said. "I want to see this lord." She nearly added, "of yours," but did not.

Rukmini smiled and said, "This is something we must do alone." She told Hari, "Come," and lifted him.

He gazed over heads and shoulders into the temple. He could see little except the heads of other worshippers. Few of them were bald. He was not a monkey, after all. He was special.

Two policemen kept their eyes on the line of people and prodded the noisy ones with short sticks. The policemen wore khaki short pants and shirts with pockets just like the Gurkha who guarded Hari and Rukmini's house. Each evening Hari tried to stay awake so he could hear the Gurkha catch thieves, but Hari only ever heard the ping-ping of a nightstick on the gate. He saw the Ghurka when he came in the day, once a month, for his payment.

Rukmini waved off ragged children who offered her coconuts. In the shade of the temple entrance, she inspected men and women who sat cross-legged with offering plates of coconut and jasmine in their laps. At last she spotted a dull-eyed man on a wheeled board. Filthy bandages wrapped the stumps of his legs. It was an omen, she thought, nodding at the man. A girl took a plate off one stump and brought it to Rukmini, who gave the girl a rupee.

Hari smiled at the man but he did not smile back. He only nodded after the girl ran to him and closed his fingers around the note.

When Rukmini stepped over the threshold, Hari shivered. It was so quiet in here, so cool. The line of people moved quickly. They followed ropes strung between columns sheathed in silver. On the far side of them, other people left in twos and threes. They smiled contentedly. None of them spoke. At last the columns ended where the low ceiling gave way to a darkened hall.

"There he is," Rukmini whispered. The lord was just as she remembered him. For a moment she felt nine years old, and she fought back tears. She wanted to say, "I have brought you my son, my only child." She wanted to say, "Please."

Carved from jet black stone, draped with a sheet of gold, Lord Venkateswara stood at the end of the hall. Garlands as thick as a man's arm hung from his neck and from a golden crown shaped like a bell. He kept his left hand curved in and his right hand open. Lamps flickered in the incense, shrouding him like mist.

Hari remembered Muttamma say, "Do you see the lord's eyes are hidden?" Yes, they were. Two white lines covered his eyes so he could not see the evil in the world; so he would not destroy it with a blinding flash.

When Rukmini turned from the lord, Hari found a priest gazing at him. Except for a lock of grey hair pulled back from his head, the priest was bald. His skin gleamed with oil. He raised a golden bell above Hari's head. Even as the priest lowered the bell, Hari saw the duller gleam of brass inside. Then everything disappeared. Cold metal touched his brow. After the priest lifted the bell, Hari looked back over Rukmini's shoulder. He could see only the lamps flickering through the incense. The priest lowered the bell briefly onto Rukmini's head. She turned toward a black bucket hanging by a chain from the ceiling. She took a knotted kerchief from the waist of her sari and undid the knot. She rolled two pearl and diamond earrings in her palm. They were a wedding present from Sharada. When Rukmini passed the earrings through a slit in the bucket, they fell with a clink.

Hari had to make an offering, too, but what? And where was the pot in which Elzabeth said children's bones were mixed with jewellery? There it was, behind the priest. Hari tore off his plastic wrist watch and threw it over the priest's shoulder. The wrist watch skittered down inside the pot. The priest started and Hari thought he would smile. He simply raised the bell and turned toward an old man. Hari wanted to ask Rukmini if the lord had blessed her as well but she seemed far away. Even after they stepped into the glaring sunshine, even after they followed a second set of ropes back to the compound, even after Elzabeth asked Rukmini, "Are you happy now?" she did not say a word.

*

Hari sat on the veranda step in his red and black uniform. He sang, "Polly Put the Kettle On," because Elzabeth was making supper. He was admiring his new, decorated tree. It was the only tree in the garden in a pot.

Rukmini was in her room. She was rereading an aerogram from America and resisting the temptation to reply at once. Sometimes, she thought, Krishna had no sense. First the years they had spent apart in America, now these years waiting for him to bring them over. Now this. She crumpled his aerogram. She sat so wrapped in anger, so confused, she did not hear the car until it stopped outside the gate.

Hari saw the car at once. It was not the Hindustan Ambassador belonging to Jagadish's father, the banker. It was a yellow Chevrolet. When a small woman in a white sari stepped from the car, Hari leapt to his feet. Lady Raman! She rarely left her huge house with the piano in the sitting room. The driver opened the gate, closed it, and returned to the car. Patting the white bun behind her head, Lady Raman walked past the decorated tree.

"You had a party, Harish?" she asked.

"See my new sword?" He pulled the golden plastic sword from the belt of his uniform.

"It is very smart. You look like Lord Mountbatten himself! Here is a gift for you." She handed him a tin box. "In England people wrap fancy paper around gift boxes, but we are not in—"

"Lady Raman!" Rukmini stood in the veranda. She adjusted her sari before approaching the door and making *namaskar*. "I wondered whose car should stop outside our gate! Babu, why did you not invite her to sit down and inform me she was here? Come in," she told Lady Raman. "Rest yourself."

Hari ran into the veranda and took his cap from the far chair.

Lifting her hem so it would clear the threshold, Lady Raman entered. "Why all this fuss, Rukmini?" she demanded. "I am your godmother only, not Mother Teresa!"

"Coffee?" Rukmini asked.

Lady Raman shook her head.

Rukmini waited for her to sit down first.

Hari sat cross-legged just inside the veranda door with the sword across his knees. He studied the picture of the Taj Mahal painted on the lid of the gift box. Should he open it now? No, later. Otherwise he might have to share the biscuits which rattled when he shook the box.

"So, the boy is cured," Lady Raman said. "I received a letter from your Aunt Sharada, but I wanted to see for myself. Your husband must be pleased."

"My husband never knew Babu was ill," Rukmini said. Her cheeks flushed. "Had he known, he would not have cared."

"Now what has happened?" Lady Raman asked. "Are you quarrelling across the ocean?"

"He does not even consult me," Rukmini replied, "and he decides to stop work on his doctorate. He has left America!"

Lady Raman's white eyebrows rose toward the dot on her brow. "*Abba*!" she exclaimed.

"I received the aerogram today itself," Rukmini said. "It seems he went to a state called Qwe-beck for a holiday. He liked it so much he decided to move to Canada. He writes me the trees there are so beautiful in autumn they look as though they are on fire." Of all things, Rukmini thought: trees! The man must be mad. "He has already secured an appointment in a town called Ot-ta-wa," she said. "Now he wants Babu to grow up Canadian."

"Canadian, American," Lady Raman crooned, "it is all the same."

"But why did he not write me earlier," Rukmini said, "and ask my advice? Have I no say in such matters?" She kept her face turned from Hari but he saw her wipe a tear from her eye. She never cried.

*"Paapam,"* Lady Raman said. She reached across the low table to pat Rukmini's arm. "This is the way of men. My husband is the same. He spent his fortune on his laboratories and instructed me to sell my jewellery to feed the children. Just because he gave his life to his work, should I have sacrificed my mother's jewellery?"

Hari toyed with the buttons on his uniform. He wished Ajja had come to visit instead but today was not Sunday. It was a school day yet Cluny Convent and the Institute were closed. Rukmini said it was a Christian holiday. She had even given Elzabeth the morning off to visit her church. He edged toward the door to look at the new tree. Its drooping branches were covered with soft needles instead of leaves. Elzabeth had gone all the way to Palace Orchards to buy it. She had brought it back in an autorickshaw with the branches waving from the back, then decorated it with red ribbons for this afternoon's party.

While waiting for the other children to arrive, Hari asked Elzabeth, "What is all this?"

"Soon you will leave India," she said. "Your *amma* wants you to learn American ways even if you are Hindu. She is very wise, your *amma*."

"Is this your Christian god then?" he asked. He pointed at the doll under the tree. The new doll had come folded. Rukmini had blown it up like a balloon into a fat man dressed in a red uniform, black shoes, and a black belt with a white buckle. His white beard hid his entire face except for the red cheeks and nose and blue eyes. He also wore a pointed, red cap.

"I do not know what this is," Elzabeth said. "Your London Uncle sent it."

Hari stared at the doll, at his own uniform, and back at Elzabeth. These days after he ate his lunch, which she brought to school in a tiffin carrier, she still recited the Lord's Prayer with the teachers and children. She still wore the clicking rosewood beads at her waist. But she no longer spoke of the one lord who had given his only-begotten son for her sins. The tree pleased her even more than it pleased him. During the party she told a story about shepherds, angels, and a babe born in a manger and then explained why Lord Vishnu came to earth as Lord Venkateswara. Rukmini gave every boy a new pencil and every girl a new hair ribbon. They stood together while she squinted into the top of her box camera. The party ended much too soon.

"*Yenbabu*?" Lady Raman asked.

Hari caught himself humming and stopped. Unable to look at her, he placed the gift box behind him.

"All this old people's talk is dull so you dream?" she asked. He shook his head and she smiled. "That is all right. My husband is a dreamer also, but he cannot carry a tune as well as you. Do you know who Lord Raman is?"

"A god?" Hari asked.

Lady Raman laughed loud and long. "No, no," she said, trying not to laugh again, "although many people think he is. He is a scientist only, my husband. He discovered that if one shines a certain type of light through an unknown compound, one can—"

Hari stopped listening. He looked out into the garden.

"Never mind," she told Rukmini. "Do you know what rubies are, Harish?"

He looked at the red and gold bangles on Lady Raman's wrists. Surely everyone knew what rubies were?

"Of course you do," she said. "Someone has discovered that if one shines a certain type of light through a ruby, one can produce a powerful beam of light. One day it may be made so powerful, it will burn a hole through a wall. Like lightning without noise."

He stared at the veranda wall and imagined a hole boring silently through it. He stared until his eyes ached. Such a beam could only be magic like the blinding flash from Lord Venkateswara's eyes. Hari decided scientists like Lord Raman must be gods.

Lady Raman stood. She rearranged her sari across her rounded shoulders. "So, Harischandra," she exclaimed, "you will grow up a Canadian it seems. That is good. Canada is part of the Empire, the Commonwealth. Canadian soldiers and Indian soldiers fought side by side under the British. Do you know," she asked, turning to Rukmini, "my husband's great regret when he received the Nobel Prize was having to sit in front of a British flag? Because we were not yet independent. Men!"

Rukmini rose without smiling. Men indeed.

"I say!" Lady Raman exclaimed. "Next time you are in Tirumala, you stay in my guest house. Your Aunt Sharada's is no better than some village *dharamsala*." Before Hari could rise, Lady Raman passed her hand through his hair. He smiled up at her. It felt short, bristly, like a hairbrush. Rukmini was forever reassuring him it would soon begin to curl.

"Lord Venkateswara has blessed you," Lady Raman said. "Not everyone gives his hair so willingly."

Hari rose and slapped dust from the red stripes on his trousers. The van driver said the same thing when he scolded two boys for teasing Hari when he was still bald. Hari had not really cared. Most of the children treated him with awe, especially after he began walking and running again. Best of all, the driver had made him a promise. He said that if Hari still lived in India next year, he alone would play Lord Mountbatten on Independence Day.

# Chapter 7

## The Ice-Water Game

Six months later, Hari and Rukmini returned to Madras for their second chance at his medical certificate. As far as Rukmini knew, there would be no third chance.

She sat in the back of Sharada's Buick and stared through the windscreen at the traffic on Edward Elliots Road. She wanted to say a prayer but could not think of one. She focused her thoughts on Lord Venkateswara instead. She also thought of Ganesha. She needed both of them now, more than ever. Once again, the gods were testing her faith. She tried not to think about Krishna. He had written to say he was renting a larger apartment, and she had replied she did not know when she and Hari would join him. If they ever did—but she could not bring herself to write this. When she tried to rearrange the cashmere shawl about Hari's shoulders, he pulled away.

He pressed his nose against a side window because he could not look at her. Staring hurt his eyes but he was playing a game: a moving game. The coconut palms lining the road flashed by so quickly, their yellow-green fronds blurred. Yet the trees set back from the street moved as slowly as the long ship off Marina Beach. So did the large buildings. The farther away a tree or building stood from the street, the longer it stayed in sight. Finally he sat facing the front. Now he could see only the back of the driver's head. Hair oil and sweat mingled to run down the dark neck. At Rukmini's insistence, the driver kept the windows closed against the draft. The car smelled of hot leather. Hari closed his eyes but they still hurt. If he failed the exam again, he thought, it would be all his fault. Even Muttamma would not be able to help him.

"Are you tired?" Rukmini asked.

He shook his head. "Is it true I was a saint in my last life?" he asked. "Muttamma said that is why the lord cured my rash."

Rukmini squeezed his arm through the shawl. "You were a powerful saint. After you died you became a star waiting to be reborn. When I prayed for a son, Lord Venkateswara sent you to me."

"What will I be in my next life?"

"You are too young to be thinking of such matters, but it all depends on how you live in this one. Being lucky and being good are not the same. Do not worry. You are a very good boy also."

He nodded. Everyone said this. He never gave Mrs. Padma, his second standard teacher, cause to punish him. Only last week she made Jagadish leave the classroom for throwing his slate on the floor. It began to rain and poor Jagadish huddled in the portico. The entire class heard him shriek each time lightning flashed and thunder boomed. Buffalo Bill did not frighten Hari. Nor did Mrs. Padma. She was not even as smart as Mrs. Kamala-Bai, his first standard teacher. When Mrs. Padma heard he might leave Cluny Convent this summer, she asked him in front of the class, "Where are you going to, Harischandra?"

"Canada," he proudly replied.

She heard it as, "Kerala," another South Indian state, west of Mysore. Hari decided she did not even know where Canada was. Surely everyone knew it was farther than Kerala? A boy could not take a train to Canada the way he could to Kerala. He would have to fly in an aeroplane and stop at places with wonderful names like Karachi and Rome, London and Gander.

At last the driver said, "We are arriving." The car turned into a road curving in front of a long, white building. Its green doors and shutters were darker than the yellowing fronds of the palms lining the driveway; darker than the faded green on the limp Indian flag over the entrance. Cool and friendly, the building looked more like a tourist hotel than a clinic. The car stopped in front of broad, white steps.

Rukmini waited for the driver to open her door. She climbed out clutching a red cloth bag against her beaded purse. She had brought her good green sweater for luck but the afternoon was too hot for her to be seen carrying a sweater. She left it in the car.

Shrugging off the shawl, Hari slid across the sticky leather seat. His eyes began to hurt from the glare of sunlight on the clinic. He sat on the car's running board and blinked. Purple and yellow diamonds flashed in front of him. They sizzled like sparklers children waved at Deepavali, the festival of lights.

"Shall I carry him?" the driver asked Rukmini.

Hari opened his eyes in time to see her shake her head at a woman in a white frock. She was pushing an old man across the lawn in a wicker chair on wheels. His head nodded as though his neck were made of rubber. He drooled on his shirt.

"Babu must walk," Rukmini said. "Otherwise people will think he is ill."

Hari pushed himself to his feet and clutched her sari. It had flowers on it like the bougainvillaea on the pillars of the Madras House. Taking the steps one at a time, he climbed to the double doors. In the shadow of the faded green awning, he looked back.

The driver finished lighting a *beedi* and tossed away the match. He saluted as if to say, "Chin up." Smoke rushed from his nostrils like steam from engines in running sheds.

"Come along," Rukmini said. She smiled when Hari threw back his shoulders to look tall like a man. She led him into the clinic and stopped in front of a desk. The clerk, who wore a black wedge-cap, was copying names from one list to another. At his elbow stood a heavy, black telephone. When he finally looked up, she said, "I am Dr. Gopal Rukmini. We have come for our medical certificates."

"Have a seat, Madame," he said. He waved his pencil at benches along the wall. A dozen people, all of them in their finest clothes, sat waiting. One read a book, another played cat's cradle with his daughter, and the rest stared at their shoes or at the ceiling fans. Each time a door opened along the corridor, everyone looked at the person coming out. The clerk licked the point of his pencil and bent over his lists.

"Lady Ramamurthy made the appointment for one thirty," Rukmini said. "It is now one twenty-five."

The clerk rose and touched the front of his cap. "Of course, Madame!" he exclaimed. "Why did you not intimate this earlier? Lady Ramamurthy herself?" He beamed at Hari after checking both lists. "You must be Master Harischandra, correct? Welcome. You are both to go to room seven," he told Rukmini. Then he frowned at his lists, lifted the receiver from the telephone, and placed it on the desk. Repeating, "Follow me," he led Rukmini and Hari past the benches. Everyone stared at her with envy. At the end of the corridor he knocked sharply at a door and opened it without waiting for an answer. The room beyond lay empty. "I will tell Dr. Kripalani you are here," he said, "though I do not believe he has returned from taking his lunch." The clerk bowed them into the room and closed the door.

Rukmini heard him run back down the corridor while shouting, "Nurse! You there, tell Dr. Kripalani to come double-quick!"

Climbing into an armchair, Hari sighed. He wanted to sleep. In spite of the awning outside the large window, light flooded the room. Photos of old men hung on one wall. They wore stiff collars and ties. Chains dangled in front of their waistcoats. On a low table next to him, someone had piled a stack of illustrated magazines and two books. The top one was called *Bible Stories for Little Ears*. Its cover showed a bearded, blue-skinned man blessing three children. Each of them held a white lamb. On the spine of the second book was a name, M.K. Gandhi, and a long title ending with *My Experiments With Truth*. Soon after his seventh birthday, Rukmini had finished her own experiments. She had brought home a book called a thesis bound in blue. People called her a doctor but she said she was not a real doctor; she was a Doctor of Philosophy.

"We must hurry," she whispered. "There is no time to dream." She untied the cloth bag to reveal a red vacuum flask. She unscrewed the white cap and placed it on the book of Bible stories. The cap had become a cup.

"Cap, cup," he muttered while she struggled with the cork. When she poured out water, a piece of ice clattered. He could feel the coolness of the water even as she raised the cup to his lips.

"Drink it before the doctor comes," she said. "It will reduce your temperature."

Footsteps sounded in the corridor.

Hari gulped the cold water.

Rukmini hid the cup and vacuum flask on the floor behind the table. Even as the door opened, she closed her hand around the cork so tightly her knuckles paled.

A tall, bearded man entered and closed the door behind him. He nodded at her and beamed at Hari. "Hul-lo," the man said. "Dr. Kripalani's occupied, so he asked me to see you instead. I'm Dr. Singh, Sara Singh." He tapped a clipboard against his chest.

"We are pleased to meet you," Rukmini said. She was about to offer her hand when she remembered the cork.

Hari liked the doctor's voice: the way he stretched out *hello*, the way he spoke slowly as though setting his words to music. How grand he looked, like a filmstar. Below the hem of his white doctor's coat, chocolate brown trousers fell to brown shoes with pinpricks on the toes. Snakes twined about staves on his pearl grey tie. His plain, brown turban looked even grander than the yellow and gold one worn by the sentry at the Madras House.

Hari chanted, "All Sikhs are Singhs, but not all Singhs are Sikhs. I learned that from Jagadish."

Rukmini said, "Hush," but Dr. Singh laughed.

"Very good, Master!" he exclaimed. "What standard are you in? First?"

"Second," Hari replied. "I can do multiplication." He licked his dry lips. "Shall I spell philosophy? P-h-i-l-o-s-o-p-h-y."

Dr. Singh tucked the clipboard under his left arm and applauded softly. "Bravo," he said. "Now, who's first?"

"I am," Rukmini said. "I shall need a moment."

"Do take your time." Dr. Singh knocked softly on a connecting door before he opened it. He winked at Hari, then closed the door.

"Are we playing a trick on the nice doctor?" Hari asked.

"This is no trick," Rukmini said. "We are playing a game, an ice-water game. You like games, no?"

Hari liked both games and toys. He especially liked toys, like the wind-up car he received for his birthday from his cousin-sisters. "Amma," he said when she reached the connecting door, "Jagadish has an electric train. The steam engine makes real smoke and has a lamp in front. Can I have an electric train when we reach Canada?" He held his breath.

The question took Rukmini aback. Here she was about to break the rules, and he was thinking about toys. Then she remembered all of this was for his benefit. "Of course," she replied. She tried to laugh at herself. "I promise. Your father will buy you the finest electric train in the world for Christmas. We will be in Canada some months before then, but if we win this game only." She opened the door and slipped into the doctor's office. She closed the door without a backward glance.

Hari drank more water. A piece of ice, the same pale green as the inside of the vacuum flask, burned his mouth. It made his tongue feel thick. He sat back to wait and thought about food. He had eaten nothing for lunch.

He had spent the morning playing with Usha in an upstairs room. It had once been her father's study. Then Hari took a short nap. He woke feeling hot. After washing his face, he went to the second dining room, the Indian one reserved for special occasions. Rukmini, Sharada, and Usha sat cross-legged on the floor under the Mysore painting of Ganesha. May spooned fragrant yellow rice onto their plantain leaves. Muttamma had refused to join them because she said the celebration would tempt fate. May returned to the kitchen.

"There you are, Harish," Sharada said. "I was about to send Usha to fetch you. Come, sit down, I say! Have your *payasam* before it grows cold."

He went to Rukmini while a tear trickled down his cheek. She tore a corner off a *chappati* and scooped up curried eggplant and potato. As he pressed one foot on the other, the tear fell on her leaf.

"What is it?" she asked, dropping the food. She bit her lip as she touched his forehead with her clean, left hand.

"Oh, no!" Usha cried.

When Rukmini pushed herself off the floor, her tumbler of *payasam* spilled. The sweet white liquid ran along the uneven floor toward the wall. "How will I get this boy to his father if he keeps falling ill?" she demanded.

"It is not his fault," Sharada said. Usha helped her rise. "You know you yourself were weak as a child. Harish does not take after his father. Usha, tell May to make hot lemon. Never mind bringing him *payasam*."

"Do not give him so much to drink, I say!" Usha warned. "We had tea an hour ago only."

"How did you make tea?" Sharada asked. "I have told you not to touch the kerosene—"

"It was play tea only," Usha said, "but the pink ice was real."

"It was delicious," Hari mumbled. He simply had to sit down. Sliding his back against the wall, well away from the spilt *payasam*, he collapsed onto the floor.

"Pink ice?" Rukmini demanded, turning on Usha. "Babu is not to eat pink ice. One never knows what kind of water these vendors use. Ditch water!"

"We did not buy it," Usha said. She shrank away from Rukmini. "I made it myself. I poured fruit juice in and sliced a banana. I put it in the icebox until—"

"Do you suppose the pink ice has given him a fever?" Rukmini asked Sharada.

"Nonsense," Sharada replied; then: "There is much truth in old wives' tales. Perhaps my mother-in-law is correct when she says those born in Bangalore can never live anywhere else. Perhaps it is Harish's fate to remain in his mother country."

"What good is all this philosophy?" Rukmini cried.

Hari stared at the empty leaf set for him. He did not feel one bit hungry, not even for *payasam*.

"Pink ice!" Rukmini scoffed. Then she exclaimed, "*Aré, baba*!" She slapped her brow and smeared the vermilion dot. Her bangles jingled when she clapped her hands in front of her mouth. "I have it, Sharada!" she cried. "Usha, never mind the hot lemon. Tell May to find a vacuum flask. Send Driver to the Connemara Hotel to fill it with ice. They want a certificate to let Babu into Canada? We will get this certificate!"

Now, finishing his third cup of ice water, Hari gazed at the photos on the wall. One of the old men looked like Ajja except that Ajja never wore a waistcoat. The man in the photo frowned as though he knew Hari was playing a trick, not a game.

Rukmini opened the connecting door. She said, "We will be one moment only," and closed the door behind her. That was easy. Now for the real test. She poured the last of the ice water into the cup. While Hari drank, gasping for air between gulps, she hid the empty vacuum flask in the bag.

Hari could not take his eyes from the man in the photo. "Amma," he asked, "is it true Ajja is a modern King Harischandra?"

"Yes," she replied, frowning. What now?

"And you named me for the king?"

"We must hurry," she said.

"But Amma," Hari said, placing a hand on her arm, "Harischandra was the most honest man in the world, correct? He always kept his word."

"What is this?" she asked. Would he never stop? First toys, now legends.

Hari looked at his sandals. "So what we are doing," he said slowly, "is dishonest. That man knows."

Her heart leapt. She glanced at both doors but they were still shut. "What man?" she demanded.

Hari pointed at the photo. "That man," he said.

"Oh, Babu," she cried. She nearly laughed with relief. Lowering her voice, she said, "This is no time to speak of such things. We are doing what is necessary only."

"But the doctor is such a nice man," he said.

"Your father will be nice to you also," she insisted. Then she had an idea. "Do you not want the electric train?" While he thought about this, she lifted him with an "Oof!" and carried him into the examining room.

From behind the desk, Dr. Singh said, "Put the boy there." He pointed at a high, black table covered with a bedsheet. The sheet was well used and rumpled. Common sense told him to change it, but there were no clean ones in sight and he did not want to argue with an orderly over the way Kripalani kept his examining room. "Remove his shirt and pants, please."

While Rukmini undressed Hari, he rubbed his eyes and looked about the room. It smelled of medicine. A fan sat on top of a grey metal cupboard. It looked like a Godrej but instead of doors it had drawers with silver handles. The fan turned back and forth. It fluttered the papers piled high on the desk and raised dust from the bookcases. He saw a tray of instruments beside two glass jars, one full of cotton, the other full of needles, and his mouth went dry. "Am I going to have an injection?" he asked. "Will it hurt?"

"I'd never hurt you," Dr. Singh replied. "I have a special way of giving injections, but you won't have a chance to see it. This is only an examination." He picked up a tongue depressor.

Rukmini moved out of his way. Behind his back she raised a silent finger to her lips. "Please," she thought. "Please."

"Open your mouth and say, 'Aah,'" Dr. Singh ordered. "That's it. A little more. Now, say—"

"Aaah," Hari sang.

The throat showed signs of irritation but nothing unusual. Bangalore people were likely not used to exhaust from so many vehicles, and the air in Madras was getting worse each year. "Very good," Dr. Singh said. He dropped the tongue depressor into a wastebasket and pressed gently under Hari's jaw. The glands were slightly enlarged but, again, it was nothing unusual though the boy's face felt warm.

The doctor stood so close that Hari could see the fine net holding the beard rolled under the doctor's chin. Hari had never been so close to a Sikh before. His hands and face smelled tart.

Dr. Singh looked up from tapping Hari's chest when he sniffed. "What?" he asked. "Oh, I see. It's called *eau de Cologne*. I don't use aftershave." He added, "You would make a good Scotland Yard man." He examined Hari's ears, which were fine. Then he picked up a stethoscope, checked that the ear pads were clean, and said, "This might be a bit cold."

Every doctor had a stethoscope, but Hari had never learned to spell it. The round metal end made him shiver.

"Take a deep breath," Dr. Singh said. "Is that all? All the way in. Better. Now, another." The airways were clear. Bending over Hari, Dr. Singh asked for two more deep breaths. He took the stethoscope off before asking Rukmini, "Have there been any lung problems in the family?"

"My father died of tuberculosis," she said. "They cut out his ribs and still he died."

"So you said," he muttered. He softly pinched the skin on Hari's back. "I meant in this boy's generation. They won't let people with lung ailments into Canada."

"Nothing," she said firmly.

"Lie down now," Dr. Singh ordered. He examined Hari's arms and legs and took off his sandals. "The boy has already been vaccinated?" he asked.

Rukmini had shut her eyes. She opened them to say, "Yes, when I took him to Mauritius."

"So, Harischandra," Dr. Singh exclaimed, "you are a world traveller already!"

"I have a wheel," Hari said. He lifted his left foot and wiggled his toes. "It is like the blue wheel on our—" He stopped when the doctor grasped the foot. Hari wondered whether he had said something wrong.

Both ankles were faintly discoloured. Dr. Singh peered at Hari's left calf and rubbed the skin to one side with the ball of his hand. The skin had good elasticity but it took too long to regain its natural colour. "What are these scars?" he asked. He returned to examining the ankle. When he straightened the leg and turned it slightly, he saw flowery splotches behind the knee. They were clear signs of recent eczema. He hoped it was not recurrent.

"Babu, Harischandra had a rash," Rukmini said.

"Who cured it?" Dr. Singh asked. "A specialist?"

"Lord Venkateswara," Hari announced.

Oh really. Dr. Singh glanced over his shoulder at Rukmini.

"I took him to Tirumala last September," she said, "and he gave his hair to the lord."

"Well, well," Dr. Singh declared. He often heard of such miracles—India was full of them—but he had never seen a case until now. "The boy is completely cured?"

"He was on his feet in six, no, seven weeks," she said. She squeezed her hands together. This was taking too long, she thought; this doctor was being far too thorough. Then again, he was nothing like the idiot last year. This one struck her as a man more concerned with medicine than with rules.

"Sit up now," Dr. Singh told Hari. "You can get dressed."

Rukmini pulled Hari's short pants up his legs. Her hands fumbled so much, he buttoned the fly himself. He pulled on his shirt and buckled his sandals. Now the doctor was shaking something in the air. After Rukmini moved away from the table, Hari saw the thermometer in the doctor's hand. Hari opened his mouth. He closed it with the silver end under his tongue. He liked having his temperature taken. It was magic—the way doctors could read so much from a silver line. He smiled at Rukmini but she kept her eyes on the fan.

Dr. Singh sat behind the cluttered desk and unscrewed the cap from his black fountain pen. He scratched his thumbnail at a spot of blue ink dried on the nib. Then he pulled the standard form toward him. "I'll ask you the same questions about the boy as I did about yourself," he announced. He hated filling out these forms. Too many people said yes to the questions. For all their supposedly simple ways, Indians were such unhealthy people. "TB, you said no. Diabetes?"

"No," she replied.

"Heart disease?"

"No."

"Bedwetting? Nervous or mental trouble?"

"None of these."

"Has he seen a doctor in the past year? Aside from the rash," Dr. Singh added.

"He was hit in the eye with a rubber ball," she said. "He was playing with a friend."

Hari nodded. He was playing with Jagadish, who had not meant to hurt him. Rukmini was so upset, she took him to a doctor, who simply put a cold cloth over the eye.

"That's nothing," Dr. Singh said. "Boys get hurt." He told Hari, "I broke my collar bone once, during a rugby match." Noticing a blank line at the top of the form, Dr. Singh asked, "Sorry, what's his birthdate?"

"Fifteenth March," Hari mumbled.

Dr. Singh looked up. He could not resist saying in a hollow voice, "Beware the Ides of March."

Hari looked at Rukmini but she did not explain what it meant. "Nineteen fifty-five," she added.

"So," Dr. Singh exclaimed, "he'll celebrate his, um, eighth birthday in Canada?" He screwed the cap onto his pen and tucked it into an outside pocket of his white coat. Rising, he wiped his hands with a handkerchief. He went to the table and eased the thermometer from Hari's mouth. Dr. Singh twisted the glass tube in the light and frowned at the silver line. Something was wrong. The boy's temperature was normal, too normal.

Rukmini held her breath with her lips pursed. She should admit the whole thing and face the consequences. They could not be worse than enduring all this. She exhaled only after the doctor shook the thermometer again.

He replaced it in a jar of liquid beside the table, then placed his palm on Hari's brow. It was also warm, though not excessively so given the heat, but it was also damp. "Are you hot, little emperor?" Dr. Singh asked.

"He finds Madras uncomfortable," Rukmini said loudly. "Bangalore has the best year-round climate, as you know, and—" She wrung her hands, glanced down and clenched them.

Even before Dr. Singh pulled gently at the lower eyelids, he knew what he would find. The nerve of the woman, he thought; to think she could fool him of all people. The blood vessels in Hari's eyes were enlarged—slightly, it was true, but enough to give the eyes a reddish tinge. One more question would do it: "Have you been crying?"

Hari shook his head. He did not like people touching him so close to the eye but he trusted this doctor. His fingertips were soft.

"He never cries," Rukmini declared. Biting her lip, she turned away to stare at the window. No matter what she said, she was making things worse. When the doctor strode past her to open the connecting door and vanish beyond it, she cried, "What—?"

Dr. Singh returned with the cloth bag. The vacuum flask poked from the top. Unbelievable, he thought; simply unbelievable—the lengths some people went to, especially the high-class ones who should know better. She would likely try to bully him next; claim her father was this high-court judge or that Congress Party member. He should throw her out right now, but he could not. He knew even as he glared at her that too much was at stake here. More than a mere ticket out of India.

Rukmini sank into a chair with her hands in her lap. She looked so sad, Hari felt like crying for her but she always said he never cried. He lay down facing the desk. Something fluttered in his stomach. He heard Jagadish yell, "Cheater, cheater, pumpkin eater, had a wife and could not keep her!" Jagadish yelled this whenever he lost a game.

Dr. Singh sat down and placed the bag on a pile of fluttering papers. When he chuckled, Rukmini looked up from her hands. "Your trick would have worked on Dr. Kripalani," Dr. Singh said. "He's usually in such a hurry, he would never have doubted the thermometer and in this heat many faces feel warm. However, not everyone's eyes are red. From fever."

"Babu never gets fevers in Bangalore," she said.

Hari nodded.

"Look at him," Dr. Singh declared. "Seven? He looks five, he's so thin. Canada's even worse than Scotland. I did my MD in Edinburgh. Improper heating, damp air—the blood nearly froze in my veins. I came down with bronchitis and had to stop smoking." Dr. Singh took a deep breath and forced himself to remain calm. He did not mean to lecture her; he simply wanted her to understand what she might face. "How will the boy manage in a cold climate?"

"He will learn to eat meat as his father does," Rukmini said. "They will play games together and he will grow up strong. Doctor, my son needs his father. They have met once only since—"

He interrupted her with, "Yes, yes, every man needs a son to leave his mark on the future. However unpromising it often looks." He wished she would not keep challenging him; he was not an ogre. He unscrewed the cap from the fountain pen and watched its gold nib glint. What he was about to do could bring a reprimand. It was not a question of malpractice, but by the time bureaucrats like Kripalani finished with him, he might just as well have injured someone. He scrawled his name on the sheet of grey paper which passed for a certificate. After selecting a stamp from a shoe box, he pressed it on an ink pad and carefully lowered the stamp onto the sheet. He smiled grimly at her while blowing at the ink. "Here," he said, holding the certificate across the desk. He wanted to say, "Take it and go," but he did not want her to leave just yet. She was a woman who knew her mind and he liked such women.

"Why?" she asked.

"Never mind why," he said. "Just take it."

She shook her head and whispered, "It would be dishonest. I apologize. You could lose your licence."

Hari's eyes grew wide at this.

Dr. Singh snorted. He tossed the certificate so it fell on the edge of the desk, just beyond her reach. "There are worse things than dishonesty well meant," he said. For a moment he wondered whether he were speaking about her or about himself. The children, he thought; we do it for the children, even the ones we never had.

Rukmini could say nothing. With his hands clasped under his chin, the doctor spoke to her in his mellow foreign way.

"If I had a son," he said, "I wouldn't want him to grow up in India either. Not the India we took back from the British and corrupted. There's no future for someone like you here. Your son deserves better. At the very least, he deserves a father." Dr. Singh glanced at Hari. "Many children can do multiplication in the second standard, but look how quickly they grow into fools here."

"Why did you return?" she demanded.

He shrugged. "I was young," he said. No, she was not one to be put off with stock answers. "I was idealistic," he admitted, "and India was about to be born. I came back in early forty-seven because I wanted to share in the glory of Independence. Hah! Already there was rioting in Punjab while the British decided how to partition it. Do you know what it's like to watch men die? It's not difficult. Hearing it, smelling it—that's different."

"My home town was shelled during the war," she said. "A Japanese ship sat in the harbour and dropped shells."

He did not mean to be harsh but he countered with, "I expect you were removed from the damage?"

"Our house was on the hill," she said. "They shelled the low-lying areas only, the wharves and godowns."

"Of course," he said. "Only the poor drown in floods."

Hari shifted his gaze from the doctor to Rukmini and back again. What were they talking about? He understood the words they spoke but it seemed other words passed between them. Still, the doctor's words echoed like those of a song. Sometimes Hari found it easier to understand people if they sang. He could feel the music. It could make him happy or sad. Sometimes it could even make chills quiver up his back. The room had fallen so quiet, he could hear only the fluttering papers and whirring fan.

Dr. Singh was playing with his pen, unscrewing the cap and screwing it back on. At last he said, "I'll tell you why I signed the boy's certificate, though I've told very few people." This was not true; he had told no one. He needed to tell her, though. He examined the pen for some time; he kept his eyes on it while he spoke. "I was working in a village near Lahore in the summer of forty-seven. One day I heard a commotion outside the dispensary and looked out to see a group of Sikhs catch up to a Muslim girl. They'd abducted her from a refugee column some days before, but she'd tried to escape. Now they dragged her toward the well even as the villagers watched. I rushed into the street and demanded they let her go. One of them asked what I would give in return. I told the bank clerk to give them what little I'd saved."

"That was very good of you," Rukmini said. She could not imagine, though, what this had to do with anything. She knew she should leave but wanted to stay; to hear him out.

"It bought time, that's all," he said. "I took the girl into my house as a servant. Her name was Inji. Within the month, I discovered she might be with child. I thought it symbolic I would become a stepfather of sorts so soon after India would attain Independence. I was so caught up in my good work, I'd become blind to the atrocities being committed in our state."

"We were blind in the South also," Rukmini said.

Hari thought of Muttamma. She, too, was blind but she could see much. Not like Lord Venkateswara.

"When I finally woke up to what was going on around us," Dr. Singh told Rukmini, "I decided to take Inji to my parents in Delhi. It was across the border by then. In Lahore we managed to get two seats on a train. Don't ask me how. The station was a madhouse. But we never reached the border. Another band of Sikhs stopped the train. They ordered us to get off and form a line. Then they went down the line searching for any Muslim fool enough to be travelling in the wrong direction." He dropped the pen on the desk and looked at his hands. He had thought telling this story would do him good—he had wanted to tell it for so long—but it was only a story now. It might just as well have happened to someone else. Perhaps it had. "This time I couldn't buy her back. Of course, when I told them she was carrying a child, they decided simply to kill her." Simply, he thought. Until that moment he had considered death a bargain only for the old or hopelessly ill. "When I tried to protect her, a stick came down on my head. It was a field hockey stick, of all things."

The doctor's voice had sunk so low, Hari could barely make out the words. Still, he could feel something in the musical voice, something which was neither sadness nor anger.

"When I woke," Dr. Singh said, "the train was gone. So were the butchers. Inji lay in the dust. So did other Muslims, all down the track. The dust was red."

Rukmini was staring at the floor. Nothing she had endured these past few years—nothing Hari had endured—was like this. It was part of their legacy, she thought; a part of what they would take with them. But they would also have to leave men like this behind: heroes of an age in which to be simply decent was to be heroic.

Dr. Singh put his pen back in his pocket and straightened. "What does a man feel after that?" he asked. He really wanted to ask, "Why do I feel so little now?" He sighed. "I threw away my *kangha* and *kara*, my comb and bracelet, and swore I would cut off my beard. I may already have violated Guru Gobind Singh's laws by taking a Muslim—by taking Inji—into my house, so what did such trappings matter? At dawn I staggered into Amritsar." He slapped the desk and rose. "I bear the *kakkars* now, the five symbols of my faith, but then I was born a Sikh."

He looked at Hari the way he looked at so many children—trying to imagine them as his own. Yes, they were all his children, and now he would even have one in Canada. Imagine. "Do you think you'll become a doctor," he asked, "and heal the sick?" He told Rukmini, "That's all one can do in this country. One can't even feed the poor, there are so many of them. But then he won't be growing up Indian, will he?"

She rose and took the certificate. "Let us go," she said.

Hari sat up.

Dr. Singh took his clipboard and walked to the door leading to the corridor. "When are you leaving for Bangalore?" he asked.

"Soon," she replied. "Before his fever grows worse."

After opening the door, Dr. Singh tapped on the silver latch. He could not leave without asking one last question. No matter what she said, if he did not ask her, he knew he would regret it. Not for fifteen years, perhaps, but long enough. "Forgive me," he said, "but could I visit you both for tea before you leave?"

Hari had never seen Rukmini blush, but she did now.

She dropped her eyes and tucked a strand of hair behind an ear. She wanted to say, "I would like that very much." She folded the certificate, put it in her purse and said, "I do not think it would be advisable."

"No," he said. "This isn't Edinburgh, after all, or— Where does your husband live?"

"Ot-ta-wa," she replied.

Dr. Singh nodded. "Good luck, young man," he said. He left before Hari could say, "Ta-ta."

Hari waited for Rukmini to help him down from the table. She turned her back on him to pick up the cloth bag. Why did she look sad if they had won? Muttamma had said they would.

He had visited her the previous evening with a pink bougainvillaea he found lying in the veranda. She recognized his voice at once when he opened her door and said, "*Namaskar. Yelaunnaru*?" And when he handed her the flower, she tucked it into her hair and wiped a tear from each of her white eyes. Then Hari and Muttamma both talked at once. He told her about his

Christmas and birthday parties; she laughed over how much he had grown in a year. After this they sat without speaking, she on her bedroll and he in her lap. While she hummed, he looked about. A moonbeam shone through the window. The room smelled of incense, camphor, and cloves. Would Canada smell this wonderful?

He let Rukmini lift him from the high table and carry him from the room. He felt like clapping but his arms were wrapped about her neck. He would get an electric train, one even finer than Jagadish's, because they had won her strange game. It was not at all like jute, in which a boy could run this way and that, then squat with his hand on his head and yell, "Jute!" when the boy who was *It* came too close. This ice-water game was played with words. It was not nearly as exciting but the prize for winning would be a splendid one: an electric train from his father, his very own father.

Rukmini carried Hari past the people waiting on the benches. When the clerk rose to bid her farewell, she turned her back on him. Perhaps she should have invited Dr. Singh to tea after all, she thought. Sharada was an excellent hostess and his manner would please her. Perhaps he would become a family friend. His visits would thrill Usha.

Outside, Hari gasped in the blinding afternoon heat. The driver was pacing beside the car and smoking yet another *beedi*. He dropped the *beedi* and turned. Hari wriggled out of Rukmini's arms and jumped up and down. "We won!" he cried. "We won the game!" He launched himself down the steps.

He did not hear her cry, "Be careful!" He could not see her, behind him now, framed by the green doors. She stood with one arm stretched toward him and prayed he would not fall. Watching him on the broad, white steps which slowed his descent—watching him flutter down toward the car with his arms out like wings—she feared he was already beyond her reach.

# Part Three

# Chapter 8

# Admissions

Announcements of arriving flights were muffled by the babble in the reception area: "Auntie? Over here!" and, "*Salut*! *Ça va*?" and, "How you've grown!" The area smelled of moist palms and face powder, of orange peels in paper bags, of slept-in clothes.

Krishna sat well back from the barrier at Customs and Immigration. Beside him were escalators between the separate floors for arrivals and departures. He was reading a paper but it was a slow day for real news. Three months before, Krushchev had proclaimed the Soviet Union's right to protect Cuba from American aggression. Now Castro was trying to bait Kennedy by reminding him that the Soviet Union had put the first man into orbit. Such clowns, Krishna thought. Still, the paper gave him an excuse to hang back. Airports made him nervous because people were so demonstrative in them. Shaking hands was one thing, but in such places people exchanged hugs and kissed. Barely ten feet away, a stout woman in a black dress laughed and cried while she hugged her middle-aged son.

Krishna also stayed well back because he didn't know how to greet Rukmini and Hari when they arrived. "How are you?"

might sound foolish since they would both be tired. "Welcome to Canada!" would sound trite. He would think of something, though. After turning to the comics, he skimmed "Rex Morgan, MD" and "The Phantom." He ignored "Hi and Lois" and "Blondie." The humour in "L'il Abner" always escaped him and "Peanuts" was for children. Lowering the paper, he glanced at the barrier and wondered what to call Hari. Not Babu. Krishna remembered the way Rukmini used to croon, "Ba-bu," when they lived in Benares. It sounded too much like Baby. Harischandra was too long and Krishna didn't like its pet form, Harish. Hari sounded too much like "*Haré*!" which was fine for a fervent Hindu but not for Krishna. That settled it. He would call Hari what he had called him in India: Boy.

There was one more reason Krishna sat well back: he disliked crowds. They were easier to avoid in North America than in India, but the few times he found himself in or near a crowd he felt self-conscious. For one thing, his height made his colour all the more noticeable. He also felt self-conscious because too many people glanced away the moment they noticed he was not one of them. If he had asked anyone, he would have learned many people found him intimidating. It was not his colour or his height that turned them away; it was his intensity. People mistook the way he glared for anger. But had he thought of asking someone why they felt uncomfortable in his company, he would not have known who to ask. The only men he called friends in Ottawa were those he met in the civil service cricket league. He wasn't a civil servant and he didn't act like a family man. They likely thought he had little in common with them. As for the other Indians and the West Indians, their complaints about Canada—its foul weather, its polite bigotry—annoyed him. He wanted to ask, "If things are so much better in India or Trinidad, what are you doing here?"

Double doors of frosted glass opened, and he saw Rukmini approaching the immigration desk. She looked nervous. Between the slats of the barrier, Krishna saw Hari and grinned. Hari wore a belted, grey wool suit and short pants, the matching cap askew. On the cap was a silver pin, wings marked BOAC. He looked much as he had two years before. "Tiny," Krishna remembered saying. "How will he play games if he is so small?" Hari rubbed his eyes and yawned while looking about. He had likely never seen so much glass or chrome and now he appeared to have discovered escalators. Krishna tried to see them through Hari's eyes. Silvery black steps slithered down to deliver a parade of sandals and shoes, many of them white canvas. The up escalator slid from a smooth, steel mat to snake out of sight beyond trouser legs and skirts. Krishna folded the paper and rose. He leaned around a pillar to drop the paper into a garbage can and, before he could prepare himself, he found Rukmini leading Hari toward him. She clutched a beaded purse and an old, Air France flight bag.

"This is your father," she told Hari when they stopped. "Remember?"

Apparently not, or perhaps he was dazed. Krishna watched Hari examine him from the polished brown shoes up to his carefully combed hair. Children's eyes always appeared larger than they should be, Krishna thought. He reached out to adjust the cap and asked Rukmini, "What's this?"

"British-made," she said. "Is it not handsome? Your brother purchased it for us in London."

Krishna tried again: "Boys don't dress up here except for costume parties." Then he glanced away and frowned at yet another noisy welcome. Why were his words so awkward, so clumsy? His jokes rarely sounded humorous these days. "It's two hours' drive to Ottawa," he said. "Let's get your luggage and push off."

Near the conveyor belt, Rukmini sat Hari out of the way on the bottom of a luggage trolley. Krishna thought she would talk about the flight. But after taking off her green sweater and draping it over the trolley's handle, she told him, "I have been corresponding with friends at a number of universities and received two promising replies. Vancouver, is it far from Ottawa?"

"Not as far as London," Krishna said.

Rukmini pointed out the luggage to him and he hefted it off the conveyor belt. There was less than he had expected: one large suitcase and a small one. She gestured for Hari to stand up so Krishna could load the luggage onto the trolley. While she followed, leading Hari by the hand, Krishna led the way through a set of automatic doors—frosted doors marked, "Exit. *Sortie*." Only then did he ask, "You're not thinking of going off to work already and leaving the boy?" He didn't mean it as an accusation. Too often, his words seemed to burst out of him without direction. Now he tried to remember where he had parked. He wished they could begin again.

"I would never leave Babu," she said.

Her use of the name irked Krishna, but he had to accept it: she had looked after Hari; she was entitled to display her affection for him. Krishna didn't know how to display his own affection but he knew he would learn, given time. Harischandra, Harish, or Babu—he was still her son. One day, perhaps, he would be Krishna's son as well.

"Over there," he finally said. They waited for an airport bus to pass before they crossed to the parking lot. "I have a new car," he told Hari. "A second-hand car like my Chevrolet. I sold it when I came here and got this. It's easier to manoeuvre." Krishna knew cars fascinated boys but Hari was either overwhelmed by all the cars in the lot or too sleepy to care. Krishna loaded the luggage into the trunk of his grey Studebaker Lark. He opened the passenger door for Rukmini and waved Hari into the back. After Krishna got in, he felt as though the car had shrunk further. It felt strange having passengers, and he wished he hadn't traded in the Chevrolet. He had slept in it during long trips, something he couldn't do in the Lark. At any rate, his days of sleeping in a car were over. It would be motor hotels from now on. He wondered what other changes he would have to make, and he wondered whether he could make them after so many years on his own.

Rukmini waited until Krishna paid the attendant and turned into a stream of taxis and buses. Then she asked, "Why not work?

You yourself wrote we cannot live on your salary alone. Toronto, is it far?" Even as she spoke she realized she shouldn't be pursuing the subject, but it had preoccupied her even as the plane had touched down. Her mother had spent her life dependent on a husband, and Rukmini saw no reason to follow suit.

"Too far to travel back and forth if you want to save your money," Krishna said. "But if you must go, you needn't worry. The boy will be too busy to miss you. I'll keep him occupied with games. His school will keep him occupied with studies." Krishna heard even breathing and glanced over his shoulder. Hari was stretched out and fast asleep.

"He is not yet seeking admission to college," Rukmini teased.

Krishna laughed then and so did she. When she tugged on his arm and tilted her head toward his shoulder, he relaxed. He was no better at reunions than he was at farewells but the three of them were finally together. He was a family man once more. While he kept his eyes on the road and scanned the gauges on the dashboard, Rukmini chatted about her relatives. She gave him news of his family but did not mention his mother; Krishna didn't ask. Airport traffic clogged the road between Dorval and Montreal, but after passing Montreal Krishna relaxed further. The miles of silence felt almost natural, somehow comforting.

Once they reached home, Rukmini woke Hari and led him into the apartment building. Krishna followed with the luggage. Riding the elevator, they watched the lighted numbers change. Inside the apartment, he placed the luggage in the large bedroom. It had two single beds, both so new that plastic covered the box springs. In the smaller bedroom lay the foam mattress he had bought when he moved to Ottawa. Rukmini laid Hari on the mattress, used the bathroom, and went straight to bed. Krishna walked to the Loblaw's supermarket. Watching the clerk ring up his groceries, he wanted to tell her, "My wife and son are with me now," but how could a perfect stranger understand his pleasure let alone appreciate it? He kept this euphoria—the strange feeling he had accomplished something wonderful—to himself. Back in the apartment, he read in the living room. Then he woke Rukmini for supper, which they ate while Hari slept. She insisted on washing the dishes, so Krishna switched on his Heathkit radio to listen to the news. After a few minutes he lost interest. He searched through his record collection while Rukmini made herself comfortable on the sofa. It was also new. She took off her glasses and placed them on the coffee table. He considered the *Goldberg Variations* but settled on the *Well-Tempered Clavier* and sat next to her.

"This is very nice," she said. "You are an expert on western music now?"

"Just classical," he replied. He was sure he told her the story once but they needed to talk about something; it might as well be music. "When I lived in Japan," he said, "people there were crazy for western things. Maybe because they lost the war and thought western ways were superior. That's where I heard my first Bach recording. It was a complete set of the *Brandenburg Concertos*, but I prefer his solo works." Seated close to her, watching her nod to the music while she toyed with the end of her sari, Krishna grew distracted. The stirrings within him were disturbingly strong. "I have the *Unaccompanied Cello Suites,"* he said. "Would you like to hear them instead of—?"

Rukmini clutched his hand when he rose. *"Yenraja,"* she asked, "are you afraid of me now?" She had expected him to be aloof at the airport, but she hadn't expected him to act so unsure when they were finally alone: unsure of the love they once felt; of whether they could begin rekindling it; of what to do next.

"Not at all," he said, sitting beside her again.

She relished the pressure of his thigh against hers. It had been much too long: not the lack of sex, which she thought didn't matter to either of them, but simply being close; having someone to talk to, someone who cared. When she kissed his temple, he finally put his arm around her awkwardly, both of them half turned on the sofa. She moved her lips over his bristled cheek until she reached his mouth, then placed a hand on his chest. She pushed ever so slightly. Before he could misread the gesture—before he could assume she did not want him—she asked, "Would we not be more comfortable lying down?"

"Yes," he said when she rose, adjusting her sari. "Yes."

✱

Hari entered the bathroom, switched on the light, and closed the door. There was a western-style toilet like the one in his London Uncle's row house but this bathroom was more dazzling, and not simply because of the shiny mirror. Light blue tiles climbed to the ceiling from a huge tub. There was also a curtain, pulled back and hooked over a spout high up on one tiled wall. He used the toilet, washed his hands, and headed down the corridor. It was disappointingly short. In front of him, past a door with a chain on the jamb, Krishna stood in a small kitchen on the far side of a dining table. The table had metal legs slanting up to the corners of a white top. The chairs were covered with brown leather and their legs were also metal. Pressing the back of one chair, Hari discovered the leather was plastic.

Krishna leaned back against the counter between the fridge and stove and watched Hari. Now the boy was fascinated by the way his bare feet stuck to the varnished parquet floor. When Krishna smiled, Hari turned away to look into the main room.

Separated from the kitchen by a low wall, the main room opened out from the dining room. Diagonally opposite him, in the far corner of the main room, was a glass door. To its right stood a metallic bookcase and a metallic stand holding a radio beside what looked like a gramophone without a horn. Above these ran a long window with white metallic blinds like the closed ones in the bedrooms. These blinds were pulled halfway up. The light in the sky was weaker than the light back home but it made the white walls glow, especially the long wall closest to him. A rug covered the floor and on the rug stood a low table. Except for a dresser he had seen in the large bedroom, this table was the only piece of wooden furniture in the house. Beyond the table, along the far wall leading to the glass door, stood a sofa covered with brown cloth. Rukmini was seated behind the table with her back against the sofa.

When Krishna again smiled at Hari, he ran to her. On the flight from London she said they would be living in a splendid apartment house. He was not sure whether he liked apartment houses, though. They were smaller than his house in Bangalore and had only one storey. Yet there was not only a light on every ceiling but the main room also had a pole with lights in plastic cones.

"Your father has a gift for you," Rukmini said. She reached for a box on the coffee table. "It is wrapped with cellophane just like the jigsaw puzzle he gave you, but see how big this is!"

He tried to read the words on the illustrated top: "Van the Gra-af—"

"Generator," she finished for him. "Van de Graaff generator. It is a model of the machine your father experiments with. Here." The cellophane hissed when she tore it away. Then she opened the box.

Eager to see Hari's reaction, Krishna looked into the living room. When Hari's brow crinkled like the cellophane, Krishna asked, "Is something wrong?"

"No," Rukmini said. "Only, there appears to be some assembly required."

"What?" He rounded the low wall.

She handed the box up to him and he lifted out the instructions. Underneath lay pieces of brown plastic, some of them painted a silvery chrome on one side. He should have known, he thought, but he hadn't looked at the box since buying the model. He had spent his holidays taking a course at Harvard and found the model in the bookstore.

Hari looked over the table at the blank, white wall. He was thinking about his electric train. There was plenty of room for a train and he was about to remind Rukmini of it when she said:

"We can piece the model together afterwards. Or perhaps you would like your father to help you?"

"Would you like that, Boy?"

Hari nodded uncertainly.

"Let's eat," Krishna said. "Kellogg's corn flakes. They will make you grow."

"I shall take my bath first," Rukmini told him. "You two go ahead."

"We can wait," Krishna said.

Alone with Hari, Krishna didn't know what to say and Hari stared back with large, unnerving eyes. What was he thinking? That Krishna was not really his father but only an Ottawa Uncle? Once Hari began school, there would be no doubt. Few uncles would do what Krishna had in mind. For now, he joined the chromed hemispheres of the Van de Graaff into a globe. There was a hole on one side so it could sit on a brown plastic shaft. When he set the globe down, it fell apart. The hemispheres rocked on the beige carpet. "We'll need glue," he said. "I'll buy some later." He sat on the sofa to read.

Hari's first words to Krishna surprised him: "May I also read a book?"

"What?" Krishna asked. "Yes, of course." He found his *Atlas of the World* on the bookshelf. When Hari took the atlas to his room, Krishna felt powerless. He wouldn't have minded if Hari had read quietly on the floor. This shyness had lasted long enough.

With her bath finished, Rukmini returned to the living room. While she towelled her hair dry, she asked Krishna about his plans for Hari's education. Krishna had given it much thought. He was tired of his assistant's complaints about the public school his children attended, so Krishna had decided on a private one. The tuition would allow him to save little, he said, but he hadn't brought Hari over to watch him grow up illiterate. Rukmini agreed, though she thought Krishna's choice of *illiterate* extreme. Noticing her frown, he wondered aloud whether Hari might not be better off in a public school, after all, which wasn't the same thing here as it was in Britain. But this was not Britain, Krishna said; it was Canada: half British, half American, with a touch of French. Then again, public schools were for ordinary children.

"You plan everything so well," she said.

The next morning, Krishna drove the Lark through the open gates of Woodbine College. It had all he had hoped for: lush grounds with a games field, a cricket pitch and a cinder track, ivy-covered red brick and even a chapel. Eton could not have been more splendid. He parked near the chapel, got out, and examined its windows. He thought he could coax more than a few words from Hari by reminding him the coloured glass made pictures like the jigsaw puzzle. When Krishna turned, he found Hari clutching Rukmini's hand with both of his. "You needn't hold his hand," Krishna called. Rukmini let go to adjust Hari's tie and brush pine needles from his jacket. Then she took the BOAC pin off his cap and put it in her purse. After this they walked farther away from Krishna, toward the headmaster's house. It was also made of red brick.

Shortly before the time set for their interview, Krishna led the way into the school. On the walls of the reception area, cricket bats were crossed over lists of blue names painted on varnished boards. When a man announced, "I'm Andrew Merlin," Krishna turned from a painting of Billy Bishop's Neuport. Its propeller was a bright blue. Merlin released the lapels of his black gown long enough to shake hands. Krishna registered a firm grasp, a dutiful smile, and a heavily veined nose. Merlin insisted everyone precede him into an office overlooking the front lawn. The Englishness of the cricket bats and the headmaster's gown pleased Krishna but he also felt uneasy, as though he were stepping back in time. He took the seat on the far left.

After climbing into the leather chair in the middle, Hari sat with his elbows propped absurdly on its arms. Rukmini sat in the far right-hand chair and arranged the pleats of her turquoise sari. Krishna wore his white flannels and navy blazer. Some years before, he had replaced the crest of Delhi University with one from Columbia but the blazer still looked foreign. He could not afford a new one.

Merlin sat behind an oak desk with a baize top. Behind him ran glass-fronted bookcases built into the wall. His gown looked newly laundered and its pleats shone with starch. With his hands on the top of the desk, he said, "I trust you've brought the lad's report cards?"

Krishna placed a bundle next to a silver inkstand on the desk. He had substituted white twine for the coarse, brown hemp. Before he could speak, Rukmini said:

"We do not have report cards for children in India, sir."

Merlin appeared surprised she had spoken. He raised his eyebrows as if to say, "Do go on."

"We have certificates only," she explained, "telling which standard has been completed. My son had nearly completed the second standard when we left." She realized she should have said, "our son," but it was too late. "I also brought some of his notebooks."

Merlin perched wire-rimmed glasses on the bridge of his nose and hooked the stems behind his ears. Then he pulled free the knot which Krishna had tied deliberately loose. Merlin put the certificates aside to flip through the top notebook. If its quaintness surprised him, he hid it well. The sheets were unbleached paper sewn together with black thread. Brown paper was folded and glued to make the jacket. On one of the flaps he pressed what Krishna knew to be a grain of rice glue. The book had been made by a servant. "Odd," Merlin said. He peered at Hari. "Did you copy these sums from a workbook?"

When Hari looked to Rukmini for direction, she said, "There is no need to be shy."

"No, sir," he said, lowering his arms.

"But look here," Merlin exclaimed. He turned the notebook about and pointed to the right-hand column of the first sums, eight digits high by seven wide. "If you add these numerals, you get fifty-two. Now, here's the two at the bottom, but where did you write the five? Our lads would have written it above the second column to show they were carrying five tens."

"I carried it in my head, sir."

Merlin thumbed through the rest of the notebook but he didn't seem to be reading. At last he put the book down and told Krishna, "I don't need report cards or certificates to prove your son will be able to hold his own against our lads. I see they don't believe in easing you into maths in India!" He sat back and relaxed as though inviting Krishna to let down his guard.

Krishna crossed his legs and clasped his hands on his knees. He nodded approvingly at Hari.

Rukmini wondered about the fuss. Her family was known for its good mathematicians. Her father had been a full professor. When she tried to smile at Hari's reflection in the bookcase, she found the reflection of a black gown distorted in the glass.

Merlin pulled back his sleeves. He leaned forward, pushed the notebooks aside, and took a silver pen from the inkstand. It looked like a miniature dress helmet. The crest on his blazer, revealed by the wayward lapels of his gown, was that of the Governor General's Horse Guards. "We discussed fees over the 'phone," he said. He spoke so formally once more, the apostrophe hung in the air. "We agreed they posed no problem if you paid monthly instead of term by term?"

Rukmini glanced sideways at Krishna. He had neglected to tell her about this.

"Would you spell your name for me then?"

"Capital K-r-i-s-h-n-a, hyphen, capital R-a-o." He added, "First initial, G."

"And your first initial?" Merlin asked Rukmini.

"Also G," she replied, confused. She had been mulling over the fees. It occurred to her now that Krishna had lied; the tuition would allow him to save nothing.

"G. Krishna-Rao," Merlin muttered while writing.

"Excuse me, sir," she said, "but my last name is Rukmini. In our part of India, we reverse our family and given names."

"Of course," he said. "How careless of me!" He stroked out the entry and said, "There." Then he asked her to spell her name and she did. "First initial G?" he added.

Both Krishna and Rukmini laughed with him. When Hari joined in, Krishna raised a finger to his lips and the childish laugh collapsed into a sulk. It deepened when Krishna tried to frown it away.

"We had the Indian High Commissioner's son here once," Merlin explained, "but that was some years ago." He touched the wisps of hair combed across his head.

Krishna, in turn, fingered the grey fanning back from his temples. He knew thirty-seven was young, but he had woken feeling that Rukmini and Hari's arrival had aged him. He welcomed responsibility, and he didn't know why he should have woken so apprehensive. When Merlin asked for Krishna's occupation and employer, he replied, "I'm a researcher with SEL. Systems Engineering, Limited. We have contracts with DND. Department of National Defence. We have a field station at Uplands Airport but you can reach me through the office on—" He stopped.

Merlin had put down the pen. He sat back, took off his glasses, and gazed over Hari's head out the window.

Krishna knew something was wrong but he continued: "I'm trying to find a way to prevent atmospheric disturbances from interrupting radio signals to planes, what we call radio interference." His chair creaked when he uncrossed his legs. Then he examined his fingernails. They were quite clean. Why was he acting like this? He knew why: he had never belonged to an old boys' club and he wondered now whether Hari would fit into this one. Krishna realized his silence appeared rude so he looked at Merlin but could think of nothing to add.

Merlin was balancing his glasses on his index finger. He placed them in an inside pocket, picked up a notebook, and rose. "Would you excuse me?" he asked. "I won't be a moment. Would you like some tea while you wait?" He was leaving the door ajar as though he couldn't trust a lowly researcher with the souvenirs of a distinguished career.

"No, thank you," Krishna replied. He rose to stand by the window. He glared at the flag hanging above an embassy beyond the school grounds. The embassy belonged to a country he couldn't place, a newly independent colony.

"Does this mean they will not admit him?" Rukmini asked.

"Let's wait and see, all right?" Krishna said. He hadn't meant to sound abrupt, but he was thinking of another uniformed functionary, an officer in the Indian Air Force.

Krishna was twenty-eight then, newly returned from Japan. Inchon and P'yongyang had nearly passed from headlines into history. He dreamt of becoming a pilot. The technical exams proved simple, the physical exams even simpler. At last he found himself interviewed by an officer with wings over his left breast pocket. A stump poked from one of his short sleeves, which bore the two and a half stripes of a squadron leader. He should have been invalided out of the service but Krishna suspected the former pilot had connections. Below his wings were numerous ribbons including that of the DFC. Krishna's gaze kept returning to the buttons on the officer's tunic, buttons stamped with the lions and wheel of Ashoka's Pillar. The two men seemed brothers in spirit, patriots charged with a sacred trust. This was why Krishna refused to believe the man at first when he said, "We can accept you, but not as a pilot. We have plenty of younger men to choose from." He paused. "They do not have your education, of course, but your vision is below our standards. However, we have need of good engineers to plan and develop—" Krishna interrupted to say he hadn't applied to the air force to work in a laboratory, and he wasn't about to prevail on his own connections to get what he wanted. The officer ignored this last. Now Krishna was faced with Hari's rejection from a private school because Krishna had no connections here. He had never buttoned on a tunic, and Hari might never wear a school tie.

The door opened all the way. Krishna turned to find Merlin leading a second man into the office. Hari was slouching in his chair. "Sit up," Krishna said and Hari did, slowly. The second man took his post between the desk and the bookcases. He adjusted a lapel of his gown as though he had flung on his costume. He held the notebook.

"My assistant," Merlin announced before sitting down again. "Hodgson, Mr. Krishna-Rao and Mrs. Rukmini."

"Doctor Rukmini, sir," she said.

"I beg your pardon?" Merlin asked.

"My wife recently earned her doctorate," Krishna explained. He forced himself to sound offhand because he didn't want men like this to assume he was boasting. Even as he took his seat Rukmini added:

"In electrical engineering."

Merlin glanced up at Hodgson. "Any lad whose mother has a PhD will be a credit to our college, eh?"

"Without a doubt," Hodgson said. "I think we'll have your son repeat the second form, though," he told Krishna. "He'll have time to fit in more easily."

Krishna tilted his head in agreement. He knew he should be glad, even ecstatic, but the morning had not gone according to plan.

Hari announced, "We learned reading, writing, and arithmetic only."

"Well," Hodgson said, rising onto his toes, "the three Rs do make for a good, sound start."

Hari wondered whether Hodgson was teasing him. Surely everyone knew writing and arithmetic didn't begin with *r*? Before Hari could mention this to Rukmini, Hodgson lowered himself and continued, still addressing Krishna:

"By the way, you've no objection to your son attending chapel on special occasions? We have some RCs here. Roman Catholics," he explained. "And a handful of ORs. Other Religions. But we're a predominantly Anglican institution."

"I intend the boy to grow up Canadian," Krishna said.

"Excellent," Merlin declared. "Would you mind signing here?" He offered Krishna the pen while tapping the admission form.

"Not at all." Krishna signed with a flourish he found distasteful since he had no intention of overacting his part the way these men overacted theirs. He lapsed into silence. The cheerier Rukmini grew during the brief tour which followed, the gloomier Krishna felt. His only impressions of the senior school and of a basement corridor, leading to the junior school, were of wooden doors and benches painted blue so often they seemed to have lost their grain. Hodgson said goodbye near the chapel. Merlin led the way back to his office, but Krishna balked at his seeing them out; at his seeing them climb into a secondhand Lark.

On the way home, Rukmini had to remind Krishna to stop for the glue. While she settled herself at the dining table to write to her university friends, Krishna returned to the model. He pierced the bevelled rubber cap of the glue bottle with a fork. Then he pressed beads of glue onto the seams of the hemispheres and gave them to Hari. The syrupy, yellow glue did not work. The hemispheres refused to form a globe. Krishna guessed the problem at last. "We need a special type of plastic glue," he said. Hari stared at the pieces as though they had betrayed him, and Krishna sympathized. The jigsaw puzzle hadn't needed glue, neither plastic nor rice. Then again, he wanted to say, this model is no mere toy. Just like a real Van de Graaff, the model could generate electricity. Not a million volts, perhaps, but electricity all the same.

Rukmini wrote aerograms now: first to Prakash and Saroja, then to Sharada, and last to Sharada's brother, Rukmini's Bombay Uncle, who had seen her off at the airport. She also wrote to Krishna's brother and sister-in-law in London and thanked them for their hospitality.

While Rukmini wrote, Hari read the atlas and Krishna moved about the large bedroom. He packed his blazer and flannels in the steamer trunk he used as a nightstand. On the trunk were souvenirs of his travels: stickers from Cunard Lines and Air France. The two from Cunard showed the *Queen Elizabeth* and *Queen Mary*; the sticker from Air France showed part of a white seahorse on cobalt blue. It had once been winged but the paper was torn. He pushed the trunk back between the beds and draped a white sheet over it. Then he set out, alone, in search of the plastic glue.

## Chapter 9

# Thanks to Mrs. Dalgleish

For the second time in as many weeks, Hari stared at the red brick of Woodbine College. This time the Lark rattled off and he stood alone until a woman appeared in the entrance. "I'm Mrs. Gordon," she said. She didn't ask for his name; she seemed to know. He followed her past Merlin's office, then a dining room with long wooden tables and benches, then classrooms filled with older boys. Their blue blazers were like the one Krishna had bought for Hari: a red maple leaf with yellow veins gleamed on the breast pocket. Even his new cricket cap was red, with yellow piping.

Mrs. Gordon turned right at the chapel doors. Hari followed her down a narrow flight of stairs into a humid basement. He had been down here only the week before, but it had been quiet then. Now he could hear noises from above and from elsewhere—the building sounded haunted—but he saw no one except her. How would he ever find his way back? Near a closed door marked Tuck Shop, she turned left up a sloping corridor. It was lined with tall, blue lockers. He thought of them as Godrejes, their name at home. Rukmini said India was no longer his home—Canada was—but he decided he could call India home if he wanted. On the walls hung narrow, black and white photos of boys in blazers and teachers in gowns. He knew teachers here were called masters, but unlike the teachers at Cluny Convent few of these masters were women. At the top of the sloping corridor Mrs. Gordon stopped and pointed to the right, toward a concrete and glass hall. "That's the junior school annex," she said. He knew without her telling him that he was a junior and he thought they would continue into the bright hall, but she turned to open a blue door. They went down an even narrower flight of stairs, which made a U-turn, and he followed her along a second corridor. Hari knew he was lost now.

At the far end stood yet another blue door. "That's the entrance you'll use from now on," she said, pointing. "Be sure to tell your father. You're not allowed into the senior school except to the Tuck Shop or the dining room." He nodded at her though he understood little. When she added, "Or to the chapel," he thought she said *chappal,* the word for sandal at home. He imagined the entire school crammed into one giant sandal. Then, remembering Hodgson had also mentioned a chapel, Hari decided they were different things.

He followed Mrs. Gordon halfway down the corridor to his new classroom and looked in. He knew he would like it because a piano stood under a window in the back. He inched over the threshold. All the boys were dressed exactly like him in blue blazers, grey flannel short pants, and grey kneesocks. The boys sat with their backs to the door. None of them wore their caps, so he snatched his own cap off when she nudged him into the room.

The teacher, who sat in the front, kept her head bowed over a book. Each time she called out a name, one of the boys raised his hand and said, "Present."

"Naismith?" she asked. "Sinclair?" When she finally looked up, Mrs. Gordon fluttered her hand. Before Hari could thank her, she pointed at an empty seat near the door and left. The teacher nodded at him before returning to the roll book. "Tully?" she asked. "Vance?"

The names were disappointingly short. They were harsh to the ear. There was not one Srinivasan, not so much as a Jagadish. Hari sat down and fingered the "JL '62" carved on his new desk. Then he looked up at the map of the world on the wall next to him. He was still looking for India when the teacher declared:

"I said we seem to have another new boy! Stop daydreaming." When he faced the front, she demanded, "Your name, please?"

Unable to see her clearly, he rose. "Gopal Harischandra, Miss," he said, and every boy turned in his seat.

The boys all looked alike. They had pinkish white faces and either brown or golden hair. Then Hari saw a boy with light brown skin, dark eyes, and hair curlier than his own. Watching him, Hari ignored the tittering.

"Quiet!" the teacher ordered. The class fell silent. She didn't wear a black gown—she wore a brown tweed jacket with coloured flecks—but she looked fearful. She reminded him of a British bulldog he had seen in London. "I'm Mrs. Dalgleish," she told him. "You can call me either that or Mrs. D, but not Miss. I'm not a waitress."

He fell in love with her name at once. It was so musical: Dalgleish, Dal-gleish.

"Spell your name," she said. "First name?"

"Capital G-o-p-a-l," he spelled, as Krishna had for Merlin.

"Middle name?" she asked.

There were only two parts to Hari's name. Still, he searched for the answer in his cap and in his new tie. It had slanting yellow and red stripes. Deciding she wanted the rest of his name, he said, "Harischandra," and began spelling it: "Capital H-a-r—"

Trying to imitate an Indian accent, a brown-haired boy whispered to the one next to him, "Capital hetch, eh, ahr."

Distracted by the tittering which followed, Hari backed up and continued with, "—r-i-s—" He paused to let Mrs. D write.

"Go on," she urged.

"—c-h-a-n-d-r-a," he spelled. Finished at last, he watched the brown-haired boy whisper:

"See-hetch-eh-en-dee-ahr-eh." This time, with Hari's eyes on them, neither boy tittered.

"Thank you," Mrs. D said. "We use only family names here. You will be Chandra. Or, if you break any rules, Mister Chandra."

Confused, Hari shifted from one foot to the other. He examined his tie again. He scrunched his cap until it looked like a red ball with yellow lines.

"Is anything wrong?" she asked.

"My family name is Gopal," he replied.

"But you just said Gopal is your first name!" she declared. "Are you trying to be amusing?" Before he could say no, she continued: "I shouldn't waste my time. The honour of being class fool belongs to Naismith here, who sits in front of my desk so I can keep an eye on him. And unless you wish to be the object of my other eye, Mr. Chandra, you'll refrain from verbal gymnastics. I have your name right here: Gopal Harris Chandra. Isn't that right?"

It sounded almost right even if she did pronounce the last part "Chandra" instead of "Chendra" and didn't roll the *r*. He nodded and sat down.

"Stand up, Nunn," she ordered, "and face the class."

One of the golden-haired boys obeyed her. He looked at the class with a smile tightening below his pug nose. He was clearly the biggest boy here.

"Nunn will be monitor this term since he's in the fourth form," she announced. "If anyone breaks the rules, Nunn will be the only one to report him. I won't have anyone carrying tales. Is that understood?"

Hari nodded with the others though he wanted to ask a question. How could anyone carry tales when, as Merlin had known, only numbers could be carried? Hari decided to wait.

"Come to the front," she told Nunn. "I'll need your help in passing out the notebooks. Class, the blue notebooks are for maths. That will be our first lesson this morning. Red is for social studies. That will be our second lesson. Purple is for French, the first lesson after break . . ."

At once Hari began imagining the subjects in colour. Numbers soon became blue, as blue as the sky he could no longer see out the small windows because the room was almost underground. Social studies became red like the swatches on the map of the world: the red of Canada and Australia. When he finally found India, it was green. He sat through the first two lessons with his head in his hands. There was too much to learn here, too much to remember: not simply that people called *chappals* sandals but that everything a boy had to learn came in a different colour. Such things were clearly more important than how to multiply by twenty-five: by adding two zeroes and dividing by four. He longed for break, a word whispered more than once by a classmate. He passed the time until then sniffing silently. Even if this classroom smelled like his old one—of wood and chalk—he didn't like the other smells. There were no boyish crops dandy with hair tonic. Here men like Krishna and boys like himself used a white paste called Brylcreem. There were no more girlish braids shiny with coconut oil and garlanded with jasmine. There were no more girls. Worst of all, the piano smelled dusty and it looked untouched.

After Mrs. D dismissed the class for break, the boys milled in the corridor. They flopped on blue benches lining the walls or jumped about. The boy called Naismith sang, "Boing, boing!" Then Nunn took charge. Everyone funnelled out through the door and into the morning sunshine. He hurtled down a grassy embankment to run across a games field. At the far side was a fence lined with low cedars. "Last one there is a rotten egg!" Nunn shouted. The class followed with Hari in the rear.

He should have known better than to run. The driveway was paved with gravel, which he had never seen at home. He had also never worn shoes for play even in the rainy season. On his third step, his right foot wrenched in. A sharp pain shot up his ankle. He collapsed in a flurry of grey flannel and blue wool. The gravel scraped his palms. He rose onto all fours and blinked through tears at his cap, lying on the ground.

A pudgy boy appeared at the top of the embankment, level with the driveway. He picked up the cap and Hari rose.

Hari pressed his stinging palms together to make *namaskar*, something he had done at home only to adults, but he guessed these boys were somehow better than him. The class was divided into four forms but Mrs. D had made it clear that, more important, it was divided between old boys and new boys. He knew this pudgy one was an old boy.

The boy handed back the cap, then pulled his own down so his dark hair jutted like a fringe. "I'm Spiro Christou," he announced. "My father's one of The Christous. He owns a bunch of restaurants and we live in Westmount. Know where that is?"

Hari shook his head.

"In Montreal," Christou declared. "Know where that is?"

Hari shook his head once more.

"Don't you know anything?" Before Hari could shake his head a third time, Christou asked, "What's your name again?"

"Harischandra," he whispered. He wiped tears from his face with the cap but ignored the blood trickling from his knee into the top of his kneesock. That could wait. As for what his father did, Hari remembered the way Merlin had acted when Krishna had talked about his work. Even if Ajja was a modern Harischandra, Hari simply had to lie. Besides, Ajja was not here so it might not matter. Hari said, "My father is the Indian High Commissioner."

"Oh yeah?" Christou said. He pointed at the rest of the boys. They chased one another in and out of the low cedars or played catch with tennis balls. "See the other Brownie?" he asked.

Hari nodded when he spied the dark-eyed boy.

"That's Ali," Christou said. "His father's the Pakistani High Commissioner. Ali's full name is Ifthakar-Ali or something like that but it's too hard to say. Chandra is, too, so I think we should call you HC, all right?"

Hari nodded. Smarting more from his lie than from his injuries, he turned to limp toward the door.

That evening, when Rukmini asked how he liked his new class, he replied, "It is wonderful." This was no lie. He could never lie to her. It really was wonderful with all those coloured notebooks and the map of the world. He knew why Mrs. D and Christou were so impatient with him. Unlike Nunn and Ifthakar-Ali, Hari was a new boy and new boys had much to learn. It was as simple as one, two, three.

*

Even if fall was the season for football, which Krishna called soccer now, he wanted Hari to practise cricket. Rukmini said Krishna was a fine athlete. He was the finest cricketer of his class at Delhi University and the finest tennis player at the Institute. She looked proud when she told Hari this. Then she said Hari should begin calling his father Appa. First, though, Hari wanted to see what kind of *appa* Krishna turned out to be.

Along with the school uniform, Krishna had bought a boy's cricket bat, which he seasoned with linseed oil. While Hari watched, the nutty yellow ooze darkened the white willow of the bat. Despite Krishna's care, the linseed soiled the red cloth wound onto the handle.

When Hari said he would rather play with a train, Krishna said, "You can't hit a ball with a train, can you?" Hari did not reply. He couldn't imagine why anyone would want to do this, and he decided not to mention the train until Christmas.

At the end of the first week of school, Krishna marched Hari onto the lawn behind the apartment building. Krishna was in high spirits. At last, he thought; at last.

"Cricket lesson number one," he said. "The crucial thing about batting is to wear out the bowler. You have to block the first fifty bowls. Then you can start hitting for runs. Here's how to block." He placed the end of the short bat in front of his left foot and raised the bat until it stood straight above his left shoulder. While he arced the bat down, he moved his right leg forward. His left leg angled at the hip, his right knee bent, and the end of the bat and his right foot touched the ground at the same time. It looked fairly simple, but each time Hari tried the motion Krishna said,

"No, no!" or, "Keep your head up!" or, "Smoother action, smoother!" He made Hari practise ten times. Hari's left leg began to ache from holding the blocking position so Krishna could check that the rear leg was angled at forty-five degrees and the front knee was over the front foot. Hari did not realize cricket was a science; he thought it was a game.

Then Krishna began to bowl. He bowled overhand, which he said all bowlers did. The red leather ball bounced off the grass a few feet in front of Hari and he tried to block. "Good!" Krishna called. "That's it!" But the more times Hari blocked the ball, the more evil it looked—not like a ball but a spinning red missile meant to crack his shins. Once, it bounced straight up off the bat and narrowly missed his right shoulder. The second time this happened, he dropped the bat and declared, "I do not want to learn cricket."

Krishna approached to scoop up the ball. "You will learn!" he snapped. He towered over Hari and blocked out the sun. Krishna shook his finger and said, "You'll show Merlin and that pompous fool Hodgson you're just as good as them. If not better!"

What cricket had to do with either Merlin or Hodgson, Hari couldn't guess, but he picked up the bat and took his position while Krishna strode away. When Krishna turned and called, "Are we ready?" Hari nodded. He decided to wait a little longer to call Krishna, "Appa."

Soon the leaves began turning from green to yellow and the wind tore them from the trees. Pine cones crunched underfoot. Geese honked and barked while they winged over the grounds. Although Hari had to wait for Krishna to pick him up after work, nearly an hour after class ended, Hari did not mind.

To keep Krishna happy, Hari took his bat to school every day and propped it behind his new raincoat with the ball bulging in a pocket. During break now, Nunn ran outside with a soccer ball for the older boys to kick. Ifthakar-Ali never joined the third and fourth formers. He played tag with the younger boys or watched Hari, who tried to play soccer. One day Hari stopped, looked at Ifthakar-Ali, and walked over to him. They laughed at Christou, who was trying to check Tully. Tully danced around him and even poked Christou's big stomach. "Come and get it," Tully said. "Hey," he cried, "all the Greeks own greasy spoons! Come on, Greasy!" This made Christou so angry he tripped over his own feet. After Hari and Ifthakar-Ali stopped laughing, they turned away from the game and walked toward the low cedars.

"Your father isn't really the Indian High Commissioner, is he?" Ifthakar-Ali asked.

Hari took a chance and shook his head.

"I knew it," Ifthakar-Ali cried. "You say you live on Montreal Road, but that's a low-class French-speaking district." He snapped his fingers. "Let me hold your bat and I won't tell on you."

Hari agreed. Soon he began calling Ifthakar-Ali by his first name, Omar. Hari didn't mind that Omar still called him what everyone else did: HC. They were friends.

Omar became Hari's hero, someone he could trust with his most shameful secrets like not being able to chew the roast beef at lunch. Hari always picked the bologna if any was left. In return Omar swore Hari to secrecy about the number of times Omar's father visited the Governor General. By listening to Krishna and Rukmini chat over supper about border skirmishes, Hari learned Indians and Pakistanis had little in common. But he decided he could like Omar if he wanted. They became like *Totor et Tristan*, the red and blue wooden soldiers in their French textbook and sometimes, when they were alone, Hari even corrected the way Omar pronounced French words. Best of all, though, Omar taught Hari songs about important historical men. Hari wanted to please Krishna, who often spoke about history at supper, but Hari could never think of anything to say. He guessed Krishna might not like the songs, and they became yet another secret.

Each morning at break now, Omar gathered the first and second formers while holding the bat over his shoulder. Omar lined them up, yelled their marching orders, and led them along the gravel driveway. The boys whistled "The Colonel Bogey March" while Hari and Omar sang:

Hitler—had only one left ball,
Goering—had two but very small,
Himmler—had something simmler,
And poor Goebbels had no balls at all.

Sometimes Hari and Omar switched tunes in the middle and left the others to lose their place. Hari's second favourite song became one they sang to a Walt Disney tune:

Whistle while you work,
Hitler is a jerk,
Mussolini bit his weenie,
Now it doesn't work.

By early October, Hari became intrigued by the chill morning air, especially when the leaves turned from orange to red. The trees looked as if they were on fire. The Gatineau Hills were Krishna's favourite Sunday haunt and Hari began his quest for the perfect maple leaf. Soon the *Atlas of the World* bulged with his collection, each new leaf more symmetrical than the last. Hari did not live October; he sensed it. The groundskeeper raked leaves into an oil drum and set them on fire, and the smoke smelled red and crackly. Unraked leaves swished and exploded under laughing boys. One thing, though: the days were shorter here, not like the days at home, and the geese became fewer week by week. And another thing: Hari saw few of the boarders after class. Not only were there old boys and new boys at Woodbine but there were also day boys and boarders. Omar said they flocked to the TV room next to the Tuck Shop. Here they ate Eskimo Pie while watching "Passport to Adventure." The only TV Hari watched was in the mornings, when Mrs. D treated the class to "The Friendly Giant" if the boys sat quietly through "*Chez Hélène*."

Hari always saw Omar off. They ran to find his father's chauffeur waiting in a sleek, black Buick with red licence plates. The CD on the plates stood for *Corps Diplomatiques*, and Omar said it got his father out of paying parking tickets. When Hari told Omar about Sharada's Buick, Omar was not interested and neither was Hari any more. Her car had not been as new as this one, with its electric windows. The first time Omar showed them off, Hari reached through the open window and pushed the silver button forward to raise the glass. He was too entranced by the quiet whine to pull his arm out until the chauffeur called, "High enough!" The edge of the glass was pressed into Hari's armpit. Omar, who sat in front beside the chauffeur, shook his head at Hari before pushing the button back. "See you," Omar said after Hari withdrew his arm.

"See you later," Hari called after the car. "See you!"

Mrs. D taught the class about Thanksgiving. She said it marked the day an explorer named Martin Frobisher gave thanks after finding his way out of the Arctic Ocean in 1578. She also said something about Pilgrims and Mayflowers in 1620. Hari memorized it all, even what he didn't understand. Then, after his first Monday off school, a strange tension settled on the masters of Woodbine and even on Mrs. D. She paraded the class into the junior school annex and into an upstairs auditorium. Here the boys found a red-faced man pacing on the stage while waiting for the auditorium to fill. Once he even stopped to frown at a piano on the side of the stage. He wore the khaki uniform of an army officer and carried a leather stick.

"That's Bully Bullion," Omar whispered to Hari. "He's the junior school housemaster. Three black marks in a monitor's book, and you get that swagger stick across your rump. Sinclair had these blue stripes. You should've seen them!"

"Shh," Nunn ordered. He glared over his shoulder at Omar. Christou, who stood beside Nunn, snickered.

Hari refused to believe Bullion could strike anyone—he looked too much like a gentleman. He didn't so much pace as march with his shoulders tilting from side to side. "Right," he finally said, "I'm to give you a special lesson on survival in case of a nuclear attack." He told them about the bombing of two cities called Hiroshima and Nagasaki. "It was necessary," he said, "so the Bolshies would keep their paws off Japan." Then he explained the measures everyone should take in case of a similar nuclear attack. "Get to a brick building and stay there," he said. "If you can't do that, dig a hole in the ground and cover yourself with whatever's handy. Even a blanket will do. If you don't have time to dig a hole, lie down with your eyes tightly shut—and your mouth, Sinclair—and hands over your ears. Don't forget to pray. Above all, though, hit the dirt!" He slapped his swagger stick into the palm of a gloved hand so hard, Hari winced. "Now we'll have a practice. On your feet."

The boys obeyed. Naismith and Vance elbowed one another. They stopped when Nunn jabbed each of them in the small of the back.

"Remove all metal objects from your pockets," Bullion said, "and take off your glasses."

Hari stood still. Nunn threw a key ring and a Swiss Army knife on the folding, metal chair behind him. Christou stacked five dimes on his chair. Tully also put his glasses on a chair but Mrs. D picked them up and held them safely with her arms crossed in front of her.

"Now," Bullion said, "on my command you will fall to the floor as quickly as possible without hurting yourselves, and you will protect your eyes and ears. One, two—wait for it, Sinclair—three!"

Chairs skidded; the younger boys tittered. Everyone except the masters and Mrs. D struck the floor. Hari closed his eyes and covered his ears. He could hear the bombs whistling while they fell through the air. He could hear explosions and smell the fire. It didn't smell crackly or red, though. He opened his eyes to find himself staring at a pair of black shoes, plump legs, and a grey-flannelled rump. He wondered why one of The Christous wore socks which smelled like a wet dog.

"Not bad, not bad," Bullion shouted. "Let's try it again and less talking this time, girls!"

What girls? Hari still missed the girls from Cluny Convent. He didn't count the young women who served lunch in the dining room. Omar said they kissed any boarder who celebrated a birthday and both of them agreed they were glad to be day boys.

After everyone stood, Hari whispered to Omar, "Christou's feet smell."

Omar softly sang:

> Great green gobs of greasy grimy gopher guts,
> Minuated monkey's meat,
> Spiro Christou's stinky feet,
> All wrapped up in pickled peppered porpoise puke,
> And me without a spoon!

Christou had heard. The second time Bullion yelled, "Hit the dirt!" someone's shoe connected with Omar's head.

Hari heard, "Ow!" He opened his eyes in time to see Omar squeeze tears from his own eyes.

"Much better!" Bullion shouted. "On your feet. Jackets a bit dusty, eh? Well, you won't have time to powder your noses when the dreaded day comes. Don't forget your rabbit's foot, Sinclair. Any questions?"

Christou turned to collect his dimes. He stared at Omar and said, "I've got one. If there's a Canadian and a nigger walking down the street, which one's the doctor?" After Omar shrugged, Christou said, "The one with the black bag."

"Be quiet, Greasy," Nunn said. He told Omar, "Don't listen to him. Everyone knows you're brown, not black."

Boys nearby laughed but Hari turned away. If he hadn't bitten his lip, he would have laughed, too.

An hour after Mrs. D trooped her class back, Bullion appeared in the doorway. Clutching his swagger stick with both hands behind the vent of his khaki jacket, he strolled to the front of the room. He nodded at her and smiled reassuringly at the boys. "In case we ever are involved in a nuclear war," he said, "it would be diplomatic of us to preserve as many of your lives as possible. You, after all, are the sons of ambassadors and statesmen and captains of industry. So, if someone comes to that door and says, 'Red alert!' you will line up in the corridor, move up the stairs in an orderly fashion, and make for the gym. Are there any questions?" There were none. "Right," he barked, "red alert!"

Hari's heart nearly stopped. The boys scrambled through the doorway. Even as they organized themselves into line, Bullion ran ahead toward the stairs. "More order!" he yelled. "Better discipline! You'll fry, the lot of you! Now, up those stairs, men!"

Up they went, hearts racing, shoes pounding, ties flapping. Round the U-turn, up and up, another turn, more stairs and into the gym. Here Bullion herded the boys into a storeroom. It was lined with shelves holding half a dozen balls for every sport played at Woodbine: football, volleyball, basketball, soccer; even two giant ones which Omar called medicine balls. The room filled quickly. Some of the boys rode wooden horses. Others bounced, ready for take-off, on springboards. A few dangled from parallel bars. Naismith, the class clown, lay like a corpse on an empty shelf. He gnawed at the end of a juggling pin. Hari and Omar climbed onto a stack of tumbling mats. Hari looked down just as Bullion swaggered into sight.

"Quiet!" he roared at Vance. Vance had taken an elbow in the ribs. "In this makeshift shelter," Bullion said after Vance fell silent, "you will find refuge from enemy attack. Cuba isn't that far away, men. In the time it takes you to say, 'Uncle Fidel loves Uncle Nikita,' birds will fall from the sky, the trees will turn to ash, your pet doggies will roast. But in here, protected by these thick walls—" He banged on one with a gloved fist. "—you will be safe. Yes, even you, Sinclair. If you move fast enough."

Mrs. D finally appeared. She was puffing, and her face looked nearly as red as Bullion's. She peered about as though she had never been in the gym, then tried to enter the storeroom.

"I'm afraid you can't come in," Bullion told her. He blocked the entrance with his arm. "You're dead, you see."

She raised a hand to her mouth, smiled, and said, "Oh dear."

✻

There were two more such drills during that short week. Then the boys heard nothing about nuclear attack, or Cuba, or Uncle Fidel and Uncle Nikita. Meanwhile Hari began dreading the mid-morning break. Christou kept calling Omar, "Nigger." Omar countered with, "Greasy." To avoid Christou during break, Hari and Omar played French cricket on the lower soccer field, past the junior school annex. It meant a long walk but Hari felt safe here, at the foot of an embankment. On top of the rise, at the edge of the upper soccer field, was a clump of pines Omar called Castle Woodbine. Hari could see why—the pines stood in a ring so close it looked like a blue-green castle—but when he asked why their game was called French cricket, Omar said, "Don't you know anything? Because it's so easy even a Frenchman can play it."

The rules for French cricket were simple. The boy who was up held the bat in front of him instead of to the side, and the bowler tossed the ball underhand instead of overhand. If the batter hit the ball and the bowler or fielder missed catching it, the batter backed up while the bowler followed him. Once the fielder threw the ball to the bowler, he could yell, "Stop!" The batter had to be good at backing up, and the fielder had to be quick. Robbie Brandon, the oldest first former in the class, was not quick but Hari and Omar liked playing with Brandon because he was easy to catch out.

One morning, as usual, Omar started at bat while Hari bowled and Brandon fielded. Omar popped the first ball over Hari's shoulder toward Brandon. The ball bounced and rolled between his feet. While Omar backed away and Hari followed him, Hari shouted, "Quick!" At last Brandon reached the ball and threw it to Hari, who caught it and yelled, "Stop!" Omar had backed five paces more than Hari had covered. Now the ball would be more difficult to field because Omar would have more time to gauge its delivery. The second time Hari bowled, Omar nicked the ball with the edge of the bat. Lunging, Hari scooped his fingers through blades of damp grass and snatched up the ball. "Stop!" he shouted.

"I want a turn!" Brandon whined.

But when Hari swung his arm back for another bowl, Omar looked over his shoulder at Castle Woodbine. He dropped the bat and threw himself at the foot of the embankment. He waved for Hari to join him, and Hari dropped the ball. Brandon gathered the ball and then the bat and ran in the opposite direction. Hari didn't care. This promised to be even more fun than French cricket. The embankment was steeper than the one outside their classroom. Hari and Omar clutched tufts of grass and pretended they were pulling themselves hand over hand up a steep cliff.

Omar stopped and peered at Castle Woodbine through imaginary binoculars. "When we get to the top," he whispered in Hari's ear, "you take care of the sentries and I'll spike the guns."

"What guns?" Hari whispered back.

"The Guns of Navarone," Omar said. He placed a finger on his lips, then continued pulling himself up.

It took ages to reach the base of the castle. Here, keeping a sharp eye out for sentries, Hari looked past the lowest branches of a pine. What he saw nearly made him laugh.

Christou knelt just beyond the pine. The heels of his shoes dug into his rump and he was looking up at another boy, who was standing. This boy unzipped his fly, pulled out his penis and snaked it this way and that. He pulled at his penis and tried to make it longer. "Come on, Christou, lick it," the other boy said. He sounded like Nunn.

Now Hari felt as though he were doing something wrong. He clutched Omar's sleeve and whispered, "He'll report us."

Christou turned and cried, "Hey!" He crawled out of the pines and grabbed Omar's collar even as Nunn tucked his penis out of sight. "Sneak," Christou snarled at Omar. "You get in here!" He punched Omar's shoulder until he meekly crawled between two grey trunks into the castle.

Hari followed. He had no choice. He couldn't let Omar fall alone into enemy hands. Hari tried to ignore the grass staining his flannel trousers and the needles pricking his palms. He stopped when his shin came down on a large pine cone. The air in the castle was cool, and it smelled green.

Christou snarled, "What'd you see?" He kept shaking Omar and even pulled his hair.

"Nothing!" Omar cried but this infuriated Christou.

Hari knew the game was over. There were no Guns of Navarone here; only his best friend being bullied. Hari finally said, "We saw Nunn's—" and stopped. He had no idea what to call it.

"It's a dink, you dink," Nunn said. He zipped his fly shut. "It's bigger than yours because I'm bigger than you and Ali. I'm nine, and I'll be able to make it go hard as a rock soon, just like my brother."

Hari puzzled over this. He didn't want to sound like a new boy by asking too many questions.

"So what're you going to tell Mrs. D?" Christou asked. He squinted at Omar, who said nothing. Christou punched him again, this time on the thigh, and Omar winced.

"No carrying tales," Hari said.

Nunn dropped to his knees next to Omar and nodded as if to say, "You heard him."

Christou grinned at Nunn. "I've never seen black dinks before," Christou said.

Nunn's blue eyes narrowed when he laughed. "Pull them out," he ordered.

Hari had no idea why either Christou or Nunn should be so fascinated by anyone's penis though he still wasn't sure what to call it. Dink sounded rude. Afraid to shift his weight too quickly, he rocked from side to side to dislodge the pine cone.

Omar shook his head first.

"You hold him," Christou told Nunn, and Nunn twisted Omar's arm behind his back. "Come on, Nigger," Christou taunted. His pudgy hand fumbled at Omar's fly, then disappeared inside. "Show us your weenie. Show us your dink." Christou groped until Omar's face darkened with shame. Then Christou pulled out Omar's penis.

Nunn stared down. So did Hari. "I thought only Canadians were circumcised," Nunn said.

In front of Omar's open fly a purplish head poked from a tight, brown ring. The colours alone made Omar's penis more interesting than Nunn's. His had been a pinkish shade of beige. When Christou tilted his palm first right, then left, Hari saw under Omar's penis. His scrotum—what Christou called a bag—was shrivelled and brown like a walnut, a soft walnut.

Christou yanked downward and Omar yelped. "Is that all?" Christou asked. "That's not a dink, Nigger. That's a worm." Dink, weenie or worm—Hari also wanted to touch it. He thought he heard wrong when Christou said, "Your turn, HC."

With his jaw quivering, Omar faced Hari. "Don't let them," Omar said. He began to cry.

"Let him go!" Hari yelled. He launched himself at Christou. Hari's head struck Christou's chin. They rolled onto the knotty roots of a pine with Hari still on top of Christou. Hari's head stung. When Christou cried out, Hari rolled off him, but before he could scramble out of reach Christou climbed onto his chest. Christou began pummelling Hari. It never occurred to Hari to cry out and gain the upper hand the way Christou had. Amazed that boys actually hit one another, Hari tried to arch his back but Christou was too heavy to throw off. Then a punch landed on Hari's windpipe and paralyzed his throat. Gasping, he clawed up needles and chips of bark. He had to fight back, yet how could he strike one of his betters? Besides, he had to regain his breath first. He lay still and scrabbled in the dirt for relief. Christou turned to slapping. The blue-green branches swallowed the first *crack*. Turning his head to avoid a second slap, Hari scraped his right cheek on a twig. He shrieked. His cheek felt wet. He could breathe again, and the smell of blood replaced the pungent smell of pine. When he saw Omar staring down at him in horror, Hari finally began to cry. Not because his cheek hurt but because he had lost the fight.

"That's enough," Nunn ordered. "You're killing him."

Omar broke free and stumbled out of the castle. Branches swished and snapped. He sounded like an animal breaking from cover, like a rabbit Naismith once frightened near the fence during a soccer game. Hunched over and trying to do up his fly, Omar managed only three steps before he skidded on dry leaves. He stumbled to his feet and ran—not toward the junior school but even farther, into the back of the senior school.

Christou rose. He brushed pine needles and dirt from his hands. "You tell," he threatened, "and I will kill you next time."

Hari jerked his head from side to side. He waited until Christou and Nunn left. They were talking with their heads close and all Hari heard was, "Mrs. D." Then he crawled out, ran into the junior school annex and shouldered the washroom door open. First he washed his face. Then he bent over the water fountain to let the water chill what turned out to be a scrape. The paper towels were rough so he pulled out his shirt tails and dried his face with them. He stared at the ceramic water fountain with its silver knob. "I hate them," he mouthed, meaning Christou and Nunn. "I hate all of them," he repeated.

The first time Hari drank from the water fountain, two boys from the fifth form had been in the washroom. They were standing at the urinals. Hari let the water fall into his palm and drank from it so his lips wouldn't touch the spout. The boys snickered and Hari looked up. He watched them step away from the urinals while zipping up their flies. They stood at sinks and combed their hair without washing their hands first. Hari didn't understand. How could such unclean boys make fun of him? More tears came to his eyes now. He hated them all: Christou and Nunn, who were supposed to set good examples for new boys; Bullion, who swaggered in his uniform and bullied Sinclair for every little thing; even Sinclair, who limped about on Friday mornings and offered to show the stripes from his caning. They were all *goondas*—hoodlums and thugs—and Sinclair was an idiot. Rukmini said Canada would be a wonderful place to live.

Hari returned to class. Mrs. D was reading, *"Totor et Tristan rentrent chez eux."* Keeping the right side of his face turned away, he slipped into his seat. She looked up at him and frowned. Then she continued with, "'*Qui a bu mon vin?' demande Totor. 'Qui a bu ton vin!' crie Tristan. 'Qui a brisé ma chaise?'*"

The last lesson of the morning was penmanship, and the class copied sentences Mrs. D wrote on the board. No matter how many times Hari tried, he couldn't catch Omar's gaze when Omar turned to lend his two-coloured eraser to Vance. When the class lined up for lunch, Omar asked permission to see the nurse. During lunch Mrs. D asked Hari whether he would also like to see the nurse but he brushed at the scrape on his cheek and mumbled, "No, thank you." He forced himself to swallow the shepherd's pie. The meat was burnt, the corn overdone and the mashed potato greasy. Omar remained absent during games period, which the class spent playing soccer. Afterward, Mrs. D said Omar had gone home ill. The next morning she announced he wouldn't be returning to Woodbine. She looked at Hari and asked, "Do you know anything about this?" Trying to ignore Christou and Nunn, Hari shook his head. They were watching him closely.

With classes finished for the day, Hari found himself with no one to see off. He kicked at the gravel and tried to sing to himself. It did no good. Even if he were punished for carrying tales, he had to tell Mrs. D what had happened to Omar. Hari returned to the room. Her tweed coat still hung in the closet at the back. He took off his own coat and cap and sat down to wait. Most of all, he wanted to tell Rukmini they should go home—back to Cluny Convent, back to where boys and girls ran barefoot and didn't have to dress up for play; back to teachers like Mrs. Kamala-Bai, who played the piano in his first standard class. Mrs. D never played her dusty, old piano.

Not caring whether he broke any rules, Hari went to the piano and pushed back the hinged cover. The white keys looked like smiling teeth, like silver bells and cockle shells and pretty maids all in a row. He ignored the black keys because they looked like gaps in the teeth. One of the white keys, in the middle, had a red dot. When he pressed it with his index finger, his little finger hit the third key to the right. The piano vibrated. He pressed both keys together and the sound lingered in the room like incense. He heard Mrs. Kamala-Bai sing a nursery rhyme which began with the sound from this other key:

> Lavender blue, dilly, dilly, lavender green,
> When I am king, dilly, dilly, you will be queen.

He didn't care if anyone heard him now. He shuffled to the right and pressed each white key in order. The sounds became higher pitched until the last few were like parakeets twittering in trees. Still on the right, he reached with his left hand to press each black key. He returned to the red dot and shuffled to the left. The keys at this end sounded like churchbells which rang along Montreal Road on Sunday mornings. He laughed then because he knew every one of these sounds by heart. He also knew only seven separate sounds came from the white keys and five came from the black. The sounds repeated themselves up and down the keyboard. This was so much easier than learning all the rules. This was magic. He climbed onto the stool and dangled his right hand above the keys. Listening to his memory of Mrs. Kamala-Bai, he played:

"Well," a voice declared, "aren't you the bold one?"

He turned to see Mrs. D standing in the doorway. "I'm sorry, Mrs. Dalgleish," he said. "I didn't mean to touch the piano. I only—"

"Touched the piano," she finished.

"I'm terribly sorry, Mrs. Dalgleish." He liked repeating her name, it sounded so musical.

"Mr. Chandra," she said after entering, "I'd feel sorrier for whomever taught you to play like that."

"No one taught me to play," he said.

"You play by ear then?" she asked.

He smiled at the thought of her tinkling the keys with the hairs growing from her ears.

"Well," she said, "there's obviously something wrong with your ear. You play like Winnie the Pooh thump-thump-thumping down the stairs behind Christopher Robin. You seem to know the difference between quarter notes and eighth notes but don't you know about rhythm and phrasing?"

"Notes," he whispered. The sounds were called notes.

Mrs. D moved behind him. She reached over his shoulder with her right hand to play the line he had tried. Her fingers were gnarled and her hand was spotted, but it moved so lightly her fingertips bounced off the keys. The notes danced in the room. "Do you see?" she asked. "You don't just press the keys in a certain order. You play them. Now, try that again."

This time Hari thought of girls dancing in a field with jasmine in their black braids. He thought of girls playing ring around the rosey, a pocket full of posies, husha, husha . . . His fingers also danced. The notes grew louder and softer, rose and fell. They touched the pulse at his temple; they tickled his chin.

"Much better," she said. "Move aside for a bit."

He slid off the stool to stand at one end of the piano.

Mrs. D had to move the stool back from the keyboard before she could sit down. "The next thing we do is add some simple chords with the left hand," she explained. Using what she called thirds, she accompanied the treble of her right hand with the bass of her left. The song reached an even greater height. "This," she said, tilting her right hand up so she looked like a queen, "is the soloist. These," she said, wiggling the fingers of her left hand, "are the chorus. The soloist plays the melody. Usually. The chorus gives depth. Do you understand that, Chandra?"

Yes, he did. She spoke a language he understood.

"Let's have a real lesson," she said. "You sit down again."

An hour later, Hari was still at the piano making friends with Do-Ducky, Re-Racoon, and Mi-Mouse. They lived in a world so much friendlier than the real one—a warm world with long days, not like these darkening ones which chased away geese; a world in which strangers were made to feel welcome, not like new boys who had to prove they weren't rotten eggs; a world in which practising meant more than blocking the first fifty bowls.

Then Krishna entered the room. Do-Ducky, Re-Racoon, and Mi-Mouse fled. Krishna apologized to Mrs. D for Hari's having inconvenienced her. She insisted she had enjoyed herself. She even suggested Hari could spend his time after class more profitably by taking lessons.

"I see." Krishna stared at her. The last thing he said before leading Hari from the room was, "Where are your manners. Did you say thanks to Mrs. Dalgleish?"

"Thank you, Mrs. D," Hari said.

"It was my pleasure, I can assure you." She looked happier than Hari had ever seen her. While he pulled on his coat and cap in the corridor, he heard her sit down again. She began playing a tune he didn't recognize, and she began to sing. Her voice sounded rusty and Krishna looked embarrassed but Hari thought it was wonderful. She sang:

Alas my love you do me wrong
To cast me off discourteously;
And I have loved you so long,
Delighting in your company.

✱

"You are late," Rukmini said when Krishna and Hari entered the apartment. She had already made coffee and Ovaltine and they were growing cold.

"I had to go looking for the boy," Krishna explained. "He was playing with a piano."

"Mrs. D gave me a lesson," Hari told Rukmini. When she poured his Ovaltine into a pot to reheat, he went to his room to change.

Krishna said the school uniform was for wearing only outside the house. Inside, Hari should wear different clothes so he wouldn't spread outside dirt in the apartment. He heard Krishna say:

"This Mrs. Dalgleish wants him to study the piano!"

Hari hoped Rukmini would agree, but she wasn't thinking about piano lessons. She placed an envelope on the dining table. The envelope bore Woodbine's crest, the red and yellow maple leaf. Inside was Hari's mid-term report card. "This came in the mail today," she said. "It was addressed to you but I opened it since it was from the school."

Krishna looked at Hari's marks while sipping the lukewarm coffee. Hari was at the top of the second form; he was a quick learner, the comments said. They were written by Mrs. D, whose signature appeared at the bottom. Under it, Hodgson had added his own signature as assistant headmaster. Krishna didn't understand why Rukmini looked upset unless it was because she disliked Hodgson more than Krishna did. But no, it was not this.

"*Yenraja*," she said, "look more closely."

Krishna did and saw that Hari's lowest mark was in games. Next to the mark, the games master had written, "Tries hard." Krishna snorted. In his day *tries hard* was the euphemism applied to boys who were chosen last for casual games. In soccer, such boys were always substitutes; in cricket, they played near the boundary, never at the wicket or in the gully. "Don't they get individual attention at a school like this?" he asked. "I'll give him soccer lessons but they'll have to wait till the weekend. The light fails so quickly now—"

"Look!" Rukmini said, stabbing her finger at the top of the form. After "Name of Pupil," Mrs. D had written, "G. Harris Chandra." Rukmini called, "Babu," and he came from his room. "What happened to my Harischandra?"

He knelt on a chair to look at the report card. He had never seen one before this and he grinned at his high marks. When Rukmini asked about his name he said, "Mrs. D changed it." He didn't describe how this had happened because Krishna was glowering at his coffee. Hari knew when Krishna was in a bad mood and at such times Hari said very little.

"This is the same woman who thinks she can teach piano?" Krishna asked Rukmini. "Wouldn't he be better off spending the extra time practising—"

"We should phone Mr. Merlin and have this corrected," Rukmini said. She poured Hari's Ovaltine back into a mug and he sat down to enjoy it.

"Why bother a headmaster about such a little thing?" Krishna asked. "Many people have their names shortened when they come over. If it helps him fit in better—"

"I will phone then," Rukmini declared.

"Ask whether the games master can't give more attention," Krishna suggested.

"I like playing the piano," Hari said.

The next morning, Rukmini phoned Woodbine and left a message for Mrs. D, who phoned back during games period. Rukmini was prepared to dislike her, but Mrs. D spoke openly of the limitations of even private schools. They chatted for some time, mainly about Hari's need for proper piano lessons and regular practice. It was Rukmini's longest conversation with another woman in two months. When Mrs. D finally said, "Now, about his name?" Rukmini told her:

"It is nothing. I am sorry to have troubled you. He is the same boy, after all." Rukmini decided that whatever damage Mrs. D may have done by changing Hari's name, she would more than make up for it with her piano. After Rukmini hung up, she wondered. No, he was not the same boy she had brought over. He could never be the same. But he was still too distant toward Krishna and she could do no more to bring father and son closer. Only the school could, she thought. It would do this by teaching Hari something he couldn't learn from her. It would teach him to be a man.

# Chapter 10

## *Halloween, Holloween*

During one of her weekday afternoon walks, Rukmini visited the Loblaw's supermarket. Without Krishna consulting the grocery list and comparing prices while she pushed the cart, she felt aimless. She walked up and down the aisles and examined products they never bought: Pure Spring ginger ale, Gagnon chocolates, Maple Leaf sausages and, in the specialty section, Canada grade A maple syrup. Then she noticed products which offered free gifts: Red Rose tea with ceramic figurines of birds; Shirrif pudding mix with plastic medallions of hockey players; Sun-Up juice powder with Vikings and Roman soldiers in the plastic bubble over the lid. Hari would have liked any and all of these, but she shook off her regret over not being able to afford them. She kept wandering until a jar of peaches caught her eye. The child on the label looked like Hari at one but lighter skinned. Those were our happiest days, she thought: when we were all together and making plans for an even better life. She calculated she had enough to buy the peaches. It would be her first surprise for Hari since coming to Canada. Besides, if she at least bought something she would feel the day hadn't been wasted.

When a man wearing a stiff apron approached to straighten boxes on the shelves, she held up the jar and asked, "Must this be refrigerated? Can I send it to school with my son for a treat?"

The man pretended not to notice her sari. "*Madame*?" he asked; then: "If your son is so old that he can attend the school, he is too old for this. It is for the babies."

"Of course," she said. Turning away so he wouldn't see her blush, she put the jar on the shelf and reached for a bottle of Johnson's baby oil. Hari had never been as chubby as the child on the label, but she liked the smile.

"*Étrangers!*" she heard the man exclaim. She watched him until he pushed open a swinging door in the back.

"Don't mind him," a voice said.

Rukmini nearly dropped the bottle. Clutching it, she turned to find a woman smiling at her from behind a fully loaded cart. She was the tallest woman Rukmini had ever seen, nearly as tall as Krishna. Curlers cinched her blue-grey hair under a lilac scarf. Lilac slacks narrowed down to burgundy pumps. Her sweater was mauve.

Rukmini glanced at the sign above the aisle and said, "I assumed baby food was meant for children only, as opposed to for adults." Embarrassed, she returned the oil to the shelf.

"That's okay," the woman said. "You just moved into our building, right? I've seen you around."

"Eight weeks ago," Rukmini said. She wanted to say, "The longest eight weeks of my life." She wanted to say, "The two of them go off in the morning and do not come back until five. How long can I read?" Instead she asked, "Do you always use the stairs? We have not met in the lift."

"Can't stand the gravity," the woman said. "I'm in one-oh-five. Drop in sometime."

Rukmini frowned skeptically.

"I never win the TV bingo," the woman said. "Not when it counts. See you."

Rukmini felt relieved once the woman wheeled her cart away. At least she had been friendly, perhaps too much so, but she sounded just like the few Canadians Rukmini had encountered since arriving in Ottawa. They took so much for granted. The Americans she had met during her graduate school days had been nothing like this, but then she had rarely ventured off campus. No one wore curlers to class; no one spoke of TV bingo. She went back to the candy section and picked out the smallest box of chocolates.

While waiting at a till, she learned something new: the supermarket not only accepted personal cheques but it also delivered large orders. Krishna always paid cash. Often he would rush to the bank during his lunch hour if they were shopping for groceries the following Saturday. And they always made two trips up the elevator with their arms laden with paper bags. There was so much he hadn't told her about simple things like shopping that she wondered whether he knew them himself.

After supper she washed the dishes while he read a biography of Horatio Nelson. Hari played with his Van de Graaff. He cranked it so the wide black band rubbed against the copper brushes and carried charges up to the chromed sphere. Then he picked up his doorbell. Krishna had made it from a Styrofoam ball on a string taped to a pie plate. When Hari moved the plate close to the sphere, a spark snapped across the gap. It pulled the ball toward the sphere and, when the ball swung back, it struck the plate with a tinny gong. He cranked the generator again and held his head close. Rukmini smiled when the static pulled at a tuft of his curly hair. She watched him put the model away at the far end of the sofa, behind the front leg, and look about. There were no other toys in the apartment. There was also little else besides the furniture and clothes, the books and records. She wondered whether this was why Krishna never invited guests, but then he never spoke of friends. He only spoke about his assistant and then only if the man had made a mistake.

Someone knocked.

Rukmini wiped her hands on a dishcloth and glanced at Krishna. He looked at her as if to say, "We don't need anything." Only salesmen knocked on their door. She opened it to find the tall woman standing behind a girl. Rukmini opened the door fully and looked back at Krishna before remembering she didn't need permission to let anyone in.

"Sorry to bother you," the woman said. "One-oh-five, remember?" She no longer wore the curlers or the scarf. Her hair was done in a beehive, which looked more fashionable on younger women. She still wore the mauve sweater and lilac slacks, and Rukmini decided Canadians didn't bother with outside clothes and inside clothes.

"Please, come in," Rukmini insisted.

"Let's go," the woman told the girl. "He won't bite."

Rukmini closed the door and gestured toward the dining table. She wished it were made of real wood and not from pressed board covered with Formica. She sat down but the woman and the girl remained standing. Both of them seemed to be examining the apartment. Rukmini suppressed an urge to stand again for their benefit. The small of her back ached from bending over the sink.

Hari was lying at Krishna's feet. He sat up when the girl's eye caught his. He kept looking at her but she looked away at the blank wall. She had golden hair.

The woman pulled two chairs out from the table, and she and the girl sat with Rukmini. "I'm Mrs. Gardner," the woman said. She sounded apologetic for having looked about for so long. "This is my granddaughter, Althea. One of them, that is." Mrs. Gardner brushed the stones on her family rings. "This one's for Al, Opal for October. She just turned nine."

Rukmini introduced Krishna and herself. "This is our son Harischandra," she said, "but children at school call him HC."

"Sounds like a juice," Mrs. Gardner said. Then she looked aghast but Rukmini smiled reassuringly. "How about if we call him Hari?" Mrs. Gardner asked Althea.

The girl shrugged.

"Turn the radio down, Boy," Krishna said.

Mrs. Gardner called into the living room, "I can hear okay."

"Hari will be fine," Rukmini said.

She watched him rise to his knees and do as he was told. At the best of times, Krishna kept the volume so low that Rukmini could barely hear the slow second movements of the symphonies, or the slow middle movements of the concertos. She was still trying to develop a taste for western classical music. Krishna never said so, but she knew he appreciated her interest.

"Hari goes to Woodbine, doesn't he?" Mrs. Gardner asked Krishna. "I've seen you coming and going, but doesn't he like playing outside?"

"There's no park nearby," Krishna said. "Just the lawn."

"There's still the parking lot," she reminded him.

"The boy might scratch a car," Krishna said. He could not imagine why Mrs. Gardner was so concerned about Hari.

She frowned at Krishna, then at Rukmini.

Rukmini, in turn, wondered why he could never bring himself to use Hari's name. She didn't expect him to use Babu, but even Harish would sound more affectionate than Boy.

"Well, it's playing we dropped in about," Mrs. Gardner announced. "Hope I'm not intruding?"

"Not at all," Rukmini insisted. "Can I get you some coffee? It is instant only."

"You sit still," Mrs. Gardner said. "We just ate. That's a lovely outfit. Is it silk?"

"Cotton," Rukmini said, "for housework and when it is hot. Nylon here is for going out and silk is for special occasions." She brushed at a wet spot, which had darkened the moss green of the cotton to a bottle green.

"I've always wanted to learn how to wear one," Mrs. Gardner said. "I've seen them on women downtown. They're just so gorgeous."

"I can teach you when you have time." Rukmini said this half-heartedly. She had already begun wondering whether she should stop wearing saris in public. They were impractical in this country but, more than this, she was tired of having to explain them to curious women. She couldn't imagine why they thought saris were twelve yards long and only made of silk, or that some of them were so stiff with embroidery they could stand by themselves like a glistening fence.

When Mrs. Gardner waved her hand, the kitchen light twinkled off her rings. "Oh, but where would I wear it?" she asked. "It's been years since I went to a Halloween party!" She looked at Krishna. "If I'm intruding, just let me know."

"Not at all," he said and reluctantly put down his book. He had reached a telling passage: Nelson, advised by his officers that the fleet was being signalled to break off its engagement, raised his telescope to his blind eye and claimed he saw no such thing. "Halloween is a popular celebration here," Krishna told Hari.

Hari liked the sound of the word. Not the way Mrs. Gardner said it; not *Halloween*. Mrs. D pronounced it *Holloween* and so did Krishna. Hari savoured the sound: *Hollow-een*.

"It is a Christian custom," Rukmini told him. "You know what customs are. Remember how on your birthday you gave out biscuits each year at Cluny Convent?"

Hari frowned before nodding.

"Actually," Mrs. Gardner said, "it's a custom held over from before Christ came to earth."

Rukmini could see Hari was confused. "Remember I told you once Lord Vishnu came to earth as Lord Venkateswara?" she asked. He neither nodded nor shook his head. Since arriving in Canada, he had rarely asked about anything they had done or anyone they had known in India. She wondered whether he had forgotten his life there completely; whether, in trying to please Krishna by acting Canadian, Hari had erased India itself from his mind. Only the week before, he told her, "Amma, last night I dreamt my father turned into an old man and he had ink spilled on the back of his neck." She said, "This was your *ajja*, his birthmark. He lived all the way out in Jayanagar, and we were the only relations he visited." Then, yesterday, Hari told her he had dreamt of gold and silver bubbles falling from clouds onto coconut palms. She kissed him and said, "Such nice dreams you have."

Mrs. Gardner said, "Al's staying with me because her parents— Well, her mom's my youngest girl, and she and her husband are— He's looking for work again, in the mines up north around Timmins."

Krishna shifted on the sofa. He didn't know whether to feel embarrassed for Mrs. Gardner because of her family problems, or because she was revealing them to perfect strangers.

"Anyway," she continued, "Al doesn't know any kids in this building. I figured Hari doesn't either, so I thought they might trick-or-treat together."

Even as Rukmini nodded, Krishna asked, "Alone?"

"It's quite safe," Mrs. Gardner replied. "They're not old enough to get into trouble." She smiled at Rukmini as though the two women understood something Krishna did not: that even children as young as Hari and Althea could develop attachments which went beyond friendship.

Rukmini smiled back, though she preferred not to think about such things. There would be plenty of time for them later.

"Don't let any bigger boys frighten you," Krishna told Hari. "Bullies are cowards at heart."

Hari said nothing. He heard the same thing often at school but he didn't believe it. If bigger boys were not bigger, they would not be so frightening.

"There's not much chance of that," Mrs. Gardner said. "The super won't let neighbourhood kids in the building. Besides, Al can hold her own. Can't you, sweetie?"

"But what costume can Babu wear?" Rukmini asked Mrs. Gardner. "Hari, I mean."

"He can have his pick," Mrs. Gardner said. "I've got a boxful, one of those old Chautauqua trunks. My kids used to love dressing up to put on plays and stuff. Never threw any of it out. What would you like to be?" she asked Hari.

"Anything?" he asked.

"I'm going as a pirate," Althea declared, "and there's only one black patch."

"Sweetie!" Mrs. Gardner exclaimed.

"A clown?" Hari said. He sat on his heels to rock back and forth. "With a red nose?" When she nodded, he yelled, "Hurray!"

"Boy," Krishna warned, "the neighbours."

"Oh, you can't hear anything through these walls," Mrs. Gardner said. "Besides, it doesn't hurt to make a little noise now and then."

"True," Krishna said, "but we're still guests here." His laugh sounded forced. Too many people still looked away when they noticed him, but he wasn't about to give anyone an excuse to suggest he "go back where he came from." He had seen this happen more than once in New York cafés when Indians talked heatedly among themselves. "Once we get our citizenship papers," he said, "the boy can make all the noise he wants."

Rukmini saw Hari frown at Krishna as though not quite believing him.

"Are we set then?" Mrs. Gardner asked Rukmini.

Hari kept nodding, and Rukmini pleaded silently with Krishna. At the same time, it occurred to her that she was not the one who needed his permission. It was Hari, and she couldn't keep interceding for him. Sooner or later, he would have to get what he wanted by asking for it.

At last Krishna shrugged and said, "Why not?" He picked up his book and searched for his place.

"Okay, Al?" Mrs. Gardner asked.

Rukmini looked at the girl. She perched on the edge of her chair as though eager to leave. There was more than apathy in her shrug, though. It was a way of hiding pleasure Krishna could never detect in a woman or a child. This girl is a godsend, Rukmini thought.

"Well, Halloween's coming up fast," Mrs. Gardner said. "Let's get started. Why don't you come down right now, and we'll find you a clown suit that fits? There's all colours, you know. Even some masks."

"Amma," Hari asked, "can I wear my soldier's uniform instead? Can I wear the red coat and black trousers and carry my golden sword? You should see it!" he told Krishna. "Amma made it for me."

The question took Rukmini aback—he had not forgotten everything, after all—but she shook her head. She went to him and helped him rise. "You know I told you we sent it by ship," she said. "It sank in a battle." She led him to Mrs. Gardner and told her, "This is very kind of you."

"It'll be good for both of them," she said.

"Race you to the elevator," Althea cried.

Hari followed her out. By trying to be quiet, he lost the race.

After Rukmini closed the door behind Mrs. Gardner, Krishna asked, "What about ships sunk in battle?"

Rukmini laughed. "It is a trick I played," she said. "When we went to board the plane at Bombay Airport, I found our luggage was overweight and could not afford to pay the added charges. I repacked and gave one entire suitcase to my Bombay Uncle. It contained most of Babu's toys. He used to ask about them, and his uniform, but not so much any more. I told him finally Bombay Uncle sent the suitcase by ship but a Pakistani submarine torpedoed it." She laughed again, not so much at her own cleverness as over how easy it was to reassure a child.

Krishna didn't see it this way, neither as cleverness nor reassurance. He asked, "Don't you think you protect him too much? He has to grow up sometime."

Rukmini returned to the sink. "Yes, sometime," she said. "Not yet. He is still a child." When Krishna began to say something else, she cut him off by opening the tap. Water splashed on her sari. Closing the tap halfway, she realized she could no longer hear the radio. He had forgotten to turn it up.

*

Hari's first impression of Mrs. Gardner's apartment was of its clutter: in the kitchen there was not only a toaster but also a blender and egg beater; in the dining room a solid wooden table; in the living room wall-to-wall carpeting, a bulky sofa, step tables, a recliner, a cabinet hi-fi, a TV set with rabbit ears, hanging baskets of ferns, dozens of family photos, and ashtrays from

Jasper and Banff. There was barely room to move, yet in the midst of all this a wardrobe trunk spilled costumes onto the floor. Then he discovered Mrs. Gardner's books. They weren't biographies or texts like his parents' books. These were real children's books, a kind he had never seen before: adventure comics. He read them while Althea gathered the parts of her pirate costume. He liked the advertisements even more than the stories, advertisements for wonderful things like sea monkeys and X-ray glasses. Next time, he decided, he would bring his Van de Graaff downstairs. He could show Althea how to charge it and even make her a doorbell from a pie plate.

Mrs. Gardner had changed from her burgundy pumps into violet mules. He watched her sit back in the recliner with her feet up. "You can borrow some comics if you like," she said.

Fascinated by her ritual of lighting a narrow cigar, he said nothing. He watched her blow a stream of smoke, blue-grey like her hair. The smoke smelled of cherries. At last he said, "My father would not like me to."

She waved her ringed fingers through the smoke. "Doesn't seem there's much he'll let you do, is there?" she asked.

Hari was not so sure about this. Rukmini had told Krishna Mrs. D wouldn't charge for the first term's piano lessons, and Krishna had relented. During the past week, Hari had divided his time after class between learning new pieces and practising. Mrs. D reminded him when it was time to go because she didn't want him to keep Krishna waiting. Neither did Hari, but he always closed the keyboard cover with regret. He had already mastered a piece called "The Skater's Waltz" and was now learning a song, "*Clair de Lune.*" It was about *mon ami Pierrot*.

Althea appeared from the kitchen with a pumpkin. "Time to carve the jack-o'-lantern," she announced. "You hold it." She placed the pumpkin in Hari's lap and returned to the kitchen. Utensils rattled when she pulled open a drawer.

"No carving in the living room," Mrs. Gardner called.

Hari circled the pumpkin with his arms and marvelled at its weight. Full; it was full. In his art class, boys cut a jack-o'-lantern from orange paper, then pasted on black eyes, a nose and a mouth. Now the cut-outs felt as empty as his apartment. While he carried the pumpkin to the dining table, he began suspecting apartments were also meant to be full. In such places, voices did not echo; they lingered like smoke. At school Halloween was orange and black: orange for broomsticks, black for witches, orange for blazing eyes, black for cats. But when he fell asleep that night, Halloween became the orange and blue of his clown suit. It became not "*Danse Macabre*" or "Night on Bald Mountain," which seeped from Krishna's radio and smelled plastic, but "Mona Lisa" and "Rambling Rose," which spouted from Mrs. Gardner's hi-fi to mingle with the cherry smoke.

✷

On Halloween night, Rukmini took Hari downstairs after supper. They left Krishna alone with his book. The woman who opened the door of 105 cackled like a witch, startling Rukmini and Hari, but she was dressed like a fairy godmother. It was Mrs. Gardner. She wore a long nose complete with warts and every second tooth was black. A mauve sash crossed her lilac evening gown, and the rhinestones of a tiara sparkled on her beehive. When she swirled a glass of amber liquid next to her ear, the ice cubes tinkled. "Come in, my pretties," she said. "The fearsome Captain Al's in the poopdeck."

Hari laughed when the toilet flushed. Then Mrs. Gardner zipped him into his baggy clown suit. The jack-o-lantern flickered on a window sill.

"Har-de-har, matey!" Althea shouted. She appeared with a flourish and bowed to the applause. Her hair had been tucked under a red kerchief, a gold ring dangled from her left ear, and a scar snaked across her right cheek. Greasepaint made her look sun browned.

"Try these on for size," Mrs. Gardner told Hari. She waved long, black shoes. "Found them in our locker today. You can stuff them with newspaper to make them fit."

When Hari finished doing this, he slipped the black shoes over his running shoes. Rukmini tied the laces behind his ankles so he wouldn't trip. Last came the perfect touch, a rubber mask. It covered his head and arched across his eyebrows. What did it matter it was so large that the red nose flopped in front of his grin? It was a real clown mask. Over it Rukmini pulled a wig made from shaggy violet carpeting. Forced by the shoes to waddle, he let Althea lead him into the bathroom. He laughed harder than Rukmini had heard him laugh since they had left India. This was how children should laugh, she thought: not in triumph over a skillful catch or a fine hit but for nonsense, because only nonsense could keep a person sane in a strange land. She rose from the floor and sank onto the sofa.

Mrs. Gardner handed each of the children a Loblaw's shopping bag. From his, Hari pulled an empty, pint-sized milk carton.

"For Unicef," Althea explained. "I brought it from school. People put in pennies for starving kids in Africa. I'll take it back and get you a ticket for the circus."

"And I'll take both of them when the Shriners come to town," Mrs. Gardner said.

"Is all this not splendid?" Rukmini asked him.

"I like it even more than birthdays," he said. He nodded, then laughed at the red nose hitting his lips. He nodded and laughed again.

"Hold still now," Mrs. Gardner said, "and stand close. Aren't you getting in the picture?" she asked Rukmini. "That's such a nice outfit, too. Better take those glasses off, though."

Rukmini stood behind Hari. She put a hand on Althea's shoulder and Althea smiled up at her. The camera pushed Mrs. Gardner's false nose in front of her lips. Before Rukmini could adjust her sari, a blue light robbed her of vision. The room flashed into a haze of orange dots. When the children scrambled for the door, Mrs. Gardner called, "Take something to start you off."

Althea grabbed tiny boxes of Sun Maid raisins from a plastic jack-o'-lantern. Hari followed her out while practising, "Trick or treat!"

Mrs. Gardner pulled off her witch's nose and collapsed into the reclining chair.

"It is so kind of you," Rukmini told her.

"Imagine getting six kids ready!" Mrs. Gardner said. She picked up her drink. "Course, I had Lawrence—Mr. Gardner—then."

Rukmini shook her head at the glass tipped in her direction. "I should be returning upstairs to wash the dishes," she said.

"There's more than one kind of gravity can wear a person down," Mrs. Gardner suggested. She reached for one of her little cigars and took her time lighting it. "I asked Hari what you give him. Rice every night gets boring. Try baked potatoes or noodles."

Rukmini stared at her *chappals*, which Hari called sandals now. "I do not know how to cook anything else," she admitted. "In India we had servants always. In America I lived in the international students' hostel." She wondered whether to admit she and Krishna had attended different universities.

"You people don't eat meat, do you?" Mrs. Gardner asked.

"My husband does," Rukmini said, "but he does not cook much of it. We have no exhaust fan above the stove."

"Sounds like Hari's eating it at school. Plenty of things you can make in the oven, you know. Chicken, pot roast if—" The telephone rang. Mrs. Gardner cursed while pulling herself out of the chair. She waved when the telephone rang again and said, "We'll talk later."

When Rukmini re-entered the apartment, Krishna looked up. He closed his book before asking, "Is the boy all right?"

"Of course," she said. She let herself laugh at his concern. "He is having a splendid time. We are so fortunate to have friends like Mrs. Gardner." Rukmini opened the box of chocolates and left them on the dining table in case anyone knocked. Then she picked up a sponge and turned on the tap. It was difficult to soap dishes while watching Krishna over the low wall, but he looked distracted and she wondered what was wrong.

He nodded thoughtfully, then let his book fall on the sofa. "How long will they be?" he asked.

"They are going about the building only," she said, wiping a plate under running water. "Why?"

He shrugged and said, tentatively, "Can't you leave the dishes till later?" He looked away at the radio.

She turned off the tap. They had never spoken of this before. They had simply allowed it to happen.

As kindly as she could, she said, "You know we agreed one child was enough."

"I went to the pharmacy again," he said.

How could she refuse him, she thought; her husband, after all their separations? How could she refuse herself? She liked the way he held her as though protecting her from the world; as though keeping her for himself. Moving slowly, she dried her hands and put the chain on the door. As a concession to practicality she asked, "What if children come for their treats?"

"Then we're not home." There was a conspiratorial gleam in his eyes when he rose and offered his hand.

"If Babu comes back and cannot open—?"

"He can buzz from downstairs," Krishna said.

They separated at the end of the corridor, he to enter their bedroom and she to enter the bathroom. When she returned from undressing, she found him lying on his bed with his knees drawn up under a sheet. She wished he had left his shirt on so she could unbutton it, slowly, but they had no time for games. She turned off the light. There was little tenderness now when they touched, though she tried to blame this on their need to hurry. Once a week, on Saturday nights, they made love as leisurely as they had long ago, but she could sense too much had changed since their honeymoon. It was in Fort Cochin, in Kerala. Moonlight had glistened on Chinese fishing nets outside the bungalow; coconut palms had rustled; the local folk in their huts had quarrelled and sung and also made love. She cast herself back to those times, back to his caresses and whispered promises. She anchored her elbows on the bed and clutched his shoulders. She tried to match the rhythm of his thrusts but he withdrew. He rolled away and sat up on the edge of the bed. Afraid to reach out for him, she asked, "What is the matter?" When she finally did touch him—when she tried to trace the muscles above his shoulder blades—he flinched.

He rose to dress without looking at her. At last he said, "You're still planning to leave again, aren't you?"

She tried to ask, "When have I ever left?" and remembered she had. It seemed he would never forget.

"You could've done your doctorate with me," he said. He wanted to sound accusing but he heard only regret. "The boy was fine with my mother. We could have stayed together at Columbia, gone to shows, taken real holidays." He looked through the venetian blinds and murmured, "We never made it to the Grand Canyon."

Rukmini sat up and pushed her hair back, away from her eyes. "He needed me," she insisted. "He was a child."

"That's true," Krishna said. "I'm not a child, after all." He slapped the blinds as though he had said too much. When he returned to the living room, she felt tears coming to her eyes.

It was true, she did want to leave—she could feel her steps slowing when she returned after her walks—but she wanted to go to something, not away from what she had here. Not from her husband and certainly not from her son. Their son. More than once, when she talked about her friends in Toronto and Vancouver, she caught Hari looking about as though he guessed they might be moving. He knew so much and yet so little. This time she would not be taking him with her, the way she had from Mauritius back to Bangalore. If the three of them couldn't be together, it was better that he stay with Krishna. A boy needed a father, and Hari had been without one for too long. She wiped her eyes before putting on her glasses to get dressed. If Krishna saw her crying, he would blame himself and she did not blame him. He scoffed when she talked of karma but she couldn't ignore its hold on her. It was still fate. They were reaping what they had sowed not only in their past lives but also in the present. If only they could begin again, she thought; if only we could correct our mistakes in this life instead of having to wait for the next.

✵

Hari and Althea had worked their way down from the fifth floor to the first. Most of the tenants had been out. Althea sat near the brass mailboxes in the foyer to examine what she called her loot. Hari felt cheated. Few coins rattled in his Unicef carton because he had kept forgetting to hold it out. A horn blared on Montreal Road. He watched a gorilla drive past in a convertible with its top down. The gorilla wore a leather flying helmet and a white scarf.

"Apartments are no good," Althea said. "People who live in houses are rich, like my folks. Come on."

"My father," Hari protested.

She was holding the inside glass door open and was looking out. "He'll never know," she said. "We'll get candy bars and candy apples, not just Chiclets. Come on!" He followed her outside. He shivered when she added, "You have to watch out for apples with razor blades, okay? I knew a kid once got fifty stitches in his mouth. From eating an apple before his mom cut it open for him."

Hari thought of turning back but they were already through the parking lot. At the first house, one with cardboard cut-outs pasted in the windows, a Swiss maid gave them a Tootsie Roll each. She dropped nickels into their Unicef cartons. At the second house he and Althea had to sing. That is, Althea sang while Hari, always behind, accompanied her. A Martian rewarded them with all the jellybeans they could clutch from a fishbowl. When Hari obliged with a shuffling dance, the Martian's wife, a Sputnik, gave Hari a dime. House by house, block by block, his shopping bag grew so heavy he thought the string handles might snap. At street corners, Althea stopped to trade information with strangers—Robin Hoods, Maid Marians, bumble bees, a railway engineer on roller skates—about who offered the best treats and who offered silly things like prunes. When Hari and Althea reached Montfort Hospital, well east of the apartment, they turned back.

By now Krishna had given up trying to tune the short-wave band of his radio to the BBC. It was past eight-thirty. Rukmini read a textbook on transformers. He stood at the balcony door with the drapes open. The apartment faced west toward a string of motor hotels. Their neon signs outshone the traffic lights. Rukmini's favourite sign had a woman springing off a board, touching her toes in mid-air, and diving head first into the word *Vacancy*. Hari's favourite sign was a pink flamingo. Krishna considered the motor hotels eyesores.

"Where is the boy?" he muttered. The speeding cars offended his sense of order. He never speeded, and he always signalled his turns. Did being born here give people a licence to break the rules? Didn't they realize there were children about? He meant to say this last to Rukmini but he said, "See how recklessly those people drive! It's like Mardi Gras in New Orleans. Put costumes on people and they change, like Doctor Jekyll into Mr. Hyde." When she rose he asked, "Where are you going?"

"I think I shall read in bed," she replied. It would be more pleasant there, she thought, but she didn't say this. She took the chain off the door. "You should also. Babu can let himself in. They are just playing, or watching Mrs. Gardner's television." Rukmini left Krishna in the light of the pole lamp.

Once in her bed, though, she couldn't concentrate on her book. Despite her reassuring words, she suspected Hari and Althea were not downstairs. Krishna seemed to consider the speeding cars as merely an affront to the law. She saw them as a hundred separate reasons for children to be frightened, perhaps even maimed.

But Hari and Althea were safely out of the traffic. They were resting on a bus stop bench. Tired of having to push the mask up from his eyebrows, Hari took off the wig and mask so the breeze could cool his face.

Althea plunged her hands into her Loblaw's bag. She let the loot slip through her fingers while she cried, "Doubloons! Pieces of eight!"

He parroted her wearily.

"There's a girl in my class," Althea said, "who heard about the witch in the bathroom mirror from Mam'selle Bouchard, our French teacher."

"What witch?" Hari asked.

"Not what witch," Althea cried. "Which witch!" She laughed. "Mam'selle Bouchard said if this girl went in the bathroom and closed the door and said to the mirror, 'Mary Square, I believe in you, come out!'—if she did this fifty times, the witch would. Come out. So she went home and got up in the middle of the night when everybody was asleep. She closed the bathroom door and even pushed a towel under so the light from the hallway wouldn't get in. Smart, huh? She tipped the laundry basket over and climbed up and faced the mirror. She kept her voice real low and said, 'Mary Square, I believe in you, come out. Mary Square, I believe in you, come out. Mary Square—'"

"Then what happened?" he asked.

"The witch said, 'Here I am!'" Althea lunged at him. "And scratched out her eyes!" Althea cackled like the witch.

Hari laughed only when a passing truck lit the bench.

They set off with their sagging bags and jingling cartons. His respect for her increased when she let them into the building with a key. They parted at the elevator. She slipped into 105, and he leaned against the elevator walls. They were padded each month-end for people who moved in and out, and he wondered how soon he and Rukmini would be moving again; whether Krishna would come with them. He often grimaced when Rukmini mentioned Vancouver or Toronto. Hari did not want to move. He liked Woodbine. Mulling this over, it never occurred to him to wonder if he had broken one of Krishna's many rules: "Take your shoes off when you come in," or, "Hang your blazer neatly." Hari found the apartment door unlocked and stumbled inside.

Krishna rose from the sofa. In the large bedroom, Rukmini also rose and listened from the doorway.

"Where have you been?" Krishna demanded. She could hear the shaking in his voice. She hadn't realized he was also worried. If only he wouldn't hide his true feelings so much, she thought.

"Trick-or-treating," Hari replied.

"Do you know what time it is?" Krishna asked.

She imagined Hari shaking his head. He still measured time by activities, not by the clock: mealtime, bathtime, bedtime.

"Nearly nine," Krishna said. "It took you two hours to go through the building?"

The shopping bag thumped and dragged along the floor. The large shoes came off one by one. "We, we went outside to the houses," Hari said. "See my costume? I'm a clown."

Krishna was relieved to see Hari but anger welled up like bile: anger at the cars, the piano lessons; anger at Rukmini. Krishna took the wig and mask and tossed them onto the dining table. "Haven't I told you not to cross that street?" he said. He didn't expect an answer but Hari replied:

"Al took me. People in the houses are rich. See all the loot? Doubloons, pieces of eight!"

"I suppose they have television sets, too, and pianos? Will these rich friends pay the doctor when your stomach aches? Or the dentist when your teeth rot?"

Hari began to whimper, "I'm sorry."

Rukmini could no longer simply listen. She pulled her housecoat over her blouse and petticoat, then hurried into the living room. Hari was cowering against the blank wall. When he began to cry, Krishna reached for him.

"Stop that," Krishna ordered. "Only girls cry. Is this what you learn from your new friend?" Krishna grasped Hari's arm, pulled him across the room, and threw him onto the sofa.

Hari pressed his face into a cushion. He felt ill, not from the candies he had eaten but from the way words could turn into snakes. They pierced his eardrums, slithered down his throat into his stomach, and churned.

"Stop this," Rukmini shouted. Krishna waved her back. She knelt to gather the crumpled newspaper spilling from the shoes.

"That's right, pick up after him," he said, and she stopped. She had never seen him like this.

"Look," Krishna said. He grabbed the Loblaw's bag and pulled the mouth open so violently the paper tore. "He isn't satisfied getting a few candies in the building. He goes begging about the neighbourhood. Look at this rubbish!"

Hari no longer felt ill; he was confused. All he had done was cross the street, and he had crossed with the light. Why was he being punished for such a little thing? Now light from the pole lamp was glinting from Krishna's eyes. Hari kept his own eyes on Krishna's hands, which he knew could snake out to grasp a wrist.

But Krishna's hands did not leave the bag. He raised it, shouting, "Children starve in India! I bring you to a better place and you want candy? Here!" He showered Hari with popcorn, lollipops, and gum; with chocolate bars, apples, and nuts. "You want more?" Krishna dumped the rest of the bag.

Hari shrieked. Lashing out, he struck Krishna's arm.

"Don't you hit me!" Krishna snapped. He raised his hand.

Rukmini finally lost her fear of him. She tried to pull Krishna away by digging her nails into his back. He cried out. He whirled, dropped the empty bag, and slapped her. She could have killed him. She could have thrown herself at him and through the glass door. Where did God find such men? She rubbed her cheek. Her glasses had flown off to land in a corner. She thought they had broken.

Hari rolled to the edge of the sofa, slid off, and knocked more candies onto the floor. He ran to her, wrapped his arms around her waist, and buried his face in her housecoat. He kept repeating, "I'm sor-ry."

"How dare you?" she shouted at Krishna. "Is it not enough I must remain home when—?" No, this was not the quarrel here. "Is it not enough he has no one to play with? Not enough that other children avoid him because he attends your fancy private school?" She thought of every injustice Krishna had done to Hari, from leaving him fatherless for so long to taking him from his mother country.

All the while Krishna muttered, "Rubbish," and, "Only girls cry," and Hari wailed, "Sorry, sor-ry!"

"You wanted him to grow up Canadian," she shouted. "Let him!"

"Keep your voice down," Krishna said. "What will the neighbours think?"

She fell silent and stood glaring at him.

"Grow up Canadian like this?" he asked. He waved at the mound of candies. It did look like rubbish now: wrappers split, apples bruised, popcorn crushed. "People starve back home and he—"

Hari broke away from Rukmini and searched near the door for the Unicef carton. "I have this for them," he said. He wiped the sleeve of his clown suit across his eyes. "Al will get me a ticket for—"

"You go begging for money, too?" Krishna demanded. "Give me that."

"It's for the children of Africa!" Hari cried. He ran for his room.

Krishna brushed candies from the sofa. He pulled the cushions off, one by one, and shook them while Rukmini crouched to feel for her glasses.

The glasses lay, unbroken, near the bookshelf. She put them on. Then she spied the Van de Graaff behind a sofa leg. The model lay on its side. Krishna moved away when she bent to pick it up. The silver globe was cracked. She jiggled it, and the globe separated from the shaft. The black rubber band slipped off the spindles. When she tossed the model onto the sofa, the hemispheres fell apart. "What kind of father are you," she asked, "expecting his son to grow up overnight?"

"I'm not going to coddle him like a child," Krishna said. She would never understand, he thought; she knew nothing about raising children. She was no better than his mother.

Rukmini made a spitting sound, a *"Thup!"* which surprised even her. "You have never treated him like a child," she said. "Were you yourself never a child?"

"What do you know about me?" he demanded. "You are my wife, are you? You have lived under my roof how long? Three years out of eight? You have shared my bed how many times? Other women have more than one child!"

This was his final betrayal of the night. He was so understanding, during their honeymoon, when she told him how she feared childbirth; how she feared bleeding to death while her child cried or, worse, how she imagined being split open when the child spewed out. They hadn't spoken of this since Hari's birth. Hari, her son. She snatched the box of chocolates off the dining table and entered the small bedroom. She found him cowering in the closet. He screamed when she reached for him but she pulled him to her and said, "Hush, it is only me." When she heard Krishna stride down the corridor, she closed the door.

But Krishna wasn't headed for the bedrooms. He wanted to be left alone. He had been so happy alone, he thought; so free of cares. His hands were shaking and he clenched them. "Oh yes," he told no one in particular, "I had a very happy *Holloween*, thank you!" He entered the bathroom. Most men would have vented their rage and sorrow by slamming the door. He closed it quietly, for the neighbours' sake.

# Chapter 11

## *The Remover of Obstacles*

Rukmini sat cross-legged on the floor with her back against the sofa. Using the atlas as a tablet, she wrote aerograms. She wrote lightly so she wouldn't damage the maple leaves pressed between the leaves of the book. She reread her letter to Sharada, then sighed. Too many of the words felt strange: "*Bagunnava?*" instead of "How are you?" Even addressing the aerogram to "Smt. S.V. Sharada" looked strange under the printed Canadian stamp. Titles like *Srimati* had no place here. She put the aerogram aside and began another, this one to Prakash and Saroja.

It was the Saturday before Remembrance Day and Krishna was at the civil service rink. He was learning to skate. She supposed he needed to convince himself he was still an athlete. She knew he was happiest on the playing field. He would be even happier if Hari were a born sportsman; then Krishna could play the lifelong coach. He still referred to piano lessons as though they were more suited to girls.

Hari was downstairs playing with Althea.

Rukmini answered the phone when it rang. The phone sat on the low wall between the kitchen and living room, and Rukmini perched on the arm of the sofa.

The operator said, "I have a person to person call for, Dr. Rook-meeny? From Dr. Hanbidge."

"This is she," Rukmini said.

"Oh," the operator said, puzzled. "Go ahead, please."

A man shouted over the static, "Can you hear me?" Also raising her voice, Rukmini said she could. "Neil Hanbidge here. I'm head of the EE department at the U of T. University of Toronto? Dr. Visvanath sent me your résumé some time back. I understand you were classmates at the Indian Institute in Bangalore?" He pronounced it "Bang-a-lore" instead of "Bang-loor."

"Hardly classmates," she said. "He was one year my senior."

"Whatever," Hanbidge said politely. "I'm sorry I couldn't write about this sooner. One of our lecturers has taken ill. I wonder if you could step in for him?"

She forced herself to sound calm. "You wish me to teach his load?" she asked.

"Among others," Hanbidge said. "Barlow—that's the poor chap's name—handles two intermediate courses, but I notice your thesis was on motors. If Dr. Visvanath could pick up one of Barlow's classes, I wonder if you could handle the other *and* take over my third-year design lab? It would free my time for more paperwork. Would that be a bother?"

Her palms felt clammy. She had taught only introductory classes at the Institute. "I suppose I could," she said, "if I had time to prepare."

"I'm afraid there's not much time," Hanbidge said, though he didn't sound apologetic. "If you could come down here—I realize it's short notice—day after tomorrow, we could go over my notes for the lab. It's more a matter of coasting till the end of term while you prepare for the next one. Barlow will be out of commission at least that long. I see you have a family, though. Could you discuss it with your husband and let me know as soon as possible?"

"This will not be necessary," she said and then lied: "He would not want me to pass up such an opportunity." To control her growing excitement, she pressed the receiver to her cheek. "I shall arrive tomorrow itself so we do not waste any time."

"Splendid!" Hanbidge said this as though he had expected nothing less. He sounded less sure of himself when he continued: "Barlow's an assistant professor, but I'm afraid we'll have to take you on as a lecturer. There's your lack of Canadian experience, and your PhD's only as good as a master's here. Besides—" She imagined him fidgeting with his tie. "—we don't have any women in our faculty. You'll be the first. Dr. Visvanath's offered to put you up for now. He'll meet you at the train or bus. You can arrange the details with him."

The call ended with her profuse, "Thank you, sir. Thank you very much."

She walked to the balcony door and took a deep breath. She wanted to shout, "Hurray!" but she was not a child. She also felt suddenly nervous: like a performer about to go on stage. She took a deep breath and pressed her hands on the door. Condensation clouded the glass around her hands. Although it was early afternoon, many cars drove with their headlights on. Thick, grey clouds were threatening to drop snow again. It would be the second storm in less than a week. She watched the taillights of cars travelling west past the motor hotels. How would Krishna react? He had always wanted to teach in a North American university. No, he would not be pleased for her. He might have been, once, but the gulf between them was widening. It had more to do with the years they could no longer recapture than with her credentials. As long as he didn't try to dissuade her by reminding her of Hari, anything but that. It was the sharpest of the swords hanging over her: one Krishna had unsheathed during her second year in graduate school. He had wanted her to fetch Hari and wait with him in India, yet Krishna had also wanted her with him in New York. The choice, for her, had been simple.

Rukmini would wait for each photograph Krishna's mother sent from Mauritius: Hari celebrating his second birthday at a picnic; Hari waving sparklers during the festival of lights; Hari with his cheeks puffed to blow out the three candles on his cake. Rukmini would show the photos to friends in the international students' hostel. The only other Indian women were also married but neither had children. The women laughed over Hari's wide eyes and serious mouth and said oh, how they hoped their sons would be as handsome. She felt proud at first, then so sad she didn't want to answer any more questions about him, so far away. They had three good years together in Bangalore. Why those years had ended, she did not know. Yes, she did. She could not have managed much longer. Hari was growing and hurting himself at play. If not a ball in the eye, a scraped knee. And that rash. The sight of his quivering lips made her own knees weak. Krishna thought getting hurt was a natural part of growing up—he said so when Hari came home bruised from floor hockey now—but Krishna was wrong. Boys didn't have to hurt themselves while growing. We hurt them enough, she thought. How could the mistakes of a past life be corrected in the present when it was complicated first by parents, then by children? Perhaps this, too, was karma.

She went to the large bedroom and sorted her clothes, those she would pack from those she had to wash. She added Hari's dirty clothes to hers but left Krishna's because he still washed his own. She pulled her suitcase from the closet, set the contents aside, and crumpled the clothes into the suitcase. Downstairs, in the basement laundry room, she loaded the washing machine. Then she returned to begin packing her books. She sat on the living room floor to do this, and fibres from the rug clung to the covers. She had sent the books by sea before leaving India.

After repacking the first layer, she stared at them. She tried to blow off the lint but there was too much static in the dry air. She glanced at Krishna's bookshelf. All his books had coloured jackets shiny with cellophane; hers were protected by brown paper labelled in ink. What was she doing, taking books which were out of date even when she had used them at the Institute? The one she held, the *Engineer's Illustrated Thesaurus* by Herkimer, had been published ten years before. The colleagues she had left behind were still trying to modernize a land in which transistor radios were status symbols. She put the book down. She had no idea how much she would earn in Toronto, but surely it would allow her to surprise Hari? She would buy him his own radio. Yes, she would buy him a transistor radio with AM and FM, a telescoping antenna, and an earplug so he wouldn't disturb Krishna. She looked at the Heathkit and reached up to switch it on. She paused with her hand on the knob and fingered the rippled surface.

Too often, Krishna reminded her of her own father. Perhaps Sharada had been right. She once suggested Rukmini married Krishna not for the new life he could provide but for the emptiness he could replace. Rukmini's father had also needed to prove himself. People called such men "complicated" when what they meant was "confused." Her mother had been courageous, though. It was the only way to survive thirty years of marriage with a man who was rarely home yet acted like a god when he was home. Switching the radio on at last, Rukmini searched for a weather report.

It was difficult to believe now—living here in such a modern place—but at one time her father wouldn't allow electricity, let alone a radio, in their house. When upper class families first began installing generators, Rukmini's mother also wanted one but Rukmini's father did not. He believed anything modern made Indians more dependent on the British. Granted, he took the train four times yearly between Madras and Delhi, but this was different. The trains were run by Indians. True, many were Anglo-Indians but they were Indians of a sort. Finally Rukmini's mother stopped mentioning electricity and her husband prided himself on having won her over. But she was simply biding her time. After he left to teach the next term, she had a generator installed in the storeroom behind the kitchen. The servants put away the kerosene lamps and Rukmini and Prakash studied under bare light bulbs. Best of all, they listened to the new wireless their mother had ordered. It was a fine Gruendig with metallic cloth over the large speaker. Below this were ivory buttons for different bands: MW for medium wave, SW for short wave. When their father returned, Rukmini and her mother watched him pace in the main room. He flicked the light switch on and off while glaring at the wireless. Then he stalked out of the house and they followed him as far as the veranda. But he wasn't going for one of his long walks, so he could fume. He was dragging the first stranger he had found, a passing tinker, toward the house. He led the tinker into the main room and cried, "See? A wireless, the first in our district!" Then he gave the tinker a coin, dismissed him, and listened to a cricket match. Although her father disliked cricket on principle, he made excited remarks like, "Well caught!" He never once noticed the dark circles under his wife's eyes from the nights she had spent worrying. He never once praised her cleverness.

Rukmini switched off the Heathkit. She packed her flight bag with the few books she had received as gifts. The remaining books went into a Loblaw's bag. She dragged it by its string handles out of the apartment and opened the door to the incinerator chute. She fed the books, one by one, down the chute. She listened with satisfaction while they fell. To Krishna, old books were useful only to people who couldn't afford progress. To her now they were merely reminders of a country she had left. Finished, she washed her hands of the soot from the incinerator door.

An hour later Hari returned from downstairs. "Amma," he cried, "you should see Al's doll house! It has fancy wallpaper and a glass chandel . . . a—"

"Chandelier?" she finished for him.

"In this perfect little dining room," he said. "Her father sent it early for Christmas. Did you know he's mining for gold up north? Al says he's filthy rich."

Rukmini sat on the sofa and held out her arms. "I have a surprise for you also," she said.

Hari came to her and stood, bouncing his knees against her legs. He looked about in case his own Christmas present might be early. A train, he thought; a train.

"I have a job," she said. "Are you not thrilled?"

He turned to sit on her knee, leaned back against her shoulder, and looked at her slide rule. It lay across an old circuit diagram. He couldn't read it except to spell out words like inductance, which meant nothing to him. "Will you do experiments?" he asked.

"Even better," she said, kissing his neck below his ear. "I shall teach in a university, one of the finest in Canada." She told him where.

"But my father says Toronto's far away," Hari said. He hopped down and turned, leaned forward, and steadied himself by pressing down on her thighs. "That's where the paper comes from." He glanced at *The Globe and Mail*, which lay on the far end of the sofa. Krishna brought it home every weekday from a kiosk at Uplands Airport. The paper was always one day late but on Saturday he bought the local paper so Hari could read the colour comics. "Will you be gone all next week?" he asked.

She took his hands and said, "I shall be back when the term ends for Christmas. That is five weeks from now only. You can have my bed in your room." Moving him aside, she asked, "Help me sort the laundry?" Hand in hand they walked to the large bedroom. "I shall leave Ganesha for you," she said.

The statue had lain in her suitcase with the photo albums. She had wanted to keep the statue on the dresser but the elephant god looked out of place among the white walls and venetian blinds. Except for her jewellery, the statue was all she had left of her mother's belongings. Rukmini shook her head with regret over the statue. The gold and silver paint of Ganesha's crown had long ago worn off, and the yellow paint on his elephant ears had begun to peel. The trunk had once broken and been mended with Scotch tape, which itself had yellowed. But he was still her Ganesha, and Hari needed him more than she did. The remover of obstacles had been removed long enough. The god of wisdom was needed once again.

"Will you phone?" Hari asked. He sat on her bed and clutched the statue but he didn't want it. She had promised they would all be together again. What if she never came back? If she could break one promise, she could break another. Worst of all, Hari wasn't sure he wanted to live with Krishna. How could a statue protect a little boy from such a big man, a man who sounded angry even when he laughed?

Rukmini looked up from sorting the wrinkled towels and bedding. Her suitcase lay half packed on Krishna's bed next to the clean laundry. She was sorting it into three piles: her own multicoloured, Hari's white and blue, the towels and bedding all white. Then she folded one piece from each pile and placed the wrinkled laundry on her own bed. There was no time for ironing. "The phone will be too expensive," she told Hari. "I shall write. Will you write back?"

"Of course!" he said. Why would he not write?

"And in the New Year, you can visit me during the Easter break. Your Mrs. D told me you will have an entire week away from class." Rukmini folded one of her cotton saris. She had stopped wearing the nylon ones after the first snowfall because static made them cling to her petticoats. "If it is not too cold," she said, "we can go to Niagara Falls. Your *appa* and I went there once, years ago. You will like the falls. The Canadian side is even more splendid than the American side. There is a boat which sails into the mist under a rainbow."

"Will I get wet?" he asked.

"No, silly," she replied. "They will give you a raincoat and—" She stopped. He had put the statue on her pillow and sat with his arms crossed. He looked worried but not about getting wet. She moved the statue to the dresser. He was kicking his heels against the box spring now. His frown was just like Krishna's. "Your *appa* will take good care of you," she said. "I will not be far away."

Hari shrugged but he refused to look at her. He knew he must have done something wrong, but what? Perhaps the silences between his parents were all his fault. They would stop in mid-sentence when he wandered into the living room looking for something to do. Then they would begin talking about motors or electricity, but he wasn't so easily fooled. They would be happier without him, he thought.

Rukmini sighed. How could she leave him like this? How could she leave him again? First to study, now to work. At least he finally had a father under the same roof and they would learn to live together. They might even learn to love one another. More important, they might learn to show their love. The few times Krishna tried to pull Hari onto his knee and tousle his hair, Hari would yell, "Don't!" and squirm out of Krishna's grasp. Kneeling in front of the bed, Rukmini pulled Hari down and hugged him. At first he resisted; then he lay his head on her shoulder. But he didn't bury his face in her neck. He was looking away. She felt his hair tickle her cheek—hair so long and fine she used to sit next to his hammock and curl the baby locks through her fingers while he slept. "I will miss you so much," she whispered. When she pulled away from him, he no longer looked worried. He looked lost. He was searching her eyes for reassurance, a promise she wouldn't leave him forever. At one time she could reassure him with peppermint and *halva* but such times had passed. "What are we talking about?" she exclaimed. "I shall be back for Christmas, correct? Let us finish packing. Do you remember where I keep our passports?"

Hari went to the dresser, and she rose. He pulled at the middle drawer with such force, Rukmini's hairbrush rolled over the edge. The statue of Ganesha toppled backward. She caught it before it could fall onto the base heater. Looking out through the grimy window, she shook her head at the snow on the lawn. The snow was covered with tracks and no longer pure white.

Only a week ago, Hari stood on the base heater in his own room while clutching the window ledge. She went to him when he called for her. It was dark outside and she switched off his light so their reflections would vanish. Then she held him up with his palms pressed against the glass and they watched his first snowfall. He kept repeating, "It's wonderful," but he frowned as though sorry everything turned white so quickly: the brown lawn, the sloping rooftops, even the bare trees. Now he loved it. He loved piano lessons; he loved playing with Althea; he loved snow. He sounded so foreign, Rukmini wondered whether she should have brought him here, from a land of brightness and women to this land of darkness and men.

❋

Krishna's first skating lesson, stopping by using a technique called the snowplow, had been simple. This afternoon's lesson, though, was difficult. The instructor gave them a drill called starts and stops, which he said hockey players did. It involved skating toward the far blue line, coming to a full stop, and returning to the starting point.

There were only five other people in the class: a bearded man accompanied by his teen-aged granddaughter, a middle-aged woman who spoke French, and two young women who looked like university students. Krishna outraced the others and reached his goal first. When he tried to stop, he took an extra step sideways and nearly lost his balance. Waving his arms like a windmill, he managed to remain upright and began again, headed back before the others finished the first leg. He gave them a wide berth when he passed. The old man's granddaughter, skating easily with her arms wrapped about him, giggled at his nervous "Whoa!" He looked more proud of her than of himself. The middle-aged woman looked tense. The two young women stopped with simultaneous scrapes of ice and laughed at one another.

Ignoring the instructor, who was encouraging everyone by clapping and shouting, Krishna approached the starting line. This time he decided to try a different technique. On his last two steps, he shifted his weight to his back skate, planted his front skate at an angle to the ice, and brought his back skate parallel until the two touched. The manoeuvre stopped him, but his weight pulled him backward. He crashed to the ice. The others caught up to him while he rose, slapping white powder from his gloves. He had fallen on his left elbow and it began to throb. He rubbed it to keep the circulation going. One of the students laughed to her companion and Krishna's face grew hot, but he was less annoyed at the laughter than he was at hurting himself. He managed a smile. He waved off the instructor's suggestion of a short break. Krishna faced the far blue line and set off again. Even if it took all winter, he would learn to skate like Bobby Hull, the Golden Jet.

After the lesson Krishna sped home. He often drove fast now but he still hadn't been caught. When he entered the apartment, he found Rukmini seated on the sofa. Her flight bag leaned against her suitcase and on the suitcase lay her purse. Her black lambskin coat, bought the previous week, lay on the coffee table. He opened the front closet and placed his skates on a rubber mat so the blades wouldn't scratch the floor.

Rukmini put down the book she was reading: his motor club guide to Ontario. She glanced at her watch and said, "You are early."

"The traffic was light," he said. Amused by the lie, he nodded at her luggage and asked, "Are we moving?"

She tried to smile by lifting one side of her mouth but she still looked preoccupied. Then, with growing excitement, she said, "I have accepted a position. I secured it through a classmate."

So that was it. Krishna unlaced his shoes without peeling off the rubber slip-ons. Trying to think of something appropriate to say—something which couldn't be mistaken for criticism—he took off his winter clothes. He always hung them in the closet when he came in but today he draped them on the back of a dining chair, first the camel-hair coat, which he folded neatly. He grasped the ends of his buff scarf, twirled it off, and held it taut behind him. Then he dropped the scarf onto the coat. "Your new employer couldn't give you much notice," he asked, "or have you been hiding the news from us to protect the boy?"

"I would have done so if necessary," she said. "You know I do not like to hurt him. The call came this afternoon only. I am to replace someone taken ill." Grinning now, she announced, "I shall be the first woman electrical engineer hired by the University of Toronto."

"An historic occasion," Krishna said. "I'm sure the boy must be proud." There was no light shining from the small bedroom so Krishna asked, "Where is he?"

"I took him downstairs to Mrs. Gardner. She will feed him supper so you can drive me to the bus terminal." Rukmini looked at her watch. "An express bus leaves in less than one hour." When Krishna didn't move to put on his coat, she asked, "Why do you stand there glaring?"

"I'm sorry," he said. "I didn't realize I was glaring." He was, though; he knew it. He checked his own watch and flexed his wrist. It ached sometimes if he spent too long outdoors and he found this disconcerting. He had assumed the wrist was completely healed and now his body was betraying him. "I was merely wondering," he said, "why a woman who claims to love her son so much would leave him motherless." Like some other women he could name, he thought, but he was trying to be civil. "Is Mrs. Gardner to feed the boy from now on? Am I supposed to pay for a baby sitter if I wish to go out?"

Rukmini rose to pull on her coat. "I shall pay for such incidentals," she said.

No, she bloody well would not. He needed no one's help to raise a child and he wasn't about to take money from his wife. "We'll manage," he said. "You can't squander money just because you'll have a regular paycheque."

"Yes," she replied calmly, "I will have a regular paycheque. I have not had one since leaving the Institute, and I have no intention of staying home any longer like the wife of your assistant."

"Stan Morely is an idiot!" Krishna snapped. "Only last week a belt on our Van de Graaff broke and we lost a whole day. It seems he hadn't bothered to order a replacement the last time it happened. He should've known the lab's already so cold—"

Krishna stopped. What did Stan Morely or his wife have to do with any of this? From what little Krishna could guess, their marriage was as dull as it was conventional. Not like this one; it had never been conventional. And with all these arrivals and departures, it could never be dull. He began lacing on his shoes. Bending reminded him of pushing himself off the ice after his fall. Blood rushed to his cheeks. After he straightened, he noticed a hanger tangled with another one in the closet. He tried to separate them but they tilted up and nearly struck his chin. He knocked the hangers off the bar, onto the closet floor, where they lay still tangled on his skates. "Let's go," he said. "You don't want to miss your express bus."

Once in the Lark he switched on the radio. Rukmini sat silently, already far away in her mind, he supposed: imagining lecture halls and ivied brick. Christmas was over a month away yet stations already played carols. He fiddled with the dial while waiting at a red light. When an announcer recited skiing conditions in the Gatineau Hills, it gave Krishna an idea. After Hari mastered skating, he could begin skiing. Stan Morely complained about how much the equipment cost, but he also said it could be rented. Perhaps the man was an idiot, but not where money was concerned.

By the time Krishna reached the bus terminal, he felt more conciliatory, almost contrite. When Rukmini caught her purse strap on the doorhandle, he said, "I'll get it." He rounded the car to open her door and shrugged off her thanks. Then, inside, he offered to pay for her ticket.

"I still have some traveller's cheques," she said.

Leaving her at the counter, he went in search of a *Globe and Mail* but the kiosk didn't carry it. He picked up Rukmini's suitcase and the flight bag and carried them to the platform. He had to say something; he couldn't let the whole episode end like this. She wasn't leaving forever but it felt like the end. Worst of all, he would miss her. It pained him to admit it, even to himself, but he was getting used to living with other people. Solitude was all very well, but it heightened a man's faults. Standing with her, first in line for the bus, he watched the condensation of her breath in the air. He wanted to say, "Wait it out a little longer. Something will come up here." He wanted to take her hand and say, "Don't go, please." Instead he told her, "Don't forget to write."

She gave him a brave smile and said, "I told Babu to be good."

Krishna left then. He didn't want to stand there, feeling abandoned, while waiting for her to leave. He sped home. The Lark felt larger now but he felt old. This was no time to feel sorry for himself. He had too many responsibilities. When Mrs. Gardner answered his knock, he forced himself to sound as though nothing was wrong. Hari was holding a comic book while Althea played with a doll house. Hari looked guilty, as though Krishna had caught him doing something wrong. Krishna crouched, balancing with ease, to look at the comic. It was called a *Classics Illustrated*, a children's version of *Ivanhoe*.

"Here," Krishna asked Hari, "do you like movies? There's a costume drama playing at the Capitol. Let's go tonight." Then Krishna remembered Hari did like movies, especially animated Walt Disney films.

"Can Al come too?" Hari asked.

"Maybe next time," Mrs. Gardner said. She lit one of her little cigars. "Al's going to help me bake a pie. You can have a piece tomorrow."

"Neat," Hari said.

Neat? Krishna wondered where he had gone wrong. He hadn't enrolled Hari at Woodbine for him to learn the same poor English other people spoke. Then Krishna reminded himself it wasn't Hari's fault. He was a child, and children adapted quickly to their surroundings, often too well.

Krishna sneezed, and Mrs. Gardner waved the smoke toward a corner. She seemed to know exactly what was happening but she didn't seem surprised. He wanted to tell her, "It's not what you think," but he simply thanked her. She waved goodbye and only then did he realize she hadn't said a word to him.

Once upstairs, Hari said he didn't want to go to a movie after all. When Krishna asked what Hari would rather do, he looked about the living room and shrugged. He settled on the floor to examine his leaf collection in the atlas. Krishna pretended not to notice the leaves were growing brittle. Leaf dust was collecting along the spine. He read his biography of Nelson. Once, when he looked up, he saw Hari listening intently to the radio, the atlas lying forgotten in his lap. Glenn Gould was performing the *Little Organ Book*, transcribed for piano. Gould was humming and the habit seemed to fascinate Hari. "You can turn it up if you like," Krishna said, but Hari shrugged again.

Later, Krishna moved the spare mattress and box spring into the small bedroom. He rolled the foam mattress, wrapped electrical tape around it, and stuffed it into his own closet. "Time for bed," he called, and Hari came down the corridor slowly. "A real bed," Krishna declared.

"I'm not sleepy," Hari said, rubbing his eyes.

"Lie down and you'll fall asleep." Krishna wished Hari would ask about Rukmini but he seemed even more withdrawn than usual. Krishna watched Hari change. When Hari turned his back to pull down his trousers, Krishna left the doorway. He switched off the radio and the lights, made sure the stove was off and the chain was on the door, and used the bathroom. Then he checked on Hari, who looked fast asleep.

Krishna took his book to bed, something he rarely did. The room felt larger, as it had when he himself had slept on the foam. He decided he would definitely enrol Hari in skiing lessons, even if it meant economizing further. A boy deserved nothing but the best. After skimming the description of Nelson's last night with Lady Hamilton, Krishna immersed himself in the Battle of Trafalgar. He heard a thump. It came from the small bedroom. He hurried down the hall and flicked on the light. Hari lay with his arm across his eyes. "What was that?" Krishna asked.

"I bumped my elbow," Hari said.

Krishna palmed his own elbow. Then he saw a dark streak on the white pillowcase. He gently pulled Hari's arm away to find a scrape under his right eye. Both his cheeks, still bearing the white indentations of fingertips, were red. So was the skin around his eyebrows.

"Why are you scratching?" Krishna asked.

"It itches," Hari said. "I used Noxzema like you say, but it still itches."

"Not enough, I guess. Use some more." On second thought, Krishna fetched the blue jar from the bathroom and spread the Noxzema himself before massaging it onto Hari's forehead and cheeks.

"Ow," he cried. "It stings!"

"No wonder," Krishna said. "The skin is so tender. No more scratching. You're not a monkey, are you?" Hari giggled. Then his eyes clouded and he turned to face the wall. From under the end of his pillow, he took out the statue of Ganesha. Krishna had heard Canadian children often took toys to bed with them. He wondered what else he would have to learn about raising a child. Not that it would be for long: a few months at most, as soon as Rukmini could find something in Ottawa. She had promised to try.

"Boy," Krishna said, "your mother is coming back." Hari said nothing. Krishna switched off the light, sat on the edge of the bed, and pulled the blankets up. Spreading his hand, he measured Hari's head and shook his own. Hari was still so small, Krishna could curve his hand from the nape to the crown. When Krishna rose to go, Hari mumbled something in his sleep.

At first Krishna thought it was "Appa," but it sounded too soft for this. When Hari mumbled again, Krishna sighed. It was "Amma."

# Chapter 12

## Snow Angels

The flag on the embassy in front of Woodbine shuddered in a constant north wind. December had arrived: red and green December with a frosting of white and its preparations for the birth of Christ. One afternoon during a piano lesson Mrs. D asked Hari, "Are you excited about your first Christmas?"

He looked up from the keyboard. "It's not my first," he said. "When we lived in India, my mother bought a potted pine."

"Do you mean your family is Christian after all?" Mrs. D asked. "You should be going to chapel then."

Only three weeks before, the entire class except Hari attended a long, eleven o'clock service in the chapel. This was in November—red and white November with the red of poppies and the white of crosses—a few days after Rukmini had left for Toronto. Alone in the classroom, Hari pecked at the piano. The keys looked yellowed and chipped and the piano needed tuning. He gazed out the high window at a pile of gravel covered with snow and wished he could be in the mysterious chapel. He wished he could be in Toronto.

"Elzabeth was a Christian," he finally said.

"You never mentioned a sister," Mrs. D exclaimed.

"She was our servant."

Mrs. D said, "I see," as though every boy at Woodbine had one. Many of them did. Some, like Christou, even had pilots. He said his father's pilot would fetch him in their private jet so The Christous could spend Christmas break in the Bahamas. Hari believed him.

"We'll switch to this book for a while," Mrs. D said. "Where is it now?" While she searched on a shelf under the window, he filled the time by playing "God Save the Queen." It was the last piece in book three of Boris Berlin's *ABC of Piano Playing*. On the inside back cover, a certificate stated G. Harris Chandra was eligible for promotion to conservatory grade one work. Not satisfied with the black seal printed on the bottom, Mrs. D had added a star. Hari thought it stood for the star of brightness, star of light. This was from a song Althea had taught him the previous Sunday, when she had taught him something even more wonderful.

They had searched for a patch of undisturbed snow. Tracks always covered the lawn in front of the building but on one side, near a chain link fence, they had found the perfect spot. "Watch this," she said. She held her arms out and let herself fall backward. The snow cushioned her fall. She waved her arms up toward her head and down toward her waist, then moved her legs out and in. "Give me a hand," she said, sitting up. "Don't stand too close or you'll wreck it." Hari grasped her hand, pulled her to her feet, and looked at what she had made:

"An angel!"

"A snow angel," she said. "All the girls at school make them. Boys, too, but only little ones. Your turn."

"I'm not a little boy!" he said.

"I know that, silly," she said, "but you're different. The other boys are no fun." She stood him next to her snow angel and held his arms out. "Remember to lie still after you fall. Don't roll, okay? Ready?" He held his breath and nodded. She pushed him, and he toppled backward. "Now wave your arms and legs!

That's it." He giggled at the snow creeping under the woolen cuffs of his snowsuit.

He liked playing with snow. If it hadn't been for all the clothes Krishna made Hari wear, Hari would have liked snow even more. Under his playclothes he wore thermal underwear, tops and bottoms. Over his playclothes he wore a thick sweater with a turtleneck which made his chin itch, a blue snowsuit, and an orange scarf. Over his shoes he wore galoshes with treads like bicycle tires. He liked the mittens, though. They reminded him of three little kittens in a nursery rhyme one of the teachers at Cluny Convent had played on her piano. He could not remember her name. He also wore a tuque.

Instead of helping him rise, Althea had fallen next to him and made another snow angel. He had wanted to get up, to look at his own snow angel, but he laughed at the clear blue sky while she sang:

> We three kings of Orient are,
> Tried to smoke a rubber cigar,
> It was loaded,
> It exploded,
> Throwing us wondrous far.
> Oh, oh, star of wonder, star of light,
> Star that's filled with dynamite . . .

Mrs. D finally placed a new book in front of the Boris Berlin. The new one was called *Christmas Carols That Never Grow Old*. She opened it and tapped a piece called "Hark! The Herald Angels Sing."

Hari licked his lips. The piece looked more difficult than "God Save the Queen." Still, he poised his hands above the keyboard, his right to sound his favourite note, middle C, and his left to strike F and A on the bass clef.

"It always helps to sing a more difficult song before you try to play it," Mrs. D said. Relieved, he placed his hands in his lap. "Ready?" she asked. "One, two, three."

Hark! the herald angels sing,
"Glory to the newborn King,
Peace on earth and mercy mild,
God and sinners reconciled!"

Hari remained half a note behind her. When they reached the end of the fourth line, she said, "You didn't tell me you could sing!" He didn't know he could except for some nursery rhymes, and the songs he learned from Omar and now Althea. "We must see about getting you into the choir," Mrs. D said. "I'll speak to Mr. Marsden about it first thing in the morning." Hari knew what the choir was: boys from every form sang in it. Marsden was the choir master. Mrs. D excused Tully for daily practices these days and the other boys watched with envy when he left. "Perhaps Mr. Marsden will even let you try the organ," she told Hari. "Not during service, of course."

The choir sang in the chapel. Hari often peeked inside while passing it on his way back from the dining room. The chapel looked bright and airy, not at all like a temple he remembered visiting in India. He dreamt about the visit often but the dreams were never exactly the same. Sometimes a barber shaved Hari's head and he turned into a monkey who played tricks on demons. Other times, Elzabeth grew wings on her feet and rose up from a playground to become a statue of Saint Joseph. Best of all, though, Hari liked dreaming about a wedding in heaven, a wedding which was so expensive that all the women he knew—even Mrs. Gardner—gave their jewellery to pay for it. Without Rukmini to listen to his dreams, he kept them to himself because he thought Krishna wouldn't care to hear about them.

The following morning after break, Hari went with Tully to the senior school. Hari kept stopping to look at the photographs on the corridor walls. The basement still made noises but they no longer frightened him. Other boys claimed the noises came from the groaning pipes and the boiler room, but he knew better: they were songs sung by old boys who had grown up and still missed Woodbine.

"You watch yourself," Tully said. Now they were climbing the stairs past the Tuck Shop. "Marsden's a real spoilsport, madder than a Hatter. He'll chew you up and spit you out."

Hari saw Marsden as a huge, hairy man with his teeth filed to points. After Tully opened the chapel door and slipped inside, Hari stopped to look about. On the back of each long, wooden seat was a rack holding a row of red books and blue books. The seat closest to him smelled of lemon oil and wax. On either side of the nave were stained glass windows with a man in each. The men wore coats of armour but their faces looked angelic. He raised his eyes to the gilded flags hanging the length of the nave. Among them were the colours of Woodbine's cadet corps, a Union Jack, and Canada's Red Ensign. The Ensign had a smaller Union Jack in an upper corner, and a shield. The shield was crammed with three lions, another lion, a harp, three *fleurs-de-lis*, and three maple leaves. The organ was on the right wall near the front. It had two keyboards and above these rose golden pipes. The pipes in the middle were thick but those on either side were as thin as his arms. To the left of the organ, above the choir, hung an arched board with rows of black numbers on white cards.

"No, no, no!" A man in tweed trousers was pacing in front of the choir. "We're not singing Papist doggerel here," he shouted. "This isn't Latin. It's the Queen's English. The syllables are *not* all the same length. I keep telling you: pro-long the vowels. Pass over the consonants, but make sure to articulate them, especially the first and last of any word. Every word. Smo-othness, smooth— Late again?" he demanded.

Hari watched Tully squeeze himself between two older boys near the end of the first row. "Brought a new boy, sir," he said, pointing in Hari's direction. "Him, behind the pillar. Mrs. D sent a note."

Marsden rolled his sleeves higher up his forearms while he approached. Hari offered the note while keeping his distance. His sweaty palm had blurred some of the blue lines. "ABCs in two months, eh?" Marsden said. "Not bad, not bad. Well, Chandra, let's hear your so-fa." Hari said nothing. A ruler had appeared from Marsden's back pocket. "Come on, come on!" he ordered. He wiggled the ruler and said, "Do, re, mi!" Hari was speechless with confusion. Marsden continued with, "So, fa, la, ti, do." Hari decided he had been wrong about Marsden. He was no ogre but Tully was right: Marsden was madder than a Hatter. Had he never heard of notes?

Marsden leaned against the end of a pew and said, "Oh, look here! Mrs. D claims you can read music. Can you or can't you?" Hari nodded. Marsden tilted his head until the tuft behind his right ear brushed his shoulder. "Yes, sir?"

"Yes, sir," Hari echoed. He was used to it: everyone at Woodbine tried to bully him when they first met. But Hari had learned two tricks: either stare at the person until he turned away, or never show how much the bullying hurt. The first was more difficult but it was also more satisfying.

"Louder!" Marsden ordered.

"Yes, sir!" Hari started when pigeons outside the nearest window cooed in fright.

Marsden pressed his palm toward the floor while saying, "A bit less volume, please. Now, Mrs. Dalgleish says you can sing, so . . . sing."

The choirboys began whispering among themselves. Hari turned sideways to face a pew, then sang, "Hark! the herald angels sing,/Glory to—" When he breathed in the middle of the second line, Marsden said:

"*Herald* angels, not Harold angels. We're announcing Christ's birth here, not meditating on the Battle of Hastings. Prolong the vowels, yes, but don't stretch them out of shape. It's *sing*, not *si-ing*. Try it again, and don't let me catch you breathing in the middle of a line." This time he allowed Hari to get further.

> Joyful all ye nations rise,
> Join the triumph of the skies;
> With th'angelic host proclaim,

"Christ is born in Bethlehem!"
Hark! the—

Marsden bombarded him with, "*Rise*, not *ri-ise*. It's Beth-le-*hem* as in *ahem*, not *aim* even if it looks as if it should rhyme with *host proclaim*. We call that a slant rhyme. Enunciate, Chandra, enunciate." When Marsden turned to the choir, the whispering stopped. He waved his ruler and chanted, "We must be sure to enunciate!" He looked over his shoulder and caught Hari backing away. "Look here," Marsden asked, "are you joining us or not?" He seemed to be pouting.

"Oh, yes, sir!" Hari cried. He ran to the choir and tripped up a step to join Tully. All this time, Tully had been polishing his glasses on his tie but now he put them on and nudged Hari as if to say, "Good work."

Marsden clapped his hands for attention. "Number fifty-nine in the blue book," he announced. "It's still Advent. The St. Thomas version, if you please. Altos, you're still too weak. And Tully, let's leave the *vibrato* to the pigeons? Ready!"

Sharing Tully's book, Hari sang with the choir. He remained half a note behind for only the first verse:

The Advent of our King
Our prayers must now employ,
And we must hymns of welcome sing
In strains of holy joy.

In the two weeks leading up to the end of term, Hari learned "*Adeste fideles*," which the boys called "O come all ye faithful"; "*Puer nobis nascitur*," or "Unto us a child is born"; and "*Tempus adest floridum*," or "Good King Wenceslas." Despite Marsden's references to Latin as Papist doggerel, he rarely used the English titles of carols and hymns.

During the same two weeks, Mrs. D led the class in "Frosty the Snowman" and "Rudolph, the Red-Nosed Reindeer." None of the other reindeer would let Rudolph join in their games but

Hari's friends let him. Still, he knew exactly how Rudolph felt. The class spent more time not only singing but also making art. Following Mrs. D's instructions, the boys built a fireplace out of corrugated cardboard and hung four patchwork stockings on it—two large and two small. Then the boys made a nativity. They smoothed the foil from chocolate bars for angel wings, shredded paper to make straw, and used cotton batten for lambs. They twisted pipe cleaners into figures of shepherds and cattle: red and yellow for the shepherds, black and white for the cattle. There was also much to learn. Blindfolded Mexican children broke open papier-mâché *piñatas* filled with treats. Dutch children who were naughty woke to find lumps of coal instead of chocolates in their wooden shoes.

Hari repeated the stories to Krishna, who listened intently over supper. But Hari did not begin his stories, as he once had, with, "Did you know?" He began them with, "Guess what we learned today!"

✷

A week before Christmas, Rukmini returned from Toronto. Hari thought he would have to give up his bed but, no, Krishna slept on his box spring and she used his mattress.

On the first evening, she told Hari about her friends, the Visvanaths, and said they envied her because they had no children. "I have a surprise for you," she said. He thought it was a present but she brought him his old, orange photo album. "I should have left this with you," she said, "not taken it away like that. I am sorry. You can have it now." When she tried to open it, Hari traced the picture of the golden-haired boy holding flowers behind his back. Then Hari picked at the fraying edges and discovered it was a sticker, like the Flintstones stickers which came with Kellog's corn flakes. He sat back and watched her turn the pages with her head bent over the album.

"Here you are waving a sparkler at Deepavali," she said. "It was taken in Mauritius. Oh and here is the safari in Nairobi National Park. See the giraffes?"

Hari looked where she pointed but the giraffes were far away, near flat-topped trees. The photos were so small it was difficult to see anything clearly, and the writing on the scalloped white edges—writing in Rukmini's hand with a fountain pen—was fading. The only photo he liked was also the only coloured one in the album. It showed Krishna leaning against the grille of a car. After this came more black and white photos ending with one of Hari in a soldier's uniform. He stood with boys and girls beside a tree tied with ribbons. After this the pages were blank. He watched Rukmini begin again—he watched her tuck strands of hair behind her ear—and wondered why she looked sad. He also wondered why it felt strange having her back.

That night, while she sat on the edge of his bed and stroked his hair, she asked, "Did you miss me?"

"Of course," he said, but he felt as though he were telling a lie. He had missed her, yes, but so much had happened in the past month—the preparations for Christmas, the choir—and she hadn't been any part of it. He turned his face to the wall and fell asleep.

The following day after school he drank his Ovaltine and ate his snack. It was a lemon tart still fresh in its tin foil plate from Loblaw's. The tart also had scalloped edges but these were round, not square like the edges of the photos. Then he decided to help by taking the dirty cup to Rukmini instead of leaving it on the table. She was washing the day's breakfast and lunch dishes. "Here, Amma," he said.

The sponge splashed when she threw it into the sink. "Is this all I am to do here?" she snapped. "Cook food and wash dishes? In Toronto I do not have to—" She leaned her forehead against a cupboard door. It creaked open and she slammed it shut. The door creaked open again.

Hari tasted bitter snakes when he swallowed. They coiled in the back of his throat. They slithered into his stomach to curdle the milk of the Ovaltine.

She turned from the sink and hugged him, so hard he thought he might smother. This was how he had felt the first time Krishna made him bundle up to play outside. Hari pulled away from her and ran to his room. He knelt on his bed to look out and wished he were playing, alone, in the snow.

The next evening, over supper, after Hari told a story about the first Christmas celebrated in New France, Krishna said, "So, history isn't boring, is it?" Hari had never said it was but Krishna still asked strange questions like this. He would laugh as though he didn't expect an answer. His next question was a real one, though: "What do you want for Christmas, Boy?"

"A piano!" Hari cried.

Krishna snorted.

"Your *appa* will get you an electric train instead," Rukmini said.

"Do you know how much they cost?" Krishna demanded.

"I can help," she said. "I have some money."

"I forgot," he said. "You're a professor now."

She tried to say, "I am a lecturer only," but he was addressing Hari:

"There's a new movie playing at the Capitol. A war movie." Then Krishna asked Rukmini, "Do you want to come?"

"You both enjoy yourselves," she said.

The theatre had a green maple leaf on its front and, below this, the title of the movie in black letters on white glass. Krishna bought tickets from a woman in a booth. He was in such a good mood, he bought Hari a drink in a lidded wax-paper cup. Even as they took their seats, the cherubs painted on the ceiling faded. Everyone stood for "God Save the Queen" while the Queen, larger than life, reviewed troops. She went on to receive flowers from little girls but Hari saw a new scene: the girls were dancing in a field with jasmine in their braided hair. They played ring around the rosey, a pocket full of posies. Then came a number of short films: one about Eskimos in fur coats who stooped over holes in the ice, an animated one about a woodpecker who laughed like Marsden, and a very short one called "Coming Attractions." When the screen went blank, Hari stood to leave but the heavy curtains drew farther apart. The screen grew wider to reveal a woman holding a torch. Hari sat down, well back in his seat, which kept threatening to fold him in half.

Hari had never seen a movie with real people in it, and he had never seen one with so much action. Men in green bowled exploding cricket balls at men in grey. The men in grey threw back exploding potato mashers. Then a woman in a gypsy dress sang a French song in a smoky café. Hari touched Krishna's arm and began describing the splendid frock Marsden had given him: a white one with puffed sleeves sewn over a longer red one with yellow piping.

When a shadowy figure went, "Shh!" Hari stopped.

Krishna turned to glare at the figure. Then he touched Hari's shoulder and whispered, "Tell me later."

Hari nodded. Yes, he would, on the way home.

Soon the movie grew difficult to follow and there was much shouting among the men in green, who then went out to shoot at the men in grey. Hari understood what was happening only because he understood the music. He felt glad when bands played briskly, sad when violins wailed in A minor, and happy when soldiers yee-hawed while a friend played a tinny piano. They were back in the café, and he played quickly to cover his mistakes. After this, Hari fell asleep. He snuggled against Krishna, who encircled Hari's shoulder with his arm. The next morning Hari remembered stumbling toward the lobby while names rolled up the screen and a lone instrument whined. It sounded like a chorus of cats, yet it also stirred his blood. After the next choir practice he asked Marsden what it was.

Marsden called the instrument a bagpipe. "How quaint," he said. "A blood-stirring chorus of cats. My sentiments exactly. There's hope for you yet, Chandra."

On Christmas Eve Hari took one last look around the living room. No stockings hung above the fireplace, but the apartment didn't have a fireplace so this was all right. Neither did Mrs. Gardner's apartment. She had hung two stockings labelled *Granny* and *Al* on the antlers of something called a jackalope. Even though the jackalope had antlers, it looked like a large rabbit. Althea said her father had shot the jackalope in the Wild West. As for a Christmas tree, there was none in Hari's living room, but no one visited the apartment so this was also all right. Mrs. Gardner had many visitors, and a mound of gifts surrounded her white plastic tree. She told him they hid the usual things: balls of wool, Laura Secord almond bark, bingo chips, cribbage boards, and pack after pack of little cigars. He looked at his own presents. Two parcels leaned against the metal stand holding the radio. One, in blue paper with jolly white snowmen on it, was tagged, "To Hari from Granny Gardner and Althea." The other, in white paper with a pink ribbon, had written on it in pencil, "To Harischandra from the Visvanaths." He knew both presents were books.

The last thing he remembered before falling asleep was Mrs. D reciting, "Visions of sugarplums danced in their heads." He dreamt he was slipping out through the closed blinds. A fence separated the apartment building from a row of town houses. For days, fallen snow had caught on the diamond links of the fence to glisten like sugar frosting or like fairies. In his dream the links broke free and the snowflakes turned into angels with golden hair, angels with wings twinkling like the stones on Mrs. Gardner's rings, angels with names like Althea.

On Christmas morning, Hari ran into the living room. He clapped and announced, "Merry Christmas!"

Krishna looked up from his new book, a biography of the Duke of Wellington. "Merry Christmas, Boy," he said. Church music played softly on the radio.

Rukmini sat on the floor with diagrams of electric circuits. On her lap lay a slide rule and a pad of graph paper. Beside her lay textbooks. "Merry Christmas, Babu," she said. She pointed her slide rule at the dining table.

On it lay a folded sweater and a jar of Noxzema. The sweater was white with red and blue bands on the V-neck. After climbing onto a chair, Hari twisted the lid off the jar. It was filled with shiny quarters, more quarters than he had ever seen in one place.

He spilled them onto the table and began stacking them in fours with the mooseheads up. He had five dollars.

"Those are from me," she said. "The sweater is from your *appa*. He searched all over Sparks Street Mall. It is a tennis sweater."

"I'll teach you how to play tennis in the spring," Krishna said. "Would you like that?"

Hari pretended to be delighted.

"What do you say?" Rukmini asked.

"Thank you, sir."

She tilted her head at him as though asking, "Can't you call him Appa at last?"

Krishna nodded over his book. "It's nothing," he said and repeated, "Merry Christmas, Boy."

After a quick breakfast, Hari ran to his room with the parcels. Yes, they both contained books. He read the one from the Visvanaths quickly because it was for a child much younger than him, but he found a good use for it. He took the maple leaves from the atlas and slipped them into the children's book. The leaves threatened to spill out. He found the rubber band from his broken Van de Graaff and wrapped it around the book. Then he looked at the one from Mrs. Gardner and Althea. It was *The Adventures of King Arthur and the Knights of the Round Table.* He opened the book and began to read. It was about a magician named Merlin and a boy named Arthur, whom Merlin took from his father, a king named Uther Pendragon. Later Arthur proved he was Uther's son by pulling a sword from a stone. And all this happened in the first chapter. When Rukmini called Hari for lunch, he ran to the dining table. He wore the tennis sweater over his pyjamas. She stood proudly at the table while steam rose from three rectangular foil plates. He smiled at her often while eating the warm turkey and gravy, the mashed potatoes and the cranberry sauce. For dessert she served a Christmas cake. It was so moist, it stuck to the cellophane on top and the corrugated, red paper underneath. Hari wanted to tell Krishna and Rukmini about the special Christmas service, the last one before the end of term, but he kept it to himself. He didn't think Krishna would be interested since it was about singing. As for Rukmini, she looked faraway.

For this last service, the choir had worn its white on red frocks with yellow piping. The congregation had worn its blue blazers or black gowns. Marsden, wearing his suit jacket for once, had conducted from the organ. Even the Vienna Boys' Choir, which Marsden held up as his ideal, could not have sounded more angelic. The Woodbine choirboys had filled the chapel with "Angels We Have Heard On High."

*Gloria, In excelsis Deo.*

The Union Jack, the cadet corps' colours, and the Red Ensign had quivered. The armoured saints—George, Andrew, Patrick, and David—had smiled at Hari from their windows. Oh, happy, happy boy, rocking from heel to toe, with his face flushed. Chills had played on his ribs and spine as though his bones were piano keys.

In the front row, Merlin had kept the lapels of his gown pulled back to show off the crest of the Horse Guards. Next to him, Hodgson had sat with his arms crossed but Mrs. D, who sat near the back, had kept her hands in her lap and her eyes closed while she mouthed the words. Beside her sat Mrs. Gordon, the woman who had led Hari down all the stairs and corridors, past all the blue lockers and doors to his new class. There had been Bullion in his uniform with his gloves tucked into his Sam Browne belt. And there had been the boys: Naismith, Sinclair, Vance, Christou, Nunn and the rest—the junior school in the front pews, the senior school behind them. Little Robbie Brandon had chanced a wave. Taking a deep breath before the next *Gloria*, which had to be stretched over eight beats, Hari had nodded back. He loved Robbie Brandon. Hari loved them all.

❋

The New Year brought a new boy to Woodbine. Hari didn't see him at first because the boy was in the fifth form, in the junior school annex, but Christou and Vance saw him in the washroom. "You should be a pal with this Engel," Christou said. "Came over on the same boat as you except he's African."

"Cut it out, Greasy," Vance said. "He's something else, HC. He can multiply in his head and he knows everything."

"Talks like you, too," Christou added. "Uses funny words like lorry and petrol."

"HC doesn't talk like that," Tully scoffed. "He's one of us now." Tully elbowed Hari and Hari elbowed him back. Not only did they stand next to one another in the choir but they were also best friends. Sometimes Tully let Hari wear his glasses and shuffle about with his hands clasped behind his back the way Merlin walked through the halls. Without telling Krishna, Hari often bought Tully an Eskimo Pie.

The next morning, Mrs. D sent Nunn to borrow a map of Canada from the fifth form teacher. "This Engel's neat," Nunn said later. "A lily-white jungle boy. Never goes out because he can't stand the sun."

That afternoon, instead of playing shinny on the rink during break, half a dozen boys from Mrs. D's class ran into the junior school annex. They reached it in time to see a dozen older boys chase a new one up to the auditorium. He didn't run like them, taking two steps at a time. He loped, bent over, with his knuckles brushing the stairs. The other boys climbed slowly so he could reach the top first. When he turned, they stopped. So did Hari, to look up in wonder at this Engel.

He truly was lily-white for an African—not only his skin, which was more pinkish than white, but also his faintly golden hair. His eyes were pink like a rabbit's. Pretending to catch flies, he snapped at the air. Then he ground his teeth and gulped loudly so his Adam's apple quivered. He beat his chest and trumpeted like an elephant.

"Tarzan!" Christou shouted.

"Monkey Man!" a fifth former yelled.

Another one added, "Jungle Jim!"

Chanting all three names, the boys continued up the stairs. They chased Engel out of Hari's sight and into the auditorium. Hari took only one step at a time. Nunn took two like the older boys. Christou also took two but he grunted from the effort. When Naismith stumbled and slapped his hand down for balance, Christou went out of his way to step on Naismith's hand. Any other time Naismith would have stuffed his fingers into his mouth and rolled his eyes, but Hari suspected Naismith had finally met his match. Hari ran into the auditorium to find Engel loping about the stage. The other fifth formers shook their fists at him and shouted, "Run, monkey, run!" He scratched his armpits and his head. He wiggled his white eyebrows, shoved his chin forward, and curled back his lips to give a shrieking laugh.

"Showtime!" a fifth former yelled.

The others chanted, "Give us a show!"

Hari thought they were already watching one but, no, Engel rose to his full height and adjusted his tie. The red and yellow stripes were not yet sagging like Hari's from daily knotting and tugging. Engel's eyebrows fell into place. They were so pale, they vanished against his skin if he didn't wiggle them.

"What'll it be today?" he asked. He spoke with an accent which was not quite British.

"Social studies!"

"Maths!"

"Music!"

Tully nudged Hari and said, "Good one."

"Music," Hari repeated and Engel nodded. Hari called, "What do all cows eat?"

The fifth formers groaned.

Engel went to the piano at one side of the stage. He played A, C, E and G on the bass clef. "All cows eat grass," he announced. He waved with the back of his hand as though dismissing Hari.

"Social studies!" a fifth former repeated. Engel nodded again. "When was the Battle of Hastings?" the boy asked.

"Ten sixty-six," Engel replied.

Then all the boys shouted questions and Engel answered them without stopping to think:

"Battle of Waterloo?"

"Eighteen fifteen."

"Columbus's three ships?"

"*Niña, Pinta, Santa Maria.*"

"What's the tallest mountain?"

"Everest."

"What's the deepest place on earth?"

"The Marianas Trench."

"Who conquered the Aztecs and Incas?"

"Cortez and Pizarro."

"Wrong," a fifth former cried. "Cortez conquered them both!"

Engel again waved with the back of his hand. This time he added, "Piss orf. Go do your prep."

Prep was the word for doing lessons at night. The boarders did prep in the classroom next to the auditorium. They followed nearly as many rules as Hari did, but theirs sounded more interesting: beds stripped each Tuesday morning, shoeshine before showers, a letter home once a month. He had learned this from Sinclair, who still broke all the rules and spent the Fridays after his caning waddling like a duck. He said most of the boys wrote to their mothers.

Hari's first letter from Rukmini arrived at the end of the week. "To Master G. Harischandra" appeared above the address. Krishna used a stainless steel knife to open the envelope, then gave the envelope to Hari. Hari took out a sheet of graph paper and spread it on the table. With his chin on his fists and his elbows on the table, he silently read: "Dear Babu, How are you? I am fine. I have settled in a rooming house. It is not very big, but there will be plenty of room when you visit at Easter. Toronto is a splendid city. In the evening I go to lectures and museums with the Visvanaths. I told them how much you enjoyed the book they gave you for Christmas. Remember to do everything Appa tells you. Love, Amma."

Hari asked to use the gold ballpoint pen, the one Krishna never used. He kept it in his good briefcase, which he also never used. Sometimes he took it out so Hari could admire the *GKR* stamped in gold on the flap. Krishna said he never used this briefcase or the pen because they were farewell presents, the briefcase from Benares and the pen from Columbia. Hari was good at penmanship and he liked writing, as long as it wasn't at school. Unlike Mrs. D, Krishna never made Hari print his letters two lines high. Krishna let Hari join his letters and write them on a single line. Hari frowned at a sheet of Krishna's ruled paper, then at Rukmini's letter, before asking for help.

"I'll dictate and you write," Krishna said. He took off his tie clip, tie and cufflinks. The tie clip went into his shirt pocket with the cufflinks; the tie went over the back of the third chair. The fourth one sat in the small bedroom so Hari could stand on it to look out the window.

He beamed. He liked doing things with Krishna as long as they didn't involve learning anything. Hari especially liked watching TV with him.

The previous Saturday, before the end of Christmas break, Krishna had brought home a TV set with rabbit ears. Hari thought it was a shame Rukmini couldn't watch it. She had gone back to Toronto so she could celebrate New Year's with her friends. Seated at Krishna's feet, Hari watched a long show called "Hockey Night in Canada." He couldn't take his eyes from the screen even during the commercials. He especially liked the Esso Happy Motoring Man. Krishna looked up from his book only when Bill Hewitt's voice climbed an octave during an exciting play or, better yet, during a fight. The Toronto Maple Leafs were at home, playing the Montreal Canadiens, who were visiting. Toronto became Hari's favourite team not only because Rukmini lived there but also because it won the game. A left-winger named Frank Mahovlich, the Big M, scored two goals and was named the first star. He became Hari's favourite player. Krishna said Mahovlich and another left-winger named Bobby Hull had joined the NHL the year after Krishna had arrived in the United

States. He had seen both of them, at different times, play the New York Rangers at Madison Square Gardens. Krishna said although Mahovlich had been named Rookie of the Year, Hull was still the better man. Hari decided he could like the Big M if he wanted.

"Are you listening?" Krishna asked.

Hari jerked his eyes back from the TV. He had drawn a maple leaf in the top right-hand corner of the sheet. Under it he had scribbled the first seven notes of "Angels We Have Heard On High."

Krishna replaced the sheet with a new one. "You can start with Dear Amma," he said. He made a paper airplane from the first sheet while he dictated. "How are you? I am fine. I have started back to school, and the choir is practising—" He asked, "What are you practising for now?"

"Lent," Hari said. Krishna nodded permission but Hari wrote, "Onward Christian Soldiers." The choir had practised it once in December and planned to sing it more often in coming weeks. It was so rousing, everytime Hari sang it he felt like linking his arm with Tully's and marching about the chapel.

"What are you writing now?" Krishna asked.

Hari read the name of the hymn aloud.

"Oh, that's all right," Krishna said. "Let's see . . . There isn't any more, so you can finish with these last two lines: Love, HC."

After Hari wrote the *Love*, he said, "She always calls me Babu. Only the boys at school call me HC."

"Do what you want," Krishna said.

Hari did. He even added a line at the bottom: "Granny and Al say hello."

Krishna sealed the letter in an envelope and wrote Rukmini's address on it. Hari was putting her letter in his pocket when Krishna looked up. "Now what are you doing?" he asked.

"Keeping the letter," Hari said.

"Why?" Krishna asked. "You've answered it."

Hari knew Krishna wouldn't approve, but he took the letter to school. He wanted to show it to Marsden once they were alone. There was never a chance during choir practice, but on the second Monday back to school Hari and Marsden spent nearly an hour together.

During the first week back, Mrs. D had announced she could teach Hari nothing new; he would have to go to Marsden for conservatory work. And so Hari took another note from Mrs. D to Marsden, who said he would gladly take Hari on—not, he assured Hari, because he had finished his ABCs in two months but because he had a good ear. Hari could sing an entire hymn, melody or harmony, after hearing it once. But when Hari told Krishna the lessons would cost a dollar each, Krishna shook his head. Hari brought his Noxzema jar from his room and spilled the quarters onto the dining table. Krishna surprised him by laughing. It was a nice laugh. "Okay, Boy," he said, "piano lessons it is," and he tousled Hari's hair. Now, approaching the Tuck Shop late on the second Monday, Hari marvelled at how easy it had been. Perhaps Krishna understood, at last, how much Hari liked playing the piano. It never occurred to Hari to ask Krishna the real reason: he was in favour of the lessons as long as Hari took them seriously and, even more important, as long as he excelled.

✱

The first conservatory lesson began with Marsden announcing, "Never mind the piano. You, Chandra, will learn to play the organ." And so, Marsden lectured while Hari sat rocking from side to side in the right-hand front pew. He rocked because the wooden pew was uncomfortable. The choir stall had cushions. Marsden stood blocking the way to the sanctuary as though afraid Hari might pounce on the keyboards, what Marsden called the manuals. "The secret to playing an organ is simplicity," he said. He tapped his ruler on an invisible head. "I don't care if the music is marked *forte*, you're not here to drown out the choir. And remember what I keep telling Tully? Leave the *vibrato* to the pigeons? The same goes for the organ. No *tremolo*."

Although he barely understood a word, Hari nodded. The thought of playing such a huge instrument made him feel small.

"Where possible," Marsden continued, "use eight-foot stops, but—" He tilted his head back and forth like a metronome. "—you can use a firm pedal bass sometimes. Remember, the choir tries to reach Him." Marsden jabbed upward with his ruler. "The congregation tries to overcome its own incompetence, and the organist supports them both. So clean playing, if you please, but not too *legato*. Lift the hands—" He did, and the ruler floated up like a baton. "—to help everyone bre-athe. When they breathe, they attack the words. And when they attack, we win!" He hopped forward and landed in front of Hari. Marsden's clothes smelled of tobacco but his breath smelled of spearmint gum. "Right?" he demanded. "Of course!" He stepped back and nodded so hard, Hari thought Marsden's head would bounce off the floor and smash through a window. Pointing his ruler at the sanctuary, Marsden shouted, "Onward, Christian soldiers!"

At last Hari sat down at the organ. But he couldn't reach the pedal-board. He could if he slouched, teetering on the edge of the bench, but then he could not reach both manuals. He wanted to quit. Not Marsden, though. He ran from the chapel and returned with four blackboard erasers. He tied two under each of Hari's shoes with the laces from his own brogues. It was still no good. Pulling on his hair, all he had left of it, Marsden said, "Apparently it's the piano for you after all." He strode from the chapel and Hari followed, leaving a trail of yellow chalkdust. He raised clouds of it from having to lift his feet straight up and plant them straight down. Marsden reached the music room first. He sat with his back to a rosewood piano and leaned his elbows on the polished cover. Hari kicked the erasers loose, untied the dusty laces, and wiped the chalkdust from his shoes.

"Today's lesson will be short," Marsden said, relacing his brogues. "A review to see if you've picked up any nasty habits from Mrs. Dalgleish. Regular lessons will be Tuesdays and Thursdays, not every day as you had before. There's a time to be the hare and a time to be the tortoise. Practices will be Mondays, Wednesdays and Fridays for an hour." Hari began to squirm. "I'll be down the hall for the first half," Marsden said, "and no cheating after I'm gone." He straightened at last and regarded Hari as though through the wrong end of a telescope. Hari stopped squirming. "No long faces here, Chandra!"

"N-no, sir," Hari stammered. "It's just, Mrs. D taught me for only half an hour. Then I practised for fifteen minutes. My father picks me up after work."

"Very well," Marsden said. "You can put in another, say, half-hour at home and— Oh, look here! Must you keep frowning like that? I can't read your mind. If you have something to say, speak up!" He went on without giving Hari the chance to speak. "Really, Chandra, if life were filled with recitative instead of dialogue, you'd sing sixty beats a minute. You act as bold as brass when you're in the choir." Stooping so his beaked nose nearly touched Hari's cheek, Marsden whispered, "Are you afraid to talk?"

"No, sir," Hari whispered back. He wondered who they were plotting against. Mrs. D? Krishna? Surely not Rukmini.

Marsden's brow furrowed. "Then why don't you speak?" he demanded.

Hari didn't know. At first he had been shy because of his accent but it had vanished since he had joined the choir. He no longer spelled his name with a *Hetch*; he spelled it with an *Aitch*. It was simply that he often had little to say. He was too busy listening to voices which cried, "Is this all I am to do here? Cook food and wash dishes?" Voices which followed him through walls and into closets: "Other women have more than one child!" He pulled the letter out of his inside jacket pocket.

"What is it then?" Marsden asked.

"We don't have a piano," Hari replied.

Marsden launched himself from the bench so quickly, Hari nearly fell off. "Incredible, simply incredible! And why not? No, don't tell me!" Marsden shook the ruler. When he wasn't using it, he kept it warm in his back pocket. "I don't want to know."

Hari slid the letter into his pocket. He decided to wait until the voices went away.

Marsden took a deep breath and brought his arms in a circle until his wrists crossed at his belt buckle. He snapped his head down. "Very well," he said with his chin pressed to his throat, "you'll stay an extra two hours after Sunday service. You'll practise in here, with that door closed, so the dining room can't distract you. Neither the chatter nor the smell of beef hash." He landed on the bench and Hari gripped its edge when the bench rocked. "This isn't ABCs," Marsden warned. "Not Boris Berlin or Leila Fletcher or whomever nursed you through *'Frè-re Jacques, Frè-re Jac-ques, dor-mez vous?'* This is sight reading, ear training, transposition, pedal work, broken chords— The whole gamut. Even a little composition. When I was your age, I dreamt of becoming a composer, not some Ottawa Valley *Kapellemeister*."

Hari wanted to ask what *Kapellemeister* was, but Marsden spoke too quickly for interruptions.

"Most of all we'll have fun," he said. "I promise. By the time I'm done with you, you'll play 'The Teddy Bear's Picnic' à la Haydn, Beethoven, and Shostakovich. Do you know who they are?" Even as Hari shook his head, Marsden chuckled. "Never mind, you will. I can see it now. If you're half as promising at the keyboard as you are in the choir, you'll have a bust of Mozart on your mantel where other boys keep pictures of hockey players." Marsden rose and left Hari to puzzle over all of this, especially the remark about hockey players. At least Hari no longer had to shout, "Yes, sir! No, sir!" Marsden said, "Now let's begin our review."

Hari gratefully pushed the keyboard cover out of sight. It seemed to him, while he edged onto the centre of the bench, that Marsden would have all the fun. Later, with Marsden's woodpecker laugh ringing in his ears, Hari ran downstairs. Passing the Tuck Shop, he heard boys teasing one another in the TV room. He had a quarter in his pocket, enough for two and a half Eskimo Pies, but he wanted to save his money for the train. He ran up the sloping corridor. According to the clock near the gym, he still had twenty minutes, enough time to look at the forts behind the junior school. Some of them had roofs of snow piled on broken hockey sticks, crisscrossed to make rafters. Tully said the senior school boys hid their cigarettes in these forts because the masters never dared crawl into the connecting tunnels. Neither did Hari; he didn't like small spaces even if they were white. Just as he reached the door leading down to his classroom, he heard someone playing a piano. "Chopsticks" came from the auditorium. Anyone who could play the piano, even something as simple as "Chopsticks," might turn out to be a friend. Hari ran into the annex and climbed to the auditorium. Here he stood quietly at the foot of three steps which led onto the stage.

The new boy, Engel, was seated at the piano. Hari could see only his back, but there was no mistaking the golden-white hair inching toward his collar. Using two fingers, Engel played "Chopsticks" again until he struck his first wrong note. Then he leaned forward. His brow struck the piano with a hollow, thumping twang.

"It's not so bad," Hari said.

Engel swiped at his eyes before turning on the stool.

"I'll show you," Hari offered. He felt proud of being able to do something an older boy could not. He climbed onto the stage and approached the piano. "Are you really African?"

"South African," Engel replied in his not-quite-British accent. He got up and Hari sat down. "There's a difference." Instead of explaining the difference, Engel said, "My old man got posted here from Moscow. That's in Russia. Napoleon invaded it in eighteen twelve."

Hari had never heard of Napoleon. He wanted to hear about Engel's father. "Is he the High Commissioner?" Hari asked.

Engel snorted. "He's just a cultural attaché. Truth is," Engel said, wiggling his pale eyebrows, "he's a spy." Engel threw back his head and laughed like an ape. He curled his arms above his head before scratching his armpits.

"It's not funny," Hari said. He meant the way Engel acted. Seeing him this close, with his shirt tail curving behind the hem of his dusty blazer, made Hari queasy. Something was wrong with Engel but Hari didn't know what: only that it made him feel worse than the voices which snaked into his stomach. The longer Engel somersaulted on the stage, pounded his chest and shrieked, the louder Hari said, "It's not funny!" Engel pushed his face close to Hari's and snapped at his nose. Even Krishna with his large hands had never made Hari feel as small as he felt now, or as ill. He cried, "Stop it!" and slapped Engel.

The slap echoed on the stage. Hari raised his hands to protect his face. He cried, "I didn't mean—!" Nothing happened. When he lowered his hands, he saw Engel on the floor. He sat with his gangly legs drawn half up and his elbows on his knees. His spindly arms wobbled. He stared at his shoes as though he had never seen them dusty. "I didn't mean it," Hari said.

Engel began to weep. He wept so quietly, Hari thought the tears were alligator tears. This was what Sinclair called them, false ones meant to stop Bullion from bringing his swagger stick down too hard. "Stop that," Hari heard voices say. "Only girls cry." The silent weeping frightened him. The snakes churned in his stomach. These snakes hadn't hatched from words, though. They came from watching Engel's white cheeks turn splotchy; from watching his pink lips quiver like his almost invisible lashes.

Hari bolted from the piano stool. He ran from the auditorium back to his class. He was in for it now. He had broken Mrs. D's rule about not fighting. Engel would tell Nunn, and he would report Hari to Mrs. D, who might forbid him to play her piano. He climbed onto the old stool and threw back the keyboard cover. This piano wasn't polished like the one in the senior school but it could still make music. He played "Hark! The Herald Angels Sing" loudly, much too loudly. It drove the picture of Engel from his mind.

Marsden had made Hari play the carol during the review. Marsden had raised his voice and pulled his hair as often as he did during choir practice. He had even slapped out the time on Hari's thigh until it stung through the grey flannel. After Hari had played it for the third time, Marsden said, "The left hand's a bit weak, but that's to be expected. Not bad, Chandra. Not bad at all. We'll make a real musician out of you yet."

Glowing now from the remembered praise, Hari closed the cover. He pulled on his snowsuit and galoshes, then ran out into the cold even as the Lark stopped at the back gate. He glowed while he climbed into the car.

He glowed until Krishna asked his favourite new question, one he had made up from a Charlie Chan movie they had watched on TV: "So, what did my expensively educated number-one son learn today?"

At times Hari thought the question was funny and he answered it. Today he sat growing cold while the glow faded.

"Nothing?" Krishna said and sighed. "A man can't win," he said, mainly to himself. He didn't expect an answer when he added, "What is it this time?" but Hari surprised him by saying:

"I don't want to learn the piano any more."

Krishna drove slowly because the sidestreets had not been cleared. He kept the Lark to the yellowing ruts, one pair of ruts in each lane. The only other cars in sight were parked in front of brightly lit houses. He waited until he reached the Rockcliffe Parkway before he said: "Is this Mr. Marsden tough?"

"No," Hari lied.

"What is it then?" Krishna asked.

Hari shrugged and looked out his window. He didn't know how to explain it and he thought only Rukmini would understand. It was the way Krishna so often spoke; the way he spoiled things. But it wasn't simply this. There was also Engel.

"You stick it out a while longer," Krishna said, and Hari nodded.

They didn't speak the rest of the way home. Hari followed Krishna to the main entrance but stood holding the outside glass door open. Unlocking the inside door, Krishna said over his shoulder, "Don't get cold."

Hari shook his head. He went in search of a patch of undisturbed snow. He found one between the parking lot and the fence. Looking up, he saw lights switched on in his apartment but he ignored them. He held out his arms, held his breath, and let himself fall backward. The snow cushioned his fall. He knew it would. He could trust snow. More snow was falling now in the darkness. He waved his arms up toward his head and down toward his waist. He moved his legs out and in. He opened his mouth and tried to catch snowflakes on his tongue. The flakes tickled his lips. Without Althea to help him, it was difficult to rise, but he managed. He picked a spot next to his snow angel and made another one, then another and another. He kept making them until he was tired of rising without help. Once upstairs, he perched on the chair at his window and looked down at what he had done. The entire area between the parking lot and the fence, lit by a single streetlight, was filled with snow angels. The latest ones were not as neatly made as the earliest ones, but he had made them himself. The white flakes in the sky were thicker now and the angels were filling with snow. Soon there was nothing left but a line of faint impressions. This was all right. He could always make more. Next time he would make enough to form a choir, his very own choir of snow angels.

# Chapter 13

# *Van de Graaff Days*

When Stan Morely asked, "How'd the skiing lesson go?" Krishna blinked at his calendar.

Mounted on a peg board above his desk, the calendar flipped up to reveal a different photograph for each month. February was represented by a winter scene: trees covered with hoarfrost in the Gatineau Hills. He hadn't been admiring the picture, though; he had been counting down to Hari's birthday. There were two days left in February, then two weeks until March fifteenth. Krishna still couldn't decide on a present. Hari liked wearing the tennis sweater but Krishna knew better than to mention tennis lessons again. Next to the calendar was the old picture of Ganesha with its lower edge neatly trimmed. He wondered whether to separate the Ganesha and the winter scene but he liked the contrast: the elephant god and the frozen trees.

He put down his coffee and turned.

Morely had a habit of changing subjects without warning. Only moments ago, he had been talking about the high cost of dental care because two of his three children needed braces. "It went well," Krishna said at last. "I took the boy to the place you recommended. He seemed to enjoy it but he was so afraid of falling, I thought he might accidentally stab himself in the foot with his pole." Krishna shook his head at the memory of standing on the beginners' slope. With five children to teach, the instructor had been unable to give Hari the special attention he needed, the finer points of technique Krishna could have taught had he known how to ski. Yes, the tennis lessons could wait for a year or two.

"Doing it's the only way," Morely said. "Know how I learned to swim? My old man rowed me out from shore one day and said, 'Get out, Stan.' I thought he was kidding till he started rocking the boat. So, I got out. For a while I treaded water hoping he'd let me back in. He just sat there hoping I'd stick my hand out. Then I thought, 'Bugger you,' and headed for shore. Paddled like a dog but I made it." Morely laughed. With his head thrown back, he looked bald. His double chin vanished into his short neck and his pot belly shook. Then he straightened and rubbed his brush cut.

Krishna also laughed. His first attempt at swimming had been less dramatic. He and his brother, Ravi, had spent many hot afternoons in local tanks, small reservoirs. One day Krishna had decided to swim to the other side of the tank, and he had. Ravi had never learned to swim—he was too afraid of drowning. Now Hari was taking after an uncle he barely knew. No longer laughing, Krishna looked at the Van de Graaff in the middle of the hangar.

Unlike the Van de Graaff in the Engineering College Museum, the sphere on this one was only five feet in diameter but the visible part of the column was longer, over eight feet high. Also unlike the museum piece, this Van de Graaff worked: the belts carried twenty thousand volts from the base to the sphere, which could store up to two million volts. No twine and orange paint here: even the grounding rod was in perfect condition. It rose from a hinged arm to a metal sphere the size of a soccer ball. Krishna insisted the large sphere be kept shiny even if he had to clean it himself. He often did, by climbing a ladder mounted on wheels, while Morely held the ladder steady. He claimed he was afraid of heights.

Krishna poured his unfinished coffee into a thermos and corked it. Then he crossed the concrete floor to his workbench. The thermometer read sixty-five degrees, not unpleasantly cool, but he switched on the space heater at his feet. He left his slip-ons at the door and remained comfortable all day in his shoes. He could do nothing about his wrist, though. The wind blowing off the river was cold and damp and February had been particularly difficult. He was getting old, he thought.

Morely had just switched on the motor, driving the belts to build up a charge, when three men entered the hangar. Parker, the head of SEL, wore a hat with a partridge feather in the band. The collar of his tailor-made overcoat was turned up. When he called, "Afternoon, Gopal," Morely smirked at Krishna, who ignored him. Krishna was eyeing the two strangers with Parker. One of them wore an air force greatcoat. The tips of his ears, pushed out by the brim of his peaked cap, were red. There was a single row of gold leaves on the peak and four stripes on each of his epaulettes. The second stranger, in a navy blue duffel coat, wore ear muffs and carried a briefcase. All five men met near the Van de Graaff. It seemed the natural place to meet though the whining belts were distracting.

"Would've phoned," Parker said, "but we wanted to catch you in the act, so to speak." He grinned as though he always bantered with employees like this and Krishna again ignored Morely's smirk. "Claude Lafortune," Parker said, gesturing to the officer. The *Claude* sounded like *Clod*.

Krishna greeted him with, "Group Captain, how are you?"

Lafortune seemed delighted while they shook hands. "Ex-air force?" he asked. He looked dapper but his speech betrayed him. He spoke with a grating accent which Krishna knew to be joual, the same French spoken by shop clerks.

"No," Krishna said. When he added, "*Malheureusement,*" Lafortune seemed even more delighted. Then he glanced at

Krishna's desk and appeared intrigued. He had seen the picture of Ganesha. Krishna didn't bother to explain. It might sound quaint if he said, "That's the Indian god of wisdom, the remover of obstacles."

When the man in the duffel coat coughed, Krishna faced him. Parker glanced at the man and said, "Sorry, this is Sergeant Warwick of the RCMP."

Warwick did not offer his hand. He removed his ear muffs, collapsed them and slipped them into a pocket of his coat. Then he pulled the rawhide loops off their bone fasteners, one by one. He didn't look like a slave to fashion and Krishna liked this about him even if Warwick did seem incapable of relaxing.

"Group Captain Lafortune is the officer in charge of funding this project," Parker said. "He's the one who got you this hangar."

"It is nothing," Lafortune insisted when Krishna tried to thank him. "The air museum types wanted to store some old engines here but this is a more useful purpose, no?"

After Krishna introduced Morely to the newcomers, Parker clapped his gloved hands. "Let's get on with it then," he told Krishna. "I filed your last report with DND and they're pleased with our progress. Good work."

Morely rocked with his hands clasped behind his back. He had written the report under Krishna's name and Krishna had edited the text for clarity. Two of the equations had contained careless errors, which Krishna had corrected without telling Morely. His usual response to such things was, "What's a power of ten between friends?"

"Now they have a new request," Parker announced.

"If I might, *M'sieu*?" Lafortune asked. Then he said, "We want that you should commence planning the next project before you are finished with this one. We are expecting to receive approval of the budget shortly, in perhaps two months. I asked my superiors, 'Why wait? Is planning not crucial to such work?' They gave me their go-ahead. I understand you are beaming radio signals to that—" He waved at the receiver on Krishna's workbench. "—so you may study the interference of the atmosphere on communications between aircraft and ground?"

"Signals in the medium wave band," Krishna said. "Yes."

Parker all but ordered, "Can we have a demonstration?"

Before Krishna could reply, Morely said, "Sure." Lafortune was admiring the large sphere but Morely pointed at the base. "Most of the interference comes from the corona discharge between the points and the belts."

Lafortune looked abashed at examining the wrong end of the column.

Morely embarrassed him further by saying, "It's not what you can see that hurts you. It's what you can't see. But you *can* see the signal fluctuate on an oscilloscope. That one," he said, "hooked up to the receiver? Mr. Krishna-Rao measures the drop in signal strength."

Only Parker and Lafortune turned to look.

Warwick was watching Krishna, and Krishna wondered whether Warwick guessed why he took the measurements himself: because Morely's could be slipshod. But it couldn't be this, Krishna decided. Perhaps Warwick didn't like foreigners, but no, this was unfair. Still, something about him bothered Krishna—the deadpan look, perhaps.

"If you listen on the headphones," Morely continued, "you hear noise. Not just hissing or crackling. Any interference is called noise. It's even worse when the Van de Graaff flashes over." This time he pointed at the large sphere and nodded patiently at Lafortune as though at a child. "You hear a whistler on the radio," Morely said. "A swishing noise that goes down the scale like, well, a penny whistle. The noise lasts a hundred microseconds but it seems a lot longer and that's the whole point, eh?" He turned to Warwick. "What if you're giving the pilot a new target and he misses part of a sentence? You have to repeat it, he loses time, the target's gone. Or what if he's surprised by another plane and has to take evasive—"

Krishna interrupted because Warwick seemed bored. He was tapping his briefcase against his thigh. "Perhaps I should summarize?" Krishna said.

Morely rolled his eyes toward Lafortune as if warning, "Be nice to him. He's a bit slow."

Krishna raised his voice over the whine of the belts. "If the signal strength falls ten decibels, communications are effectively wiped out. But we've found we can keep the attenuation, the fall in signal strength, to less than three decibels at certain frequencies. What we call windows." He had meant to sound less technical than Morely, but once Krishna began lecturing, he found it difficult to stop. "We could decrease the interference by installing filters on the plane's receiver, but that adds weight—"

Now Lafortune interrupted. First he told Morely, "My minister, he sells such projects by pointing out how they benefit civilian aircraft as well."

"Oh," Morely said. "Right."

"At last we reach our purpose," Lafortune told Krishna. "Once you have completed this project—by the spring, I think?—we want that you should see the effect of these corona discharges and the flashing over on much higher frequencies."

"I don't think the effect itself will be much different," Krishna said. "A radio signal is a radio signal." He caught Parker staring at him coolly. Parker didn't like his researchers to dismiss projects out of hand, however simple they might sound.

But Lafortune also seemed to know the research on higher frequencies might tell them nothing new. "Perhaps yes, perhaps no," he said. "You see, the aircraft of the future will receive many more telemetry signals than those of voice. That is to say, signals directly from machines on the ground. After you have solved this problem of avoiding atmospheric interference on the medium wave band, we want that you should begin the same research on the telemetry. We know that in America they are already doing similar work because of President Kennedy pledging two years ago to win the Space Race, but will they share their results with us?" He spread his hands to suggest not.

Parker looked intrigued by the reference to space; pleased to be part of such exotic work. If he only knew, Krishna thought. Parker rarely visited the lab and had little idea of how much drudgery was involved.

Warwick, on the other hand, still looked bored. He was examining the wooden studs of the unfinished walls and the A-beams of the metal ceiling.

"They'll share the theoretical work," Krishna told Lafortune. "Through journals."

"We're doing applied work here," Parker said. He looked proud of this. "I believe theory belongs in the classroom?"

Krishna turned to hide his annoyance. He pulled the grounding rod away from the column so quickly, the weight of the small sphere set the hinged arm wobbling. Parker always wanted practical answers before theoretical problems were solved. He wanted every contract not so longlived as to upset his clients, yet not so shortlived as to upset his cash flow.

"Enter Sergeant Warwick," Parker told Morely. "Your security clearances will have to be upgraded before Mr. Lafortune delivers the new equipment. You'll lock it up every night and—" Krishna looked over his shoulder to find Parker addressing Lafortune. "It can actually communicate with other machines?"

Nodding in reply, Lafortune told Morely, "They are formalities, these clearances."

Warwick finally spoke. "If they were, I wouldn't be here," he said. "Sir."

Lafortune pursed his lips at the insulting pause before the *sir*.

Warwick propped his briefcase on a raised knee and took out a sheaf of flimsy paper, which he tossed onto the base of the Van de Graaff. "These are like the ones you probably filled out before," he told Morely, "but we'd like you to go back farther."

Krishna tensed. His wrist was beginning to throb and he flexed the fingers of his left hand. He heard Morely laugh.

"This is a joke, right?" Morely demanded. Much of life was a joke to him, but Krishna supposed there were worse ways of dealing with inconveniences, or surprises.

"Since the Missile Crisis, sir," Warwick replied, "we've stopped joking. Some of us have been around long enough to remember a certain Russian cipher clerk named Igor Gouzenko. Not much has changed in eighteen years. The war's gotten colder, that's all."

Krishna scanned the top form, which Morely picked up and held between them. The first item read, "Have you visited a Communist-dominated country since 1945? If so, list date(s) and reason(s) for visit(s)." As though implying long answers were suspect, only one blank line followed. The second item read, "List your addresses with dates for the past 20 years, beginning with the most recent. Account for significant time spent travelling." Only half a dozen lines followed. Krishna would need twice that number.

Morely fanned through the remaining forms and asked, "What's involved in checking us out this time?"

"The usual thing," Warwick said. "Interviewing neighbours, though we can't tell you who. Checking bank accounts, police records . . ."

Krishna could no longer remain silent. He forced himself to sound calm when he asked, "For convictions?"

"And warrants," Warwick said.

"Something wrong?" Parker asked.

Krishna lied: "I believe I forgot to pay a speeding ticket in Brooklyn some years back."

Everyone laughed with him except Warwick. "Don't worry, sir," he announced. "We'll let you know if you did."

This time only Parker and Morely laughed. Krishna grew cold. The statement sounded so ludicrous—so much like, "We have ways of finding out." It baffled him why only Lafortune looked disgusted. His eyes widened as if asking, "Where have we heard this before?"

"I think that's all then," Parker announced. "Mr. Krishna-Rao, I wonder if you could meet with the Group Captain so you'll know precisely what's involved with the new project?"

Krishna inclined his head.

The three visitors turned to leave. Just as they neared the exit, Morely pushed the grounding rod toward the column. A jagged blue line arced while the Van de Graaff discharged. The air between the spheres buzzed. Tensing, the three men turned. Even as Krishna moved to switch off the motor, there was a brilliant flash followed by a loud, crackling snap. Despite himself, he ducked.

He straightened to find Parker looking annoyed. "See me in the morning when you stop in, please," he called to Krishna. Now what? Parker followed the others out before Krishna could nod.

"Why did you do that?" he demanded, pulling the grounding rod from Morely's grasp.

"They forgot their demonstration."

Shaking his left hand—pretending he was trying to loosen a cramp—Krishna laughed even harder than Morely.

That evening, on checking the mail, Krishna found an advertising flyer from Ogilvy's department store and a phone bill. Rent was also due, tomorrow. While flipping through the flyer in the elevator, he discovered a squarish envelope from Rukmini caught in the furniture pages. Hari was so eager to open the envelope, he counted the slowly changing numbers while the elevator rose to their floor. Krishna supposed it was only natural. Two weeks before, she had sent a Valentine's card in reply to one Hari had made in school. The card from her stood next to the Noxzema jar of quarters on Hari's window sill, where the statue of Ganesha had been.

Hari still missed it. Rukmini had taken the statue back to Toronto. She had said, "I will trade you your photo album for this," and Hari had reluctantly agreed. He liked her Valentine's card, though. He had made yet another Valentine, for Mrs. Gardner, but not for Althea. They no longer played together because her father had returned from northern Ontario, and she had gone back to her parents. It didn't seem fair: losing not only Ganesha but also Althea.

After entering the apartment, Hari pulled off his galoshes, shoes and snowsuit, then ran to his room. Sitting on his bed, he opened the envelope. Inside was a birthday card—a clown with a red nose and large shoes who said, "On Birthday No. 8." He opened the card to find a folded square of grey paper. Rukmini had written a note in the card and he had to read the note twice before it made sense. Then he unfolded the grey square.

Still in the dining room, Krishna heard a "Hurray!" followed by the thump of sock feet. "Boy!" Krishna warned.

Hari ran down the corridor. He simply could not believe it. This was better than a jar of quarters. It was even better than a train. "A piano!" he cried. "A piano!"

"What piano?" Krishna asked.

Hari gave him the card first, then a cheque for $500. Krishna had to read the note only once. It began with Rukmini's usual, "How are you? I am fine." Farther down it read, "Here is your birthday card and a gift cheque. Give it to Appa and tell him it is for a piano and anything else you want. It is every penny I have saved since coming to Toronto. You must enjoy it for me."

Krishna sat down. "Five hundred dollars!" he muttered. Unbelievable. He thought he was only thinking the words but he heard himself say them: "Wouldn't she be better off here than buying you expensive presents?" Hari was watching him uncertainly. "I'll put this in the bank tomorrow," Krishna said. He tucked the cheque into his shirt pocket. "By the time you grow up, the money will have doubled or even tripled because the interest is compounded—"

Hari wasn't interested in lectures about banking. "No," he said. "It's for a piano!"

"Where would we put a piano?" Krishna demanded.

"In my room," Hari said. He could feel himself wanting to cry but he knew crying would only make Krishna angry. He sounded angry enough when he said:

"I'm not lugging a piano with us every time we move!"

"Where?" Hari asked, astonished.

"Who knows? I don't have a fancy job or a PhD like— Never mind. Go and change."

Hari did, but not before grabbing back the card.

Krishna took the cheque from his pocket and shook his head. It never rains but it pours, he thought. The phrase jarred. It was one of Morely's favourites because things never went wrong in the lab one at a time. Krishna tried the phrase aloud: "It never rains but it pours."

*

The next day, before lunch, Krishna drove to the SEL office on Laurier Avenue. He normally picked up his cheque from the bookkeeper but she said, "He's got it." She meant Parker, who handed it over himself after Krishna entered the inner office and took a seat. The cheque totalled $490 after deductions. It was enough, but always less than Krishna knew he deserved. Parker drove no mere second-hand Lark. He owned a Chrysler, ordered each year from the factory, and he lived on Clemow Avenue. His youngest son's paper route included the house of a cabinet minister.

"I just wanted you to drop by for a chat," Parker explained. "We never seem to have enough time for chats." He swivelled his chair so he could look at Krishna and also out the window. The office overlooked the Rideau Canal. It was frozen and Krishna glimpsed a lone skater. Parker asked, "Do you really think two men are necessary for this project?" He had asked the same thing only a few months before.

Krishna said, as he had then, "Our underwriters require us to have more than one man if we're working with anything over six hundred volts." This time he added, "If there's an accident, one of the men can get aid."

"Fortunately we've never had one," Parker said. He swivelled back and forth. Although he added, "Thanks to your methodical work," Krishna guessed Parker would never forgive anyone who caused an accident. "As I was saying?"

Even as he spoke, Krishna knew he was being too honest, perhaps too critical: "Mr. Morely has great technical ability, but his theoretical knowledge—"

Parker stopped himself from swivelling by laying a hand flat on his desk. "You seem to have trouble remembering theories belong in universities," he said. Before Krishna could decide whether to respond, Parker asked, "How are the skating lessons going, by the way?"

Krishna wanted to reply, "It's really not your business," but it was in a way. "I'm afraid I had to drop them," he said. "I've been spending more time with my son. He's learning to ski."

"Can't your wife do that?" Parker asked. "She came over with the boy, didn't she?" Krishna was not about to go into details. He didn't have to, since Parker moved on to one of his pet topics. "It's not my concern, of course, but I can't help thinking you need to use the system more. We're not called Systems Engineering, Limited for nothing." Krishna didn't smile and neither did Parker. "Why do you think I got you into the civil service rink? The name of the game is making contacts. Contacts lead to contracts."

Krishna forced himself to say, "Yes, sir." In the outer office, when the bookkeeper asked how it had gone, Krishna allowed himself to say, softly, "Contacts lead to contracts." She laughed and waved goodbye. Later, while he sped through an amber light, he wished he had said something less obliging than yes, sir; something pithy like, "I try to keep my private life separate from my professional life. Sir." But men like Parker would never understand this. He was an old DEA hand—Department of External Affairs—and still made the round of Ottawa cocktail parties. He called himself an engineer but he was a businessman. One day, Krishna thought, he would say this aloud: "You, sir, are not an engineer. You are merely a businessman."

Krishna drove south to Uplands. He had planned to go to the bank during his lunch hour but Lafortune had phoned early this morning and insisted, politely, that they have lunch. He had suggested a restaurant on Sussex Drive near Byward Market, but Krishna always took sandwiches to work so he had suggested a grille next to the airport. It was the Golden Jet Grille, named for the RCAF aerobatic team. During his first year in Ottawa, Krishna had eaten here once a week.

Lafortune was already in the restaurant, at a table next to the window. He surprised Krishna with, "You look as jolly as I am feeling."

"Something wrong?" Krishna asked. He hung his coat and scarf on a hook, pulled out the chrome and vynil chair, and sat down.

"It is why I phoned you to meet today itself," Lafortune said, tapping his menu. "This Sergeant War-wick—"

"War-rick," Krishna said. "The second *w* is silent."

"Ah yes, British English," Lafortune mused. He tilted his head while parroting a line he must have learned in school: "Never pronounce it as it is spelled." He laughed. "I believe it was George Bernard Shaw who said the word *fish* should truly be spelled g-h-o-t-i. The *g-h* is pronounced *f* as in *tough*, the *o* is pronounced *i* as in *women*, the *t-i* is pronounced *sh* as in . . . What was it now? I just—"

Krishna wanted to say, "I thought this was urgent." Instead he asked, "About Warwick?"

"Ah yes, the *t-i* is pronounced *sh* as in *nation*." Lafortune smiled self-consciously. "I beg your pardon. I am still fascinated by the intricacies of English. Yes, our friend War-wick." He grinned as though taking revenge on the man by mispronouncing his name. "He may prove to become a bother for the both of us."

"I'm not a Communist," Krishna said. He tried to sound flippant. He was tired. He had slept poorly.

"It is not that," Lafortune insisted. "During the Korean War you lived in Japan, it seems." Krishna stared at him and he chuckled. "Your M'sieu Parker loaned me your résumé yesterday afternoon. He did not tell you? Hmm. Probably we have it on file somewhere but files are so dusty. It is very impressive, this résumé."

Krishna looked at the menu to hide his pleasure. Solid, yes; impressive, why not? He decided on the soup of the day.

Lafortune ignored his own menu. Either he had decided what to order, or he was less interested in eating than talking. "I am certain the records of the police in Japan and India will show nothing, but—" He spread his hands to suggest otherwise. "—let us be frank. People have suspicions of anyone who has been, what is the word? Unorthodox? Not even that. Adventurous, hah!"

Krishna laughed. Impressive, adventurous—what next? "Life in Japan was hardly that," he said. "I worked in a factory helping to design heavy transformers. I played shuttlecock—badminton. And climbed Mount Fuji once a month. That was my adventure."

"Perhaps," Lafortune said, "but we are dealing with men who were born here. Like me, they do their duty overseas—" He brushed down from his embroidered wings to his blue and white UN ribbons, a fading one for Korea and a recent one, perhaps for the Sinai. "—and they return to stay. You have travelled much, and even I was surprised you left Columbia University so soon before having completed your thesis. For this position, too. Hardly a secure one, I can see."

Krishna raised his guard. "How do you know so much?" he asked.

Lafortune's shrug of the hands looked less mechanical now and more reassuring. "I leave the knocking on the doors and the telephoning to the types like War-wick. I merely noted your résumé and consulted your existing security clearance. But even without such things, one can draw conclusions. One might even jump at them." He looked up when the waitress approached. "I will have the steak, if you please," he said. "Medium, and my friend—?"

"Soup," Krishna ordered.

"That everything?" she asked. She glanced at the fraying cuffs of his suit jacket. He had worn the old, cream linen jacket especially for this meeting.

Lafortune was looking away, pretending he hadn't noticed her glance, but Krishna thought Lafortune was going too far when he said, "Steak also. It is on my bill."

They went through the obligatory, "It's not necessary," and, "But I insist!"

Krishna finally gave in and said, "I'll have mine well done."

Lafortune waved off the thanks. He leaned forward and clasped his hands. The pressed blue sleeves of his uniform looked incongruous on the paper placemat. It was covered with black and white drawings of the Golden Jets, with various commercial aircraft in the border. "Let us face it," he said. "You are still a landed immigrant, and M'sieu Morely is a citizen."

Krishna lowered his guard enough to snap, "Then let them make me a citizen. That way I won't have to wait another three years."

Lafortune waved as though at a bad smell. "Poof, many immigrants have received clearances more high—higher, I meant to say—than you will need for this new project. It is not that either." He sat back and looked out the window.

Krishna also looked out, between the checkered café curtains. The stiff, orange windsock beyond the airfield fence showed the wind blew north by northeast. Would it never stop? With his hands under the table, he massaged his left wrist. Then he realized Lafortune was watching him note the wind direction. There was something amiable about this Quebecker, something which went beyond his lack of guile; something Krishna hadn't expected in a senior officer. When Lafortune spoke again, he seemed to have switched subjects the way Morely often did:

"Do you know that Georges Vanier is the first *Québécois* appointed to be the Governor General? Do you know I will be blessed to receive a second row of gold leaves for my cap? Why, when this nation was founded by two races? I went to the CMR at St-Jean, the Collège Militaire Royale. But when I went to RMC in Kingston to finish my training, the types there called me Clod, not Claude. You know what Lafortune is. Lucky Clod, they called me though I was anything but lucky at first. The drill instructor, he was Inspector Javert to my Jean Valjean. It was truly *le temps misérable*. But I surprised him. Oh ho, I surprised all of those *Anglaises* with the stiff upper lip. I passed the top of my class in spite of my atrocious English. It is the only reason I wear these four stripes. Canada, it is still a British *bastille*, my friend."

"And I'm a British subject," Krishna said. "If Warwick checks closely enough, he'll even find I applied for the Indian Air Force." Krishna wanted to take his words back but the annoyance in Lafortune's eyes changed to admiration.

"They refused you?" Lafortune asked.

"I refused them."

"But why?" Lafortune demanded, incredulous.

"It doesn't matter."

"You are certainly a man of principle," Lafortune declared. "People like you, like me also, we do not go far with ease. People like Sergeant War-wick, they plod onward, upward. Be frank with him if he should question you. If you stand on your principles, he will become suspicious, or at least unco-operative. I suspect, for example, that you left Columbia partly because of a difference in personalities? Do not look so surprised! It occurs all the time. But admit it if you are asked. Do not say something he would not understand like, 'My supervisor was not guiding my research properly.' Or whatever happened."

"I got tired of marking papers for him," Krishna said.

"And Sergeant War-wick, he must have got tired of rubbing down his horse, or whatever these Mounties do in their training. But he stuck on. This business of principle, it is not truly my point anyway. Neither is the Lucky Clod business. Do you see my point yet?"

Yes, Krishna did, though he wished Lafortune had reached it earlier. "People who play by the rules are rewarded," Krishna said. "People who don't, aren't." He straightened the cutlery on his placemat.

*"C'est ça!"* Lafortune exclaimed. "Exactly right, I meant to say. It is why I want to help you." He leaned forward again. His voice dropped, but it gained intensity while he spoke. He jabbed a fin-

ger on his own placemat until he dented a Lockheed Tri-Star. "I see this all the time. They let types like you into this country. They cry, 'Oh, we need educated men from abroad to lead us through the twentieth century.' The century Wilfrid Laurier said belongs to Canada. Even a *Québécois* can be wrong, sometimes." Lafortune jerked the corners of his mouth up into a brief smile before continuing, once again serious: "Or they encourage types like me. They cry, 'Oh, let us give our French-speaking brothers a chance at last. It is not their fault they lost the Battle of the Plains of Abraham.' But even with their own people, even if they were born here and grew up here and lived on Clemow Avenue instead of on Montreal Road—even with their own people, they try to clip the wings. This is a great country, my friend. I am not ashamed to love it, but it was not made great by men like us. Nah, it was made great by men like Mackenzie King and Sergeant War-wick. The plodders. By now you are thinking, 'Such elitism!' And yet you would not even be here if you were not more advantaged than millions of your fellow countrymen. Those who have no hope of leaving there."

"I've never claimed to be humble," Krishna said.

Both men laughed. They looked out the window again and Krishna forced his shoulders to relax. They were tight from keeping his hands clasped on the table.

Lafortune sat back again and wiped his brow. "You are like me," he said. "You wish to be blunt, but you are afraid to be openly blunt. Listen, this is not an easy project you are working on. Neither is it crucial to the scheme of things. It is simply another piece of a jigsaw puzzle with no final picture. I am told the work we are having done on contracts one year will be *passé* the following. Yet it is imperative you succeed. If you fail, they will hold the failure against you. If M'sieu Morely fails, he will have another chance and another. Me also, but with me it's if this project or any of the others goes over the budget. How or why money is approved, it does not matter." He threw something invisible over his shoulder. "Give a thousand dollars to design a new toilet for a transport plane— Do not laugh. I have seen it done. And pay that, but not too much more. It is not the way it was ten years ago, when I returned from Korea to pilot my desk. But then we were still recovering from the shock in nineteen hundred and thirty-nine, the shock in twenty-nine. Now we have confidence. The economy is shaking, but we are still rich. We see a war brewing and we say, 'Permit us, *messieurs-les-foux*, we shall bring you peace. And if you should bestow another Nobel Prize on us, we will not be ungrateful. We are a nation of grovellers, after all.' Well, perhaps not. I like these new times, but it is necessary for a man to step carefully. I can get you this security clearance perhaps, but only if I know in my own mind what is troubling you."

Krishna lied once again: "Nothing, why?"

"Do not play the *ingénue* with me," Lafortune scoffed. "I was watching when Sergeant War-wick said the search will contain police records. What have you done?"

Krishna's watch felt too tight. He slipped the end of the leather strap back through the loop and eased the pin through a hole closer to the end. After tucking the strap into the loop, he twisted his hand. Much better.

"Do you not see?" Lafortune demanded. "If the Mounties find anything, it is possible I could appeal to my superiors and say, 'We need this man, this man only.'"

"Can you get me a new position?" Krishna asked. He thought he heard wrong when the waitress announced:

"Here you go." She placed two bowls of soup on the table. "Comes with."

Lafortune peeled the cellophane off his crackers and crumbled them into his soup. It was cream of tomato. Krishna placed his packet in the middle of the table. "Thank you," Lafortune said, "but I have enough. I could perhaps provide a useful reference, nothing more. Where would you like to work?"

"In a university?" Krishna asked. "U of T. The boy's mother, my wife, recently started there. I prefer teaching. This research is all very well, but there's no end to it, as you said. If we start looking at telemetry, we might as well study ionospheric disturbances. Satellites are more affected, after all."

Lafortune spooned up pieces of cracker with his soup. "I do not believe it is a state secret someone is already looking into that. At civilian establishments I know few people. But CMR, why not?"

"My French isn't good enough to lecture," Krishna said, "though if I took lessons—"

Lafortune dismissed the subject with, "We shall see. But you stop avoiding my true question. Do you have anything to hide?"

Krishna tugged a serviette from the chrome dispenser. The serviette tore. He wiped soup from his lips before admitting, "Not really, but you might think otherwise." If he had to trust someone, it might as well be a man who offered friendship. Krishna pulled back the cuff of his jacket and the French cuff of his shirt to reveal the scar. It ran diagonally under his watch, then along the back of his wrist. The doctor had cut into the flesh to remove shards of bone. He had used local anaesthetic and Krishna had watched the entire procedure. It had amazed him—the ease with which a blade could part flesh. "I'll tell you a story," he said.

The waitress approached with the steaks. He hadn't finished his soup but he pushed the bowl toward her. She set the steaks down, then brought a bottle of ketchup for the French fries. "Can I get you anything else for now?" she asked.

Lafortune shook his head.

"A story," Krishna repeated after she left, "about a struggle that lasted, oh, fifty years, but the fellow I'll tell you about didn't join it till near the end, in forty-four, at Delhi University. He knew little about politics. He soon learned, in his very first year, when he became secretary of his students' union. What we would call president here."

"But how could this happen?" Lafortune asked.

"It doesn't matter," Krishna said; then: "Maybe it does, considering he had to learn so quickly. The sweepers went on strike, what we call garbage collectors here. The rubbish piled up on the university grounds until people feared cholera would break out. So he organized the students in his hostel. Early one morning they started the clean-up. By noon, the grounds swarmed with helpers even though the students' union was supporting the strike. The union was run by arts students, those who had time for such nonsense. I think they actually wanted classes to be cancelled."

"He thinks," Lafortune said. "The fellow in your story."

Krishna could not bring himself to smile. He had taken it seriously then and he still did. "The student leaders didn't know he'd secretly met with the sweepers and asked whether they would go back to work if the students agitated for the increased wages. The sweepers hadn't trusted him. He'd held no office, after all, and he was from a much higher caste, a Brahmin. The first night of the clean-up—it took two days altogether, from morning till night—the students' union held a special meeting. For once, the engineering and science students attended, and the so-called leaders were impeached. The assembly elected the fellow secretary, and his friends to other offices. They even elected a number of women after he made a speech about Gandhi's—" Krishna stopped to regain the thread of his story, then continued. "Suffice it to say, he went to the principal of his college and threatened all classes would be boycotted if the sweepers weren't given their demands. The principal didn't believe him either, so the boycott started. It spread to other colleges in the university. Three days later the board of regents ordered a settlement with the sweepers and the fellow became—not famous, notorious. He'd just turned nineteen, but those were different times."

Nodding, Lafortune examined a charred piece of steak before eating it.

"At any rate," Krishna continued, "the fellow's ambition grew. By his second year, in forty-five, he'd thrown the entire student body into the freedom struggle. The British had promised India its independence if it helped in the war, but no one trusted Winston Churchill. He had made fun of Gandhi once—

called him a half-naked fakir in a loincloth—and never been forgiven. To think that such little things can affect history. Even though the fellow refused to join the Congress Party, his job was to organize speeches by this Congress Party leader, that Congress Party leader and even members of the Socialist Party. When he finally decided—don't ask me why—that Churchill wouldn't keep his promise, the fellow organized a true show of will: a march. They were forbidden according to war regulations, which were still conveniently in effect. The authorities sent a troop of mounted policemen to block the road out of the university." Krishna shook his head. It amazed him how easily everyone had played into his hands. He might just as well have led the police—they had responded so predictably.

"Imagine five thousand students facing perhaps a hundred policemen on horseback," he said. "The closer the two groups came, the more the students in front began to scatter. They were better known than the fellow, who still tried to remain in the background. He turned to urge his followers to continue. When he turned to face the front again, he discovered he was the real leader now. The mounted policemen charged. They swung *lathis,* bamboo sticks weighted with lead. Nothing happened to him at first. He was nimble, after all. He even caught a *lathi* and pulled the policeman off his horse, but none of the students struck a blow. Not a one. Not even with the foam from the horses' mouths flying into everyone's eyes, or the *lathis* raining on their heads. Then he stumbled. A horse reared up in fright, and its hoof came down on his wrist." Krishna pulled his cuffs forward to cover the scar. He had left out so much: the fear in the eyes of the students, the horses, and even the policemen. The blood-soaked *khadi,* the screams.

"His colleagues rushed him off to the dispensary. That's where he heard the police had issued a warrant for his arrest and those of all the other leaders, Congress and Socialist alike. What should he do? Go to prison peacefully as Gandhi always insisted? No, the fellow was still too young, still too brash. He wanted to continue fighting, but he had to recover first, so he fled to the South, back to his home town. He learned to like its peaceful ways again, not like those of the North, always in turmoil. He was still in the South when Churchill lost the election and Clement Attlee announced he was sending Mountbatten to Delhi. As far as the fellow knows, the warrant for his arrest lapsed on the night India became independent."

Lafortune dabbed at his lips with his serviette. He let it fall on his plate. "No," he insisted when Krishna raised his own serviette, "you finish. Ah, I wish I could meet this fellow. But I seem to have read in some résumé that he received his degree from that very university? With first class honours."

"He went back after Independence," Krishna said, "but he never again lived in the North. Well, he did, once." Krishna reached for the ketchup. The days in Benares saddened him now. They had been the best days of his life. He had been newly married, respected by all, and still unbeatable on a cricket pitch.

Lafortune brushed a crumb off the stripes on his cuff. "You come to dinner and tell more stories, *mon vieux*," he said. "My wife, she likes *les histoires*, the stories. She has a more balanced outlook on life than I. She says I will begin walking lopsided from the chip on my shoulder. I say the only way to cure this is to find a chip for my other shoulder." He used a toothpick to free a shred of steak from between his teeth. "If this matter comes to light, I shall deal with it. If you ask me, it is nothing. The way these Mounties work, it will be a few months yet before we hear. Perhaps I will even have a chance to singe our favourite sergeant's wick." He laughed.

Krishna also laughed, though not as heartily.

"As for your relations with M'sieu Parker," Lafortune said. He paused. "Your employer speaks highly of you, yet I detect some tension. I would not rush out to make the deposit on a house or a sailboat. Our budget must still be approved by the estimates committee. You should take this time to make your peace with your employer. A man cannot afford to keep leaving places because of a difference in personalities. Or because of his principles, not every time." Lafortune signalled the waitress for the bill.

*

While Krishna drove home that evening, Hari seemed unusually quiet. He went directly to his room and did not want a snack. After changing, Krishna sat down with *The Globe and Mail.* He looked at the employment opportunities first. All the good university positions required a PhD. Trying not to think about Rukmini, he turned to the news. For once he read entire articles, not simply the first paragraph of each, so he could put irritants like money and fools like Parker from his mind. A federal election was pending. Five years before, the Conservatives had reduced the Liberals to a pitiful few in the House of Commons, but a year ago the Conservatives had themselves been reduced to a minority government. Krishna wouldn't be able to vote but if he could, he decided, he would vote Conservative. Not because he liked their policies but because they had been in power the year he arrived in Canada. He considered them the people who had let him in. Besides, Parker was a Liberal.

The paper was not helping. Krishna put it aside. Perhaps music would help. He put on a record, the *Little Organ Book* again. After listening to the first piece, he washed the breakfast dishes and made supper. He called to Hari when it was ready and Hari took his place at the table.

"Do you want milk?" Krishna asked.

Hari nodded. He speared a tube of macaroni onto each tine of his fork, then one of the green peas Krishna had added to the mix. Hari liked the peas better than the macaroni, which was colourless. The cheese sauce was lumpy.

"Do you want to go to a movie tonight?" Krishna asked. "There's one about cowboys and Indians."

Hari shook his head. He was no longer angry with Krishna; Hari simply had nothing to say. He had been listening to the voices.

Despite the music, the apartment seemed as quiet as the lab in the hangar; as quiet as those few seconds before the spark jumped the gap. Hari stared at Krishna balefully.

Krishna threw down his fork and snapped, "Say something!"

Hari stopped eating. He put down his own fork, sat back with his arms crossed, and pursed his lips into a thin brown line.

Krishna tried to make a joke: "You can't eat like that."

Hari leaned forward and finished eating. He left the table without saying, "Excuse me," as he had been taught at school. The previous fall, the first time he had said, "Please pass the salt," Krishna had reminded him he could reach it himself. Since then he had continued only with, "Yes, please," and, "No, thank you," and, "Excuse me." He went back to his room.

While washing the supper dishes, Krishna felt his annoyance grow. He scraped burnt macaroni and cheese out of the pot, dumped the blackened mess into the garbage, and scrubbed the pot with steel wool. Normally he washed out the steel wool and pressed it dry so it wouldn't rust but today he threw the clumped fibres into the garbage as well. He hated doing dishes, and now he had a surly child on his hands. He went to the small bedroom, crossed his arms and leaned in the doorway.

Hari was bent over *The Adventures of King Arthur and the Knights of the Round Table.* He wasn't reading—the words refused to keep still on the page—but he could feel Krishna blocking the doorway. Hari was trapped.

"That's enough nonsense," Krishna said. "Are you coming to the movie or not? You can pick. There's a Walt Disney movie at the Museum of Man. *Swiss Family Robinson,* I think."

Hari looked up briefly before dropping his eyes to the book.

"All right," Krishna said, "sit there and sulk." He strode down the corridor and pulled on his coat. He tried one last time. "Are you coming, Boy?" he called. There was no answer. When he left, he slammed the front door. It almost felt good.

The movie turned out to be a waste of money. There was too much dialogue and not enough action. Even the obligatory lost soul, who tripped and fell while being pursued, acted annoyingly helpless. Krishna left after the first reel. Perhaps he should have taken Hari to Mrs. Gardner instead of leaving him alone? But he was a big boy now, nearly eight. He knew better than to play with the stove. He was likely in the living room with the radio turned up.

Krishna found only the dining room light on. From the doorway of the small bedroom he heard steady breathing yet the bed seemed oddly flat. Krishna snapped on the light. The bed was empty. A moment later Hari crawled out of the closet and rubbed his eyes. Krishna couldn't imagine what Hari had been doing in there. What was he frightened of? Again Hari changed into his pyjamas while keeping his back turned but this time Krishna didn't leave. He wanted to ask, "Can't you see a piano is such a trivial thing?" but he couldn't trust himself to ask this without losing his temper. It wouldn't stop at a single question. He would only make things worse. Krishna went away and read his book on the Duke of Wellington. When he looked in on Hari again, Hari was asleep. Krishna sat on the edge of the bed and stroked the curly hair.

"Boy," he whispered. "Boy."

Next morning after dressing for school, Hari came to the table. He knew he was late but Krishna said nothing. The only sounds came from the rustle of corn flakes pouring into the bowl. Hari even dug into the bottom of the box for the Flintstones sticker. Normally he had to wait until the box was half empty so he could shake the cereal aside, but he wanted the sticker now. He wiped off corn flake dust and pocketed the sticker, still in its cellophane. He and Tully were trading so each of them could complete a set.

The silent battle continued outside. Ever since the first snowfall, Krishna had played out an early morning ritual. He unplugged the block heater, started the Lark, and switched on the defroster. Then he cleared the windows and windshield, sometimes with a scraper, sometimes with a whisk, often with both. This morning he needed only the whisk. He cleared snow from the windshield with long strokes which revealed Hari arc by arc, speckled with snow. As always, when Krishna cleared the passenger window, he tapped lightly. This morning Hari did not grin. Krishna finished clearing the other windows, his own last, and whisked the snow off his coat. He climbed into the chugging Lark and asked, "Are you cold?"

Instead of saying no, Hari shook his head. He tried crossing his arms but his snowsuit was too bulky. He looked out his window at smoke rising from nearby town houses. The smoke rose straight into the sky.

This morning's traffic crawled even more slowly than usual, west along Montreal Road and north along St. Laurent Boulevard. Krishna couldn't drive quickly even on the Rockcliffe Parkway and twice he honked his horn at the driver in front. He gripped the steering wheel so its rippled surface dug through his gloves.

At last he wondered—and it occurred to him he should have thought of this before—what his own father would have done. They had never disagreed. Not wanting to follow Ravi's example, Krishna had obeyed their father's every wish. Looking back on it now, Krishna wondered whether he might have made a mistake. Obedience was one thing, subservience another. Even as a child Ravi was difficult. He ran away from school—something Krishna never did, no matter how many times he was tempted. Often, to strike back at their father for his rages, Ravi threw household items down the well: once a shaving brush, once an umbrella. He rebelled even in his sleep.

After Krishna's grandfather had died, the Brahmin community had helped Krishna's father finish school. The Brahmins prized education. It was the source of their power. Krishna's father had not only earned his SSLC—his Secondary School Leaving Certificate—but had also become the first man from his village to earn a college degree. Many years later, after he had been appointed a superintending engineer based in Mysore City, he had announced he would house any nephew or niece who remained in school. Sometimes it had seemed half the village children lived in his house near the sandalwood factory. When Krishna and Ravi came home from boarding school, they enjoyed sleeping on the veranda with their cousins, the boys on one side, the girls on the other. The visits home were the only time Krishna could enjoy the company of girls, though he rarely knew what to say to them. With the veranda so crowded, Krishna's father established a simple rule. He drew chalk marks on the floor and ordered the children to sleep in their designated spaces. He even made the spaces different widths to accommodate differences in size. When he rose at six to have his morning coffee, he came out to the veranda. If he found so much as an elbow across a line, he prodded the offending child awake and said, "Straighten out here!" Ravi never slept straight. Although he was two years older than Krishna, Ravi slept like a baby. He lay curled with his knees drawn up to his chest, his head across one line and his feet across another. Krishna's father slapped the bottoms of Ravi's feet with a walking stick but it did no good. For all his scientific methods, Krishna's father was at a loss. Not completely, though. One evening he rubbed out the lines and washed the floor himself. While it dried, he recalculated the space each child would need. He drew an arc in a far corner of the veranda. The arc threw off his system, but he compensated by drawing the remaining lines diagonally. This left an unused rhomboid near the steps but it was a small price to pay for his peace of mind.

Krishna edged the Lark onto the roadside near the junior school gate. He tried not to smile. After Hari slid out of the car, he turned to close his door. Krishna leaned across with his arm extended and palm up. "Talk to your Mrs. Dalgleish and Mr. Marsden," he said. "Ask if they know of anyone with a second-hand piano for sale."

Hari slapped his mittened hands against his snowsuit. He looked at Krishna, leaning across the seat; at the large, gloved hand, which was open now.

"Did you hear me?" Krishna asked.

Hari leapt then. He shouted, "Hurray!" He ran so fast over the snow-covered gravel, Krishna thought Hari would fall, but he kept his footing all the way to the blue door.

The piano arrived ten days later, on the Saturday before Hari's birthday. Hari liked Saturdays: first a TV, now a piano. He had woken early and Krishna had made pancakes for breakfast, which Hari ate while watching cartoons.

Krishna waited by the elevator after he buzzed the movers in downstairs. The elevator was padded at his request. As an afterthought he had asked the superintendent whether it would be all right to have a piano in the apartment, but only as an afterthought. The superintendent had said yes, of course. Once the elevator arrived, Krishna watched two men in coveralls push the used piano out. He stared in disbelief at squiggles of white paint on the orange wood.

"Orange?" he exclaimed.

One of the movers, a husky man with red hair, said, "Roxatone. It was a fad a few years back. Bars, pianos, you name it. Do it yourself if you want. Put the Electrolux on reverse and the paint comes out. Blop, blop."

His younger but taller companion chuckled. "Could be worse," he told Krishna. "Might've been tiger stripes."

Both men laughed. Krishna strode into the apartment to hide his scowl. He didn't want them to leave the piano in the corridor, after all. It had cost four hundred dollars. He had bought Hari a soccer ball at Ogilvy's department store and banked the rest. Besides, Krishna was in a good mood and he wasn't about to let simple-minded fools spoil it. He had imagined a huge instrument, but the piano was small enough to fit along the blank wall across from the sofa. This would mean putting up with Hari's practising but Krishna preferred having Hari in the living room. It turned out Hari preferred this as well.

The men eased the piano off its skid, padded with old carpeting. Then they wiped their faces with rags, which they kept in their back pockets. "You should get it tuned after it settles in," the husky man suggested. "Say a week or two. But it doesn't sound bad." He flipped back the cover, hunched over the keyboard, and began hammering a tune. Krishna closed the door so the noise wouldn't disturb the neighbours. He had heard a similar tune in the cowboy movie. It was an Indian war dance.

"Here's your money," he snapped.

The man straightened with a fading grin. After taking the twenty-dollar bill, he handed back two two-dollar bills. He stared at the change as though expecting a tip.

"What are you waiting for?" Krishna asked.

"Uh, nothing," the younger man said.

Krishna could feel the men's eyes on him when he went to the door. "Then," he said calmly, "please leave."

After they left, he placed a dining chair in front of the piano. On second thought, he added a cushion from the sofa.

All this time, Hari had sat on the sofa and kicked his legs. He kicked them straight out in front of him and grinned while he watched the men unload the piano. His piano. Now he climbed onto the makeshift stool and fingered the orange wood between two white squiggles. It was the most beautiful piano in the world.

He no longer needed a red dot to find his favourite note. He hummed while it echoed in the room. "This is middle C," he explained. "Mrs. D calls it Do-Ducky. Not Mr. Marsden, though." Lately Marsden had begun saying things like *Father Charles Goes Down And Ends Battle*—this was the order of sharps. Hari pressed the two black keys to the right of middle C. "Do-Ducky lives next to the garage, C sharp and D sharp." He pressed another white key. "This is Fa-Furry-Fox, or F. He lives next to the house, F sharp, G sharp, A sharp." These were a group of three black keys.

Krishna had never heard Hari speak about his classmates or his studies, even history and maths, the way he spoke about these black and white keys. They were like old friends. Hari sat forward and began playing a tune. Krishna was careful to chuckle before he asked, "Is that it? Your mother spent all this money on a fancy piano so you can play Christmas carols? You're three months late."

Hari flushed and his shoulders sagged. He kept frowning at the keyboard until he remembered Krishna had never heard him play. Hari looked at the turntable.

Krishna sighed and sat on the sofa, well away from the missing cushion. He watched Hari hop down and go silently to the metal shelves. He looked either angry or determined—Krishna could not tell which. It wouldn't hurt to be more careful, he thought. It would take practice, that was all.

Hari looked under the *Little Organ Book*. He wasn't sure what he wanted but when he found an album with a picture of someone named Glenn Gould, Hari knew this was it. He slid the record out of the album and the dust jacket, placed the record on the turntable, and switched on the Heathkit. After pressing the phono button, he lowered the needle and let the record play for some time. Then he turned down the volume. Once more seated at the piano, he played:

He stopped when Krishna rose to pick up the album cover.

It was one of the first records Krishna had bought after coming to America. This 1955 release of the *Goldberg Variations* had made Glenn Gould famous. Krishna had rarely listened to it since his early days in New York. He sat down with the album on his knee and listened to Hari repeat the notes. This time he kept playing. He played softly, slowly, so slowly Krishna thought Hari was having trouble remembering the next note. It was not this. He was forcing Krishna to listen, forcing him to wait for the next note and the next. The *Goldberg* sounded like a keyboard exercise and yet, and yet it contained such contradictions. It sounded both sacred and profane. Krishna had never felt so amazed. He seemed to be discovering something about himself, and he was discovering it in music which had been with him for years. He simply had not listened to it often enough. At last he understood. The best music, music like this, could take a man out of his everyday world and bring him back to a world which could never be the same. Hari, the boy, his son seemed to know this. He led, and Krishna followed.

Hari stopped before the end of the sixteenth bar. He stopped here because it was as far as he had let the record play and because it was the end of the basic Aria theme, the end of the melody. But many years later he would realize he had chosen to stop here even though, and perhaps because, he had reached a point of harmonic instability. Next came a very slight variation which would pull the listener toward the end of the Aria. But even this was not the end because all the variations followed, each of the thirty variations which had to be played one after the other until the entire work ended. And one thing more: there was no room for halfheartedness, neither for Gould nor for Hari. Each time he performed the work at recitals, Hari would play as though it was his final, perfect performance.

When he stopped at last, Krishna said, "That's . . . incredible, Boy! Very—" He didn't know what to say; *nice* felt inappropriate. "—moving."

Hari turned with a questioning frown and Krishna recognized the problem at once. "No, you're not a boy any longer," he said. "You're a real piano player, HC! Why don't we put a sign on top that says, 'HC—his piano'?"

Hari grinned. He turned back to play three pieces without stopping: "Lavender Blue," "Hark! The Herald Angels Sing" and "God Save the Queen." His head tilted left and right. His hands moved surely, with such authority that even a mere nursery rhyme sounded like an aria which demanded variations. Finished, he slipped off the chair. Before closing the cover he stared at the keys as though afraid he were dreaming.

With the sound of the piano stilled, the apartment had fallen quiet, so quiet the needle hissed while the record still turned.

Krishna began to clap. Hari ran toward him with his arms outstretched, and Krishna rose to scoop him up, to hug him while they whirled and the apartment resounded with laughter. Krishna found himself savouring how warm Hari felt, brittle but warm. It barely bothered Krishna, when he finally kissed Hari's cheek, to find it wet. They sat close on the sofa, well away from the missing cushion. Hari wiped his sleeve across his eyes and leaned against Krishna. Then Hari looked up when Krishna snapped his fingers and said:

"I nearly forgot." Krishna went to the front closet. Tucked in a back corner of the shelf was the soccer ball he had bought. Next to it lay the old calendar picture, rolled and secured with an elastic band. He had brought it home the previous evening and said, when Hari had asked about it, "Circuit diagrams." Now Krishna said, "Here's your birthday present from me." He tapped the soccer ball aside and took down the picture.

Hari watched, puzzled, while Krishna climbed onto the makeshift piano stool and tacked the picture on the wall above the piano. Hari stood up and moved to one side. Ganesha had come back: Rukmini's remover of obstacles, the god of wisdom. Hari grinned at the elephant god with his four arms and his belly large from eating sweets. Next to a pyramid of sweets was a mischievous rat.

Krishna stepped down and also looked at Ganesha. Both of them had travelled a great distance, farther than Krishna had ever intended. When he scooped Hari up once more, Hari shrieked. Krishna carried him, dangling, to the sofa. Hari squealed all the way, then climbed into Krishna's lap. "Tell you what," Krishna said. "After lunch we'll go for a drive and I'll show you my lab. Would you like that?"

Hari measured his hands against Krishna's, first the right and then the left and then both together.

"We'll have a good time," Krishna promised. "I'll even show you how a real Van de Graaff works. I'll charge it up and help you move the grounding rod to pull the charges off the big sphere. Nothing you've seen or heard is as magical as when that spark jumps the gap." He glanced at the piano, then tousled Hari's hair. "Almost nothing." Krishna closed his hands around Hari's, two small hands which could coax such grand music from ivory and felt, metal and wood. "What do you say?"

Hari looked at the piano and nodded. It would be fun to play with a real Van de Graaff, yes. Afterward, though, he would practise, watched over by Ganesha while the jasmine girls danced. At last he said, so softly that Krishna had to bend: "Thank you, Appa."